ALSO BY CHRISTINE DeSMET

The Fudge Shop Mysteries
First-Degree Fudge
Hot Fudge Frame-Up

PRAISE FOR
THE FUDGE SHOP MYSTERY SERIES

Hot Fudge Frame-Up

"An action-filled tale with a very likable main character as the core ingredient. Not to mention some amazingly delicious recipes that will have all readers running to their kitchens. . . . Readers will 'eat' this particular tale up while also drooling over the fudge recipes in the back. The same can be said for DeSmet's mysteries that can be said for actual fudge: There is no way you can consume just one."
—*Suspense Magazine*

"I love culinary mysteries and this book seems to have everything. A deliciously lighthearted mystery, a love triangle with hot guys, and of course, yummy fudge . . . *Hot Fudge Frame-Up* is a delightfully decadent addition to the series and I'm looking forward to reading more about Ava and her adventures in Door County, Wisconsin, in the near future."
—*Books-n-Kisses*

"With captivating characters and a suspenseful mystery, *Hot Fudge Frame-Up* was a thoroughly enjoyable read. I can't wait to see what Christine DeSmet has in store for us next. In the meantime, with the mouthwatering recipes at the back of *Hot Fudge Frame-Up*, I will be eagerly heading into the kitchen with this book in hand to try them out."
—*Cozy Mystery Book Reviews*

"Lucky Harbor, a fudge brown American water spaniel, plays a rather large and important role for a dog. And rightly so. Great reading for beach time." —*BookLoons*

"Tasty recipes are included in the sweet-themed mystery. The fun only escalates with the high jinks of the Oosterlings and their friends as they meddle in one another's lives as only loved ones can." —*Kings River Life Magazine*

Dec 2015

First-Degree Fudge

"Will tingle your sweet tooth at the first mention of Cinderella Pink Fudge, even if this pastel treat may be a murder weapon." — *The Washington Post*

"An action-filled story with a likable heroine and a fun setting. And, oh, that fudge! I'm swooning. I hope Ava Oosterling and her family and friends take me back to Door County, Wisconsin, for another nibble soon."
— JoAnna Carl, national bestselling author of the Chocoholic Mysteries

"Christine DeSmet has whipped up a melt-in-your-mouth gem of a tale. One is definitely not going to be enough!"
— Hannah Reed, national bestselling author of *Beewitched*

"The first in a new series set in the 'Cape Cod of the Midwest,' *First-Degree Fudge* is a lighthearted confection that cozy mystery readers will devour."
— Lucy Burdette, author of *Death with All the Trimmings*

"As palatable as a fresh pan of Belgian fudge, this debut will delight candy aficionados and mystery lovers with its fast pace, quirky cast, and twist after twist. A must read!"
— Liz Mugavero, author of *A Biscuit, a Casket*

"Will have readers drooling with its descriptions of heroine Ava Oosterling's confections. Set in a small Wisconsin town on Lake Michigan, readers will enjoy the down-home atmosphere and quirky characters." — Debbie's Book Bag

"Interesting characters enhance this mystery . . . plenty of romantic tension. The mystery evolves nicely with a few good twists and turns that lead to a surprising villain."
— *RT Book Reviews* (4 stars)

continued . . .

Five-Alarm Fudge

A FUDGE SHOP MYSTERY

Christine DeSmet

AN OBSIDIAN MYSTERY

OBSIDIAN
Published by the Penguin Group
Penguin Group (USA) LLC, 375 Hudson Street,
New York, New York 10014

USA | Canada | UK | Ireland | Australia | New Zealand | India | South Africa | China
penguin.com
A Penguin Random House Company

First published by Obsidian, an imprint of New American Library,
a division of Penguin Group (USA) LLC

First Printing, April 2015

ISBN 978-0-451-41649-0

Printed in the United States of America
10 9 8 7 6 5 4 3 2 1

To those who volunteer in small communities such as Namur, Wisconsin, where history is preserved, neighbors are cherished, and everybody attends the fall harvest festival.

Chapter 1

The royals were coming in two weeks to our tourist haven of Door County, Wisconsin—a thumb of land jutting into Lake Michigan called the "Cape Cod of the Midwest."

The momentous event had put a panic in me, Ava Oosterling. It was why I was in an unused, stuffy church attic and heading to the basement with my two best friends, Pauline Mertens and Laura Rousseau. We were looking for a divinity fudge recipe.

Divinity fudge is a white meringue-style confection and an American invention, though this type of fluffy nougat candy can be traced to ancient Turkish Europe and back thousands of years BC, when Egyptians combined marshmallow root with honey. Local lore said that a Catholic nun may have served school children divinity fudge. She allegedly left the handwritten recipe inside the church that Pauline, Laura, and I were cleaning.

Finding and making this divine recipe would help improve my reputation. Immensely. Since returning to Fishers' Harbor last spring, I had unintentionally combined my Belgian fudge making with helping our local sheriff solve two murders. I was determined to stay out of trouble and focus on fudge.

Nature was cooperating. Three hours ago I had been in my fudge shop, and everybody had been talking about how we'd be at our colorful best for Prince Arnaud Van Damme from Belgium and his mother, Princess Amandine. Today was the second Saturday in September. Door County's famous maple trees overhanging ribbons of two-lane country roads bore leaves tipped in scarlet. The leaf-peeper tourists clogged our streets and roadside markets on weekends to snap up pumpkins, apples, grapes, and everything made from our county's famous cherries.

I'd increased fudge production at Oosterlings' Live Bait, Bobbers & Belgian Fudge & Beer. I'd also opened a small roadside market in the southern half of the county near my parents' farm with the hope of catching more tourists coming to see the prince. My six copper kettles were constantly filled with fresh cream from my parents' Holsteins, the world's best chocolate from Belgium, and sugar. Favorite flavors flying off my shelves included maple, butterscotch, double-Belgian chocolate with walnuts, and pumpkin. But I couldn't wait to serve the prince and princess my Fairy Tale line of fudges—cherry-vanilla Cinderella Pink Fudge and Rapunzel Raspberry Rapture Fudge.

This brouhaha over a prince could be blamed on my grandpa. Finding a divinity fudge recipe from the 1800s for the prince was Grandpa Gil's idea. So was asking the royals to travel here to tour our famous Saint Mary of the Snows Church in Namur, Wisconsin. The tour would occur during our fall harvest festival, called a kermis. Last summer, Pauline's boyfriend, John Schultz, had found an antique cup during a Lake Michigan diving expedition. The initials on the cup were AVD, which Grandpa thought might belong to Grandma Sophie's ancestor Amandine Van Damme. Grandpa searched Sophie's ancestry and found, lo and behold, that a few of her shirttail relatives were part of the current noble class in Namur, Belgium!

Our Namur—pronounced *Nah-meur*—was a wide spot in the road, a collection of a half dozen buildings amid farm fields about forty miles south of my fudge shop. It was within a stone's throw of my parents' farm near Namur's neighboring village of Brussels. Some of our towns were named for places in Belgium because the southern half of Door County was settled by Belgian immigrants in the 1850s, including my ancestors.

We were all shocked that Grandpa had called up the royals on his cell phone as if they were mere contacts. He'd reached some assistant, of course, but it had turned out Prince Arnaud was eager to bring more tourists to *his* city of Namur. The prince had accepted Grandpa's proposal to visit, to our shock. But the prince saw this as a tourism mission, which could benefit both Namurs.

Jubilation here over this development was tempered by my reputation. The fishermen and tourists coming in to buy fudge kept saying that "Things happen in threes." One smiley-faced man asked, "Do ya think that prince is gonna take a powder? Ava, you stay away from him, ya hear?"

"Taking a powder" meant he'd die in yet another murder involving me and my fudge.

"I'm not superstitious," I insisted. "I'm scientifically minded."

Fudge making is about the exactness of heat and the precise crystallization stages of sugar. Depending on what type of fudge you're making, that sugar has to bubble and get to the "soft-boil" stage temperature of two hundred thirty-eight degrees. Divinity fudge—what the prince had said he wanted to try—needs two hundred sixty degrees.

Truth be told, even my scientific side was on tenterhooks. Divinity fudge is notoriously hard to make; you can't have a speck of humidity, or the egg white meringue will flop. And Door County is a peninsula surrounded by water and humid breezes. In addition, every time a climacteric event had been planned lately in my life, a body showed up, with my relatives wringing their hands over my involvement.

Ironically, this time my parents and grandparents wanted me involved.

Why? Because Prince Arnaud Van Damme was thirty-six (only four years older than me) and a bachelor who was going to inherit a castle.

My relatives weren't hot about my current boyfriend, Dillon Rivers. They had their reasons. My mother still slipped at times and called Dillon "that bigamist." A part of me couldn't blame them for trying to distract me with a handsome prince.

Oddly enough, my grandma wasn't enthused about her royal relatives traveling to Wisconsin. Ever since Grandpa contacted them a month ago, she'd been acting aloof about the visit, as if she didn't want to own up to being related to them.

"Grandma, how come you never told me about them before?" I had asked her last week while she was making one of her famous cherry pies. We had been in her cabin on Duck Marsh Street in Fishers' Harbor. I lived across the street.

"I guess I forgot. They're so far back in my family tree they're barely a twig."

A twig? She forgot royalty! My scientific mind said something was amiss.

I asked her, "Are you mad at Grandpa for inviting them? Did he make up the story about the divinity fudge?" I had assumed he did all along. My search today in the church was merely to please him.

She'd heaved a big sigh as she pulled a fresh, steaming cherry pie from the oven. "He didn't make up that story about the Virgin Mary."

My overzealous, matchmaking grandfather, Gil Oosterling, told the royals the divinity fudge had allegedly been enjoyed by the Blessed Virgin Mother after she'd appeared in front of Sister Adele Brice in 1859 in the nearby woods.

The Blessed Mother?

Yes. That Mother.

Here? In Wisconsin?

Yes. It's true. A bishop even sanctioned it as the only such sighting in the entire United States. In December 2010, the *New York Times* did a big article on it.

Grandpa said that Adele—from the Belgium province of Brabant, where Prince Arnaud was from, too—hid the original, handwritten recipe within the bricks of Saint Mary of the Snows to protect it from the fire dangers presented by wooden structures and stoves in the 1800s. Grandpa told the prince I would make Sister Adele's divinity fudge recipe for dessert at the kermis, with the meal being served in the beautiful little church. Not only that, but Grandpa said we'd present the original recipe document to the royals. Grandpa had learned the prince wanted to build a museum in Namur that would highlight the history and culture of our sister communities. Housing a priceless recipe in the museum would be like the famous Shroud being kept in the church in Turin, Italy. Thousands of people would visit Belgium each year. Grandpa said the recipe would come back to us on a two-year cycle or some such thing, and thus, thousands might visit Door County, too.

The prince had suggested the divinity fudge I made could be part of a fund-raiser for the church, which was now used as the Belgian Heritage Center. Princess Amandine was enthralled, too. She called divinity fudge "heavenly candy, white and pure as the robes worn by the nun and Blessed Virgin Mary."

Princess Amandine had told Grandpa that divinity fudge was a rare treat. She'd eaten it only once, and that was when she was a little girl. I'd attempted to make it once and given up because all I'd made was goo. Supposedly, there was something special about Sister Adele's recipe that made it foolproof. I was intrigued by this, but Grandpa was obsessed. There was mention that Grandpa and I might receive some special governmental medal of honor for this divinity fudge recipe.

This royal visit had gotten out of hand quickly.

But I tried to keep a cool head. All the fuss came down to raising funds for the church. It lacked a steeple. It had crumbled long ago. Selling tickets to see a prince and eat fudge would give a proper home to the three white crosses perched precariously on the peaked roof.

Pauline, Laura, and I had volunteered to be on the church-cleaning committee, a handy excuse to spy in every nook. We had just finished going through the beastly hot, stuffy attic bedroom above the kitchen. The bedroom was about eight by ten feet. One small window in the slanted roof let in light. The room had been used by a traveling priest back in the 1860s before a rectory was built. After finding no divinity fudge recipe, we had hurried down the narrow stairs and back into the kitchen, panting.

Pauline glugged from her water bottle. She was red faced and sweating, her long brown-black braid frizzed from heat and humidity. "I'm done. This is stupid, you know."

"We have to look in the basement yet," I insisted. My long auburn ponytail had gone limp, sagging on the back of my hot neck.

Laura ran a hand up her sweaty forehead and through her blond bangs and bob. "We need a break before the basement. I like your grandfather, but this isn't my idea of a fun way to spend a Saturday morning. Besides, I've got to go home yet and bake bread all afternoon."

Laura ran the Luscious Ladle Bakery. She supplied fresh-baked goods to our five-star restaurants. I sold her mouthwatering cinnamon rolls with gooey icing dripping off them at Ava's Autumn Harvest on Highway 57.

I waved a hand in the air, giving in, but only a little. "Take a break. I need to check on Grandma, anyway, out in the graveyard. I'll be back in ten minutes. Then we head for the basement."

Pauline said, "All we'll find will be mummified mice and musty dust motes. At least I hope that's all we find. Things happen in threes, you know."

I hurried out without responding, though inside my head a voice reminded me that Pauline was always right.

Grandma Sophie was only a few yards east of the front doors, tidying what always appeared to visitors to be an odd grave-yard. In a boxy space under a giant maple tree, about thirty headstones sat in rows within *six inches* of one another. A joke around here said the people were buried standing up. What really happened was that in 1970 the priest had moved the headstones from the graveyard located along the east side of the church, where the lawn spread between two maple trees and continued to the back of the church. Nobody had been buried there for at least a hundred years, by that time. The ground was resettling, and the stones were sinking or toppling. To save the lichen-etched stones from disappearing altogether, they were moved. Because the collection sat in front of a blacktopped parking lot next to the church, people mistakenly believed the priest paved over the old church graveyard. But it was a myth that cars parked atop Belgians at rest.

On her knees, squeezed in between the headstones,

Grandma was fussing over the placement of potted yellow and orange mums.

Grandma's wavy white hair buffeted about her shoulders in the breeze.

"That looks really nice, Grandma. You look nice, too." She wore a red, long-sleeved T-shirt, black denim jeans, and sturdy walking shoes.

"Thank you, Ava honey. Did you find the recipe?"

"No. Are you sure Grandpa didn't make that up? Has he had the three of us looking for a nonexistent recipe?" Grandpa liked a good joke, so I was still suspicious.

Grandma Sophie grunted as she shoved at the ground to get up off her knees. I rushed to help. Last spring she'd broken a leg. She still experienced pain.

Once we stood together in front of the headstones, with my arm secured around her waist, she said, "My grandparents used to talk about that fudge recipe. My great-grandparents were there at the time of Sister Adele. They knew her personally. So I believe it's true, honey."

Her great-grandparents Amelie and Thomas Van Damme were buried behind the church. Their headstone sat in front of us—gray and weathered, a couple of inches thick, a foot wide, and three feet high, with a chipped, arched edge.

I said, "Maybe what they were really remembering was the Communion wafers. They're white, just like divinity fudge. Maybe Sister Adele made sweet wafers, and thus people just said they were sweet as fudge. They both melt on the tongue, after all."

"No, Ava, my grandparents were pious. They would not have joked about that. They weren't eating fudge for Communion."

A giggle escaped me, despite my trying to be serious for Grandma. "Maybe church enrollments would rise if they served fudge. It would be a whole new market for me."

"Honey, please be respectful. Your grandpa believes there's a recipe hidden here somewhere. People have looked for it off and on for generations now. It's time we find the darn thing and send it home with those people."

Those people. Her disdain for her relatives silenced me. A little research had told me that the prince and princess were active in charities to help the poor. They had assured Grandpa the recipe would travel back to our community to help with fund-raisers to benefit Door County. The royals appeared to be good people. What wasn't she willing to share with me? Grandma stood as still as the statues before us, her physical being as sturdy as her conviction. I said, "I'll do my best to find that recipe, I promise."

Grandma pushed a pouf of white hair off her face. "Your grandfather will be over the moon."

"The moon, wafers, divinity fudge, your hair—all white. Your hair is as divine as divinity fudge, Grandma."

That got her to smile, finally. Then she shook her head. "This graveyard is so embarrassing. Your grandfather should never have invited them."

"But the prince and princess are related to the people laid to rest here. They'll want to pay their respects. They're interested in the early settlers from Belgium and the generations carrying on here now."

Many of the other names in front of us were familiar to me because the families still lived in the area. I recognized Coppens; a high school classmate of mine, Jonas Coppens, owned a small farm up the road from my new market. He was spreading mulch around right now several yards across the lawn at a historic schoolhouse. I growled because I recognized a woman with him, Fontana Dahlgren.

"Fontana is supposed to be helping us dust and polish the inside of the church," I said.

"The floozy? Don't count on it." Grandma shuddered next to me, my body absorbing her tiny earthquake. "I suppose she'll be flirting up a storm with the prince. Maybe that's good; at least we won't have to entertain him and his mother."

"Grandma? What's wrong? You haven't liked this idea of them coming since the moment Grandpa broke the news. But Grandpa and my father—your own son—and my mother would love to marry me off to the prince. Not you?"

The fine wrinkles around her mouth quirked with a grimace. "The prince and princess are barely related to us. They're all about fuss and appearances. There's a reason some of us sawed ourselves off from the branches of the family tree and departed for America. This visit is going to end up in a disaster."

She began limping away toward the historic schoolhouse. She'd meet up with her church lady friends who were on cleaning detail, too.

My heart held a dull ache, and my stomach felt as if it were a dryer with a bunch of old bolts tumbling in it. I vowed to figure out what was upsetting Grandma about this visit and fix it for her. Certainly a little fuss wasn't the issue, because Grandma loved her kermises and making her famous pies. Could it be *me* she was embarrassed about? Or our entire family? We were plain people, just farmers, fishermen, and fudge makers. I thought that was good enough. But Grandma was confounding me, something I confessed to Pauline and Laura when I got back inside the church a minute later.

My girlfriends and I were standing near the bottom of old wooden stairs leading into the dim, dusty concrete church basement. The room was about ten by twelve feet. It was empty, save for a row of plumbing pipes lined up in the middle of the floor. A meager bulb lit the area, turning shadows into muddy brown in the corners of the floor and joists overhead. Cobwebs hung down; they stirred from our sudden appearance.

Pauline stood directly behind me on the wooden stairs. "I tell my kids all the time not to go into strange places." She was a kindergarten teacher in Fishers' Harbor. "This is the dumbest thing you've ever gotten me into. No recipe is hidden down here. I think your grandmother's upset because your grandfather has gone lulu."

"It feels like more than that, Pauline. She mentioned something about the royals being about fuss and appearances. Do you think I embarrassed her?"

"Heck, I'm embarrassed by you all the time. Including now. You bought into your grandfather's fudge story hook, line, and sinker. He's a fisherman and he knows how to reel you in with a tall fish tale. Or fudge tale."

Laura, bringing up the rear of our human train on the stairs, said, "Can't we just say we looked and not?" She sneezed.

I told them, "I can't lie to my grandfather about looking for the recipe. I owe him a lot."

Last spring, Grandpa Gil had resuscitated my life. I'd spent eight years in Los Angeles in a grunt job for a TV show. Then Grandma Sophie broke her leg in April. Grandpa asked me to return while my show was on spring hiatus. He had the idea of moving his minnow tank over in his bait shop to let me turn half of his building into a fudge operation. He'd also moved the singular apostrophe in his sign to make it the plural Oosterlings' Live Bait, Bobbers & Belgian Fudge & Beer. That kind of love couldn't be ignored. I quit my show and stayed.

With Grandpa's kindness resonating in my soul, I stepped onto the concrete basement floor. As I walked over to the pipes, I held on to my ponytail while moving to the right to keep away from a cobweb trailing from the joists.

Laura wasn't so lucky. "Ick. They're all over in my hair."

She'd somehow missed copying my stealthy move. Her blond bob looked as if it were snared in a hair net. As a baker she was used to wearing hair nets, so maybe she'd cope with this better than Pauline. She was six feet tall— taller than me by two inches, and too dressed up for cleaning a church and poking around for recipe scripture. She wore her favorite designer sleeveless tangerine top and shorts. Laura and I had on denim shorts. I was in a faded pink T-shirt, while Laura wore a threadbare blue-and-white-striped, short-sleeved blouse.

Pauline shook her brown-black braid to rid it of a cobweb that had broken loose from its mother ship overhead. "I've seen enough."

"There's a doorway over there," I said, pointing toward a passageway, intentionally ignoring Pauline's whimpering.

I was enjoying the exploring. Although I'd grown up nearby, I'd never been in this basement or the attic of the church, because their doors were located within the kitchen. The kitchen used to be the sacristy where priests and altar boys would get ready for Mass.

I also hadn't been inside this church since I'd jilted my fiancé here the night of our wedding rehearsal eight years ago. That was the same night I'd eloped with another man—

Dillon Rivers, whom I divorced a month after that, then didn't see for eight years, and now was dating again. Memories—bad, embarrassing ones—had been hitting me like darts from the moment I promised to look for the recipe in this church. At first, I couldn't force myself to come back here. My stomach had rolled for days, as if it wanted to purge my mistakes. That would take a long time. But I knew if I was going to fully embrace living in Door County again, I had to do a mea culpa and face what I'd done. Pauline and Laura were gems to volunteer for the kermis cleaning committee with me. Entering the church this morning had caused my breathing to stop for a moment, but the search for the fudge recipe had helped take my mind off past romantic disasters.

The next room in the basement was empty. Another small space, it smelled of chalky dust and time standing still. It spooked me. A brick chimney stood in the far corner. A rusty lid covered a hole in the brick where a furnace pipe used to fit.

I said, "Check the sills at the tops of the walls and the joists. I'll check the chimney. I can almost sense that Sister Adele was here."

Laura said, "Do you honestly think Sister Adele came down here? With a recipe?"

"Sure," I said. "She may have had to toss wood in the furnace now and then. Maybe she spent a whole bunch of time down here. This space would've been cozy with the furnace blazing. She probably had a rocking chair in a corner at one time. She could have built a secret cubby behind a brick for her valuables."

Pauline scoffed. "What valuables? She was a nun. Don't they vow a life of poverty?"

Laura answered for me. "She had a rosary. I'm sure she thought that was valuable."

"And she had the recipe," I reminded them.

Pauline said, "Have you ever thought that your grandfather made up this story to keep you busy looking, and thus keep you from spending too much time with Dillon?"

"I've thought of that, but both Grandpa and Grandma are sincere about this fudge story."

"I still don't get why nobody found it before now."

"Pauline, it took a gazillion years for people to find and authenticate the Shroud of Turin."

"So now you're comparing this divinity fudge recipe to the Shroud?"

"Yes. If the Blessed Virgin Mary ate this divinity fudge, then the recipe is just as priceless."

My fingers scrabbled and scraped across the rough, dust-laden edges of the brick and cracked mortar, checking for a secret hiding place.

Pauline backed away a step. "Watch it. I can't get these clothes dirty."

My BFF had worn her favorite outfit today because she'd be meeting up with her boyfriend, John, a tour guide, at the potluck lunch for the church cleanup committee. John was on a bus somewhere in the county with thirty leaf-peeper vacationers from Chicago. The lunch would be held at my new market.

I popped off the metal covering over the chimney hole. Rust and soot flakes spewed out. They fell to the floor near my feet, sullying my running shoes. There was no recipe. I reached down for a handful of rust, wiped it on my pink T-shirt, then bombed the front of Pauline's shorts.

Pauline gasped, brushing at shorts and legs. "What are you doing?"

"Proving to Grandpa that we were trusty fudge archaeologists doing our best to unearth ancient, sweet divinity hieroglyphics."

"When Lent comes around next spring, I'm giving you up instead of booze this time. And forget your Christmas present this year."

With a smile, I pushed the wafer-thin metal covering back in place. "Must I remind you that it was Grandpa who rescued John last summer when John got left behind on his diving expedition by that creep? And John is the one who found the ceramic cup at the bottom of Lake Michigan that Grandpa thinks belongs to Grandma's ancestors. That's why Grandpa called up the royals in the first place. The initials on the cup are AVD, which might be the other Amandine Van Damme way back in Grandma's lineage. John's finding the cup led to the idea of bringing Princess Amandine here for the kermis, and that sparked Grandpa's memory about the story of Sister Adele and this church and the divinity fudge. So you're the cause of this search for a recipe, not me. I'm actually the one getting filthy in order to help you and John."

Laura was giggling.

Pauline pulled madly on her long braid to vent her frustration. "You always manage to turn things upside down and around so that you're never at fault."

"And you love me for it. What're you getting me for Christmas?" I peered up at her in a wide-eyed dare.

Pauline took a deep breath, looking down her nose at me in a double dare.

A dead black-and-red box-elder bug was stuck in her hair above one ear, which I didn't mention. Instead I reached up with my thumb and smudged the tip of her nose.

She smudged me back.

Laura said, "Hey, what about me?"

We burst out laughing. Pauline and I wiped our hands on Laura's blue-and-white-striped blouse and gave her cheeks a sooty pat.

"Perfect," I said. "Grandpa will believe we did our best and we can put his silly story to rest."

Laura took a selfie photo of us with her cell phone. "It's almost noon. I have to get back to start the bread and relieve my babysitter."

Laura was the mother of twins born in July. Little Clara Ava had my first name as her middle name, and Spencer Paul got his middle name from a shortened "Pauline."

I said, "Nobody's leaving yet. We still have the choir loft to inspect."

"Your grandpa will never know if we skip that," Laura said.

Pauline huffed, "But Ava won't lie to him. Cripes, let's go get it done."

"Thanks, Pauline," I said. "Just ten more minutes, Laura, and then you'll be free to go home to Clara Ava and Spencer Paul."

We headed up the stairs to the kitchen, then went into

the nave. We marched up the center aisle and through shafts of colors striping the pews from the stained glass windows.

Laura said, "Wasn't a Fontana Dahlgren on the list for helping us clean the church? We could leave the loft for her to clean. By the way, who is she?"

Pauline and I shared a mutual snort. Laura was our new friend, whom we'd met last spring when she opened her bakery, so she didn't know Fontana.

"Fontana's outside bothering Jonas Coppens. My grandmother called her a 'floozy,'" I said. "Fontana is mad at me, and that's why she's not in here helping."

Fontana, divorced from Daniel Dahlgren, ran Fontana's Fresh Fare, another roadside market a few miles south of mine on Highway 57. She sold her own homemade soaps, perfumes, lotions, and makeup, along with a few pumpkins to lure the tourists. My market, which focused pairing fudge flavors with local wines and fresh organic vegetables, fruits, and dairy, sat on land owned by Daniel and his new wife, Kjersta. Fontana had already stopped by my market to suggest that it was unfair competition of me to be located so close to hers, despite our goods being so different. I suspected the real reason Fontana was upset was that I'd made friends with the new wife of her ex.

Pauline added, "I heard she didn't qualify for the choir that will sing for the prince at the kermis. Maybe she's pouting and refuses to step inside the church now."

I said, "It's more likely she took a look at our names on the cleaning crew and discovered no men to flirt with, so she said the heck with it."

"Well, Jonas is a hottie," Pauline said, spritzing lemon oil on a long pew stretched across the back wall.

Laura set to work dusting the white railing of the loft while I tackled the antique pipe organ.

I filled Laura in on Jonas. We'd grown up with him. He'd lost his parents in a car accident when he was in his twenties. He now ran the family farm northeast of our farm and across Highway C, which intersected with the village of Brussels. He'd never married, but I'd heard plenty of times from my parents that he'd be quite the catch.

Pauline said, "Fontana is merely practicing on Jonas. The

prince is her target. I'm surprised she's not at one of the spas getting a pedicure so her feet look good in glass slippers."

Poking about for hidden doors and drawers in the organ, I moaned that we hadn't even found odd scraps of old newspapers I could take to Grandpa. He and I loved treasure hunting in old books and anything with the printed word.

Laura, who was wiping the organ's pipes halfheartedly, said, "At least we didn't find a body in the church."

"Yet," Pauline said, coming to stand next to me at the organ.

I gave her a punch in the upper arm, then raised my right hand. "I swear that no bodies will be found in this church now or during the prince's visit. Grandpa won't have to add 'and Bodies' at the end our shop sign, though the alliteration should be appreciated by you, Pauline." She loved word games for her students. "Besides, I've changed."

Their loud guffaws echoed from the altar at the opposite end of the church. Two tall angel statues with candles on their heads stood sentry at the steps up to the altar. I imagined they were laughing, too.

Laura pulled a piece of cobweb from her hair. "Does your family believe you've changed into somebody who doesn't always get in trouble?"

Pauline said, "Not if they're hot to marry her off to a prince and have her move over to Belgium. Sounds like a way to get rid of her. We should chip in for plane fare."

With smugness, I said, "I won't invite either of you over to my castle, at this rate. Pauline, a dead box-elder bug in your hair just dropped off to the floor."

She bent down with a paper towel to pick up the bug. "Aha! It's the dead body we knew we'd find."

"And that's the last one," I reassured them. "I have no time for crime anymore."

With Dillon's help, I was refurbishing the Blue Heron Inn in Fishers' Harbor, which my grandfather and I had recently acquired with a big, frightening mortgage. It sat on the steep hill overlooking our bait-and-fudge shop on the docks. With the inn, my new roadside market, my fudge shop, the prince's impending visit, and keeping a semblance of a romance alive, I was doing my best to stay out of trouble.

I stopped inspecting the organ for secret doors, then plopped my butt on the bench, giving in to frustration. "I was really starting to like the idea that the recipe might exist."

"What about the bench you're sitting on?" Laura asked.

With gleeful, silly hope, I launched myself up, opened the bench lid, then screamed as I jumped back, letting the lid drop with a loud clap.

Pauline came closer. "What—?"

I pointed at the bench. "A bloody knife."

We three huddled around the closed bench, staring at the lid. I said, "Open it, Pauline."

"No way. Maybe it was just your imagination."

We gave Laura an imploring look. She shook her head. "I faint at the sight of blood."

I lifted the lid. Slowly.

We stared down at a hunting knife—about seven inches long and smudged with red on its blade and white bone handle.

I said, "I work with cherries in my Cinderella Pink Fudge. That's not cherry juice."

The smeary knife lay across sheets of music. Dried blood droplets mimicked musical notes on the five-lined staff of "Ave Maria."

I leaned closer.

"Don't touch it," Pauline said.

"I'll call the sheriff." I had my phone out already.

She snatched it from me. "You're not getting involved. You know you have bad luck. We're walking away from this and letting somebody else find it."

Laura had paled. "That's a good idea. I need to get back to my babies."

Pauline shut the lid of the bench with a bang.

A sudden corresponding loud *thud* from below made us jump. We stared wide-eyed into one another's eyes. My heart was racing.

Voices—chattering—drifted up to the loft. The loud noise had been a door likely slamming against the wall after being caught by the breeze.

We scrambled to look over the railing. It was John's tour.

I whispered, "Crap. They're not supposed to be here. This is cleaning day."

Pauline plastered on a smile, then waved at John below. She whispered back to me, "I don't want John involved in whatever your bloody knife means. The last time he tried helping you, he almost ended up dead."

"It's not *my* knife."

"You found it. And I know how you are. Criminally curious." She looked down her nose at me with her sternest teacherlike demeanor. "I'll make sure they don't come up here. Forget the knife. Promise me."

But she hurried down the stairs to the nave before I could actually promise.

Chapter 2

I eased up the bench lid.

Some of the blood splatter on the sheet music for "Ave Maria" had underscored the lyrics *Safe may we sleep beneath thy care.* The irony hit me. Somebody had not been playing it safe with the Buck knife.

Then someone was calling my name.

I lowered the bench lid quickly, stepping away and into the choir pews.

Fontana Dahlgren stood on the top step of the stairs to the choir loft. Her red, wavy hair cascading past her shoulders hailed me like a warning flag. As always, her petite, cheerleader persona caused me to stare out of envy and curiosity.

In fifth grade I'd thought that if I stuck close to her I might acquire her looks. In science class we'd been introduced to the concept of living cells absorbing other cells or their qualities. Fontana possessed startling minty green eyes set in a face with enough freckles to keep her from looking too porcelain. A short-sleeved yellow cotton sweater showed off movie-star breasts that were all her own. Knee-length shorts floated silkily about her toned legs. She carried two big designer bags hooked on one arm—a purse and one filled with the homemade soaps, perfumes, and makeup she was always hawking.

"Well, hello, Ava Mathilde Oosterling." Her melon-colored lipstick shimmered. "Practicing a song for the prince? I guess since your family invited him, you get to sing something despite not making it into the choir. Let me coach you. Perhaps we could sing a solo during the kermis."

"A solo means one person alone, Fontana. Not two." She knew I had what my mother called a tin ear. Grandma said I couldn't carry a tune in a bushel basket. Fontana didn't want to coach me; she wanted to make me over—yet again—and use me to flirt with the prince.

She stepped into the loft. "Why don't you go on down to join your friends while I dig around in the music for us? I'll pick something simple for you."

The last thing I needed was for her to find the bloody knife. After her scream, John's tour would be ruined and Pauline would disown me as a friend.

A lie was in order. "Fontana, go back down. We just waxed everything. It's slippery and you'll fall." Her ankles looked spindly atop sandals with tall, wedge heels.

In faked stealth, I crept across the floor in my sooty sneakers. As I came within a yard of Fontana, her spicy perfume pricked my nostrils.

Instead of turning around to descend the stairs, Fontana stayed in place, her teeth chewing off a portion of the dewy melon-colored lipstick on her lips while she strained to look behind me in the loft. I was focusing on wiggling my nose to avoid sneezing when a premonition hit me—one accompanied by a chill.

"What's the matter, Fontana? Did you leave something behind after the choir tryouts?" *Like a knife?* Tryouts had occurred over the past week, but I recalled my grandmother telling me that a few singers had returned early this morning with the organist to decide on some songs. They'd left before Pauline, Laura, and I arrived to clean the church.

After a dramatic sigh, Fontana said, "I suppose I can come back for it later."

"What is it you left behind?"

"You certainly are nosy. I'll return after taking the tour group to my roadside market."

Now her competitiveness was making me grind my molars. "The tour is supposed to go to my market, not yours. We're doing a wine-and-fudge-pairing event for their lunch treat. And a grape stomp."

"I spoke with Mike about that. He doesn't have enough grapes."

She referred to Michael Prevost, the winegrower and vintner. His vineyard was located on the property behind the farm where I had set up my roadside market.

I stepped closer into her perfume cloud. "Fontana, can we please go down the stairs and join the discussion below in the nave?"

John and a university specialist were talking about the church's history and rocks.

"Oh, sure. Sorry. I'll come back after lunch."

"No," I said. "The floors and benches need to be left alone for a full day so the wax sets properly."

After a sigh, she said, "I can come back tomorrow."

"You'll have to ask me for the key. You'll need to come all the way up to Fishers' Harbor to pick it up at my fudge shop." Another lie. And inside a church. "You've forgotten that my family is the keeper of the church key."

Since my parents lived nearby, they kept the key and also kept a log of who went in and out of the church. The sheriff had requested they do that to help with security precautions before the royal visit. At the moment, my grandmother had the church key.

Fontana gave me a pointed look with her phosphorescent eyes. She knew I knew something. She flashed her engaging, cheerleader smile. "Let's hurry before Cherry and John leave us behind on the tour."

Before I descended the stairs behind her, I scanned the crowd from my perch in the loft. Pauline's boyfriend had a bandaged hand. His guest expert, Tristan "Cherry" Hardy, sported a bandaged arm and hand. What had happened to them?

I had a bad feeling about today.

I eased down the staircase quietly, glad that its entrance was in the vestibule and didn't spill me out directly into the crowded nave. The more I looked at the busload of people gathered inside the church, the more bandages I saw, and the less suspicious I became about them. The tourists had the usual scuffed knees, blisters from new sandals, bug bites, and sunburn. Maybe Pauline was right. The knife wasn't anything to worry about. Maybe some kid had stolen the knife from a parent, nicked himself, then raced up here after the choir tryouts unnoticed to hide the knife. That had to be the answer.

I tried to pay attention to the speaker, but my gaze kept drifting to his forearm with its approximately three-inch white gauzy bandage.

Tristan "Cherry" Hardy was a good friend to many of us. The tour group hung on his every word. Tall, boyishly handsome in his forties, with short brown hair, Tristan hailed from the University of Wisconsin at the Green Bay campus. He was conducting research on cherry orchard and vineyard improvements for the local extension office. He wore a royal blue polo shirt with the UWEX logo on it. Our area was a leading producer of Montmorency tart cherries. Tourists flocked here to pick and buy cherry everything, from cherry salsa to pies to my fudge.

Tristan stood in the nave's aisle, his back to the altar. Not far from him were the angel statues, as tall as fifth graders with candle wreaths on their heads. The tourists filled the open area at the back where pews had been removed for occasions like this. Laura was inching toward the door to head home. Pauline was on the opposite side of the crowd with John listening to Tristan go on about the history of the local forests and the Belgians who flooded into Door County in the 1850s to fish in the Lake Michigan bay called Green Bay.

"Door County is about stone and water," he said. "Because of the Niagara escarpment created by the glaciers long ago, we're built on stone. The stone formations here continue all the way out to Niagara Falls. Our topsoil is thin and precious. Building a basement for a church would have taken a lot of work—and probably some dynamite. Any stone removed from here was used to help build foundations or even stone barns like the one Ava Oosterling uses for her new roadside market."

Cherry waved his arm my way. I waved back to the crowd.

Cherry continued. "Being built on stone means we can

dry out fast, leaving our orchards and vineyards susceptible to pests, fires, and the harm done by drifting chemicals in the air, perhaps even the exhaust of so many tourist vehicles and supply trucks going by on Highway 57."

John almost leaped out of his Hawaiian shirt in shock. The crowd was muttering about themselves being blamed for pollution.

John jumped to the front alongside Cherry. "That didn't come out the way he meant it."

"Anything we put into the air has an effect," Cherry assured us in a calm voice. "Can food be organic, if the organic food stand is next to a busy city street choking with fumes?"

Oh, egads, this day was getting even worse. Who would want to eat fudge if they believed the cars whooshing by polluted it?

John leaped in with facts on the water quality of the bay, where he explained he'd been diving. He didn't say, but I assumed he'd cut his hand on the expedition. John was in his fifties, with brown hair graying at the temples and a joking manner that tourists enjoyed. Today he wore his usual tour-guide outfit: baggy tan shorts and billowy Hawaiian shirt—this one festooned with purple grapes and red wineglasses.

John encouraged everybody to snap pictures of Saint Mary of the Snows. He raised a small camera to videotape everybody. Ordinarily, I found John a bother. He was hoping to mount his own food and travel show on a cable channel. He often videotaped me stirring fudge in my copper kettles. But right now I would almost kiss his hairy feet in a thank-you for distracting Cherry from his ill-advised presentation.

"Cherry," John said, "we need to move on now for lunch at Ava's Autumn Harvest. Your talk was originally scheduled for after the lunch, so why don't we continue this after we all imbibe in Ava's wonderful fudge and Michael's wines?"

A lot of wine might be needed to help people forget about pollution on their food.

To my shock, Fontana stepped in front of Cherry and John to address the crowd. "The tour is stopping first at Fontana's Fresh Fare, Cherry."

John tried to speak up about his tour—it wasn't Cherry's tour, after all—but Fontana went on about free natural lip balm made from local beeswax and perfumes made with thistle flowers and dill seeds. The women outvoted the few men in the crowd, which meant they were not coming to my outdoor market.

My grandpa and I needed all the sales we could get. We had a prince and princess coming and we wanted them to enjoy a freshly refurbished Blue Heron Inn.

In a loud voice, I said, "There's fresh Rapunzel Raspberry Rapture Fudge today at Ava's. Served with whipped cream from my parents' farm. And Mom brought cheddar curds. They squeak in your teeth."

The curds announcement got heads nodding. Tourists loved Wisconsin's famous squeaky cheese curds.

Hands shot up.

But then Fontana got in my face. Her homemade perfume polluted my lungs. It smelled like a combination of mincemeat pie spices and rosewater.

Fontana pulled a huge bar of pink soap from her bag of products to wave around. "Look at you, Ava. What is that black stuff all over you? My new cherry-infused goat milk soap is just the thing to take care of grime."

I ground out, "Some of us were cleaning the church as we'd promised to do. This is only a little soot and dust."

An older woman called out, "Working amid the cinders. You're Cinderella."

A man said, "Ava, are you the one the prince is coming to see?"

A woman my mom's age said, "Wash your feet, honey! You want clean feet in those glass slippers!"

Laughter galloped through the throng.

Fontana waved her soap again. "Let's take her down to Fontana's Fresh Fare for a makeover. In an hour she won't look like an ugly stepsister at all. Did I tell you that all my makeup and lotions are half off today? Let's get back on the bus and head on down there."

Cherry raised his bandaged arm with a brochure in his hand. "Sorry, Fontana, but John was right. I'm hungry." He chuckled. "We're having lunch at Ava's Autumn Harvest.

Then we have the rest of my presentation at one o'clock. Folks, we expect several area farmers to be there, so it should be interesting. After that, we're visiting the Prevost Winery where you can participate in a grape stomp."

Fontana pouted petulantly, then addressed the crowd. "I can show you where Sister Adele saw the Virgin Mary walk right up to her in the woods. My vegetables and plants for your face are grown with the blessed dirt touched by the Virgin Mary and Sister Adele Brise. And of course, we might return to the church to find Sister Adele's divinity fudge recipe hidden somewhere in this holy edifice."

The crowd gasped.

So did I. I exchanged a look of horror with Pauline, who stood a few feet away.

How did Fontana learn about the recipe? That was my grandfather's secret. Only my family, my girlfriends, and the prince and princess knew about it. We wanted to announce it at the kermis in two weeks.

Even John—who could never keep a secret about anything—appeared shocked, though he was smiling. He was probably dreaming up a new tour that would follow the trail of Sister Adele between Namur and southwest of us to Champion in Kewaunee County where her shrine resided.

The tourists were flipping their heads every which way as they began imagining where the recipe might be hidden.

John addressed his tour. "Hold on, everybody. The divinity fudge recipe is merely a story made up by Ava Oosterling's grandfather to help celebrate the prince's visit. But Ava will be making divinity fudge for the kermis. So all of you should come back here in two weeks to try it. Your donations will help us restore the steeple above us and help support our local volunteer fire department. Ava's fudge is heavenly tasting, a miracle all its own. Did you know that Ava's Autumn Harvest is in a historic stone barn that escaped the Great Fire of 1871? Did you know that fire took over one thousand lives here the same day the Great Chicago Fire took three hundred lives?"

Just like that, John wrestled the crowd's attention away from Fontana while also squelching the rumor about the fudge. I wanted to hug Pauline's boyfriend.

A school bus waited for them on the blacktopped road in front of the church.

Cherry hustled after John out the door. Fontana wiggled along in her wedge sandals at Cherry's elbow.

Pauline and I piled into the front seats of my yellow Chevy pickup truck. I had pulled onto the road heading east when a flash of red and yellow appeared in my side mirror. I stopped.

"What's wrong?" Pauline asked.

"Double-fudge trouble." I shifted into reverse.

"Don't hit the bus."

"I won't." I backed up enough to let Fontana see me. "Fontana is trying to sneak back in the church."

After spotting me watching her, she headed in the opposite direction toward Jonas over at the historic schoolhouse east of the church.

Pauline growled, "Let her sneak back in. She owes us for not helping us clean the church."

"I think she knows something about that knife, Pauline."

"I told you to forget that knife. And don't get involved with Fontana. She's been too unpredictable since her divorce from Daniel. Let's go."

Fontana was waving her hand in the air toward Jonas, who was pushing a wheelbarrow filled with garden tools. Through our open windows we heard Fontana yell, "Jonas! I need a ride."

"A ride, my foot," I muttered. "She's waiting for me to leave. Then she'll duck into that church to look for that recipe and hide that knife."

I pulled my cell phone out of my shorts pocket, intending to call the sheriff.

Pauline groaned. "Don't call Jordy. That woman isn't somebody you want to tangle with. Daniel nearly lost his property in their divorce because she was sentimental about the tree in their yard where she'd carved their initials. Who knows how she'll get back at you for having her arrested inside this church? We don't know for sure she had anything to do with that knife."

I stared at my phone, then sagged in my seat. "You're right."

"Hearing you say that is music to my ears."

"Thanks, Pauline. And thanks to your boyfriend for deflecting trouble."

"I'm hungry. Did you and your grandpa bring along any of your Rose Garden Fudge that won your contest last July? Chocolate with rose petals tastes heavenly with a cabernet."

As she rattled on, I watched with great trepidation as the church ladies, including my grandmother, toddled out of the old schoolhouse with their brooms and mops. Over at the church, Fontana seemed to be leading Jonas toward the church's side door near the parking lot. She probably thought she was hidden behind the vehicles still parked there.

"My grandmother is responsible for locking up the church today. Fontana's going to cause Grandma Sophie trouble if I don't do something."

Pauline gave me a cross-eyed look. "I give up. Call the sheriff, but then let's leave so you don't end up blamed for this trouble."

An hour later Sheriff Jordy Tollefson showed up during the postluncheon presentation by Cherry at Ava's Autumn Harvest on Highway 57 to tell me the bad news.

Chapter 3

It was a good thing Sheriff Jordy Tollefson showed up when he did at my roadside market. The neighbors were arguing—not good for selling pumpkins and fudge to tourists.

Everybody was gathered on the large grassy area outside the stone barn. Ava's Autumn Harvest was located on property belonging to Daniel and Kjersta Dahlgren. My barn was about forty yards from their house, large garden, and garden pole shed. Their apple and cherry orchards lay beyond behind the house. Highway C ran by in front. Vehicles were parked up and down the blacktopped road as well as on the grassy land between the driveway and my stone barn.

Cherry's presentation about the harm done to our local orchards and vineyards by drought, bugs, and chemical drift from neighboring farms exacerbated a months-long, simmering disagreement among my friends who lived in the area.

Grape grower Michael Prevost was the most vocal, accusing Jonas Coppens of using too many chemicals on his cornfields north of Michael's property. The cornfield bumped up against both the Coppens and Dahlgren properties where their properties intersected in a triangle about forty yards behind the Dahlgrens' brick house.

Jonas had shown up without Fontana, which pleased and worried me. I wondered if Grandma had tangled with her in the church. Calls to my grandmother had gone unanswered.

John's group of thirty people seemed embarrassed by the heated discussion. Cherry, Michael, Jonas, and Daniel Dahlgren were debating "proof versus no proof" that chemicals had entered the local groundwater and grapes.

I plied the busload of tourists with plastic cups of wine. Michael had provided several Prevost Winery wines, from crisp whites that tasted like sweet morning air, to luscious purple-red pinots that reminded one of watching the strip of sunset on the horizon when light leaked out of our autumn evenings.

As the sheriff strode from his car, Pauline escaped to be with John.

I went inside the barn to warn Grandpa Gil that the sheriff was here. "Gilpa, you didn't tell Fontana about the recipe, did you?"

"Surely not, A.M. Why?"

I told him what had transpired over in Namur.

"You're sure that was a Buck knife?" Grandpa Gil ran a hand over his wavy silver hair. I still hadn't gotten used to Grandpa not having engine oil or grease all up and down his person and in his hair. Since he'd junked his beloved but decrepit fishing trawler this past summer, he'd turned into a dapper guy I didn't recognize. Today he wore a clean red plaid shirt and tan pants.

He said, "Your grandmother gave me a new Buck knife for Christmas last year, but mine is back at the house. Had to be kids. You know how it is at a certain age they all want to play with knives."

"I suppose, but maybe you should go see what's keeping Grandma."

"Sophie will be fine. You better scoot. Those people out there tasting your fudge want to know all about the ingredients. Point across the road to your daddy's farm and tell them the cows they see are making that cream you use to create a slice of Heaven with Belgian chocolate."

"I'm not so sure they're going to care unless Cherry stops talking about chemicals floating all over in the air. Pretty soon nobody will want to eat my fudge."

"What's gotten into that guy? Never seen him be such a zealot about his research."

I hurried outside. I paused to breathe in the sun-drenched air. In the far distance, maples that limned the horizon meeting the Green Bay of Lake Michigan showed spots of orange and red. The bay shimmered beyond the treetops.

The beauty should have calmed me. Instead I saw the sheriff in his squad car talking on his phone. Something was up.

I joined Pauline behind a flatbed wagon loaded with pumpkins. We helped a few kids pick out the best ones for carving.

Nodding toward the fray not far from us, I asked, "What's going on now?"

"He's talking about finding dead bugs in the Dahlgrens' cherry orchard."

"Dangerous bugs?"

"I don't know. He moved on quickly to talking about some rot and cancer diseases that could hit the cherry trees. I couldn't hear over Kjersta's agonizing complaints about their business being ruined."

"I'd scream, too, if my business were about to tank." My fudge shop almost did just that last May when it'd been found tainted with hidden diamonds, of all things. I'd had to close down for a couple of days until the sheriff and I figured out I was being set up in a murder case. "How's the pairing event going?"

"So far the favorite pair is Cinderella Pink Fudge with Mike's new sweet white wine made from the grapes introduced to the Prevost vineyard by Cherry about eight years ago. Cherry explained it all, hogging the microphone. Poor Mike couldn't even talk about his own grapes."

It took grapevines several years to establish themselves and bear fruit. This should have been a celebratory year for Michael Prevost. However, it was not because of the crop problems he and the Dahlgrens were experiencing.

Kjersta was arguing with Cherry again. Daniel had married the opposite of Fontana when he wed Kjersta. She was a farm girl like me, shapely and tall. Unlike me, she kept her wavy brown hair in a pixie cut. She had big brown eyes with eyelashes so lush they looked fake, which I knew bothered Fontana.

Kjersta and I had attended twelve grades together. Her husband, Daniel, was forty—eight years older, and proud of his family's role in our county's history. His ancestors had been planting cherry trees in Door County since Professor E. S. Goff planted the first trees in Door County in 1896 not far from us near Sturgeon Bay.

The Dahlgren cherry orchard's yield had dropped by half in the past two years, which was what Cherry Hardy was studying. To compensate for the loss of income, Kjersta had planted a vegetable garden that covered two acres. I'd helped earlier today with digging up the potatoes. Kjersta got to sell anything she wanted at my stand in exchange for no rent and use of the small barn.

Dillon had replaced rotted beams and a rusted tin roof for me with fresh Shaker-style wooden shingles. The shingles were of the kind the early Belgians, Swedes, Finns, and Norwegians might have made when they sent millions of shingles south to repair Chicago after its famous fire that happened the same October days as ours. Back then, the stone barn's space probably sheltered up to a dozen cows in winter, a team of Belgian horses for logging, and maybe a barn cat and some chickens. Today, it held islands of fudge, jellies, and jams, and a dozen Belgian pies in as many flavors made by my grandmother.

Pauline and I jerked our attention to the presentation when Daniel's voice rose. With his height of well over six feet and shoulder-length, wavy blond hair, Daniel stood out.

Cherry was holding up both arms as if he were stopping traffic. "We're not sure what's really causing the orchard damage. I'm buying more fudge, cheese, and wine today from this market to see what we might detect in the food chain."

I yelped to Pauline, "He's going to test my fudge for chemicals?"

"Your fudge contains cream from your cows that feed off the land nearby. Cherry wants to see what's getting into our food chain."

I stood up straighter behind the pumpkin wagon. "That's nonsense. Jonas has always been careful because my family's farm is across the road. He knows we're a certified organic dairy."

But Michael Prevost, my retired high school math teacher who operated the vineyard to the east of the Dahlgrens' orchard and Jonas's farm, wasn't so generous with Jonas. Mike was in his late fifties, robust and muscular, with a big round head like a basketball on his shoulders. He maintained a rather tall but thinning crew cut that was almost a Mohawk in the front. The robust sienna color of his hair looked dyed.

He held up a piece of naked grapevine. "Jonas, you're lying. Your crops are perfect, not a weed in sight, not a bug in sight. What's it going to take to stop you from ruining the rest of us?" He shook the vine. "This is all that's left of several of my grapevines planted within fifty feet of your property."

I found Mike's accusation about lying interesting, because when he was a high school teacher, or "Mr." Prevost, he had a habit of feeding answers for tests to some of the so-called slower kids to help them get a D or C grade instead of an F. We students noticed, too, that his briefcase held an unusual bounty of pens and notepads that were likely purloined from the supply room. The other teachers always complained about not being given enough supplies, but not Mr. Prevost.

Jonas looked like a copper pot ready to boil over. He had a deep tan, as most farmers did, and the tan garnered respect because it represented hard work. His dark auburn hair was streaked from summer sun, and his gray-blue eyes looked like sleepy moons in his face.

"I believe 'ruining' is a strong word," he said in his even but stern voice. "Let Cherry work on the tests back at the university and report back."

"Where's Fontana?" I asked Pauline. "And my grandmother? She and the church ladies never miss free fudge, cheese curds, and wine."

The sheriff was still in his car talking on the phone, which I found curious.

Pauline wound her long, dark hair around a hand in worry, too. "Why don't you go back to the church to find out what's going on?"

My phone buzzed in my pocket. I took a peek. "A text from the sheriff. He probably wants my help solving the case of the bloody knife in the church loft."

Pauline tossed her hair back off her shoulders. "I'm going home. John's picking me up by five o'clock."

"Another date? Where?" I was envious because Dillon Rivers and I didn't go on dates nearly as much as John and Pauline. Dillon and I had vowed to take our relationship slow this time. Eight years ago, we'd ended up like a doomed Bonnie-and-Clyde pair careening through life doing what we wanted on impulse. Now at age thirty-two, I wanted the experience of true, old-fashioned courting. Dillon had agreed. Now we were like archaeologists, sifting carefully through our hearts one cupful of attention at a time to see if we might unearth the secret to our future. But sometimes the sifting felt mighty slow and boring.

Pauline tossed into her big purse a sack of fudge, a bag of cheese curds, and a bottle of wine. "We're catching a new play at the American Folklore Theater in the park."

"Did you pay for those, Pauline?"

She went bug-eyed. "These are payment for you ruining this outfit in the church. You should buy yourself some new clothes sometime. See how it feels. Go on a date."

My dates entailed me taking sandwiches to the inn for Dillon, where he'd been smashing down old plaster as of late. We would eat amid the dust. Then I'd go back to my fudge shop on the harbor to set up for the next day. I'd retire to bed early so I could get up at five in the morning to start making fudge. After Cody Fjelstad or some of the church ladies stopped in to take over the cash register, I'd bring fudge down here to my lower Door County market. It was a routine that I should have loved, but I found myself jealous of Pauline. Once her school day was done, she was free as an eagle to soar.

My father arrived behind the pumpkin wagon as Pauline took off in her car. Peter was tall, like all of us Oosterlings. His sported our family's lush head of wavy chestnut brown hair and the Belgian nose. The nose was slightly aquiline with a tiny ridge in the middle. My dad said the Belgian nose was specially made for use in creating the best in beer, booyah, chocolate, and fudge.

"What're you doing here, Dad?"

Noontime was one of the milking times for his big herd.

Mom must have taken over for him, which meant this trip over here was serious. He had cleaned up in a pair of black church slacks and a blue chambray shirt, the cuffs rolled up on the sunny fall day. "Thought I better see what Cherry had to say about the chemical drift issue and support Jonas."

Dad and Mom had known Jonas's parents for years before they'd perished in the car accident.

Cherry was saying, "The early test results should be coming back by Monday, and the test samples that we're taking today will further prove or not what's really going on."

The professor's teaching and lab assistants, Nick Stensrud and Will Lucchesi, had just driven in. They were familiar guys, and from a distance they looked like brothers with their short brown hair and slim builds. They'd been to our farm several times in the past couple of years with Cherry, as well as his colleague and dean, Professor Wesley Weaver. As early adopters of organic farming, we Oosterlings had given ourselves over to research projects for the university. Nick and Will usually did the "dirty work" of gathering samples for Cherry.

A woman in the crowd asked, "But can we still eat the fudge?" She held a piece of my Cinderella Pink Fairy Tale Fudge in front of her.

I held my breath.

Cherry said, "We all live with chemicals. It's hard to escape them in our world. It's my job to moderate the effects as best I can by teaching good practices in farming, or grape growing, or fudge making for that matter."

I gulped. I looked at my dad, whispering, "I guess I've arrived if the university extension service is taking note of my fudge."

Kjersta asked Cherry, "But we have rights, don't we, to make Jonas cough up his chemicals? He's using illegal chemicals."

"I'm not using anything illegal."

Dad muttered under his breath, "That's the spirit."

A car door slammed. The sheriff had gotten out of his squad car. I'd forgotten his text. He stalked toward where Dad and I stood behind the pumpkin-filled wagon.

Three other vehicles pulled into the grassy parking area, including my grandmother in her sports utility vehicle. From a car, Fontana bolted out of the backseat, heading straight for Jonas.

"You left me back there. How could you leave me like that?" Fontana said, her shrill voice mocking the twittering of a flock of sparrows sitting on the eaves of the barn behind us.

Fontana was like a fox heading into a flock of chickens. The crowd split up or backed off. She trotted from Jonas over to Cherry, talking loudly about seeing him later and how she'd explain everything. I wondered what.

Kjersta hurried to Jonas with a cup of wine, asking if he'd like to try some, which I thought was a neighborly gesture considering how they weren't getting along. But I saw the wisdom in breaking up this unfortunate scene. I grabbed wine cups and followed Kjersta's lead.

Fontana then headed toward her ex-husband, Daniel, but he escaped by grabbing a bottle of pink wine right out of Mike's hands. He began pouring a new round to anybody noshing on my pink fudge.

Dad disappeared inside the barn to help Grandpa.

John told his tour it was time to get on the bus so they could go down the road and around the corner to the Prevost Winery.

Sheriff Jordy Tollefson followed me back to where I took up sentry again at the pumpkin wagon. Customers scattered, to my chagrin.

My grandmother limped up behind him but spoke to me. "The sheriff badgered us about some knife being found in the organ bench. Maria Vasquez was there, too."

Maria was a deputy sheriff. Guilt rattled me. I'd called the sheriff.

The sheriff looked through his aviator sunglasses at me. "Your grandfather around?"

"In the barn."

Jordy sauntered to the stone barn.

Horrified, I asked Grandma, "Was that Grandpa's knife in that bench?"

Grandma grabbed her white hair to keep it from whipping in the breeze across her face. Her dark eyes looked like blisters of pain. "This whole mess is Gil's fault."

"What do you mean?"

By now, only a few feet from us, the church ladies were buzzing with the tourists about "blood" and "Ave Maria" and "organ bench" and "knife."

Grandma said, "Maria kept asking about the prince and princess, and who might want to do them harm."

Grandma was shaking all over.

Over her shoulder I spotted Fontana heading to a car with Cherry. Cherry had his arms full of the fudge and other goods he'd bought to take for testing. Fontana seemed to be arguing with him. Cherry was shaking his head vigorously.

John was herding his group into the bus.

My grandfather and father had emerged from the stone barn, walking on either side of the sheriff. While my father was always reserved, my grandfather was gesticulating wildly in the air at the sheriff.

As they approached, I asked, "What's going on?"

The sheriff, tall and menacing in his brown and tan uniform, gun at his hip, with his hat brim set straight over his sunglasses, said, "I'm going to have to cancel the royal visit. I'll be contacting the prince and princess."

Chapter 4

Grandpa scooped Grandma next to his side with a long arm around her waist. "Prince Arnaud and his mother are my wife's relatives and I invited them. Sheriff, I can do what I darn well please with family."

My grandfather was itching to get himself in handcuffs. Again. He and I had something twisted in our DNA with a chromosome that looked like the chrome of handcuffs.

I appealed to Jordy. "If Prince Arnaud doesn't attend, the kermis will be ruined. It's only two weeks away from tomorrow. We need that money to restore the church steeple. Would you deny people their religious freedom? Go against the Constitution?"

The sheriff removed his aviator sunglasses and then held up a hand to quiet me. He gave me a penetrating look, as if we were in a private bubble. Last summer I had realized Jordy might have intentions concerning me that went beyond mere law enforcement. But he was a gentleman and kept a respectful demeanor. "Ava, and all of you, we don't have a big enough staff or budget to protect royalty from some nutcase. I was called to look at a knife. Maria's taking it into the lab. This has to be taken seriously as a possible threat to your visitors. We live in a different world now. It's my job to be cautious."

I muttered, trying to sound respectful, "Jordy, you don't have the authority to stop a royal visit." Then doubts set in. "Do you?"

His hands fiddled with his sunglasses. "I have the authority and responsibility to inform our governor and the royal visitors if I feel we lack the resources to properly protect visitors to our county. I'm sorry if that would end up canceling their visit or harming the kermis."

Grandpa piped up again. "I'll call Arnaud Van Damme and ask him to bring along bodyguards."

My grandma said, "Now, Gil, if it's not wise for Arnaud and Amandine to come, let's listen to the sheriff."

"I'll find farm lads to protect them," Grandpa said.

Jordy slipped his aviators back on. "Bodyguards at their expense would be a good idea. This is the height of the leaf-peeping tourist season and I have my hands full with important things."

My grandfather said, "Like what? Too many people stopping at Ava's market? Could you help us with the traffic tie-up out there on the road before you leave?"

My father and I winced at Grandpa's directive, but he was right. The country road was clogged with all the cars leaving and the bus trying to turn around in the driveway.

My grandmother left us to hoof it back to her sports utility vehicle with her church friends Dotty Klubertanz and Lois Forbes.

After my father left, I said to Grandpa, "Grandma's not so excited about her royal relatives."

"Honey, I've been trying to figure that out. It could be my gift is too big for her. You know how humble we Belgians are. We don't need fancy stuff in our lives."

"She said something like that earlier to me when she was cleaning around the gravestones. But I sense there's something deeper going on. She'd be relieved if the prince and princess never came."

Grandpa caught my hand nearest him and gave it a gentle squeeze. His rough hand sported the accumulation of years of calluses that had weathered a lot of storms, like our ancient oak tree in the middle of our pasture that we could see from where we stood. "Let's give Sophie plenty of space. Sooner or later we'll know what's going on and then we can help."

"I'm sorry I found that knife."

"You didn't do anything. The knife was there. You did the right thing by calling the sheriff."

Grandpa's mere touch reassured me. I said, "I'll give Grandma space. I promise."

He laughed. "Thank you. You do have a way of not letting well enough alone."

"You calling me stubborn?"

"I'm calling you a Belgian."

"Same thing, Gilpa. And I inherited it from you."

Because the sales were so good, I stayed longer than usual. I checked in with my helper at the fudge shop in Fishers' Harbor, Cody Fjelstad, who was nineteen and busy with college classes. He said he'd be able to stay on for a couple more hours.

Grandpa and I rang up good sales after the arguing quit. The Rose Garden Fudge sales were neck and neck with Cinderella Pink Fairy Tale Fudge. Rapunzel Raspberry Rapture— served at the outdoor picnic tables with fresh whipped cream—was gone within an hour along with Mike's pinot.

Grandpa accelerated the speed of money from the wallets by telling everybody about the impending visit by the prince. A couple of tourists from New York said they'd be back in two weeks to see Prince Arnaud. Grandpa told them a Belgian had negotiated the sale of land that created New York City.

I endured more jokes about wearing glass slippers to a ball, but I didn't mind. The cash register's steady ding was music to dance to in any kind of shoe.

My brain returned to thinking about Fontana and the knife as I pulled to a stop in front of my rental cabin on Duck Marsh Street in Fishers' Harbor around four o'clock that Saturday. While glancing across the street at my grandparents' cabin, I saw that Grandma's SUV was there. It was unfortunate she'd been caught up in the mess.

I was vexed by Fontana's sneaky behavior and her open and almost desperate flirtations with Jonas and Cherry, though I recalled Cherry was seemingly telling her no about something. She was probably trying to get him to hold some special event at her roadside market. The great sales happening before her eyes at my market likely created jealousy.

I had barely stepped from my yellow Chevy pickup truck in front of my log cabin when Lucky Harbor planted paws firmly on my sooty front. My weariness evaporated.

The American water spaniel was a brown, curly-haired dog invented in Wisconsin that looked like a short golden retriever that had gotten an old-fashioned permanent. His eyes held golden flecks that could soak up the sun and mesmerize me. Lucky Harbor had wandered into my fudge shop last May as a puppy. Cody named him Harbor because of our location. But when my ex-husband showed up later to claim the runaway puppy, we learned the dog's given name was Lucky. I had assumed Dillon had named the dog after his famous bad habit of gambling. Instead Dillon had kicked the habit and felt himself lucky to be starting over with his life. That sentiment unlocked something soft toward Dillon again inside my heart. I, too, was lucky to start over in Fishers' Harbor. So all of us now called the hunting dog two names: Lucky Harbor.

"What's all the excitement?" I asked the dog.

He plunked his butt on my lawn.

"You want fudge, don't you?" Chocolate wasn't good for dogs, so I never gave him fudge. I had learned that every time customers said "fudge" they said it with such exuberance that the tone excited the dog. Now my pockets were always filled with tiny Goldfish crackers to use as "fudge" for Lucky Harbor.

I tossed a handful of crackers into the air. His teeth clacked as he snatched most of the crackers. He snuffled about in the blades of grass for the two he'd missed.

On his collar I noticed a floatable key holder—an orange plastic tube about three inches long. I smiled. Dillon had taken to sending me messages in it this summer.

I unscrewed the key holder, then pulled out the paper. It read *I miss you*.

I got a pen from my truck, and wrote on the note *I'll be right up*.

With the note in the key holder on his collar again,

Lucky Harbor took off toward Main Street, a block and a half away. He veered right, streaking in a brown blur up the steep hill to the Blue Heron Inn.

The inn stood on a bluff overlooking the marshy cove at the end of my three-block street as well as the harbor and a good portion of our quaint downtown. By the holidays, I planned to move into the inn permanently. Lucky Harbor paused at the top of the hill to peer back at me. His tail wagged. He wanted me to follow.

A thrill tickled my insides. After such a strange day, I couldn't wait to fall into Dillon's strong arms.

After I entered the Blue Heron Inn, Dillon wrapped me against his bare chest and ignited an instant fire with his lips on mine.

He smelled of fresh wood shavings and the pine scent that always spun off his saw blades when he was working on the gazebo out back. My lungs filled with his manly essence.

"I needed this," I muttered.

"I needed you," he whispered in my ear.

We parted to look into each other's brown eyes. His eyes were the color of the deepest, darkest chocolate fudge in my shop. He was six feet four inches tall, which gave him enough height over me that I could fully appreciate his dreamy eyelashes and strong chin.

His bare chest and six-pack stomach sported a bronze tan from summer, begging my hands to explore. My breathing was ragged. I pressed my hands on his pectoral muscles and nuzzled his neck.

A guttural, wild growl emanated from him and then he took me to the floor.

Giggling, we rolled about on the giant floral rug in the reception hall of the historic inn. The chandelier above sparkled like stars winking down at us.

Dillon rolled to a stop, with him over me, cradling me under him. "You're overdressed," he murmured, a gleam in his wild eyes.

Then a big slurping tongue alongside my cheek made me go, "Ugh."

Dillon said, "Lucky, bad timing."

I rolled out from under Dillon, then got up off the floor.

"He's reminding us to keep our promise to ourselves. Sex only on Wednesdays."

Dillon rose to his feet. "I don't need a watchdog. I'm a grown man."

"Think of him as our guardian angel," I said, rearranging my clothes back into proper order. "We promised to date like real people and not let sex be the only thing that attracts us to each other."

He gave me a petulant, steamy look.

I almost caved. "If we're going to make it as a couple, we have to control our impulses sometimes. What if Cody had walked in on us? Or my grandma? Or your mother? They're always popping in."

"Darn, but do you always have to be right?" He winked.

"With this, yes."

Dillon conceded by combing through his shoulder-length hair as he caught his breath. He'd let his hair grow longer over the summer, and it gave him a wilderness persona that was new. I'd married him before at a time in his life when he was trying to be just the opposite—as polished as the casinos in Vegas, where we'd been married.

Dillon pulled on a black-and-white-plaid flannel shirt, and then a red sweatshirt over it. September late afternoons and evenings grew chilly.

Dillon picked up a toolbox. "How was your day?"

I always melted at that question. *How was your day?* So simple, yet it defined "love," I felt. It showed he cared. We'd promised in our new pact to always ask each other how our day had gone.

When we first met back in college in Madison, he'd talked mostly about his schedule of gigs as a standup comedian. I was in awe of him. We eloped. A month later in Las Vegas I found out he'd dated other women pretty seriously—even married another woman in one of those crazy one-night stands that are supposed to be annulled the next day. After being accused of bigamy, he got the mess cleaned up, even spending a few days in jail rather than having his parents bail him out.

I realized that everything I'd done—including eloping—had been done for him, not me or "us." Sure, I had tremendous fun. But that's all it was. I hadn't taken responsibility for "us" or "me." I hadn't spoken up. Now I was making up for that, though Pauline and the sheriff didn't much like that sometimes.

In our pact to date the old-fashioned way, Dillon and I said Wednesdays would be our day for "fooling around." We had to practice impulse control because the lack of restraint had been the bane of our existence when we first married. Today was Saturday. I was regretting our rule.

He checked the tools in his box.

I petted Lucky Harbor. "My day was weird," I began.

"So was mine, but let me show you the good news first."

"Meaning there's bad news?"

"I'm afraid so," he said. "You, too?"

"I'm afraid so," I said.

Outside, under the canopy of the towering cedars and maples, the beautiful bones of a new gazebo nestled amid the lawn. It overlooked the Lake Michigan bay and our harbor.

The gazebo's roof was mere plywood, but it looked ready for shingles. Eight corner posts held up the roof. One cornice was in place, its loveliness lifting a window in my heart. Dillon had cut a pattern into the pine plank depicting a mother duck and her ducklings trailing from one post to the next.

"What do you think?" Dillon asked, putting down his toolbox.

"Enchanting."

"Hold that thought while I show you the bad news."

When we went back inside, he surprised me by scooping me up at the bottom of the staircase in the foyer. Somehow he loped up the powder blue carpet of the staircase with ease. He put me down in front of the second room to the left. It was a mess of plaster, piles of old wooden laths—and a huge hole on the outer wall. I could see the cedars outside.

"What happened?" I asked.

"There's no insulation in this outside wall and some of the lapped boards on the outside are rotted in places. I'm going to have to check the entire upstairs for insulation. And make sure the wiring is up to code."

"Maybe the bank will let Grandpa and me add a little to our mortgage."

"It's not the money I'm worried about. It's the time. I don't think the prince and princess can stay here."

My mouth went dry. "They have to stay here. They expressly said they wanted to. This inn is historic and is now in our family."

Dillon squatted down near a wall. "Some of this wiring is a fire hazard. I already asked the fire chief to stop by and he concurred."

Dillon was a trained civil engineer, usually working on things like streets, roads, and bridge construction and repair. His family also ran a construction company. He was expert on construction codes. In addition, he'd recently joined the Fishers' Harbor Volunteer Fire Department and was in training, along with my young fudge shop helper, Cody.

"Isn't there any way we can get this done in two weeks?"

Still down on the floor, Dillon shook his head. "It's meticulous work. You can't go out and hire just anybody."

"And I guess I can't afford them anyway. What if I helped?"

Dillon's dark eyes took on a knowing look. "You already have too much on your plate." He got up to give me a hug.

We went back downstairs.

"I'll just have to make a batch of fudge and conjure a solution."

Whenever I had troubles, I escaped into fudge making to help me think. Because making fudge required focus, it acted like meditation.

Dillon said, "Let me buy you a burger and fried cheese curds from the Troubled Trout. You brought me lunch yesterday, so I owe you."

With all the events of the day, I'd forgotten to eat. The fried cheese curds at the Troubled Trout were renowned. The curds came from my parents' creamery. They were rolled in dough and then deep-fried.

We set off to walk the few blocks to the bar at the other end of Main Street.

With Lucky Harbor on a leash, we sauntered along until I was startled by a sign in the window of our town's bookstore, the Wise Owl. It was going out of business and everything was on sale.

"This can't be. Milton Hendrickson's retiring? Grandpa never said a thing. We have to go in and find out what's going on."

We left Lucky Harbor outside, his leash hooked over a small gateway post that marked the few steps of flower-lined walkway to the bookshop door.

The store was aptly named because Milton looked like an owl. He wore eyeglasses that sported round, dark frames. The only remaining white hair he had stood out in a tuft on each side of his head, much like a horned owl's feathers.

Milton was in the back shuffling through old maps and documents. His bookstore was filled with a variety of objects in addition to books. He had at least a dozen old globes, and wooden chests on the floor filled with undecipherable old tools. The place smelled of the pleasant musk of an attic and old books.

"Mr. Hendrickson," I called out. He was hard of hearing and refused to wear a hearing aid. "Are you really retiring?"

"Oh, hello, Ava." He turned too fast, his shaky hands fumbling and dropping the stack of documents. The papers— all yellowed—skated around us on the dark wood floor. We helped him pick them up.

I handed back my stack. "Is anybody taking over the shop for you?"

"Some gal by the name of Jane Goodland is coming tomorrow afternoon. Driving over from Green Bay."

"That's good, then. We need a bookstore."

"Oh dear. I'm sorry to disappoint you." He exhaled a withering breath. "She said she was looking for office space. She's a lawyer."

"Oh no. This has to stay a bookstore." Memories were bubbling inside me. "This is where we stopped with Grandma and Grandpa every Christmas to buy books from you. What will I do for Christmas now?"

He gave me a quirky grin. "Maybe reread those old books?"

I had to laugh. "Maybe you're right. It's been a while since I dug out my childhood books." An idea popped into my head. "Do you still have picture books and early readers?"

"Around the corner, near the floor. All half price."

I found them and scooped them up, taking them to the register. I explained to Dillon, "For Pauline. She has a baker's dozen of kindergartners this year and she's always in search of Christmas gifts. This year they'll all get a book, and of course my fudge."

Dillon's arms were full of what looked like old maps, architectural renderings of the outsides of buildings, and blueprints.

I asked, "Did you find something interesting?"

He laughed. "I'm hoping to find the blueprints for the Blue Heron Inn. It might help us solve the wiring issue."

I liked the sound of "us."

We took our bags of purchases, got takeout from the bar, and then ate our burgers and fried cheese curds on the dock in front of Oosterlings' Live Bait, Bobbers & Belgian Fudge & Beer.

Dillon took off later with his dog to go back to the inn. He stayed in the downstairs suite. Since I couldn't pay him much, I gave him the free room there. By Thanksgiving I'd be moving in and Dillon would find a condo.

I relieved Cody, who went to pick up his girlfriend, Bethany. She was in rehearsals for a play at the American Folklore Theater at the nearby park.

I made fudge until about eight o'clock that night, setting out pink loaves of Cinderella Pink Fudge on the white marble table near the window to cool overnight.

By the time I was done with the loafing, I thought I'd feel restored. But I wasn't.

My head was in a stew about the knife, Fontana, and Grandma.

I went home to my cabin. It was about thirty feet across the lawn behind the fudge shop. My resident field mouse, Titus, scurried under the couch as usual when I came in. I left a nibble of fried cheese curd on the floor for him and then went to bed.

The next morning at seven thirty, back in my shop, I was

cutting the pink fudge when my phone buzzed in my apron pocket.

My mother was screeching on the other end of the line. I set the fudge cutter aside.

"Mom, calm down. I couldn't understand a word you said."

"I said I came over here to clean the church, and, and, and . . ."

"What church?"

"Saint Mary of the Snows."

"But I just cleaned that yesterday."

"I know, but you miss stuff whenever you clean. We have a princess coming. She's going to wear white gloves and touch everything. Oh, this is horrible. I don't want to be involved! You have to come over here. Then you can call Jordy."

"Why, Mom? Because you found dirt?"

"No! I fell over it!"

"Mom, you're not making any sense. You fell over dirt? The dust bunnies that I left behind can't be that big."

"I fell over a body!"

Chapter 5

My mother wouldn't stop screaming. Florine hated anything in life being out of order. I'd been "out of order" all my life, according to her standards.

"Mom, get out of the church. Run! I'll call Sheriff Tollefson."

Grandpa came in the shop then with a group of fishermen and their sons—maybe six years old—grinning and carrying fishing poles.

All smiles, too, Grandpa said, "We need to find some bobbers for these young fishermen, and fudge. Got any of your Worms-in-Dirt Fudge?"

The little boys yelled their approval about eating worms.

It was one of the flavors in my Fisherman's Catch line of fudge for men and boys. "Yeah, Gilpa, coming right up." The dark Belgian fudge was made with wiggly candy worms in the top layer with dirt made from chocolate cookie crumbles.

While my voice sounded strong enough, my hands were shaking. I couldn't blurt to Grandpa in front of these little boys that my mother had stumbled across a body in a church. I realized, too, that I didn't even want to tell my grandfather. He was whistling and the happiest I'd seen him in a long time. He liked kids. Last summer he'd had to let go of his beloved but clunky boat he'd been pouring money and hours into for years. Now he hired out to our dock neighbor, Moose Lindstrom, and piloted Moose's fancy new, big *Super Catch I*. But Grandpa complained a lot that he didn't have much to do, seeing as how the boat was new and ran so smoothly.

I hurried through wrapping the fudge for the boys and their fathers.

Then I ducked in the back in my tiny kitchen to call Jordy.

Not surprisingly, he screamed at me, too. "You found a what?"

I had lied and told him I'd been on my way to Mass at Saint Francis and stopped at the church. "I found a body."

"Whose body?"

Crap, I didn't know. Mom never said. I hadn't asked. "I didn't wait around to look closely."

"Where is it?"

I'd forgotten to ask that, too. "Just come."

After we rang off, I called Pauline as I headed out the back door of my shop.

"What time is it?" Her voice sounded muzzy, even sultry.

Jealousy pinged inside me. "Pauline, it's going on eight o'clock. Get out of bed. I need you. My mother found a body in the church."

"I'm not in the mood."

I was getting upset as I walked across the lawn to my cabin. "I need you, Pauline. This is the last favor I'll ever ask in my entire life."

"Liar."

"I know."

"Okay."

Pauline and I arrived at the church in my yellow pickup truck at around eight thirty that Sunday. With few cars on the roads, I had sped the whole way to Namur with Pauline covering her eyes. We'd been in a rollover accident last summer and she was still skittish of my driving.

I pulled to the side of County Road DK in front of the church. The small parking lot next to the church and behind the gravestones was taken up by the sheriff's squad car, another car with MEDICAL EXAMINER on the door, and an ambulance.

The front door of the church was unlocked. Pauline and I hurried inside. The church was chilly and smelled of smoke.

I hugged my Wisconsin Badger hoodie sweatshirt. Pauline wore a new, navy-and-white-striped cotton sweater over a white turtleneck and new skinny blue jeans that had designer rivets on the pockets. Since meeting John, she seemed to buy new clothes every other week. Her long black-brown hair was as loose and beautiful as a TV commercial, while my hair had been hastily gathered into a ponytail that was already drooping on the back of my neck.

The tart, bitter taste in the air made me roll my tongue around my mouth. "Mom didn't mention a fire."

Pauline said, "Up in the loft. Look."

Feathers of smoke had marred the high ceiling area stretching from the loft and partway into the nave. The smoke had dulled the west wall and one of the stained glass windows.

Yellow crime scene tape crossed the bottom step of the staircase. There was no noise up there. "They must be in the basement."

"Who do you think was murdered?"

I thought about Fontana trying to sneak back inside the church yesterday morning. "Fontana?"

"That's wishful thinking."

Pauline and I walked up the center aisle. With the morning sunlight doing a direct hit on the stained glass windows to our right or toward the east, the nave seemed surreal with the refracted light. The two tall angel statues had light dappling the candles on their heads, as if the candles were lit.

When we reached the kitchen to the west of the altar, we heard voices. The basement door was open.

Pauline hugged her purse, whispering, "I'm not going down there. I'm only here to drive your truck back home after you get arrested."

I whispered, "We're doing this to protect my mother. You like my mother, don't you?"

"Do *you* like your mother?"

"Very funny. Of course I do. Come on."

With me in the lead, we trooped down the ancient, short staircase to the basement.

Muffled voices came from the far room. We passed under the hanging cobwebs, then around the old plumbing pipes.

I walked first into the last room where we'd gotten sooty yesterday.

The sheriff swung toward us with a hand out. "Stop. Don't touch a thing. Where'd you go? I thought you'd be waiting for me here."

A body lay prostrate on the hard floor, feet to this end and the head—bloodied—near the wall. A woman was putting small bags around the hands of the dead person.

"I ..."

Pauline said from behind me, "We were at church. I mean, I was at church. She came to pick me up."

Jordy looked at his watch. I cringed. I knew he was tucking away facts about my comings and goings. "So when did you discover the body?"

My head was muddled. The man was facedown, with dark, coagulated blood on the back of the head. He lay near where the old furnace might have sat, not far from the covered vent hole. The man wore dress shoes, tan pants, and a dark suit coat that looked navy in the harsh light somebody had set up next to the body. The man's arms were outstretched somewhat toward the wall over his head.

I didn't know our medical examiner, a woman who'd recently taken over following the retirement of a doctor who'd been in the position for a couple of decades. The woman was maybe forty, shorter than me by four inches, with blond hair worn in dreadlocks down to her shoulders. A camera was slung around her neck.

She was taking off rubber gloves. "I'm done. You can remove the body." She flashed a suspicious look my way, then addressed Jordy. "I'll have a report in a couple of days. But it looks like death from blunt trauma to the head."

I was dying to hear the details, but with the way she was peering at me I realized she harbored uncertainty about my status.

"I only found the body," I blurted, pleading to her. "I didn't do it. Who is it?"

She removed the camera from around her neck, then packed up her small case of tools, snapping it shut. She ignored me, saying to Jordy, "Let's talk tomorrow, say at nine? I'll be in the morgue."

Jordy nodded.

"I'll get my assistants," she said.

The woman left, stepping gingerly around us, careful not to touch us or the walls or doorway.

After she left, I asked Jordy, "Who is it?"

"Tristan Hardy."

"Cherry?" My stomach flip-flopped. I took a step forward toward the body, but Jordy pushed me back in place next to Pauline near the doorway. I said, "It can't be Cherry."

Jordy squinted at me. "You found the body. Why are you so surprised?"

Heat flamed up my face. I couldn't let my gaze meet his, so I stared at the back of Cherry's head, so still on the floor with blood in his short brown hair. His bandaged right forearm drew my eyes next. The bandage looked loose, partially ripped from his wound, as if he'd been fighting. I wanted to see his knuckles but couldn't because of the bags.

"How long do you think he's been down here?" I asked, ignoring Jordy's previous question.

"You didn't find the body, did you?" Jordy said, his trim but muscular body stepping into my line of sight with Cherry's body. "What's the real story?"

I swallowed hard, glancing at Pauline next to me, pleading silently for help. "The real story?"

If my mother were brought into this, the Oosterlings' lives would fall apart. My mother wasn't capable of handling stress. She wouldn't be able to work in her dairy store and creamery. She'd take to cleaning things incessantly.

I said, "The real story is that I love making fudge and I want to keep my life just the way it is."

Jordy withdrew a pad of paper and pen from his front pocket.

"What are you writing down?" I asked.

"What you just said. Sometimes suspects talk in riddles. What were you doing here this morning?"

"Looking for a recipe."

"What recipe?"

"The divine one for divinity fudge. Made by a nun who saw the Mother of God."

Jordy clicked his pen a couple of times as his eyes bored into me. "This isn't one more of your far-fetched stories, is it?"

Pauline said, "She's telling the truth. Her family believes the recipe may have been written down by Sister Adele Brise in the 1860s or later. Some people call her Adele Brice, with a C. This church was founded in 1860. It's been rebuilt and rededicated several times over the years. There could be one of those time capsules hidden away containing holy artifacts touched by Sister Adele, including the divinity fudge recipe. We've been looking for it because Prince Arnaud Van Damme told the Oosterlings that he wanted to taste the saintly divinity fudge of Door County."

Pauline began smacking the gum in her mouth.

Jordy appeared confused by too much information, which was perfect.

The ambulance attendants and the medical examiner trundled down the stairs and into the room. They bagged Cherry's body and hauled him away.

When Pauline and I turned to leave the basement, the sheriff asked, "Did you kill Tristan Hardy?"

"No way, Jordy."

"Do you know who did?"

"No."

"And do you know who might have set that fire upstairs?"

I almost blurted out "Fontana Dahlgren" but held back and said instead, "A lot of people were upset over Cherry's research."

I filled him in on the chemical allegations that had fomented into ugly feelings among the local neighbors. "In addition, he had concerns about the dry weather, and pests getting into the weakened orchards and grapes. Kjersta Dahlgren told me he'd been collecting bags of things on their property as well as next door at Michael Prevost's vineyard. He and his lab assistants also tromped around Jonas Coppens's farmland."

Jordy made me list everybody who'd been at my roadside market yesterday during Cherry's presentation. Then he asked, "Anybody else in here yesterday or in that loft?"

"Tourists with John Schultz's tour."

Pauline elbowed me hard in the arm.

"I'll talk to John," Jordy said. "Isn't that the same guy who found that cup that might belong to your grandma's family? The guy who almost got himself killed by the murderer of Lloyd Mueller last summer?"

"The same guy."

Writing, Jordy said, "The same guy who was staying at the Blue Heron Inn in May when that actress keeled over from your fudge?"

"She didn't die from my fudge. She was choked to death using my fudge, at the hands of a wily woman who was after her money and jewels."

"Nevertheless, John Schultz seems to have the same talent you do for getting involved with illegal activities."

Pauline groaned.

Jordy snapped his notepad shut. "The church is off-limits for now. You'll need to explain to folks that they'll have to move the kermis, or cancel it."

"Not this again. You can't cancel anything and we don't want to move it. The church is special. Can't you hurry up the investigation?"

He gave me a sharp look that sent chills down my back. We walked ahead of him out of the church.

When we were outside he confiscated my church key and locked up. After he drove away, Pauline hit me in the butt with her big bag.

"Ouch. What'd you do that for?"

She tossed her hair off her shoulder. There were tears in her eyes, so unlike Pauline. "You've ruined John's fall tours. People are going to be really mad at him if he doesn't let them inside this church where they think Sister Adele hid the divinity fudge recipe."

She was loping toward my truck ahead of me.

"Pauline, John wasn't supposed to be telling people about the recipe anyway. We don't want people breaking into the church and stealing mementos. We wanted the recipe all hush-hush before the prince arrived. John violated my trust. And it's not my fault that Cherry got killed in the church."

"There you go again. You're always right." She hadn't turned around. She charged into the truck cab, closing the door with a bang.

Something was wrong. Pauline was never petulant.

I eased in on the driver's side. "I'm sorry, but John wasn't even supposed to be in the church yesterday when he was. Why was he there so early? And with Cherry? Cherry was going to give his presentation about his research at lunch after the tour, not during the tour."

To my shock, Pauline's tears turned to a sob. She dug a tissue out of her purse.

"Pauline? What's wrong?"

"Tristan Hardy bullied his way onto the bus during a tour stop earlier. It wasn't the first time he'd done that. John didn't like it. You saw how they were in the church yesterday. Cherry was trying to take over the tour."

"But what does this have to do with Cherry's murder?"

The tears flowed faster. "John and I didn't go on our date last night."

"But you were together this morning, right? When I called, I thought you sounded sultry . . ."

"Like you'd interrupted a blissful morning after sex? The truth was he was so upset about Cherry that I told him to skip our date because I didn't want to talk about it over dinner. I was sick of hearing about Cherry."

"I'm sorry, but I still don't see . . ."

She wiped at her nose with the tissue. "We were together last night at my house, but John was determined to reroute his tour so that he could somehow avoid Tristan Hardy. So he spent the night on the phone with some guy and got all excited about his TV show idea all over again. We'd gone to bed around ten o'clock when minutes later he got up from the bed and then never came back. I felt bad and got up to go find him, but his car was gone. I think he went to meet up with Cherry."

Panic punched my stomach. "No, Pauline. I doubt John came to this church last night to meet Cherry."

She had red eyes. "John loves treasure hunting. He found that precious cup with AVD on it in that big bay. What if they both came here thinking they could sneak in at night to look for the divinity fudge recipe? What if they ended up in a fight? What if John killed Tristan Hardy because of fudge?"

Chapter 6

I tried to reassure Pauline that a mere fudge recipe couldn't be the motive for John killing Tristan Hardy.

She started crying harder as I put my yellow pickup in gear.

"Sorry. I said that wrong. John didn't kill anybody, I'm sure."

We headed back toward Brussels, passing green cornfields bursting with fat ears for harvest later on. It was a little after nine o'clock. I decided to stop at our farm. It would cheer Pauline up.

We bounced over our long gravel lane. The sun was heating up the day fast and small whirlwinds were stirring the dust enough to nettle my front hood.

Pauline sniffed. "Everybody knows that John has gold rush fever. He's obsessed with proving himself after that company fired him last spring."

"He did threaten to sue them for age discrimination, which saved Fishers' Harbor and my fudge shop this past summer. They were about to buy up all kinds of property if they could swing it. John is our hero. He sent his former employer packing. John is not a killer. You know what I think?"

"What now?"

We were jostling over ruts. "John probably can't sleep for his nerves. He sent his demo tape to some producer a couple of weeks ago. He's on pins and needles waiting to hear. That's why he left your bed last night."

Pauline's heavy sigh almost sounded like a tire going flat on the truck. "I suppose you're right."

"I'm always right."

"No, you always *want* to be right. There's a difference."

Pauline and I traveled in silence, then down the remainder of the long, straight gravel lane that parted the pastures and strips of hay, wheat, and corn. Far off to the southeast I could make out Ava's Autumn Harvest.

We stopped in the gravel circle in front of our redbrick farmhouse and next to Mom's SUV. The house was to the right or north of the gravel, and the big red barn with its attached creamery and other outbuildings sat to the south side of the gravel area.

Giving Pauline's forearm a squeeze in friendship, I said, "Let's see what Mom knows. She might have clues to solve this before the sheriff even has a chance to have his Sunday noonday meal."

Pauline stared back at me, agape. "Sometimes you say the strangest things. Even I know what your mother must be doing inside your farmhouse."

Mom was in the hallway between the living room and kitchen vacuuming the beige-carpeted stairs up to the second floor. She was still in her good church clothes—patent leather ballerina flats and a lovely muted forest green A-line, short-sleeved dress. It had a matching jacket, but that was tossed over the corner of a sofa in the living room. Her elbows jabbed the air as she pushed the sucking nozzle over the carpet.

"Mom!" I called above the noise.

I had to take the nozzle from her and turn off the vacuum.

"Mom, Pauline's here. We went to Saint Mary's. The body was Tristan Hardy."

Mom fell into me, wrapping her arms around me. Her shoulder-length, wavy dark-brown hair fluffed about my face. "Oh, honey, no, not Cherry. I didn't know. I got the heck out of there fast." She let me go, taking back the hose and vacuum. She was gripping the appliance so hard that her fingers were white. "Please tell me the paramedics got there in time and shocked him or something."

I grimaced.

Mom stared down at the vacuum. "He's been here in our home as a guest with his professor friends and those PhD students from the university so many times. We're all family. He was always working on new ways to manage our crops and pastures. And he liked my cheese curds. He and Professor Weaver always bought several bags to take back to their department."

Pauline and I led her to the kitchen.

I said, "Let's make some coffee."

When we got to the kitchen, Mom set to work washing breakfast dishes by hand. There was no use reminding her she had an automatic dishwasher. I dried dishes while Pauline ground coffee beans and then plugged in the coffeemaker.

While we worked, I asked my mother, "Did you go into the choir loft?"

She paused with her hands in the soapy water, staring out the kitchen window that overlooked the farm buildings and pasture. "No, why?"

"There was a fire up there sometime between the time we cleaned the church yesterday and the time you found Cherry."

"I smelled smoke but thought it might be coming from the kitchen appliances, so I checked on them and then went into the basement. I didn't smell the smoke there and assumed somebody was burning leaves nearby. I started cleaning in the basement. It smelled down there, a little like pickling spices, so I knew I must have been whiffing somebody's kitchen next door. What was on fire? What damage did it do?"

"I don't know." The imagery of the knife and blood on the music for "Ave Maria" flashed across my memory. I took a guess. "Maybe the music in the organ bench."

"Do you think somebody meant to burn down the church? To hide the murder?"

"All conjecture, Mom. And we don't even know for sure if he was murdered."

Mom pulled the plug on the sink drain, letting it slurp down the soapy water. "You don't think Cherry would have started that fire, would he? How strange of him."

"I'm sure the sheriff will figure it out. Let's have some coffee."

When I went to the cupboard for cups, I was surprised to find the antique collection of floral china cups that had been willed to my grandmother by my grandfather's deceased friend Lloyd Mueller.

Before Lloyd's death, I'd been invited into his large library in his home and discovered he collected history books and community cookbooks that contained references to my ancestors. Pauline, Laura, and I also saw his extensive collection of delicate china cups and saucers in his dining room, including those made in the late 1800s, such as the Redon Limoges cup and saucer made especially for sipping chocolate drinks. Laura knew a lot about antique chinaware and enlightened Pauline and me about their value. The Limoges cup in front of me had pink roses on it with a gold-trimmed, scalloped rim with gold at the bottom of the cup. The saucer was scalloped, too, with a gleaming gold edge.

"Mom, these are Grandma's precious cups from Lloyd. Why are they here instead of at her cabin in Fishers' Harbor?"

"She made me take them. She said they were raw reminders of the past."

"But these cups aren't from her past. These are Lloyd's past."

"Yes, but Sophie said there's already too much fuss about cups."

Pauline said, "She was referring to the cup that John found."

"Mom, do you know why Grandma isn't keen on the princess coming here to look at that cup?"

With great care, I set some of the Royal Albert and Royal Doulton cups on the counter for us to look at, along with a German chocolate cup with a large pink rose on it from Silesian Germany that had a crown and swords between the words. There were large green leaves with a peach color in the background.

Pauline said, "So delicate. All with roses. I loved his rose garden." She touched the rose on the German china cup with a finger, stroking it lightly, as if she were touching a baby's cheek for the first time.

I said, "I'll take these cups and saucers back to Grandma this morning."

Mom reached for one of the chinaware sets. "Let's use them. I need something to calm my nerves. Let's pretend we're ladies of leisure, like the princess."

We settled into the opposite end of the kitchen around the table that could seat twelve. A large bay window overlooked our backyard and Mom's garden.

I asked Mom again about Grandma.

She said, "I don't know, honey. She won't tell me."

Pauline said, "Maybe she's sad. Sometimes family reunions make us sad as well as happy. We think about everybody that's not there anymore. I learned that long ago from my kindergartners. One of them told me once he was sad when Christmas came because his grandpa could never be there again."

I remembered Grandma fussing with the flowers amid the gravestones yesterday. "I hadn't thought of that."

Mom rose abruptly and left the room. Pauline and I exchanged a curious look.

Soon, drawers in the living room desk whooshed in and out, closing with *click-clack*s and *bang*s. When Mom returned to the kitchen, she was wearing a big round button on her short-sleeved green dress. She sat down across from me again. The oversized button, maybe four inches across, said on its perimeter Ava's Fudge — Fit for Royalty.

She handed us each a button. "I wanted everything to be perfect for you, Ava. My little girl, part of royalty."

The buttons had a depiction of the Namur church amid the farmland in the top half, with a picture of Oosterlings' Live Bait, Bobbers & Belgian Fudge & Beer on the harbor in the bottom half. My heart swelled with the thoughtfulness.

"Thanks, Mom. This is beautiful."

My mother patted the button on her chest. "I was going to surprise you with these at the kermis. Instead we need them now. I had Father Van den Broeck bless these."

"The priest at Saint Francis?"

"Yes. They looked enough like prayer cards to him that he obliged with a sprinkle of holy water on them. They'll protect you as you do something about this mess, Ava. We must have the church for the kermis. And Cherry would want that, too. He'd love to know there was a royal requiem for him, and the kermis will do that. You have to help the sheriff and his people get this mess cleaned up before the kermis."

A requiem was a Mass said for the dead.

"Mom, do you realize what you're saying? You never want me involved with trouble."

"I got you into this mess. I found that body. I should not have been there vacuuming in that basement. I should have had more faith in your ability to clean. I keep forgetting you're not a teenager anymore. I shouldn't have called you and put the burden on you. I should have walked away entirely."

Pauline and I exchanged a look.

I said, "But then nobody may have found him for days. Mom, you did the right thing."

Mom thought for a moment. "Don't tell your father I found that body." She raised her delicate cup up from its saucer in a salute. "Ava, Pauline, put your buttons on. Those are your badges. Nothing much of any import has happened in my life but marrying Pete and birthing you, Ava, and raising you, Pauline, like another daughter. Now I'm about to meet a prince and princess. Nobody is going to ruin this for me. Even Cherry wouldn't want the kermis ruined. Why else was he in that church? He must have been looking for the fudge recipe, too. You have to save our fall kermis."

Mom was making sense, which scared me even more than blessed buttons. I was starting to recognize my own thinking patterns in the way she had worded that little speech. Things that shouldn't make sense were sounding logical. When you turn into your own mother, you know you're in trouble.

After Pauline and I got into my truck, I said, "I should tell Dad about these buttons. Maybe Mom needs a vacation. She didn't sound right."

Pauline took off her button and buried it in her voluminous bag. "You and your mother are totally on the same wavelength. For once. Your father wouldn't believe it." She put a hand out. "Give me your button."

"Why?"

"It's a holy button. Your priest said some incantation over it. Let's keep them out of sight until we learn their powers."

I stared at her for a millisecond until we both burst out laughing.

She said, "Your mom said they were supposed to be a surprise at the kermis. Let's save them for then."

"Those things really are blessed. Mom wouldn't lie about that. She never lies. Except about finding that body, of course." I started the truck. "That was really nice of her to do for me. Mom's hard to figure out at times."

"She's practical, pragmatic, and polite."

"Is it *P* week for your kindergartners?"

"Yup. The *P* words are going up all over the room this afternoon for tomorrow."

"Add the words 'prince,' 'princess,' and 'perpetrator.'"

After we pulled out of our circular driveway, I said, "We have to get a look in that choir loft. But first we're going to talk to John about last night. Your problems are more important, Pauline. Try calling him again."

"Why bother?" Her voice cracked. "He didn't come back last night and he hasn't returned any of my calls. He's in love with the thought of fame, not me. Ava, I think he and I are over."

Chapter 7

Pauline was not happy with us stopping to open up Ava's Autumn Harvest that Sunday morning. But tourists were like chipmunks; once the day warmed up, they came out of their burrows, and I needed the dough. I put Pauline to work setting up the pecks of apples on the flatbed wagons with the pumpkins.

Pauline said, "I need to get back so I can work on my classroom."

"No, you need to hunt down John. You two are not splitting up."

"Though I know you're dying to say 'I told you so.'"

"He's older than you by around twenty years and sensitive about his age. I just want you to be careful. You're young and pretty."

"Arm candy. I know."

Her agreement made me feel worse. When Pauline and I disagreed, there was vitality in our relationship. "You'll find him and then you'll talk. Did he mention what he was up to today?"

"I don't remember."

She didn't remember, because she was upset with him. She couldn't think, because she didn't make fudge to help her think. But she had me.

I had Pauline help me set out what little fudge I had left under a shady umbrella. Although fudge doesn't melt unless you torture it with direct fire practically, I still didn't like its sugary crystals bombarded with sunlight. A cool fall breeze feathering around us as we worked would give the fudge a perfect, sapid soul when it touched the tongue. Like wine, which I asked Pauline to set on the outdoor tables as well, fudge flavors intensified on the tongue when they went from cool to warm.

A phone call to Grandpa revealed he was on the *Super Catch I* on the bay with his fishermen and their boys yet. He sounded bored. Cody was manning the bait-and-fudge shop.

While still on the phone, I wandered inside the stone barn so Pauline couldn't hear me. "Is John out on the water with you?"

"No, and funny thing, A.M., Moose was expecting him. But he never showed up."

"What do you mean?"

"Moose had another boat arranged for him to take out for some filming. Moose couldn't rouse him with phone calls and messages."

I hung up with Grandpa, then called Dillon. Blackbirds were chattering in the background in the backyard of the Blue Heron Inn.

After I asked Dillon if he'd seen John, he said, "Maybe he had too much to drink last night and ended up sleeping it off on the side of the road somewhere."

"That's not like John."

"Depends. It's a guy thing. He's had a lot on his mind lately. I guarantee he'll be mortified when he wakes up any minute now with a hangover. He'll want to buy two dozen roses for Pauline. Let me drive around and look for him."

His offer warmed something elemental in me. "That's why I love you. And I never thought it'd be reassuring to hear that somebody got too drunk to drive. I'm sure that's it. I know he loves Pauline."

After I hung up, Kjersta Dahlgren showed up in the barn while I was putting price signs up on the shelving island with the jams and jellies. Her face appeared drawn.

Kjersta said, "I heard about Cherry."

"Already?"

"The sheriff stopped by only minutes ago to ask me and

Daniel questions about Cherry and all the disagreements we've been having with his lack of action with Jonas Coppens." She shivered, crossing her arms in an obvious attempt to hide her nervousness.

Dread kicked me in the backside. "You and Daniel are suspects?"

"I'm scared. The sheriff asked if we saw anything last night."

"Did you?"

"I saw two cars pass here around eleven maybe, heading toward Brussels."

And taking the turn in Brussels took a person to the Namur church. My head naturally connected everything to John, who seemed missing. "You didn't recognize the cars?"

"It was dark. But one car didn't have lights on. I only saw it because the car behind it was traveling close and then the one in front braked. I saw the brake lights. Then after a few moments, they both sped up and kept on going. I figured it was teenagers."

"Had to be," I said, admonishing myself for jumping to conclusions.

I helped Kjersta harvest a few cabbage heads and pumpkins. Her cabbage heads were nearly as big as bushel baskets, as were many of her pumpkins. It took two people to lift some of them.

In exchange, Kjersta offered to take over the cash register in the stone barn, so I grabbed Pauline. We got in my yellow pickup and headed north to Fishers' Harbor.

I skipped telling her what Kjersta had said about the cars last night. The county had twenty-eight thousand residents plus thousands of tourists in it; anybody could have been on that road heading toward the church. I told her what Dillon had said.

"But why would he go out drinking like that? What's weighing on him?"

"Maybe he's thinking about proposing to you."

The truck cab went silent for a full thirty seconds.

Pauline said, "I never thought of that."

We listened to the engine hum for a moment.

She said, "I've felt him working up to a proposal several

times, but then he backs off. This TV dream of his has always been his priority."

She was delving into her doubts again, which wasn't like her. Was that what love did to a person? I said, "He's nervous because he wants everything to be perfect for you. Maybe John's going to surprise you at the school this afternoon. Think about it. You're there all alone, after all. No kids. No principal. All very private. John loves drama."

I wiggled my eyebrows.

Pauline laughed. "All right. I won't worry about John. Tell Dillon thanks. By the way, when are you going to let him propose? Have you two hammered out the date for that in your silly agreement?"

I almost ran off Highway 57. "It's a verbal agreement and it's not silly. There's nothing wrong with us wanting to let our love grow the old-fashioned way."

She scoffed. "Liar. You're dying to act like rabbits."

"If only your kindergartners could hear you now, Miss Potty Mouth."

That got a laugh. "I want to be married to the right guy and be married for a long time like your parents and your grandparents. Their love is solid. I've never had 'solid.' Except with you and your family."

That touched me so that I had to grip the steering wheel extra hard. Her parents weren't always happy. I remembered being seven and ten and twelve and Pauline would stay a week at a time because something bad was going on at home between her parents. They argued a lot and threw things. Her house was a mess of broken dishes and broken hearts. There was probably special meaning this morning in the way we shared the coffee in those priceless antique cups. Such things weren't possible in Pauline's parents' house.

After Sturgeon Bay, where the canal zone split Door County into its lower and upper halves, the road also divided, with Highway 57 leading to the southeast shore and Highway 42 heading toward the bay side of Lake Michigan. We were in Fishers' Harbor on Green Bay within a half hour. Main Street, which was also Highway 42, was clogged with cars and people—those chipmunks—out now for lunch and shopping.

At around eleven o'clock, I dropped off Pauline at the school on the southeast edge of the village, then doubled back to the harbor and Oosterlings' Live Bait, Bobbers & Belgian Fudge & Beer. Cars lined the parking lot. The bay sparkled. Sailboats and touring boats glided by. The *Super Catch I* was in its slip, so that meant Grandpa was back.

The cowbell on the door clanked when I went through the front door. The place was packed. I gloried in the awesome smells of chocolate fudge, vanilla, cherries, and coffee.

Cody called out, "There's Miss Oosterling! Princess Oosterling! Glad you're here to put a sparkle in our day like a crown atop your head."

Customers laughed. Cody had always been like that. He made me smile no matter what. Since the first day I'd hired him in May, he called me "Miss" in the shop. He coped well with his Asperger's condition by using laughter. Now at nineteen he'd entered technical school to pursue a degree in criminal justice. His goal was to be a police officer or fire department captain or warden overseeing the local parks. Cody's dream was to wear a star on his chest. He liked me calling him "Ranger."

After wending my way through the crowd, I whispered, "Ranger, Sunday is usually a good day for us, but this seems especially packed. Any clue why?"

"Yeah. They're going on a wine tour with John. He told them to meet him here when they bought the tickets yesterday. We haven't seen him, though."

I shrank into myself.

Cody noticed. "What's wrong with John?"

"Dillon thinks John was out too late last night and overslept. He'll be here, I'm sure."

I tied on one of the fancy aprons that my shop sold. This one was pink crisp cotton, with ruffles on the edges and straps, and red cherries on the front bib and the skirt pockets. Aprons weren't my style, but last summer I'd learned their power. Men loved to salivate over a woman in an apron. Women loved wearing them because their grandmothers had worn them, but the women also didn't mind the looks they got from the men. I now sold aprons that sported my fudge flavors on them, such as my signature Cinderella Pink Fudge.

Cody said, "Don't leave before you give Sam the cookbooks. He's waiting in back."

I hurried to the back. My ex-fiancé, Sam Peterson, was in the storeroom across from the small galley kitchen. He'd opened a box and was pulling out slim cookbooks.

"Hey, Sam. You found the right boxes, I see. Everything else in here is pretty much bait shop supplies and kilo chocolate bars."

I'd brought several boxes of the cookbooks I'd inherited from Lloyd Mueller to the shop to peruse during my downtime. Sam had called me about taking cookbooks to his office for his Monday group meeting. He ran a group for people like Cody with mild forms of autism spectrum disorder. During their meetings, they worked on life skills, which lately included learning how to cook. Sam also wanted to use the old community cookbooks to encourage discussions about the emotional connections to food. Sam had explained to me last spring that some with Asperger's could experience difficulty with comprehending emotions, but talking about what their grandparents served at meals was a tool that helped them learn one meaning of "love."

Sam's presence always gave me pause because he was perfect. Today he wore a crisp white button-down shirt. He was two years older than I, and taller, blond with short hair combed with a side part. He had been a football hero in our high school. He still maintained massive shoulder muscles that made a white shirt look sexy as heck.

His blue eyes twinkled, even in the dim light of the storage room. "You look good in pink." Although he knew I was dating Dillon again, he didn't hide his hope to win me back.

"Thanks, Sam. Want me to help haul these to your car?"

"No, I can manage. Just the two boxes, right?"

"Yeah. I still have to look through the others. I'm looking for connections to the prince and princess."

He stood there, staring at me, stalling. Sam stood like a statue when he had something really important to say.

"What's wrong, Sam?"

"Fontana Dahlgren called me. This morning."

"Oh? She interested in dating again?"

Sam, despite being a mature man, turned red. His hairline twitched a little, which always marked his nervousness. "I don't know about that, but she asked for my help. She said the sheriff had asked to meet with her. She said that her ex-husband's wife had fingered her in a murder investigation."

I sagged. "Kjersta said the sheriff had been asking her about who had been driving by her house. I'm sure he asked about anybody who had been with Cherry yesterday before he died. That would include Fontana. She was all over him during the tour in the church."

"So why would she feel like a suspect in his death?"

My mind recalled the scene at Ava's Autumn Harvest. "Sam, maybe you should stay away from Fontana. Fontana and Cherry were arguing about something yesterday at my market."

Sam's eyes widened in shock. "You didn't say that to the sheriff, did you?"

"No."

He picked up the two boxes of cookbooks, flashing me an accusing look.

"Sam, stop it. I didn't finger Fontana for murder."

"She says you want to run her out of business."

"That's silly. She sells soap and perfume and I sell pumpkins and fudge."

Sam shrugged. "Okay. Sorry I accused you."

"Sorry that you believe everything Fontana tells you. Sam, you're not getting together with her on the rebound, are you?"

He chuckled. "I'm not pining for you. You and Dillon deserve each other."

I arched an eyebrow, and he continued quickly. "That came out wrong. You're two dynamic people who are like matches and dynamite. You work as a couple. Me? I don't need explosions in my life."

"Then leave Fontana alone. I hear there's a lawyer by the name of Jane Goodland who's maybe moving into the Wise Owl. Why not say howdy to her? Milton can let you know when she stops by."

"Have you seen Jane? I don't think I could handle her. Or her dog."

Shaking his head in derision, Sam escaped fast, heading into the shop and then disappearing into the sea of customers.

I was cutting a new batch of Worms-in-Dirt Fudge at the front window, giving away tiny samples to customers, when the school bus that John used for his tours pulled into the parking lot. To my surprise, my nemesis, Mercy Fogg, lumbered out, her mop of blond, curly hair whipping about in the breezes buffeting off the harbor. She was dressed in a dark uniform that shockingly included a tie. For once, she didn't look too clownish. She had a habit of putting together odd combinations of clothing and colors. I was so stunned at her attire that my mouth stayed open the whole time she strolled through the parking lot, across the docks where people milled, and then into my store.

"Ava O," she said. "What gives?"

"What do you mean, Mercy?"

"John and I have a tour right now."

I sagged. "I know. We can't find him."

"I found him."

I raced from my end of the table toward her near the door, but she backed off, bumping into a customer on his way out. I realized I had the fudge cutters in my hand yet. I put the sharp tool down on my white marble table, motioning her closer for privacy. "Where did you find him?"

"In my bus." She motioned over her shoulder with a thumb. "Came outta my house this morning to clean it up for today's tour, and there he was, lying in the aisle on the rubber tread like a big coho salmon. I thought he was dead."

My heartbeat skittered about. "But he's not dead."

"No."

"He's still in the bus?"

"Hell no. Something happened to him. He didn't wake up at first. I had to dump cold water on his face. He mumbled something about a church and a fight, and then things went black."

The blood drained from my head. I looked over her shoulders and out the window toward the bus. "Where is he now?"

"My house."

I reached out to grab her shoulders.

She flashed a look of disdain. "The uniform is new."

I backed off. "Sorry. You look nice."

"Nicer than usual is what you really want to say."

"Mercy, take the compliment before I stuff it somewhere you won't like. I need to see John. To help him. Pauline's worried."

"She better be. The guy could be a murderer."

A groan escaped me. "You heard about Tristan Hardy already?"

She popped a piece of the dark-chocolate fudge with gummy worms in her mouth, munching. "This stuff can stick to your bridgework, you know that?" She dug around in her mouth with an index finger.

Mercy was stalling on purpose to frustrate me. Ever since I'd moved back to town and found success with fudge, she niggled at me. But I felt for her. She'd once been our village president, then gotten ousted by a nineteen-year-old bartender in the election. Mercy was trying to regain her position in the herd, as my dad would say. And you never trusted the alpha animal, because she could charge at you when you least expected it. "Mercy, what did you hear about Tristan? And why would you think John is a murderer?"

"I got on my bus, plunked down in my driver's seat, and I'm eating a doughnut, one of those cherry doughnuts with the glaze with the cherry bits in it—"

"Stay on the point, Mercy. What did you hear about Cherry?"

"I turned on my bus radio. The radio said he was bludgeoned to death and they're looking for the murderer. I get up then thinking about blood, looking at my hands stained from the red cherry doughnut, then turn toward the back of my bus and I find John Schultz sprawled on the floor with blood on his hands."

I screeched, "Blood?"

The entire fudge shop went silent as customers looked at us. I hustled Mercy outside.

Chapter 8

I trotted onto the yellow school bus in the harbor parking lot. The aisle was narrow. John Schultz was a hefty guy.

I asked Mercy, who stood behind me, "How did you get him out?"

"He drags okay. It's wider down there on the floor."

"You dragged him? Out of the bus? Didn't his head hit on the steps?"

"Hell no. I only dragged him to the front. Then I was able to turn him around. His shoes fell off on my lawn, though. They disappeared. I think my neighbor's new golden retriever puppies stole them. They're cuter than sin, but those dogs are mouthy."

"Never mind about the puppies. Give me your house keys."

Mercy lumbered off the bus steps and back into the sunshine. "He's fine. Just needs some sleep."

I followed down the steps. "Give me your keys. I'm going to get John while you're taking those people in my shop on their tour."

"I drive. I don't yack at people like you. I'm not their tour guide."

My head felt ready to explode, but I wouldn't give Mercy that satisfaction. She had a brochure hanging out of a pocket. I snatched it. "You don't get paid unless the tour runs, right?"

"Yeah."

"Wait here."

I hurried inside the shop, hustled past the minnow tank and onward to the far aisle where I found my grandfather giving a little boy a plastic set of bright orange bobbers. After the boy and his dad sauntered on, I asked, "Gilpa, you know everything about Door County, right?"

"Not everything. What's going on, A.M.?"

"There's an emergency. John's not feeling well. I have to go pick him up at . . . at . . ." I gulped. Grandpa didn't much like Mercy. "At Mercy Fogg's house."

"Holy Hannah, what's that woman done to us now?"

"I'm not exactly sure. That's why I need you to be a tour guide to all these people." I waved toward the women and girls lined up buying fudge, cute aprons, purses, and sparkly kids' stuff that sported logos for my special flavors. I unfolded the brochure. "They're going to a couple of lighthouses, the farm with the ostriches, a vineyard, and the White Fish Dune's State Park and its nature center."

"I'll fetch your grandma. This'll take her mind off her royal relatives."

Gilpa and Sophie had the people on the bus in no time. Mercy was impressed with my quick work that earned her some dough. She loaned me her house keys.

Cody agreed to man the shop, but I encouraged him to call his girlfriend, Bethany, to help. I usually gave a fudge-making demonstration at the copper kettles around one o'clock. Cody might have to pinch-hit for me.

I hopped in my yellow truck in the parking lot and within a minute was at the Blue Heron Inn. Dillon, covered in plaster dust, was in an unfinished bedroom upstairs.

Breathless from the race up the stairs, I said, "I need your help."

"Of course, Ava." He dropped his hammer and then loped toward me. "What's up?"

Once he heard the ghastly story about Mercy and John, we hopped in his white construction pickup truck with Lucky Harbor in the backseat, his tail slapping the vinyl.

We wended over to the school to pick up Pauline. She shared the backseat with the panting water spaniel.

Dillon skidded and fishtailed through the back streets

and alleys until we found Mercy's quiet street. Houses were set back in lots filled with cedars, pines, and maples, with forest land behind the homes and a rural road not far beyond that. Her house was a modest bi-level, brown with white trim and a white door in the middle with a garage to the right. We parked in her driveway.

I unlocked the front door, and then we hurried up the steps to the main floor.

Pauline called out, "John? Sweetie? It's Pauline."

For a moment we stood in place, adjusting our eyes to all the colors. Mercy was apparently in love with folk art. Her walls, furniture, and furnishings sported every mismatched color and pattern imaginable, but it was all rather quaint in a county fair way.

Lucky Harbor set to work sniffing around the house.

Dillon said, "Now we know what she's been doing since she lost her job as village president last year."

Every chair in her dining room was painted a different color—lime green, shocking pink, yellow with black polka dots, and one with purple and teal stripes. But there was no John. The living room was the same.

Pauline said, "If John is here, my eyes can't pick him out."

Dillon yelled, "John, where are you?"

A muffled noise emanated from a short hallway.

We found John in a bedroom festooned with flower patterns. The bedspread sported splotches of yellow daylilies against a white background.

Pauline rushed to John, easing her hips onto the bed. "Honey, what happened? How are you?"

"Where am I? How'd I get here?"

Pauline collapsed on him, hugging him, her black hair shifting like a river's currents over his face and chest. Then she kissed his face several times.

Again he said, "Where am I?"

Pauline took one of his hands in hers. "You're with me, sweetie."

Dillon and I exchanged a look. He put an arm around me, but the pleasant gesture didn't cure my wooziness over my secret: John had told Mercy something about being in a church and a fight. And John was disoriented now.

He appeared okay physically. But then as Pauline went to help him up, the bodice of a nightgown appeared on John's burly chest. It had little yellow ducks on it.

Pauline screwed up her nose. "What are you doing wearing a nightgown?"

Dillon chuckled. "You look mighty pretty, John, but let me find your clothes." Dillon started pawing in a clothes hamper nearby.

John sat up against the pillow. Pauline stuffed another pillow behind him. He said, "Not sure how I got into this or why. I remember being naked in a bathtub, though, with somebody washing me off. That wasn't you, Paulie Pal?"

Pauline gasped, "No, John." Her shoulders straightened. "You left our bed to come over here with Mercy?"

He said, "Is that where I am? How'd I get here?"

I sat down on the opposite side of the bed. "Mercy said she found you on the bus. With blood on your hands." I'd told Dillon and Pauline about the blood previously. "John, do you remember how you got on the bus?"

"No."

Pauline asked, "What did you do last night?"

"I got in my car to go buy something. I don't know what now. I remember driving, but I don't know where I went. I remember being outside my car. Maybe checking a tire? I vaguely recall somebody had stopped, or maybe I stopped behind somebody else. Maybe I had stopped to help them. I don't know." He lifted a hand to the back of his head. "I got a bit of a knot somehow."

Dillon said, "I can't find your clothes. But we need to get you to the hospital. Do you feel up to me helping you down the front stairs?"

John nodded, one of his hands examining the knot on the back of his head. "I'm not feeling dizzy anymore. Maybe I slipped and fell on the road and Mercy found me. I can't remember if she said anything. You find my car?"

Dillon said, "We only learned you were here minutes ago. I'll find your car."

Pauline scurried about the room, opening closet doors and drawers. "You and Mercy are probably about the same size around the waist." She held up baggy denim jeans. "Will these do?"

John nodded. "But they're Mercy's clothes."

Pauline said, "All that matters is that we get you out of her house."

Dillon found a Packers-logo sweatshirt, and then he had the audacity to hold up a giant pair of grandma-style panties. "She's got clean undies, but I think you'll want to let the boys hang loose for this ride."

"You got that right," John said.

We all shared a needed chuckle.

Pauline and I left the room while Dillon helped John take off the nightgown.

In the living room, Pauline said, "That woman has gone over the edge. I bet she murdered Tristan Hardy, ran into John for some reason, or ran him off the road, then brought him here to wash off all the evidence."

"You've been reading suspense novels again."

"What of it? There are only so many picture books about puppies that I can handle. Why aren't you suspicious of this? We just came from your mother's place and the church where the sheriff and medical examiner found the body. We saw the body. There was blood. What if that blood on John was Tristan Hardy's blood that came off Mercy's hands after she killed Tristan? What if John had gone down to the Namur church for some reason and stumbled across the murder?"

With Pauline's imagination, I wasn't going to need to tell her what Mercy told me about the church and the fight.

She collapsed into a nearby chair covered with a quilt. "We need to find his car. Why can't he remember things, Ava?"

"I don't know, Pauline."

"I'm scared."

A sharp bang caught our attention.

I said, "The dog. We forgot about Lucky Harbor."

Pauline and I rushed to the kitchen. A large roaster pan sat upside down on the vinyl floor. Lucky Harbor had already scarfed up whatever had been in the pan. He was mopping the floor with his tongue. I tossed the pan on the counter, and then we got the heck out of there.

After Dillon dropped me off at the fudge shop, he and Pauline headed to the hospital with John.

I whipped on an apron with orange pumpkins embroidered on it.

Cody was handling both sides of the shop. Bethany wasn't there; she was studying for a test, Cody explained.

But efficient Lois Forbes in her red-dyed hair and Dotty Klubertanz, a plump lady with short white hair and dressed in her usual pink sweats with sequins, were ringing up sales of fudge and aprons on my side of our little outpost on the harbor. Both ladies were in their sixties and part of the church ladies brigade that always seemed to frustrate me as much as it helped me. If I didn't keep a firm hold on my shop as manager, Dotty and Lois could turn the place into a church bazaar fund-raiser within the time it took to recite the Lord's Prayer.

Dotty rushed over to help me tie the back of my apron. "Honey, we sold out of the Rapunzel Raspberry Rapture Fudge."

"How am I doing with the Cinderella Pink Fairy Tale Fudge?"

"Getting low on that, too. And Kjersta called. She can hang in there another couple of hours, she said, but several cars have stopped for lunch and the cheese selection is getting low. She said the mild cheddar paired with the Cinderella Pink cherry-vanilla fudge is a combo that's selling fast."

"I'll call my mom. Thanks, Dotty, for coming to the rescue today. Again."

"No worries. That nasty business in Namur isn't getting you down, is it? Kjersta said you discovered the body."

"It's unfortunate. I think Cherry and his colleagues were coming close to finding out why Kjersta's orchard and the Prevost vineyards weren't performing the way they should."

Dotty leaned in close, motioning me to her. She was shorter than me, so I lowered an ear toward her. She said, "It has to be about the divinity fudge recipe."

"How so? Can we talk while I gather ingredients in the kitchen?" I wanted to get out of earshot of the customers.

In the galley kitchen, I began collecting Belgian chocolate kilo bars, a twenty-pound bag of sugar, butter, and cream. Making fudge was helping me build big muscles in my arms. In spring when I first started, I'd made and sold fifty or so pounds of fudge a week. After my first fudge festival in July, I'd begun seeing my sales go up. Then with the introduction of Ava's Autumn Harvest this fall, I now made and sold over three hundred pounds of fudge a week. It scared me to think of what would happen in winter, because I'd have no roadside market. The tourist trade went way down and my sales would, too.

Dotty was loading her arms with ingredients, too.

I asked her, "Why are you so sure Tristan Hardy's death is about the recipe?"

"Holy wars."

"Holy wars?"

"Yes. The other ladies and I were online today discussing it. People are willing to kill for two reasons: love and beliefs. My friends and I doubt that anybody would use the church to hide a love affair, so it has to be about finding the recipe."

"Because it could be worth a lot of money."

Dotty stacked one more pound of Oosterlings' organic sweet cream butter on the load in her arms. "Money is good, but this is about somebody wanting to live in the steps of Sister Adele Brise."

Dotty said the name with an inflection and flair, as it might be said in the French patois in the Walloon regions of Belgium. Belgium is a country divided into Wallonia with its French-speaking provinces, and Flanders with its Flemish provinces. Namur is the capital of the Wallonia region.

"What are you saying, Dotty? That a woman killed Cherry?"

"I don't know that. But I'm sure people want to touch all the spots that Adele touched and walk the paths she walked. They want to bask in her love."

"If this is about love, how could anybody murder Tristan Hardy? For a fudge recipe? What would be the motive?"

"You haven't been listening. This is about somebody lost in their faith."

"Well, Dotty, that's a given. Murder is a mortal sin."

Dotty's sweet pink face grew a bit red in obvious frustration with me. She led me out of the kitchen. Both our arms were overloaded. Pausing in the hallway, Dotty said, "This murder is about the glory that somebody needs. Holy wars are about claiming glory. Somebody wanted glory from this murder."

"What do you mean by glory?" I felt as if I were back in grade school catechism class.

"They want to triumph, Ava. Somebody wants revenge about something. Revenge is why Tristan Hardy was killed. At least that's how we church ladies voted online about an hour ago. Money came in third."

"What was the second-place motive?"

"Sex."

Chapter 9

The dark chocolate, sugar, and cream had barely started heating in the copper kettle when questions arose about Tristan Hardy and the divinity fudge recipe. About twenty customers had gathered near my kettle at the front of the shop after lunchtime on Sunday. Raindrops splattered the big bay windows overlooking the harbor.

My arms were on autopilot stirring the fragrant, sweet concoction in the kettle. My brain was stirring the motives for the murder voted on by the church ladies: glory, money, and sex.

A woman in the crowd said, "Divinity fudge didn't become popularized until the early 1900s, after Sister Adele passed away. Why would you think the holy recipe even existed?"

The crowd quieted at this bold question that had apparently caught all of Door County and me—the fudge expert—in a huge mistake. But it was not a mistake.

"Not so about fudge," I said. "Yes, the meringue-type candy became popular here after the invention of corn syrup, which was introduced in the United States in 1902, but it existed far earlier in various forms."

Thanks to the cookbook collection in Lloyd Mueller's house that I had inherited, I knew that divinity fudge was made by 1915 at least, but it was evident it existed earlier, because a form of it was a candy for the Egyptians, which I told the crowd.

"Divinity candy is related to marshmallows."

A giggling boy of maybe six with curly red hair and freckles said, "Marshmallows? The Egyptians roasted marshmallows outside their pyramids?"

"They could very well have done that," I said. "What's your name?"

"Josh."

"In only a few minutes, you can help me with the fudge if you like."

"Sure!" His mop of red hair flopped as he nodded.

Stirring, I said, "In two thousand BC, the Egyptians boiled the root of the marsh plant called the mallow, or marsh mallow, then combined it with sugar and honey. The candy was made expressly for royalty."

Josh said, "Like your prince? If the prince likes your fudge, will he marry you?"

Everybody laughed, including me.

"I'm not sure fudge would make him marry me, but he's very interested in divinity fudge. That's one reason why he's coming to Door County."

The woman with the earlier questions, who appeared to be Josh's mother, asked, "So, what's the connection between the old marsh mallow plants and today's divinity?"

"Modern marshmallows were made in France in the 1800s using corn syrup, water, and the mallow sap, and egg whites to bind them. The introduction of egg whites into the recipe—which is what is used now in divinity fudge—tells me that Sister Adele could very well have made divinity fudge in the late 1800s."

Josh said, "How'd she get eggs? Did she steal them from wild turkeys?"

I brought my ladle up into the air to test the state of the chocolate-coated crystals. A ribbon of chocolate whipped about, to the crowd's delight.

"Chickens," I explained, "including Belgian breeds like Brakels, were probably brought over on the early ships with immigrants to Door County. The term 'fudge' appeared in newspaper articles at the same time in the late 1800s when the Vassar College women made the candy for fund-raisers using a cooking method over a Bunsen burner, not unlike what I'm doing right now."

Another woman raised her hand. "My grandmother made divinity with coconut."

"Oh yes, divinity fudge loves to have a few things added. Peppermint flavoring is a favorite at Christmastime, and in the South confectioners make divinity with pecans. What should I put in my recipe to create something that Sister Adele might have found back in the 1860s and 1870s here in Door County?"

The crowd shouted, "Walnuts" and "wild blackberries" and "blueberries."

Josh added, "Fish."

Laughter resounded.

I invited him up to stir the Rapunzel Raspberry Rapture Fairy Tale Fudge.

I told the crowd, "Josh is doing a great job with that four-foot maple paddle. While he's stirring, I'm going to add the organic butter. We add the butter at the end—often frozen butter—to regulate the temperature a bit."

I showed the crowd the thermometer dangling off a hook nearby, which I could use if needed. I was experienced enough now that I rarely tested officially for the temperature. I could tell by the look of the concoction in the kettle how it was doing. "The colder and drier the air in the shop and outside, the lower the temperature it takes for fudge. However, if I were making my Cinderella Pink Fudge, I'd want a slightly warmer temperature. Vanilla fudge requires about four degrees more than dark chocolate. Okay, Josh, that looks good. Let me take over again. Thank you for your fine help."

The crowd applauded him as he raced back to be with his mom.

The fudge was soon ready for loafing. I poured it on the marble table. The glistening, rich, dark chocolate flowed like sweet lava, steaming.

I exchanged my heat-proof gloves for sanitary plastic gloves, then grabbed my loafing tool—a large flat knife made of wood—to massage the molten chocolate.

"Josh, would you like to help?"

He nodded. I slipped plastic gloves over his hands. The gloves were oversized for him, but he was smiling proudly. I picked him up to set him on the stool I kept near the table. Outside, the rain had stopped. The sunshine was causing steam to rise off the docks.

"The marble table pulls the heat out of the fudge. By loafing—or massaging—the fudge, we coat all the crystals with the fat that comes in the butter and cream, which makes the fudge smoother. After loafing about four batches of fudge in a row, I have to let the marble table cool down again or the fudge won't set up properly."

Josh massaged the goopy mass of raspberry fudge, sending a wonderful aroma into the room. To appease the crowd, I brought out a batch of fudge made yesterday and showed them how to eat it with a dollop of whipped cream on the side and fresh berries or some homemade raspberry jam to dip the fudge pieces in.

Everybody flocked to my glass cabinet to buy several flavors of fudge to take home. I gave Josh a free bobber from Grandpa's side of the shop.

About an hour later I drove down to Ava's Autumn Harvest. It was going on three o'clock. Dillon had texted twice but had no news yet about John Schultz's condition.

How had John lost his memory? How had he gotten the goose egg on the back of his head?

Daniel was helping Kjersta load pumpkins in the back of a customer's car along with a box of pickling cucumbers. He called over, "Your fudge sold out."

"I brought some."

I put out pumpkin fudge I'd made yesterday, maple fudge, and my unique Rose Garden Fudge. This rose fudge was white with what looked like confetti in it made from yellow, pink, and red roses I plucked from Lloyd Mueller's backyard organic garden. I also brought along small bags of crystallized rose petals. The fragrant, delicate chips the size and texture of cornflakes always sold well alongside the rose petal fudge. I froze them, too, for making rose-flavored fudge later in winter.

The wine stock seemed low on one outdoor table. "Didn't Michael bring us more bottles?"

Kjersta shrugged as she placed a bucketful of her freshly dug potatoes on a corner of the flatbed wagon that held cucumbers, cabbages, and green and yellow peppers. "Mike is practically having a party over at his winery. I called him, but he said he was too busy pouring free wine."

"Why the party?"

"Michael said he's celebrating that Tristan is gone."

Stunned, I said, "He's celebrating Cherry's death? And telling people that? That's foolish."

We began walking together back to the stone barn.

Kjersta swung her empty bucket. "I can't blame Michael." She paused at the door of the barn, her big brown eyes showing weariness. "Cherry was causing the huge rift between Jonas and Michael. Jonas was fed up with Cherry. I know that Jonas complained to the university about Cherry. He told me he wrote to his dean."

"When was this?"

"A couple of weeks ago. Start of the university's semester."

"Did you tell this to the sheriff when he stopped by earlier?"

"No. He only asked about cars going by last night."

We went inside. The barn smelled of something sweet, like clover hay. "What's that?" I sniffed Kjersta. "A new perfume?"

Kjersta laughed. "My new soaps. I figured I could best Fontana at her own game." She led me to a small stack of soap cakes wrapped in clear cellophane on a shelf across from the cash register.

Giving her a sly smile, I said, "You're not jealous of your husband's ex-wife, are you?"

"Ha, she's jealous of me. Now she'll be even more jealous. These soaps are far better than what she sells."

She showed me the soap bars. They were a pale pink, the hue of clover when it first blooms after a rain.

I said, "They match the color of my Cinderella Pink Fairy Tale Fudge. Women will love buying these as gifts."

Kjersta said, "I use the milk from sheep and goats. Fontana uses cow's milk."

"You use Jonas's goats and sheep?"

"Yeah."

"But you seem to think he could have murdered Tristan Hardy."

The pained look on Kjersta's face showed me she was conflicted. "No. It must have been a bad accident. They must have argued in the church basement and shoved each other and Cherry fell."

"But you've no proof."

She shook her head. "I just have this bad feeling about Jonas sending that letter to the dean. Cherry would have found out, I'm sure. It could've been Cherry planning to harm Jonas, but it turned out the other way."

That chilled me. My family respected both men. "Are you still using Jonas's animals to mow in your orchard?"

Daniel Dahlgren and Michael Prevost had used Jonas's goat herd and flock of sheep for a few years to eat or "vacuum" dead leaves and weeds. The goats were turned into the Dahlgrens' orchard, but not the vineyard because they would eat the grapevines in addition to anything else except for the wire fencing. The sheep ignored the grapevines, though, and thus were used in the vineyard to eat the ground cover there. Eating the fallen leaves prevented molds from forming and growing.

Kjersta said, "Daniel is suggesting it'd be best if we cut ties with Jonas entirely. Especially now."

The sweet smells inside my little barn took on a sour note. I remembered that Sam had told me Kjersta had said Fontana had something to do with the murder.

After swallowing hard to drum up courage, I said, "Fontana says you blamed her for Cherry's death."

Kjersta didn't even blink. "She had some role in the death, if you ask me. Don't you agree that she loved having two men fight over her?"

My friend returned to her own gardening chores with her husband while I finished the afternoon working at my roadside market wondering what had really happened in that church basement. Was there a lovers' triangle? Could Fontana and Jonas be harboring a horrible secret?

Thankfully, a steady stream of customers saved me from my maudlin thoughts.

As I was heading to my truck at six o'clock, the sheriff's squad car pulled into the grassy flat next to the empty wagon where pumpkins had sat earlier. Jordy got out, shutting the door with a solid *ker-thunk*.

I sighed. "Hello, Jordy."

He touched the brim of his hat in salutation, then removed his sunglasses. The sun was lower now and behind his broad shoulders. "Just talked with your friend."

"Which one? I have more than one."

"The one without a memory."

"John Schultz? How is he?"

"Something called transient global amnesia. Can't remember where he's been in the last day. Seems mighty convenient." He took a deep breath, expanding his already-broad chest. "And connected to you."

My goose bumps were back. "Why do you say that?"

"He can't remember where he's been. He can't remember where his car is. And I can't seem to find Tristan Hardy's car. Two cars are missing, a man is dead, and you found the body. Want to tell me the truth now?"

I fingered the keys in my right hand. "You forgot the knife. How is all that connected to the Buck knife in the choir loft and the blood on the music sheets? And the fire? What burned anyway?"

"I can't tell you. I'd like to hear the perpetrator tell me."

"Sorry, Jordy, but you're messing with me. I found the body and the knife. I'll give you that much, but you know I didn't kill anybody. Or set a fire. In the organ bench." I was guessing, but it worked.

A hiss escaped across his lips. "Are you holding back information about your friends?"

My blood pressure was surging. "Do I need a lawyer?"

"Wouldn't hurt. Probably wouldn't hurt for whomever you're protecting, too. You willing to come down to my office tomorrow for a chat?"

"No, Sheriff Tollefson, sir. Because I don't know anything."

After a long moment in which he glared at me, he got in his car, then drove away.

All of a sudden the breeze sweeping across the treetops

and farmland from the Lake Michigan bay felt frosty. I ran for the barn to grab my sweatshirt I had left there, sucking the air to catch my breath. I couldn't let my mother be questioned by Jordy. His ability to thrust a laser stare through a person would wilt Florine. She would confess without even realizing it, then end up vacuuming a jail cell.

Chapter 10

By seven that Sunday night, I was alone with Lucky Harbor in my cabin. The dog had thrown up on my kitchen floor. I wondered what he'd eaten at Mercy Fogg's house. It appeared to be raw meat loaf, replete with chopped onions, but I could swear there were also colored marshmallows in it, of all things.

I called Dillon. Dillon said, "He's eaten and regurgitated worse. As long as he's breathing okay and wagging his tail, I wouldn't worry about it. Want me to come clean it up?"

The water spaniel had lain down already in a corner of the kitchen next to the refrigerator, his head between his front paws. His contrite eyes followed my every move.

"No, I can handle it. You keep an eye on John." He'd volunteered to keep John with him at the Blue Heron Inn for the night.

"Pauline's here."

"Tell her hi."

I turned my attention to the vintage cookbooks that filled boxes in my cabin. Like panning for gold, I kept flipping pages for anything about divinity fudge or history related to my family.

A knock on my door startled me.

It was Mercy Fogg, of all people. She had never graced my door in all the months I'd known her. She still wore her bus uniform. I got the feeling she was proud to wear any kind of uniform that took her a notch above her usual coveralls worn when driving our county's road-grading equipment or the snowplows in winter. She'd prefer a crown and an ermine robe, I felt sure, with a scepter in one hand.

"Something wrong, Mercy?"

"Why do you assume that something's wrong?"

"Because you don't like me much, for starters. Why is that, anyway?" I knew it was jealousy, disappointment, and a general mad-on against most of Fishers' Harbor, but I loved pimping her anyway. "Why don't we put all the cards on the table, as we say, and be done with it?"

"Life is more than a game of cards." She practically shoved me out of the way as she tromped into my small rental cabin.

She sniffed the air, flipping her head about, her blond bouffant curls bouncing. "What is that putrid smell?"

"The dog upchucked whatever it was you had in that pan at your house."

"My venison meat loaf," she growled. "And that was the last of my stash, too. Now I have to wait for the deer hunting seasons to start to replenish my larder."

"So you hunt?"

"Bow and gun. Since a little girl. With my dad."

"You still hunt with him?"

"He's . . ." Her voice caught. "He's in a nursing home. I made the meat loaf for him and his friends there. I was going to bake it after I drove the bus."

I didn't feel as tall as usual. We were both looking at Lucky Harbor lying in the kitchen. His tail thumped once.

I said, "You make your meat loaf with marshmallows. I've never heard of that."

"I ran out of eggs to bind it together. I figured they'd do."

"If it helps, Lucky Harbor loved it going down."

Mercy gave me a sideways glance. Her eyes were watery. "Thanks, Ava."

Then she perused my small cabin. "Quaint. These cabins almost belonged to me, you know."

"Almost. You would have had to buy this property from Lloyd Mueller. It's the fudge shop you 'almost' owned."

"One piece of real estate begets the next."

When Mercy was village president, she'd swung a deal several years ago that could have made her the owner of the bait-and-fudge shop if my grandfather missed paying his taxes for too many years. She had also wanted the village to buy up the cabins on Duck Marsh Street to tear them down and expand the harbor with fancy condos and shops. She was all for Lloyd Mueller selling out to a Milwaukee tour and travel company to plow us asunder. That was the same company that had fired John Schultz. All of Mercy's fancy plans, however misplaced, were nixed when John threatened the corporate vultures with a hefty lawsuit over age discrimination.

Everything turned out well for Grandpa and me because Lloyd had left a will that put Cody Fjelstad in charge of Lloyd's estate. Cody could take over when he turned twenty-five. He had just turned nineteen, which rankled Mercy because another nineteen-year-old, Erik Gustafson, had ended up as mayor. Mercy was turning sixty soon, but she was increasingly hemmed in by youngsters. Based on my own angst about turning thirty-two I guessed the dreaded feeling of getting older was pressuring her, too. Despite our differences, I understood Mercy sometimes.

Mercy was inspecting the living room area's stone fireplace. Then she picked up the cookbooks on the couch and sat down. The springs popped.

Titus, my ever-faithful mouse, appeared under the back of the couch, his pinkish nose wiggling, sniffing for an escape route. He noticed the dog, then left stage right.

I stepped around the couch to face Mercy. "You've got a reason for this visit."

Mercy capped her knees with her beefy hands, tapping her fingers, nervouslike. "You should know something about your grandparents."

My heart startled. "What?" I crossed my arms.

"It's about today's vineyard tour they were on." She tapped her fingers on the couch arm. "They were quite entertaining. At least your grandmother was."

"How so?"

"Your grandmother got stinking drunk."

That made me lurch. "She never drinks to excess."

"When we got to the Prevost Winery, Mike wasn't only

giving away sips in those dinky sample cups. He was handing out full glasses."

"But that still doesn't explain her drinking to excess."

"Everybody was toasting her relatives."

"Oh no." I slumped onto the raised hearth.

Mercy nodded. "I could tell something was wrong about the relatives. The more people asked her about Prince Arnaud and Princess Amandine, the more she glugged the wine. Your grandfather finally saw what was going on, but too late. He helped her on the bus, where she passed out."

"Passed out?" I rushed over to the window to look across the street. Their lights were off or I would have gone straight over there. "It looks like they went to bed early."

"Is there something wrong with her relatives? Do they have a disease? You're not a carrier of something awful, are you? Is that why you haven't had kids yet? You're afraid they'll be born with whatever your prince and princess have?"

Mercy sounded ridiculous. But then I wondered if she'd put her finger on what might be troubling Grandma about her royal relatives. Maybe there was one of those whispered secrets families hand down through generations.

"Thanks, Mercy, for telling me this. My grandmother is going to be really embarrassed in the morning. I'm sure she'll apologize to you."

Mercy pushed her hefty frame up with a grunt. "Don't worry about it. No locals were on the tour. All Chicago people. But Mike Prevost saw her getting tipsy." We were at the door when Mercy added, "He's got his own troubles."

"How so?"

"Mike said he ran into somebody last night with his car. He said the person was parked along Highway C down there where you're from. Mike says he swerved for a raccoon and slammed to a stop behind the parked car. Wrecked a headlight on Mike's car. The other guy started to get out, then thought better of it, it seems, and took off. Probably a drunk."

This was corroborating Kjersta's story. "Did he say what the guy looked like?"

"He said he only got a glimpse. Some kind of Hawaiian shirt."

I winced. John Schultz wore those shirts. "Did Mike say who it was?"

"No. He said he never saw the guy's face. But you and I know who it was."

Mercy gave me a look filled with more subtext than a soap opera scene, then left. Lucky Harbor sailed out the door after her, heading up the hill to Dillon.

I couldn't concentrate on my cookbooks. I had to tell Pauline what I'd learned. I called Dillon to see if she was at the inn visiting John.

"Sorry, Ava. Pauline left. I made popcorn and rented a couple of Grand Prix racing documentaries for John and me to watch."

I felt like a discarded autumn leaf left to drift in the wind. "Did he remember anything of importance yet?"

"No, but it's only supposed to take a day and not over forty-eight hours."

That would mean it might take him until Monday night. "Take notes."

"Of course, Ava. I miss you."

"I miss you, too. I sent Lucky Harbor back to you. Good night."

Like sugar crystals scrambling to make sense of the heat in my copper kettles, my brain sought meaning in the maze of happenings I'd experienced in two days. Why had John been on that road? A road that wasn't far from the Namur church? What had he seen? What had Michael Prevost seen? Had he been on his way to the church? Heck, that church was starting to sound like a late-night party place, if Michael, John, Jonas, Fontana, and Cherry had all been there.

Although it was early, only about eight now in the evening, I shut off the lights, ready to fall into bed.

A scratch at my front door signaled Lucky Harbor was back. He was wagging his tail as he trotted inside. His collar had the bright orange, floatable key holder attached. A warm feeling came over me.

I opened up the key holder, then withdrew a piece of paper. *Forgot to say I love you. Dillon.*

I smiled. A bit of peace washed over me.

Lucky Harbor trotted to the bedroom. He adored sleeping on my bed curled up at my feet.

As I headed to my bedroom and my borrowed dog, the pitter-patter behind me on the floor indicated Titus was running from the kitchen back to underneath the couch. The normalcy of Titus's routine soothed me, too.

But I still had a tough time sleeping. My grandmother had gotten drunk. Sheesh.

On Monday morning I was at the fudge shop by five o'clock to cut and wrap the Rapunzel Raspberry Rapture Fairy Tale Fudge that had been loafed near the window the day before. My thoughts weren't on fudge, however.

I was thinking about my grandmother and what awful secret she might have about our ancestors. I tied on a pink apron with a bib top and frilly skirt over my jeans and long-sleeved pink T-shirt.

I shoved my horrible thoughts aside for Pauline. I texted her to say I'd walk up to the Blue Heron Inn later in the morning to check on John for her.

My grandfather wasn't at the shop early as usual, which didn't surprise me today. If Mercy had been correct about Grandma Sophie's condition after the winery tour yesterday, Grandpa was administering lots of coffee and juice to my grandmother.

When my grandfather finally popped in, he was wrinkly in the face from lack of sleep. My hands began to shake as I continued cutting fudge into one-inch squares.

His silver hair wasn't combed; swatches of it stood up in every direction, making him look like an aging rock star. He wore a blue-and-black-checked flannel shirt that he'd buttoned crooked. The shirt collar was pushed up on one side of his neck toward an ear. He wore tall rubber boots over his denim jeans, as if he were ready to march through the marsh at the end of our street looking for minnows to add to his tank.

With gentleness, I called over, "Gilpa, are you going fishing today?"

He growled, making his way to his coffeemaker behind

his register. Amid the popping of the can lid and scooping of coffee, he said, "Not in the mood. I feel like skydiving without a parachute."

Hmm. "Mercy Fogg told me about yesterday. How is Grandma?"

"Hmmph. Ornery as hell. I thought she'd be pleased as punch going along yesterday. I thought it'd get her talking about her history here in Door County and she could feel pride. Inviting that prince and princess here was the worst thing I've ever done, according to her."

Bad karma sparks showered off my grandpa.

I said, "She hasn't liked your surprise so much, I know." I hauled a pan of the Rapunzel Fudge over to my counter to wrap individual pieces.

Grandpa took the coffee carafe and marched by me to the kitchen in back for water. When he returned, he said, "I'm thinking it might be a good thing to ask the prince to cancel the trip."

I almost squished the fudge I was wrapping in pretty red wax paper. "Don't do that, Gilpa."

I told him about Mercy's theory concerning some hereditary condition that might be worrying Grandma.

Grandpa punched on the coffeemaker button so hard he pushed the machine back against the wall with a bang. "Hogwash. Your grandmother is not diseased. Neither are you."

With that, he tromped out in his boots through the front door. The cowbell almost fell off from the force of him slamming the door. I knew he wasn't mad at me; he was mad at himself for not being able to please my grandmother. He loved her deeply. Whenever he displeased her, it was as if an eclipse happened and his heart went dark.

For the next two hours I made fudge, cleaned (not to my mother's standards), took inventory after the weekend sales, and restocked gift items, including the aprons. We'd sold a dozen of them yesterday after my fudge demonstration. I called the church ladies to order more. They made them by hand. Lois Forbes, who lived over in Jacksonport on the lake side of the county versus our bay side, said she'd come across an entire bolt of pink satin that was begging to be trim on Cinderella Pink Fairy Tale Fudge aprons.

Around seven thirty, Lucky Harbor showed up outside the front door, panting and scratching on the glass. I let him in. He was soaking wet. He immediately shook, spiraling water all over my jeans and pink, long-sleeved T-shirt and white bib apron, the floor, and nearby shelves.

"Thanks, Lucky Harbor. Somehow getting drenched by you feels appropriate this morning."

The brown dog sat, panting up at me. On his collar under his neck I spotted the buoyant key holder.

I heard Dillon's strong, manly voice as I read, *When the sun rises, I think of you. Love you.*

I took the note to my counter, then scribbled on the back *When my heart beats, I think of you. Love you.*

After placing the rolled notepaper back in the capsule, I tossed Lucky Harbor two Goldfish crackers from my pocket. I gave him a good hug, despite him being wet. "What a good messenger service you are, Lucky Harbor. I love you, too, you know."

He barked. Then I sent him on his way.

As I closed the door, I peered about but didn't see Grandpa. The *Super Catch I* was still at its slip at the other end of the harbor.

By eight, when Grandpa hadn't returned yet, I began to worry and called his cell phone. There was no answer. I hoped he'd gone back to his cabin to be with Grandma Sophie. I called her. No answer.

I decided enough was enough, took off my apron, and set out a change jar on my counter with a sign for customers to use the honor system.

I marched across Duck Marsh Street to my grandparents' front door. Finding the door unlocked, I stepped inside.

The smell of bacon and eggs drew me to the kitchen, where I halted in surprise.

My friend and former fiancé, Sam Peterson, was sitting at the table sopping up a sunny-side-up egg with a piece of toast. Across from him sat Grandma in a pink fuzzy robe, sipping coffee from a large mug. They peered up at me as if I were a burglar.

"What's going on?" I asked.

Sam put down his toast. "Your grandmother called me an hour ago to come over for a chat."

"Grandma, is something wrong?" I rushed to give Grandma Sophie a hug. "How can I help? Why is Sam here? Why didn't you call me?"

Grandma winced. "My head, Ava honey, slow down. This is about you."

I plunked down in the chair between them. "Me? And I wasn't invited to the conversation?"

"I asked Sam to come over and give me some advice about lawyers. Your father called earlier and the authorities have arrested Kjersta Dahlgren for the murder of Tristan Hardy."

"Oh no."

"You're one of her friends, and you found Cherry. I'm worried about you."

I patted her hand nearest me. "Don't worry about me. What about Kjersta? This is all wrong. It's Michael Prevost they want. Or Jonas Coppens. Or . . ."

I didn't want to bring up Fontana's name, since Sam had dated her.

Grandma and Sam stared at me. The refrigerator's buzz filled the room.

I told them, "Kjersta told me her theories about everybody being upset with Cherry, but that's all I really know."

Sam fingered the toast on his plate. "Your father is concerned, too. He called me this morning to help you."

"I'll call Parker Balusek."

Sam got off his chair. He poured me a mug of coffee, then topped off Grandma's cup. "Fontana called me this morning. She gave a statement to the sheriff last night. She says she's sure Kjersta killed Cherry."

"Sam, just because she's an old girlfriend . . ."

"Fontana was sobbing."

"Of course. She's a good actress when she wants to be. Be careful. You know she's jealous of me and Kjersta because of my new market doing well. And let's not get into the issue of her wanting to torture her ex-husband by dating the entire male population around Brussels and Namur. I don't believe she's a 'floozy' as my grandmother calls her. Fontana isn't the type to go to bed with men indiscriminately, but she wants to be loved by somebody. In her desperation I'm not sure she makes the best decisions concerning her actions."

"Maybe I could discuss the issues with her."

The urge to do something with my hands—either make fudge or throttle Sam—overwhelmed me. "Sam, Fontana isn't one of your social work clients. The issues are clear. The wrong person is in jail. Kjersta is our friend."

I had to do something. I got up. "Grandma, can you cover the fudge shop? Grandpa's not there, so don't worry about having to talk to him about yesterday." I hugged her. "He's concerned about you, Grandma. He's sorry. He loves you buckets."

She was sniffling as I said to Sam, "Don't worry about lawyers. I'm turning myself in."

The Door County Justice Center in Sturgeon Bay was a contemporary edifice of brick with limestone rock accents and four gray rock columns out front. Yellow lilies that hadn't succumbed to early frost waved in the breeze. A stained glass window depicted Miss Liberty. I went through the maroon-colored doors, then walked to the protective glass window and spoke through the tiny holes.

"I'm Ava Oosterling. I'm giving myself up." I didn't really want to say that, but I knew it would fast-track me to the sheriff.

The woman behind the glass gave me an odd look, then consulted her computer. "Yup, the sheriff is expecting you."

That rankled me. Somehow Jordy knew I'd show up after he arrested Kjersta.

When I was being patted down, I suddenly knew why the woman gave me the odd look. I was still wearing the pink apron from my shop. I'd worn it over to Grandma's house, too, evidently. I decided to leave it on. Maybe it would soften up the sheriff.

A deputy escorted me to the little room with the blue

plastic chairs and six-foot table. Pauline and I, as well as my entire family, had gathered here in the past to discuss a few matters of accidents and murder.

Ten minutes went by in the frigid room. The cold wait was a sheriff's tactic. Jordy wanted me to be shivering so I'd spill everything fast and then leave.

Sheriff Tollefson finally stomped into the room, sharp as usual in his tan uniform, his brown hair short but with fashionable waves in it. He plopped down a pad of paper and pen, then eased into the chair across from me.

His brown eyes ogled my attire. A corner of his mouth twitched. "Thank you for saving me the trouble of tracking you down today."

"You can't really think you're going to arrest me."

"You and Pauline."

I shivered for real. "We were merely cleaning the church. His body was there. That's it. And there's no way Kjersta killed Tristan Hardy. Come on, Jordy, you know the Dahlgrens."

"Must I continue to remind you that it's *Sheriff* Tollefson when I'm on duty? We went through this last summer."

He was starting to waste my time, which always turned up the heat inside me. "Well, *Sheriff*, there is no way Kjersta killed anybody. She grows organic vegetables and cherries and apples."

"So 'organic' somehow inoculates a person from committing murder? What if I think she committed an organic murder? It was organic to her personality. Now, tell me about her. I know Daniel, but Kjersta is fairly new to me. She married Daniel when?"

"A couple of years ago. Right after his divorce from Fontana."

He made notes. "Your family was upset with Tristan, too?"

My instincts said I was toying with a rattlesnake. "He and Professor Wesley Weaver and their students came to my parents' home a few times to talk about the study they were doing. It was through our own county cooperative extension service. My parents were both very cooperative."

"Cooperative with the cooperative?" Jordy shook his

head, then made notes. "Wesley Weaver and Tristan Hardy were friends?"

"Colleagues. I suppose they were friends, too."

Jordy's pen scratched again on the paper.

He asked, "What do you know about Jonas Coppens? In relationship to Tristan Hardy and Kjersta Dahlgren?"

It was another rattlesnake question that could bite Kjersta. She'd told me she thought Jonas capable of murder. But that was supposition. I shuddered.

"Cold?" the sheriff asked.

"No. My apron keeps me cozy." I searched my brain for things to say that would keep my friends safe. "Jonas was getting the blame for a lot of trouble. He and Kjersta weren't on good terms, but all of us were questioning the slowness of Tristan's research. We were tired of the mystery about chemicals and bugs not getting resolved."

"Kjersta said that Tristan Hardy took samples of food on Saturday from your roadside stand, including your fudge."

I brightened. "Yes, he did. He likely ate it before it went anywhere."

"I've been told he dumped stuff off at the university that afternoon. But we can't find his car. There are likely more materials in the car we'd like to look at. Have you seen a blue Ford Fusion around?"

"No."

Jordy harrumphed. The sheriff then sat back in his chair, his hands going behind his head, where he laced his fingers together in a relaxed mode probably meant to trick me. "Maria Vasquez says that your friend's boyfriend got some knock on the head."

"How does she know that?"

"Incidents of violence are reported to us by the emergency room doctors. She also heard this morning that the guy who owns Prevost Winery had a headlight on his passenger side broken when he ran into somebody who he described as wearing a Hawaiian shirt. I recall somebody who wears those things. Do you?"

The rattlesnake in the air between us had just bit me. Jordy had the upper hand. But there was no way I was going to give up my best friend's boyfriend this easily. "I didn't witness anything. And if you're going to question Mike Prevost and believe him, think again. The guy got my grandmother drunk yesterday. In my way of thinking, Mike is not a very reliable witness."

Jordy popped his hands from off his head, then leaned across the table at me. "Drunk?"

I told Jordy the tale of woe about my grandparents leading the tour yesterday to help out John Schultz.

He shook his head while scribbling across his pad with his pen. "I hope Sophie's feeling okay this morning."

"She'll be fine after about two pots of coffee to get over the dehydration. Sam Peterson is with her."

"Ex-fiancés are good for something, I guess."

"That was uncalled for, Jordy."

"You're right. Sorry, Ava."

I was getting the upper hand back. "What evidence do you have that Kjersta murdered Cherry?"

"I can't give you all the details."

"Can I talk with her?"

"That's not advised."

"But not illegal. You forget I'm familiar with the rules here. She's allowed limited visits. Maybe she and her attorney put me on the preapproved visitor list."

After scowling at me, he went to ask the status. He evidently had no intention of arresting me. I suspected that was only what my panicked parents thought might happen.

I was shown to Room B117, which was labeled ATTORNEY VISITS. Kjersta and I, sans sheriff, sat in blue chairs again, but this room was much smaller, more like a church confessional.

Kjersta wore a jail jumpsuit. With her pixie haircut and big brown eyes, she almost looked fashionable and straight off some TV show about women in prison. But the whites of her eyes were red from crying.

"I didn't do it, Ava. I didn't kill Cherry."

"I know." Oddly, my gut betrayed me with a tiny lurch. I felt ashamed for doubting her. Sam and the sheriff had done a number on me. "But they must have something on you. What's the alleged evidence?"

"Evidence, ha. The evidence is perfume."

"Perfume?"

"They say that perfume was detected on Cherry's clothing that matches what I wear and sell."

This amazed me. "Are you sure there's no other evidence?"

"I can't think of anything else. And my lawyer hasn't been told anything much yet."

"They must have something else on you, Kjersta, that they're not telling you."

She shuddered. "Sheriff Tollefson seems fixated on the perfume for now."

"The sheriff has a good nose?"

"He got a whiff of me yesterday, and he decided I smelled like the clothing they took off Cherry. The sheriff was aware of how upset I was about Cherry's lack of action to stop the chemical drift from Jonas's farm. He also found out that I make homemade organic scents now. He put two and two together."

I sat back in my chair, flummoxed. "But you wear natural scents, like the new soaps you created. You create scents from clover."

Kjersta leaned forward, tapping her worn fingernails on the table. "Yes, and we both know who else wears natural scents, though more pungent. Fontana."

"Did you tell the sheriff you think it's her?"

"I tried. He doesn't believe me. I told the sheriff that Fontana and Cherry were arguing and she's been dating him. But she only dated him to work up to this—me being jailed. She wants me out of the picture so she can have Daniel back. Somehow she manufactured this murder to get rid of me. And watch out. You know she wants you out of business, too. Before this is over, you and your family will be ruined. I guarantee it."

Chapter 11

The notion of my family possibly being ruined by Fontana sent me straight to the farm to warn my father.

It was midmorning, but my dad was still milking cows with the help of his herd manager.

The milking parlor sent cows through on an assembly line. It had ten milking stalls—five on each side of a pit area that put my dad and the herdsman at almost eye level with each cow's udder. Dad would do what's called the "dip and strip" first, or washing the teats and making sure each was healthy by squirting out a little milk by hand.

Then the herdsman put the milking cups on each teat. Whooshing suctions and pulsations in the hoses drew the milk out of the udder. The glass vacuum tubes along the top of the stanchions that looked like hamster trails sucked the milk all the way to either of two rooms, depending on how my dad flipped the switch. One room had a holding tank for that milk to be shipped away for packaging as milk and yogurt people bought in a grocery store. The other room was the creamery where Mom made cheese and butter, and skimmed cream for my fudge.

With the milking machines set up on the cows, Dad sauntered over to me at the area reserved for visitors. To honor our upcoming visitors, he'd painted the black, yellow, and red Belgian flag on the wall behind me as well as the Wallonia Province flag, which was yellow with a red rooster in the middle.

Dad wore clean blue jeans, a blue chambray shirt, and

tall black rubber boots that were spotless. He walked them through a shallow rubber tub filled with disinfectant.

"Hi, honey."

I relayed to him what I'd found out in Sturgeon Bay.

"Perfume?" He wrinkled up his nose. "Seems a bit flimsy to jail somebody based on perfume."

"I know. I'm sure the sheriff has some other evidence that he's not sharing with Kjersta or anybody in the public yet so that he can get a clean confession from somebody. Do you remember anything weird in the last few days? Anything that could help get Kjersta freed?"

"Such as?"

"Did Fontana Dahlgren stop by?"

"No." He trained his eyes on the Holsteins. "I've been seeing Fontana a lot, though, in her little red Mustang zipping around the countryside."

"Really? Like where?"

"All over. I was out baling hay over near Highway C one day last week and she had stopped near that roadside chapel at Jonas's place. She pulled on the door, but it appeared to be locked."

"How odd. She's not the church kind. Though it wouldn't hurt her to attend."

My dad chuckled, then sobered. "Maybe you should lock up the stone barn and call it quits for the season. At least until this murder case is solved. With Kjersta in jail, and Daniel doing his chores off in his orchards, you're there all alone now. I don't like that."

His caring almost brought me to tears. "Thanks, Dad, but I'll be fine." Then Kjersta's words echoed in my head. *"Watch out. You know she wants you out of business, too. Before this is over, you and your family will be ruined. I guarantee it."*

"Did you notice anybody driving by our farm on their way to Namur the night of the murder? It could have been past ten o'clock."

Dad said, "I was in bed by that time and sound asleep. Maybe your mother recalls something. She's a light sleeper, always complaining about waking up at three in the morning and never getting back to sleep until it's time to get up."

Mom was next door in the creamery. She was dressed in white and wore a hair net. "Thank goodness you weren't arrested yet, Ava. Do I need to worry?"

"No, Mom."

At the front counter, I helped myself to blocks of cheddar cheese and bags of fresh cheddar cheese curds to sell at Ava's Autumn Harvest. I marked down what I was taking on a pad of paper. Mom entered items on her computer tablet in the evenings.

After she finished swishing water in a big stainless steel sink, she came over, still wringing her hands. "I haven't told your father I found the body. I just can't do it."

I sagged. That was not what this family needed—more secrets being kept from one another. We were going to implode with secrets.

But I respected my mother, and after all, I was the one who volunteered to take the rap for finding Cherry's body. After catching up my mother on what had transpired with Kjersta, I asked her about cars going by on Saturday night or very early Sunday morning.

Her brown eyes went as wide as Kjersta's. "Come to think of it, I did hear cars. But not at three when I'm usually awake. Around midnight. One roared pretty good. I figured it was high school kids laying rubber on the road like they do sometimes."

Her answer gave me nothing. Fontana loved to show off in her Mustang, but a lot of people showed off by speeding on our back roads. The killer could be in Chicago or Chechnya by now. But Kjersta thought Fontana was a suspect. I'd known Kjersta since first grade. She'd never bossed me around or tried to make me over like Fontana. Fontana had always wanted to shape the world to her liking. It was so darn easy to blame her for Cherry's death. But could I believe it?

Daniel Dahlgren blamed his ex-wife, Fontana, but not Jonas. After I set out the cheese and curds at my stand, Daniel had come out of his house to join me.

The wind whipped his wild blond waves. He had that

same rangy, cowboy demeanor that Dillon possessed. A big belt buckle cinched his confident gait. As he drew close, though, I could see that worry clouded his blue eyes.

"Daniel, I'm so sorry." I updated him on my visit with Kjersta at the Justice Center.

He was fussing with my price signs.

"I can do that, Daniel. Why don't you head off to see your wife?"

"Kjersta asked me to help you. I saw her earlier this morning. She told me to make sure nothing happened to your market. She wanted to be sure Fontana didn't make us shut down."

"But what could Fontana do?"

"She'll think of something."

"I'm not afraid of Fontana."

"I am." Daniel was restacking blocks of cheddar cheese. "My wife is in jail because of my ex-wife."

He said that with a catch in his throat that ruptured my soul. These people were my friends. But I'd been away for eight years. I'd missed a lot of growing and changing among my friends. Maybe some changes weren't so good. I ached to feel as though I belonged to my tribe again, but I wanted my tribe to get along as it had done long ago. An urgency to help them—to be meaningful to my friends— overwhelmed me.

Daniel and I brought the vegetables out of the barn from their overnight storage and stacked them on the flatbed wagon and tables. I put out the fudge I'd brought along. Two customers pulled in right after we were set up. Daniel left to do fall pruning in his orchards.

After I made the two sales, nobody else showed up for an hour.

On a whim, I set up an honor jar for money, then got in my truck and headed down Highway C the short distance to Jonas Coppens's property.

I pulled to a stop past his driveway and a few feet this side of the roadside chapel along the road. Jonas's parents had built it years ago when I was a kid. The chapel's foundation was about the dimensions of my pickup truck.

As my dad had told me, the door was locked. That was unusual. Most roadside chapels were open to the passersby who wanted to escape their busy world and take a moment for solitude and prayer. With the way my life was going lately, I wanted to lock myself inside one of these chapels and never come out again. I wondered why Fontana had been trying to get inside.

This chapel had a small window to the west. I peeked inside.

The interior looked the same as when I was a child. Jonas and I and some other farm kids would sometimes play house here. Statues of the Virgin Mary and Jesus stood on the compact altar, which had a gold-painted cross on the wall above it. Pudgy, unlit white candles sat on either end of the altar. A box with the word DONATIONS sat in the east windowsill. A padded kneeler and railing in front of the altar had enough room for two people.

"Hey there, Ooster."

I leaped. "Hi there, Jonas. You gave me a start."

He ran a hand through his short dark auburn hair, his gray-blue eyes sweeping me up and down while he smiled. He'd always called me "Ooster" when we were young.

He said, "The last time we were in there, you had sprouted and were taller than me and you pushed me off the railing, which I was imagining was a horse that I was riding."

While we chuckled over that, I noticed a bicycle lying on the road behind him and in front of my truck.

He waved an envelope in his hand. "Just bringing a letter to the mailbox before the mailman gets here. What's up?"

"My dad said he saw Fontana trying to get into your chapel last week."

"That's why I keep it locked." He shook his head over the matter.

"She comes around a lot?"

"Isn't Fontana everywhere at once?"

"True. But I wonder why she'd want to get inside your chapel. It's not like she's religious. The only higher power she believes in is herself."

He shrugged. "But she sure squawked when they passed on her being part of the church choir for the kermis."

"Yeah, I heard. But we can't have somebody who sounds like a crow cawing in the choir for the prince."

Jonas chuckled again. "That's exactly how she sounds."

"Were you there at tryouts?"

He picked up his bike. "Not inside. I worked on the lawn around the church last Wednesday when they made the semifinal selections, then did the mulching when they made the selection for the final two on Saturday morning."

"I thought Saturday morning was about music selection."

"No. There was a sing-off, too. They were singing 'Ave Maria.'"

My mind went to the Buck knife and blood on the sheet music. "Who were the final two?"

"I'm not sure. It was real early. The sun was barely up. Fontana showed up. But the guy sort of sneaked in and out. When he saw me, he asked me not to tell anybody."

"A guy? I assumed it was women who were vying for the final choir positions."

Jonas's farmer's tan had turned almost magenta. He put a foot on a bike pedal. "I gotta get into my fields. Got some early corn to check on."

"Jonas, wait." I stepped quickly, pulling at his arm before he could put the bike in motion. "Who was the man?"

"You haven't heard it from me, Ooster. Cross your heart and hope to die if you tell?"

"Jonas, this is silly."

"It was Pauline's man friend. I've never formally met him. But I recognized him from another time when a bus tour stopped to look at my roadside chapel. On Saturday early, he called over to me and asked me not to tell that he'd been there. I gotta go. Just remembered I left the water running to the livestock tank."

Jonas pumped away fast, passing his mailbox without leaving the letter. He pedaled down the gravel lane that led back to his farmstead.

So John Schultz was at the church early on Saturday. Before his tour. Pauline didn't know about his trying out for the choir. She would have told me about that.

He'd had a bandaged hand on Saturday. So had Cherry.

What did they know about that knife I'd found in that organ bench? And why did I have a feeling Fontana knew something about it? What was going on in my midst?

I hoped John's memory was coming back soon.

Mom took a shift at Ava's Autumn Harvest. When I returned to Fishers' Harbor around twelve thirty that Monday afternoon, I spotted my grandfather wheeling his garden wagon—my childhood Radio Flyer—down the sidewalk along Main Street. I honked, pulled into an empty parking spot, then ran across the street.

The wagon was stacked high with DVDs and videotapes of old movies still in their cardboard sleeves. We were standing a few yards down from the Wise Owl.

"Gilpa, what's all this?" I restacked a few videotapes that threatened to topple from the wagon.

"For Sophie. Milton let me have them for a quarter apiece." His grin was that of a kid again, and on a Christmas morning at that. But now he was playing Santa Claus. "She's going to love these, don't you think?"

Grandma loved old movies. She often talked about how she and Grandpa would drive over three hours to Madison in their courting days and early marriage to see movies at the Orpheum Theater on State Street. They'd make a weekend of it, seeing four or five movies sometimes. These days, they liked going to Door County's outdoor drive-in theater nearby, called one of the best in the country for its sound system and snacks. But autumn nights were getting too chilly for hanging out at the drive-in.

The titles in the wagon included *Pillow Talk* with Doris Day and Rock Hudson, a 1959 classic. There were also several lighthearted movies starring Cary Grant, including *Arsenic and Old Lace*, from 1944, and silly movies with Elvis Presley and Frank Sinatra. The wagon included a couple of films with Sophia Loren, including *Grumpier Old Men*, from 1995. I had to smile. Grandpa often called my grandmother his Sophia Loren.

"What a nice thing to do, Gilpa." I kissed him on the cheek.

His face flushed, and his eyes twinkled with friskiness.

"I'm going to make her forget about yesterday and her relatives. Nobody is as royal as my Queen Sophie. I'm making the rest of today and tonight all about her. We're watching movies all day. I'm even going to make her popcorn just the way she likes it."

"In the fry pan on the stove?"

"You betcha."

I've never forgotten the sound of my grandparents shaking the fry pan back and forth over their electric stove burner, the action sounding like metal zippers opening and closing fast, punctuated by the popcorn popping. Grandma always poured melted butter over the popcorn in a Tupperware tub. When Pauline and I were young girls, Grandpa would pick out the burned kernels of popcorn and tell us, "Be careful, those'll put hair on your chest."

As we were parting, my grandfather looked back and me and said, "I met that new lawyer lady taking over Milt's store. She's a looker, the likes of which Fishers' Harbor has never seen."

I realized I hadn't tried to look up Jane Goodland on the Internet yet. "I wouldn't let Grandma see that look on your face when Jane's name comes up in conversation."

Grandpa laughed. "As they say, I can look at the menu. Doesn't mean I want to order anything."

A minute later, I came upon Lucky Harbor sitting next to the front door of the fudge shop like a sentry. His collar had the orange key holder on it.

The note read *News about John and memory. Weird.*

Chapter 12

Lucky Harbor rode in the shotgun seat while I drove up the steep hill to the Blue Heron Inn to see what was going on with John and his memory.

Hammering led me to the backyard. To my shock, Dillon stood in front of a finished gazebo. His dark eyes sparkled over a lopsided grin.

Dillon wore a black T-shirt that showed off every sexy fiber of his upper arms, shoulders, and trim torso. The wind played with his dark, wavy hair, making my fingers itch to participate in mussing it.

I didn't see John.

All around the top cornice of the gazebo, the wooden cutouts depicted mother ducks and ducklings paddling around and around in a merry-go-round fashion. The gazebo floor was big enough to hold a kermis polka band or even a small orchestra.

Dillon planted a big kiss on my lips. He smelled of wood chips and pride.

After a second and rather long kiss that reminded me we hadn't sneaked away for a tryst since last Wednesday, I asked, "How did you finish it so fast?"

"John. You know how he is, full of bursts of energy and ideas. He grabbed a hammer and saw and then I could barely keep up."

"Where is John? Did he get his memory back?"

Dillon began cleaning up the area, tossing scrap wood

into a red wheelbarrow. "John told me he was going to be the lead singer of the choir for your prince and princess, but he said that I couldn't tell anybody, especially Pauline. He wants it to be a surprise. She thinks he can't sing."

"Jonas told me about John sneaking into the church early on Saturday. And then he came back later of course on tour, with a bandaged hand. Did you ask him how he cut himself?"

"That's where it gets weird. It came about because he got himself a real Hollywood manager." Dillon gave me a knowing look.

"Oh no. Not my manager."

"Yeah. John said he heard you mention him a couple of times, so he looked him up. John didn't know anybody in Los Angeles, so he started with Marc Hayward."

"He's not here, is he?" I pivoted about with a feeling that I should duck. Marc was nice, but he'd pressure me to work on scripts and get back to Los Angeles. Marc felt bad that the bullies on the writing team at the *The Topsy-Turvy Girls* television show usually voted down my script ideas. So now he hoped that I'd write movie scripts instead and somehow strike it rich. I sensed that he dreamed of going to pitch meetings with me to the big studios where we'd also collect big checks.

Dillon said, "Evidently, Marc showed up late Friday night and asked to meet John at the church on Saturday morning to listen to the auditions and scope it out for filming."

"Jonas never said anything to me about somebody else showing up early."

"Your manager never showed."

"Marc does that but with a good excuse. He always has a plan cooking." My common sense kicked in. "Marc is here to make money off my grandmother's prince and princess."

Dillon continued picking up wood. "John said he was so excited about meeting the guy and filming that he fumbled with getting equipment in his car trunk and cut his hand. He thought it was okay on Saturday, but it started bleeding again Saturday morning when he got a paper cut with some of the sheet music."

"Crap. So some of that blood on the sheet music is John's?"

"Probably."

"Jordy's thorough. John's going to get questioned in a serious way."

"Well, that won't happen now, not with John losing his memory about Saturday night."

I picked up several wood chips off the lawn. With unease, I asked, "Do you know why John might have left Pauline's place late on Saturday night?"

"He got a text from Hayward. We looked on John's phone and it was there. Seems your guy wanted some night-time shots of Saint Mary of the Snows. John drove him down there. He remembered that part this morning."

Relief ran through me. John's disappearance had nothing to do with any panic over his relationship with Pauline. "John's eager to become famous with his TV show. I bet they were on the road, stopping to look at the roadside chapel when Michael Prevost hit them with his car. Mike may have had too much to drink that day." I still wanted to throttle Mike for letting my grandmother drink too much yesterday.

"John said that he recalled Hayward told him to drive on because they didn't have time to get into trouble." Dillon tossed the last of the small boards into the wheelbarrow.

I helped him gather his tools from the lawn. We put them on top of the scrap wood in the wheelbarrow. "But how did John get his bump on the head and lose his memory?"

"He remembers going to the church with Hayward. The place was unlocked."

"That's odd that it was unlocked. There's only a handful of people with keys, including my mother and grandparents, the parish priest, and the foundation people. They're all very careful."

"Well, John and Marc got in without breaking in. John then remembers falling down in the nave. But he's fuzzy about that. He thinks he was hit from behind with something. He recalls a scuffle and Hayward cursing. I suspect your manager hauled ass with John out of there."

"That could've been the roar my mother heard that night."

"John says he recalls a snippet later. He saw the yellow bus he uses for tours, and having lost his sense of orientation, told his manager to drop him off there."

"So Marc Hayward drove onward in John's car to where Marc was staying?"

"That's my guess. You'll have to ask your manager about all this."

Indeed. Dillon picked up the handles of the wheelbarrow. We walked around the inn over the uneven lawn to the front. Dillon's white construction truck wasn't there. "Did you let John drive your truck?"

"I'm not worried. John knows where he is now. It's Saturday night that disoriented him. He and Hayward are scouting locations for shooting."

"I'm not excited about this new friendship. Marc is rather ruthless about money and fame."

"John would like a piece of the action, though."

"That's what worries me. What if they succeed with this TV series proposal? Do you think John would move to Los Angeles?"

"You're worried about Pauline."

I nodded. Dillon took me in his arms, kissing me on the forehead. "They'll work it out."

"She'd be devastated if he left. She's so in love with the lunker."

"No, you'd be devastated if Pauline ever left Fishers' Harbor."

"Well, yeah. We've got our groove back."

Dillon began unloading the wheelbarrow on the edge of the street. "Let's not jump to conclusions yet about John. Please don't tell Pauline any of this. John swore me to secrecy. He wants to spring this good news about Hayward on her. For him, getting a Hollywood manager is a big deal."

I sighed heavily, trying to relieve the tightness in my stomach. "Wait a minute. You said John felt like he'd been hit from behind in the church?"

Dillon laughed. "I guess we got sidetracked. Yeah. That's how he lost his memory."

"John and Marc probably stumbled across the murderer in that church on Saturday night."

Dillon stopped stacking wood scraps to enfold me in his arms. "I was hoping you hadn't noticed that part."

"John and Marc could be in danger. Somebody could be scared that the two of them could turn in the killer."

"Maybe they did. Maybe that's why Kjersta is in jail."

When I got back to the shop, my grandpa left to lead a fishing excursion using the *Super Catch I*. After serving a couple of women tourists who wanted Cinderella Pink Fudge for a party, I called my mother to see how Ava's Autumn Harvest was faring on a Monday afternoon.

"Honey, the cars keep whizzing right by. I got suspicious and finally hopped in the SUV to see what was going on. I found several cars parked at Saint Mary of the Snows with people milling around and taking pictures. One man was hoisting another guy up to look through a stained glass window. Word has gotten out."

"About the prince coming?"

"I don't know about that. I pretended I was a tourist, too, and only heard people talking about finding holy fudge."

"They didn't get inside the church, did they?"

"No. Somebody put more yellow tape up this morning. That church is wrapped like a Christmas present. All it needs is a bow on top."

"It needs a steeple. Maybe we should put out a donation jar there."

"I thought of that. But I didn't have one. I only had your Ava's Autumn Harvest brochures in my pocket, so I left those on the doorstep. Several people picked them up."

"Did that help our sales?"

"No. Some people looked confused and put the brochures back."

I was crushed, but then she added, "Then I told them my daughter was the one appointed to make the holy fudge. One man said you must have holy hands and he wanted any kind of fudge made by you."

"Holy hands?" A groan escaped my throat. "This isn't good."

"But maybe it is. I know this is wrong to say, but if tourists break into the church, they'll mess up the crime scene, right?"

"And you're thinking there'd be no way to connect it to you. Mom, you didn't murder anybody. And nobody is going to find out you found the body. I found the body. That's our story and we have to stick to it."

She sighed over the phone. "Did you find out anything more from the sheriff?"

"No, but Kjersta warned us to watch out for Fontana. Have you seen her around much? Dad said he saw her trying to break into Jonas's little chapel."

"I don't know why she'd be trying to break in. That woman could just get Jonas's key anytime she wanted."

"How's that?"

"Everybody around here knows they've been sleeping together."

That didn't surprise me, certainly. "So, why do you think Fontana would have to break into Jonas's chapel?"

"Maybe they had a little fight after she was seen driving around with her top down with Michael Prevost. I mean the car's top, of course, though sometimes there's very little on her top, too."

"Fontana and Michael? When was this?" My old math teacher didn't seem like her type. I wondered why Mike Prevost would bother hooking himself up with a woman who wanted her ex-husband back but who also seemed after Cherry and Jonas.

Mom said she'd seen Fontana and Michael together that very afternoon.

After hanging up, I made a new batch of Rose Garden Fudge. The rose petals and rose flavoring infused the shop with a perfume beyond compare.

Next, I checked the barometric pressure. Because of the fishing and boating that we loved, Grandpa had all kinds of thermometers and barometers on the walls of his bait shop. In my research in Lloyd's books, one person had written that you can't make divinity fudge unless the barometric pressure is thirty inches or over, which meant clear weather was at hand. We had that this afternoon. But humidity also had to be low, around fifty percent.

One of the earliest references I'd found for divinity candy came from a 1905 recipe. It was a simple recipe using a pint of "golden drip syrup," a pint of sweet milk, a cup of granulated sugar, and a tablespoon of butter. That seemed simple enough, yet I couldn't imagine Sister Adele Brise having access to much "golden drip syrup," though perhaps she could have used honey or maple syrup if they'd tapped trees in the late 1800s.

Another recipe from 1907 was more to my liking. The ingredients were simpler, and possibly what the nuns would have had on hand in the late 1800s. This recipe called for melting a cup of sugar in a pan, then pouring that into a cup of cold milk. That was set over a fire to cook; then two more cups of sugar were added, with yet another cup of cold milk. The milk and sugar concoction was then cooked again. How clever of them back then. They were expanding and contracting the crystals, and expanding them again.

The ingredients were then taken off the fire. A teaspoon of butter was added, just as I would do today. The whole batch was beaten until it cooled, finally being spread into a buttered pan.

Another recipe basically took that concoction of milk and sugar and poured it over egg whites that had been beaten stiff.

I was assembling ingredients in the kitchen of my shop when the cowbell *clink-clanked*.

"A.M.? A.M.? Where are you?"

It was Pauline. It was a little past two thirty in the afternoon. Her kindergartners had gone home. She must have broken all speed records in Fishers' Harbor to get here.

"I'm in the kitchen."

She appeared in the doorway, bracing herself against the doorjamb. This had to be serious, because she hadn't bothered to bring her giant purse with her. She was still dressed in her washable polyester black slacks and a simple red blouse that could stand kindergarten accidents. But her long brown-black hair looked messy as a horse's mane after a harrowing quarter-mile derby. She was breathing so hard she couldn't talk.

"What the heck is wrong, P.M.?" When we were kids, and

sometimes in trouble, my grandpa started calling us the shortcut initials of "A.M." for Ava Mathilde and "P.M." for Pauline Mertens. He'd say things like "This shines on you all A.M. and P.M., but now tell me what trouble you two girls have gotten yourselves into." These days, the initials that signified our bond as friends often slipped out of our mouths when things grew serious.

"Haven't you turned on the news, A.M.? Or gone online?"

"No, I've been busy doing research on divinity fudge."

"Forget the fudge. The medical examiner held a news conference. They've arrested Daniel Dahlgren for murder and John was taken in for questioning. He's under suspicion."

I was already flinging ingredients back into the refrigerator. "I'll drive. He's still in Sturgeon Bay?"

"Yes. But that's not the worst of it. That Buck knife we saw in that organ bench allegedly belongs to your father. And it's tied to the murder."

I jerked in place. "Who says?"

"Fontana Dahlgren. She was at the press conference. Crying about Cherry's murder. As if she ever really loved him."

"As if, indeed. Come on." There was no way that knife belonged to my father.

We raced back out to the parking lot, found her nondescript gray sedan, and were soon out of town and flying down Highway 42.

Within minutes, a squad car pulled up behind us.

Chapter 13

With the squad car's red and blue beams strafing me through the rearview mirror, I had to pull over. Pauline was shuffling about in her purse on her lap, muttering.

Deputy Maria Vasquez leaned into my open window. "A bit of a hurry?"

Pauline said, "It's about the murder."

Since the deputy had to know everything said at the press conference, I focused on John's plight. "It's unfair, Deputy. John got hit on the back of the head in the church on Saturday night, probably by the real killer. But that wasn't the worst of it. John lost his memory and ended up sleeping at Mercy Fogg's house. She found him in her bus."

Maria winced, leaning closer. "Is this for real?"

Pauline corroborated it.

I continued. "We found him in Mercy's nightgown. Mercy was going to feed him meat loaf with marshmallows in it. Colored ones at that. John shouldn't be questioned at the Justice Center. He's not well. Anything he says will be tossed out by a judge."

I turned to Pauline and rolled my eyes. I had no clue about judges.

Maria said, "This is probably the stupidest attempt ever to get out of a ticket. But . . ." She sighed. "Your father is somebody I respect. Since he may be involved, you can follow me."

As we pulled back onto Highway 42 behind the county

cruiser, Pauline took her hand out of her purse with one of the buttons my mother had given us. Pauline waved it in front of me. "Touch your button."

"What for?"

"Swear on it you won't keep stuff from me again."

"What stuff?" But I knew. I'd kept things about John from my best friend. I wondered how much she knew. I waved off the button so I could keep my eye on the speeding squad car in front of us. "I'm sorry. Dillon made me promise. Besides, you were still in school this afternoon when I learned about John and Marc."

I told her most everything, but I kept the secret about John's singing at the choir tryouts. That was his surprise for Pauline and one that I didn't have the heart to spoil for her.

Pauline rubbed the button. "At least these work."

"How so?"

"I was rubbing this the whole time you were talking to Maria. No ticket. And we're getting a department escort all the way to jail."

"That doesn't sound so lucky. And I didn't think you believed in hocus-pocus. But thanks for helping me by rubbing the button."

"Oh, it wasn't for you. I was rubbing that blessed button to save John. You're on your own."

"Thanks a lot." I knew she didn't mean it. "Can you rub it some more for my father? I can't believe they think that Buck knife is his. My father had nothing to do with Tristan Hardy's death. My father was never at that church much at all. The churchwomen were the ones inside most of the time."

Pauline said, "What if your mother brought his knife along to use it to clean crevices or scrape wax from candles off the floor or pews?"

I called my father, put him on speakerphone, then handed off the phone to Pauline.

"Where are you, Dad?"

Pete said he was home. "They said it'd be okay to talk with them later, after the milking. Jordy came out to confirm with me that the knife is mine."

My heart lurched. "It can't be. No way."

"Ava, calm down. Somebody must have stolen it. We get a lot of visitors here to watch us milk and watch your mother make cheese."

That was my dad, so even-keeled. "What about Mom?"

"She's still at your market. I doubt she heard about the press conference. I'll tell her everything once she comes home. I've already hidden her vacuum cleaner."

A chill came over me. This shouldn't be happening to my family. "Take care, Dad. I love you."

"Love you, Ava Mathilde."

Once we were at the Justice Center on South Duluth Avenue in Sturgeon Bay, I texted Dillon with a quick update. We also saw John's car in the parking lot, so that had been found.

The woman behind the window handed us name tags to wear.

Pauline peered at hers. "These are really nice. Better than our school tags."

"We'll ask the lady on the way out where they order them."

"Sarcasm will not help, A.M."

"Just keep rubbing the buttons in your purse, P.M."

We had to cool our heels in the waiting room for a half hour, reading and rereading all the plaques to the officers who had served our county. Sheriff Jordy Tollefson's picture made him look older, I thought, even weary. There was justice in that if he were about to drag my father and mother into his murder investigation of Tristan Hardy.

Finally, a door burst open. Out marched John Schultz with my manager, of all people. John fell against Pauline in a bear hug.

While they babbled about his needing a lawyer, Marc and I met in the middle of the room, shaking hands cordially. Marc was bald, but had one of those rare, perfect heads and was handsome in a fish-out-of-water sort of way. He flashed the typical Hollywood, expensive killer smile. His blue eyes were seductive behind the black designer eyeglasses. He probably owned a year's worth of glasses. I'd never seen him in the same pair twice. He was shorter than me by a couple of inches, and was reported to be sixty-two years old in online listings, though he told people fifty-five.

He played tennis, racquetball, and ran in every charity race he could find. Among the L.A. crowd, he was known for being against drug abuse. But he was too earnest when it came to making money. Money was Marc's drug.

"Hey, hey, hon, it's awesome-sauce nice to see you." He rose on his toes to air-kiss me on both cheeks. "You've been working on product for me? Not much else to do here, right? Where am I, anyway?"

He'd said that with a smile.

"You call it the flyover zone, Marc. Wisconsin. In Door County," I said. "It looks different in the daylight."

He didn't respond to my hint about his activities on Saturday night. I added, "I hear you've taken on John Schultz as a client."

Marc's blue eyes seemed to turn green with dollar signs. "I like to think of John as a partner. He's a man of ideas, like me. Say, you want to catch a drink later and talk about your next script?"

It intrigued me that Marc thought John's idea for a show based in Wisconsin would be popular with a broad audience, but it didn't totally surprise me. Agents and managers loved discovering new talent and "product." Discovering new "product"—which might include a proposal for a new travel series—garnered respect in Hollywood. Marc also loved being a manager. He truly enjoyed discovering new talent, and if the next "find" came from the flyover zone, all the better. But being dogged about such things was both Marc's skill and his flaw.

"Sorry, Marc, I'm not writing at the moment. I operate a fudge shop north of here and a roadside market south of here near Brussels." With a forced smile, I added, "I told you about the fudge shop last spring."

Marc adjusted his glasses. "I don't understand what you could possibly write about a fudge shop, but I admire you for the research. It'll play well in interviews."

"Marc, you're not listening. I'm not writing anything about a fudge shop."

"That's good, because scripts, books, plays—anything that pays—about a fudge shop won't sell, babe. So this fudge shop thing is temporary between gigs?" He winked.

This was the same old Marc, kidding with me, but underneath it all he liked to nudge me. I said, "Did the sheriff ask you about Saturday night?"

"You bet, babe. Great questions, too. You should write a script about this."

"What were the questions?"

"Why did I go to the church? Did I see some guy named Tristan Hardy? Why was I there so late? Late? I just get started after midnight back in L.A."

By now Pauline and John were sitting nearby on chairs, oblivious of us. I led Marc to the other side of the room, where we sat under portraits of officers.

I asked, "So, why did you go to the church?"

"To get a look at it by night when nobody was around. You know how it is in production. We do a lot of our indoor filming at night. I wanted to see what the setup would be for the prince's visit. Figured we'd get a head start on storyboarding."

Storyboarding was essentially creating a comic-strip version on paper or computer of a movie or TV show before it was committed to filming.

I asked, "Did you see who hit John in the back of the head?"

"No. It was dark in there and the light switch didn't work. I brought out my penlight. As soon as I clicked it on, John got hit and I heard somebody running. I half dragged, half walked John out of there. My college days came back to me. Buddies and I got bounced out of L.A. clubs at four in the morning now and then."

Marc was slim compared to pudgy John, and Marc was in excellent shape.

"Did you tell the sheriff about the light switch not working?"

"Of course. Hey, hon, are you a detective? We could package a Belgian detective as a series."

"That might have been done. Poirot. And I'm not a detective. I'm a fudge confectioner. You don't listen, Marc. I care because these are my friends who are involved. And my family. Evidently, the knife they found in the organ bench allegedly belongs to my father."

Marc leaned into my personal space. "Do you know who did it?"

"No."

"Why not? You used to be pretty good in the writers' staff room at *The Topsy-Turvy Girls* show."

That confused me. I sat back. "No, I wasn't. If you recall, they usually ignored my ideas. I fetched their food. That's how I started making fudge."

"Yeah. I did like that batch of pink perfection my assistant ordered recently online. Served it at a party."

"You did?" I was feeling better about Marc instantly.

"Everybody swooned over your fudge."

"Thank you."

"You always were talented, had darn good ideas. Maybe we should create something like a staff room here and you could brainstorm the solution to this murder case. We'll film it all, of course."

I smiled knowingly. Marc's agenda to make money off my family and friends didn't interest me. I left Marc to go find Jordy.

When I found out that Jordy was busy still, I corralled Pauline in the bathroom. I told her we had to go over to the church. John could ride home with Marc Hayward.

Pauline gave me her teacher look, tossing her hair off her shoulders and looking down her nose at me. "I'm going with John."

"No. He's fine with Marc. They'll yuk it up with talk about filming the prince. You and I are going to the church in Namur."

"You heard it had more yellow tape around it, didn't you?"

She knew I was drawn to yellow police tape. It called to me with subliminal language that dared me to break through it. "There's something I don't get about the church. Tristan's body was found in the basement, but somebody was in the nave or choir loft when John and Marc came inside. And yet the light switch didn't work, which meant somebody had shut down the circuit. The blood on the music appears to be from John, but the knife is my father's and that was apparently stolen. I don't know about you, but I think there was a heck of a lot of people involved with this."

"You think it was more than one person responsible for killing Cherry?"

"My manager said something that sparked the idea. Plots for TV shows usually take input from several people. Why not a murder plot?"

Pauline shivered. "So you think Kjersta and Daniel are guilty? Add Fontana and you've got three people involved."

"The sheriff wouldn't arrest Kjersta and Daniel without good cause. He likely has more on them than just those perfume smells I heard about."

"So, what brilliant plan do you have that I will need to refuse to have anything to do with?"

"We need to talk again with the individuals whose names keep popping up, including Michael Prevost, Jonas Coppens, and Fontana Dahlgren, as well as Professor Wesley Weaver and his teaching assistants."

Pauline finished washing and drying her hands in the restroom. "Your folks know Weaver and those teaching assistants. Do you really think . . . ?"

"Not Weaver or Nick or Will. They and Cherry traveled around together, and Will and Nick were working on the research project with Cherry. But I wonder about other colleagues. Jealousy among colleagues is one of the oldest motives for murder, Pauline."

We walked out of the restroom at the Justice Center, then told the guys a lie about stopping by Ava's Autumn Harvest before heading back to Fishers' Harbor. They took off north in John's car, and Pauline drove south of Sturgeon Bay, heading to Namur.

Pauline drove like a schoolteacher—lawfully.

I said, "Can't you step on it a little?"

"There's a squad car following us."

I turned in the passenger seat to look behind us. "It's Maria again."

"So now what do I do? We can't drive to the church. She won't let us break in."

"Keep driving. I'll think of something. We have to get into that church."

After we'd turned off Highway 42 onto County Road C,

we stopped at Ava's Autumn Harvest to see how my mother was doing. The deputy pulled her car to the side of the road, which my mother noticed right away. She looked up from rearranging pumpkins on the flatbed wagon.

"We're under surveillance, aren't we?" my mother asked, panic scoring her tanned face. Her long, dark hair was frizzed from the humidity.

"Mom, the deputy is only protecting us."

"Do you think they're working on any theories involving me? They're wondering about that knife."

"Mom, they don't know anything. They think I was there, not you. And he wasn't stabbed with the knife. He was hit on the head or he hit the wall."

"But I was . . . there. Honey, I'm going through menopause. What if I forgot something strange that I did in a panic?" She restacked a pumpkin into a new position. "I need to sweep."

Mom hurried back inside the barn. My heart went out to her, recharging my vow to protect her and figure out what had happened in that church.

It was around four thirty, so Pauline and I pitched in to close the market. I brought in the few pumpkins that hadn't sold. My fudge had sold out, as had the Dahlgrens' potatoes and cabbage heads.

Their large garden had plenty of bounty in it, but we'd never keep up with picking everything. I hoofed it over to the two acres of garden. Tomato plants were loaded with red fruit hanging down onto straw mulch.

Pauline joined me. "Fontana never did anything like this when she was married to Daniel. All she did for work was her nails."

Her words made me think about the act of murder. "It takes a lot of work to kill somebody. As much as I'd like to blame her for Cherry's death, I don't see her busting a nail over such a thing."

"Though if there were a crowd in the church that night, she could still be involved. She was a cheerleader and pretty strong. Remember the flips she used to do? And the way she could walk across the gym on her hands?"

"True." I turned around to the *ker-thunk, ker-thunk* of a

baling machine punching out bales of third-crop hay not far away, including across the road in my family's field. Hired help was driving the tractor.

I sagged from the thought of the dozens of workers who might have stolen a knife from my dad, then entered that church and killed Cherry. Yet I knew Jordy was smart. He was looking for perpetrators with a strong motive. He had likely questioned a lot of workers already. I wondered whether any temporary farm help were on the suspect list. My father hired such strangers all the time. A chill fizzed like frost across the fine hairs on my arms.

I did an about-face and then marched for the squad car out on the road.

Pauline ran to catch up. "Now what are you doing?"

"Asking Maria who they've questioned."

But Maria wouldn't talk about the case. I didn't even have any fudge left to bribe her. So I slammed myself in behind the wheel of Pauline's car and then we headed down the road.

"Slow down!" Pauline yelled, buckling up.

"Maria's following us again."

"I don't care. This car needs TLC."

"Tender loving care? It's not human."

"It has over a hundred thousand miles. It needs a rest after we were speeding earlier."

"It's a car, Pauline, a machine. Machines don't need rests. You need a new car anyway. This thing is boring."

In a last-minute decision, I yanked the wheel into a sharp right turn into Jonas Coppens's driveway. To my dismay, Pauline's small sedan slid on the gravel, then fishtailed into a doughnut spin.

Chapter 14

The car landed in the stubble of a chopped cornfield a few yards off Highway C on Jonas's land. We were facing the highway, staring at Maria's squad car hood. She'd driven in with us. We got out of our vehicles.

Maria waved dust away from her face, then removed her aviator sunglasses. "What the hell were you trying to prove?"

Pauline echoed, "Yeah, what the heck?" She slapped at her black slacks and red blouse.

I said to Pauline, "You need new tires. Those have no tread left."

Maria peered up at me with brown eyes evoking the ferocity of a bear. "The last time you did this sort of thing, you rolled your truck."

"I'm sorry. Really. I won't do it again. But I am on private land, Deputy."

Maria put on her aviator sunglasses in clear disgust. Then she got in her car and drove it onto the road, heading toward Ava's Autumn Harvest. She was obviously keeping an eye on me from a distance, but at least she wasn't at my elbows.

"I turned in here to get rid of her. My plan worked."

Pauline choked on the dust still whirling in the wind. "You had no plan. You were driving like an idiot. If you wrecked anything on my car, you're going to pay for it."

"Nothing is wrecked. But you need new tires." I wanted

to tell her that her gray sedan was a dusty, forlorn heap of metal.

Jonas came roaring down the driveway on a tractor. He pulled to a stop and shut off his motor. "Are you all right? Need a tow?"

He alighted from the tractor and the first thing he did was head to Pauline's car to inspect the tires. Then he peered at me. "No flats. You didn't rip anything on the undercarriage?"

I said, "The car's undercarriage is fine."

Pauline huffed. "We'll see."

Jonas said, "Why don't you start it up and drive it back onto the lane and we'll see if it's okay?"

Pauline pushed around me to get to the driver's seat. While I stood next to Jonas, she started the car, then drove the gray car slowly from the cornfield back onto the gravel lane. A rattle that sounded like *clunkety-clunk-clink, clunkety-clunk-clink* made me wince.

After she got out of the car, Pauline whipped her hair back, firing at me, "You wrecked my car, Ava Mathilde Oosterling."

I held up my hands because she looked as though she wanted to wrestle me to the ground for a pounding. Her face was redder than a tomato. I felt awful. "I'll get it fixed. There are probably rocks in your muffler."

"My muffler is new. It doesn't have holes in it."

"You bought a new muffler for this old thing?"

"I love this car. You didn't throw away your grandma, did you, when she broke her leg?"

Jonas laughed. "I'm sure it's nothing. Do you want to come up to the house for a beer?"

Pauline said, "No, thanks."

I said, "Sure. We need to talk about helping the Dahlgrens with their harvesting."

Jonas flinched. His gaze flitted toward the Dahlgren house to our south and across the fence.

I said, "You don't really believe they killed Tristan Hardy?"

"With the shovel covered with Tristan's blood? What else am I supposed to believe?"

"What shovel?"

"The garden shovel. I was working on the fence near their place early this morning after Kjersta was arrested when the sheriff came back with some help, some expert on blood and evidence of that sort. They rousted Daniel from the house. I guess to get keys. They entered your market, then the Dahlgrens' garden shed, and then the sheriff came out with a shovel. I heard Daniel yelling something like 'that's not his blood.' They obviously didn't believe him. They hauled him off in handcuffs."

A chilly breeze rattled around my ribs. "So that's what they have on him. They think Daniel used a shovel to kill Tristan."

Pauline said, "There's not much use for us to go over to the church now."

But I thought otherwise. We got in Pauline's car, with her driving, and went *clunkety-clunk* back onto Highway C. I asked Pauline to turn right toward Brussels and Namur.

Pauline grumbled, "I hope this means we're stopping at the station so a mechanic can look at my car while you pay the bill."

I ignored her. "Jordy has a shovel as evidence, and even if it's got blood on it that belongs to Tristan, why would Daniel and Kjersta be dumb enough not to wash it off by now? Something's not jibing with this."

Her shoulders heaved in a sigh. "Good point."

"Somebody planted that shovel in their shed."

"But it was locked."

"I doubt that. My market is always locked, but I doubt that a mere garden shed is locked all day and even at night. Most of us don't lock our sheds and barns."

"So somebody stole their shovel?"

"It might not even be their shovel. A pointed shovel or spade is standard equipment around here."

"So Fontana bought or found a shovel, whacked Cherry, then snuck it back to Kjersta's garden shed?"

"Maybe." I hesitated voicing my next thought. "Kjersta told me she thinks Jonas was involved. It wouldn't take much for him to walk over to the Dahlgren place. But . . ."

"Jonas is a nice guy."

I told Pauline what Kjersta had said about Jonas writing to Cherry's dean two weeks ago, and that Fontana enjoyed fomenting jealousy between Jonas and Cherry over dating her.

Pauline turned at the intersection in Brussels. "Being upset with the professor doesn't strike me as much of a motive for whacking him over the head with a shovel. And think of all Jonas has been through after his parents were killed in that car accident years ago."

"I know. He held on to the farm by himself through his hard work. But I've noticed he seems nervous or odd lately, not himself. When I was looking at his roadside church earlier today, he came down his lane on his bike with a letter for the mailbox, but then he didn't put the letter in the box. And just now, back in his field, he got off his tractor and looked first at the car tires and not us, as if he wanted to avoid direct eye contact."

"He has a right to be nervous, don't you think? He didn't like Cherry dragging his feet about the research. Jonas must realize he's as much a suspect as you are."

"Thanks."

"Ava, you make Jonas nervous. You would make me nervous, too. In fact, I don't even want to be with you right now. I'd rather be like your mother—doing something like sweeping. By the way, send her over to my classroom. The school doesn't have enough budget for a janitor."

Although she was speaking the truth about the school budget, that lightened our mood. We checked the rearview mirror a few times to make sure Maria wasn't following us, then stopped in the blacktopped parking area next to Saint Mary of the Snows in Namur. Pauline grabbed her bag. I checked my pocket for my cell phone.

A corn chopper was grinding through the field north of the church, but there wasn't anything else going on around us. Nobody was outside the handful of buildings on the east side of the church or across the road.

The redbrick church had yellow tape across all the doors, including the side door next to the parking lot.

Hefting her purse onto her shoulder, Pauline asked, "So, what are we looking for? Footprints outside in the grass?"

I held up a key. "We're going inside. My grandmother's key."

"Does she know you have it?"

"Of course not."

Pauline shook her head as if I'd be getting detention for this.

After I reached around the yellow tape, we ducked under it to enter the church. We passed the space for the wheelchair lift and went up the short stairs and past the restrooms.

The taint of smoke still hung in the air. The smudges on the wall up near the loft stairs were still evident, reminding me of the days ticking away before the prince would arrive to visit the church. The low sun pushed through the stained glass windows that needed to be washed, giving the interior a sepia tinge.

I led the way to the loft stairway where yellow tape remained.

Pauline grabbed my arm. "There's going to be soot all over up there. They'll be able to tell we've been here."

"Nobody's going to look for us here today. It's Jordy's dinnertime."

"We'll get dirty."

"Did you forget you're still wearing your classroom clothes?"

She peered down at her red blouse and black slacks. I had on my usual blue jeans and a long-sleeved pink T-shirt and sturdy athletic shoes. I twisted my hair into a knot at the back of my head. Then I ducked under the tape.

The tap of Pauline's black flats on the stairs echoed behind me.

In the choir loft, there was smoke residue everywhere, which saddened me. All our cleaning earlier had been for naught. It would take a lot of elbow grease to get the church back into shape before the royal kermis.

The piano bench was charred, with the lid closed.

"Don't touch it," Pauline said. "It could still have John's blood in it."

I opened it anyway. There was nothing inside. The sheriff had taken all the music sheets, ashes and all. "There's no blood, Pauline."

"So why was the knife tossed in there? And by whom?"

"My dad said that anybody could have stolen it from the farm. I'm sure he gave the list of visitors we keep to the sheriff. But I suppose anybody could sneak around our farm in the dead of night and take a knife if it were left out in the barn or creamery and the doors had been left unlocked."

"Wouldn't you hear people? What about your dogs?"

"The dogs sleep with Mom and Dad." We had an old cattle dog that snored louder than Mom and lay on the bed, and a tiny white, fluffy bichon frise that burrowed under Dad's pillow to sleep. "But Mom said she heard a car out on the road around midnight on Saturday night."

"That could have been somebody on your place who was leaving, roaring as they hurried out of your driveway, making a fast getaway."

I hadn't thought of that. "Thanks, A.M., that's brilliant."

"Just trying to keep up with you, P.M."

"What if Cherry and Fontana were on the road and coming up behind the person who'd been at our farm? Fontana lives only a few miles away, by her market."

Pauline began to tiptoe carefully between the smoky choir loft pews toward the staircase. "So you're thinking the person sneaking around your parents' farm thought Cherry had taken down his license plate? Then when Cherry and Fontana stopped at the church for whatever reason, the person followed Cherry and Fontana into the church, and the person killed Cherry."

"Supposition totally, but plausible. You're getting into this, Pauline."

"No. I'm eager to make sure John isn't pulled into this murder thing. That was his blood, after all, in that bench."

"Yes, but we found the knife on Saturday morning and Cherry was killed on Saturday night. Until we find a connection between the murder and the knife, John's free, though the sheriff may have questions." I held back telling her that Jonas had seen John in the church Saturday morning early. "I'm sure he must have done some errand in the loft before we went up there, cut himself, freaked about finding a knife, and now he doesn't recall it because of the bump on his head."

"If only he'd get his memory back. The bits and pieces he recalls aren't reliable."

We went back down the staircase to the nave.

On our way to the basement, we had to go through the kitchen. We found it ransacked.

"This is ridiculous, rude, and wrong," Pauline said.

Tomorrow was probably an R day in school. "It sure doesn't look like anything the sheriff or his crew would do."

Flour and sugar were spilled out of their sealed containers. Every box had been tossed out of the cupboards.

Pauline asked, "Do you suppose they were looking for the recipe?"

"Maybe," I said.

I tiptoed around the mess, trying to avoid the flour so I didn't make tracks. Pauline stayed at the door to the nave clutching her purse.

A banging suddenly resounded from below us.

Chapter 15

Marc Hayward called to us, "Who's up there?"

I yelled back as I hurried to the basement, "What are you doing here? How did you get in? And where's your car?"

We soon stood together in the doorway to the room where Cherry's body had been found. My manager—and now John's manager—was holding the steel cap that went over the vent in the wall.

"Hi, Ava." He wiped off a hand covered with a white substance, then reached out to Pauline. "You're Pauline, right?"

After her nod he said, "Isn't this a great place for filming?"

I panicked. "This is a crime scene. What are you doing down here, or even in this church?"

"I have to ask you the same thing."

"Trying to . . . get myself off the hook."

"Ah yes, but John explained that it was your mother who found the body down here."

I gave Pauline an evil look for spilling that secret to John, then said to Marc, "You're not going to tell anybody, are you?"

"Heck no." He pulled a roll of masking tape out of his pocket. "Can you show me exactly where your mother found the body? I'll mark it for the actor so he knows where to lie."

"Actor?"

"For John's travel and food show. It's imperative that we make a short trailer right at the scene of the crime in this church for authenticity. It'll be a great way to introduce this tourist site and the hunt for the fudge recipe. We need a trailer to show around to the executives in order to sell the show. Nothing too involved, really. We'll be in and out of here in no time, upload it to the Web, and then send it to a head of development or two or six."

I wanted to grab Pauline's purse and bop Marc on his bald head. "Get out of here or you can be arrested." And then my mother and I would probably be found out. "Did you cause the damage in the kitchen?"

I got my answer when he abruptly turned to put the steel plate back in place in the furnace chimney hole. The white substance on his hands had to be flour from the kitchen.

Pauline filched about in her purse, probably to rub those darn holy buttons again.

Marc said, "The kitchen is set up for filming a scene about this story."

"But that's a lie. There was no messy kitchen when my . . . when I found the body. And how did you get in here?"

He held up a key.

Pauline sighed. "Does everybody in the county have a key to this church?"

Marc put it back in a pants pocket. "John had one."

Pauline asked, "Where's John?"

"Over at the school looking around. We thought we'd film that, too, with an actress pretending to be Sister Adele Brise. We could use a stand-in. Want to help?"

A headache threatened to throb in my forehead. "Marc, please, get out of here before you get us all into serious trouble."

"You've changed since you moved back to Door County."

His words gave me pause. "How?"

His gaze flicked up and down my person. Finally, he said, "You seem taller."

With that, he marched up the stairs. Footsteps shuffled about in the kitchen, then echoed across the nave.

Pauline had a way of raising one dark eyebrow that made her look like an eagle about to scoop up a fish off our bay.

"Pauline, I didn't invite him here, so don't blame me."

"He's going to end up getting you into deep trouble. I feel it coming."

"Never mind me. What about him? He was snooping for the recipe. Why else would he be looking inside that pipe? He and John have gold fever."

"Don't go blaming John for the mess upstairs in the kitchen."

I headed for the basement wall and the blood smear that was still evident on the concrete. With care, I braced myself with my hands on either side of it for a close look. The smear wasn't much, it seemed to me. Cherry could have pushed back against the wall and hit his head, but I wondered if he'd come off the wall and fought back. If he had, I didn't see how Fontana on her own could have gotten Cherry to turn around again so that he could be whacked on the back of the head before falling facedown on the floor. But it could happen if somebody had been helping her.

I told Pauline my thoughts, then added, "I don't think Cherry was killed here at all. I think he was placed here and this smudge is from somebody's hand."

"Whose hand? Not John's."

"Of course not John's. But whose?" I splayed a hand and fingers out in the air above the stain to size it up.

Pauline ventured near me to peer at the bloodstain on the gray concrete. "It's awful to think that somebody was wrestling down here with Cherry when John and Marc came into the church Saturday night."

As we ventured from the old furnace room, we noticed the electric breaker panels on the south wall. I hadn't noticed them before because we'd been intent on stepping around overhanging cobwebs.

I opened one of the two-hundred-amp panels. "Go upstairs, Pauline."

"Why?"

"Do you have to question everything?"

"Yes. Sometimes you do stupid stuff. Like wreck my car."

"Just go upstairs. And give me a tissue. I want to see which breakers take out all the lights in the nave and choir loft."

Pauline handed me a tissue, then trundled up the basement steps. Soon, she hollered, "I'm in the nave!"

I yelled, "Turn on all the lights!"

"They're on!"

With her tissue over my fingers, I nudged one circuit breaker switch after another. Between each flip, I waited for her to respond. On the fifth try, we knew which ones had been flipped to cut any lights. We knew which one cut all the lights at once.

When I rejoined Pauline in the kitchen disaster, I called the sheriff. "Hey, Jordy. Did your team look at the circuit breakers for fingerprints?"

I had to hold my phone away from my ear. He was yelling at me. I put my cell phone on speaker mode.

Jordy yapped, "What the hell are you doing in that church? I'm going to arrest you. You're tampering with evidence, which suspects often try to do. Don't you move. You Oosterlings are a big bunch of bothersome Belgians!"

I grinned at my BFF, then said to him, "Pauline just gave you an A for that."

Jordy barked, "You got that right because it's *A* for aggravation."

"Listen, Jordy, I think the person who killed Cherry had to know how to work the church's breaker box in a pinch. They didn't have time to think. I don't think Kjersta was in this church much at all, and Daniel's pretty tall, so I don't see how his hand could cause that smudge on the basement wall. He and I reach up higher than that when we brace ourselves against the wall. Have you thought this through?"

Click.

Pauline had gone white. "You shouldn't badger the sheriff when you're a suspect."

"He knows very well I didn't knock off Cherry."

"It doesn't matter. Jordy has to go by the book. I think he really meant it when he said he's going to arrest you."

We gave the flour-strewn kitchen a final glance, then left the church.

Pauline wanted to go straight to the historic school to see John.

But when we got there, it was locked. We turned in time to see a long black limousine leave Namur. Obviously, it had been hidden on the west side of the church, maybe even on the other side of Chris and Jack's Belgian Bar and that was why we hadn't noticed it. Such a thing was so rare and out of place in Door County that Pauline and I stood there, mesmerized. The big tree overhanging the fake cemetery rippled in the reflections as the glamorous vehicle glided by.

Pauline muttered, "Wow."

"You do realize that John is being seduced by my manager and that you likely won't see him until we figure out a way to get rid of Marc. He's convinced that something about Door County, Wisconsin, is unique enough to draw a big audience on television."

"But you're not so sure."

"I'm never sure about Marc Hayward. He has this earnest edge about him, and he does know a lot of Hollywood people. He gets too caught up, though, in the game of pitching scripts and selling new product. Being near him feels like I'm a footstep away from landing in the jaws of a bear trap. I'd be happier if he weren't around.

"Yes. But I'd love to get a ride in that limo with them before he leaves. And maybe this will give John ideas about hiring a limo the night he proposes to me."

"When is this night going to be?"

"It could come at any time."

"He needs to get his full memory back first. You're lucky he remembers you."

Pauline laughed. "No man forgets what I offer him."

"Pauline!"

I walked around the pale yellow historic school and sister house until I found the window that I knew was loose. Mom and I had been cleaning the building one day when we learned which old screens and sashes had faulty latches.

Pauline gave me a boost up and over the windowsill. "I'll wait by the car and whistle a warning if somebody comes," she said.

"Nothing doing. Grab my hand and get in here to help me look around."

"What are we looking for now?"

"The murderer could have hid in here before or after they killed Cherry. They could have left a clue behind."

Pauline leaped up and got over the sill far faster than I had.

The inside of the main room had rows of chairs for the Belgian Foundation meetings on Thursday nights. Most of the dark, scarred wooden floors were the original planks from when the school had been built in 1860. An old-fashioned chalk blackboard dressed one wall. At the front of the room were two wide, ceiling-high doors on wheels. Pauline and I pushed them aside, the doors rattling, to reveal the altar where Mass or worship had been held for the sisters and the schoolchildren long ago.

Pauline said, "This simple school with this ingenious door always makes me stop to think about the life of the sisters. It had to have been very harsh, yet they kept their faith going no matter what. Their first winter here they had nothing but *sabots*."

"Wooden shoes."

"And people would walk ten miles or more in them to come here for Mass." Pauline stepped closer to the altar. "Didn't your grandpa wonder if this building had the recipe, instead of the church? After all, didn't the sisters stay here for weeks at a time to teach?"

"But this is made of wood. He's sure they would have stored precious things in the brick church so that fire couldn't take them."

After the famous fire of October 8 and 9, 1871, that killed so many in our county, practices changed. It was considered a miracle that the church made of wood in the neighboring Robinsonville community withstood the fire. That church was where Sister Adele Brise took refuge. The church—in the community now renamed Champion—marked the spot where she saw what she called the "Queen of Heaven," a woman with a long white dress and a yellow sash, and a crown of stars around her forehead holding back long golden hair that hung past her shoulders. Despite Sister Adele's blessed luck with wooden structures, brick and stone became the norm for new structures. I was certain my grandfather was right about where the recipe had to be stored, if it existed.

As we wandered about the school, I recognized plenty of places for hiding sacred recipe cards, though. Maybe there was a clue here, a journal hidden behind a panel of the wall, for example. There were bookshelves, a pantry on the first floor, cupboards, and a dining room where an antique clock that looked like a castle sat on a table by a window. I gave the clock close scrutiny, but it didn't appear to have secret compartments.

We went upstairs, the warm air growing stuffier as we ascended the narrow staircase.

A room that must have served as a parlor and library was filled with shelves on the walls and a shelving unit in the middle. The stand-alone unit held antique tools, cooking utensils, and more. The foundation was gathering and preserving historical items.

The first small bedroom on the south end didn't hold much. A door in the middle of the two bedrooms went to the attic. It held the usual assortment of forlorn furnishings and lamps, and appeared to be a dead end when it came to clues. Nobody had been living in it, for sure, and nothing seemed odd or out of place.

The last bedroom gave us a surprise. The dust on the floor had been disturbed, brushed clean mostly. The vestiges of footprints remained.

Pauline said, "Who's been sleeping in my bed?"

"Exactly. It looks like somebody camped out in here."

"Not the three bears, I bet."

"But maybe the killer."

Pauline hugged her bag to her chest. "I'm getting out of here."

She took off, tromping down the narrow staircase. I followed. We went through the kitchen and through the door leading to the church lawn.

Once we were outside, to my surprise Lucky Harbor bounded toward me.

Dillon had parked his white truck next to Pauline's car.

As he loped behind his dog across the green grass lawn, my heartbeat quickened. The breeze tossed Dillon's wavy chestnut hair, giving him a rakish, piratelike aura. He wore jeans and a black T-shirt, putting his muscular build in silhouette against the golden light of the sun.

As he approached us, a scowl on his face put me off-kilter.

I asked, "What's wrong, Dillon?"

"You've spent all day with Pauline and not me, that's what's wrong. Excuse me, Pauline, while I take her off your hands."

He scooped me up in his arms. I yelped in surprise. He strode fast back across the lawn to the parking lot.

Lucky Harbor barked and ran in circles around us.

I had to hang on with both hands looped behind Dillon's neck, which wasn't bad, since it allowed me to stare right into the deep wells of his eyes. He smelled of fresh soap.

Pauline shouted after me, "Just in time!"

The faint sound of a siren seared the air. Could that be Jordy coming to arrest me?

Dillon plunked me in the front passenger seat of his white construction truck. The siren was growing louder. He let Lucky Harbor in the seat behind me. The dog's tongue licked one of my ears in greeting.

The siren was like an irritating cicada in the background. I said, "Let's not sit here."

"That's why I'm here. To rescue you. We need to talk about an issue."

Dillon burned rubber out of the church parking lot.

Chapter 16

Dillon had a serious edge about him as he barreled down the county road. Since our pact in July to try to be different people instead of our old reckless selves, he'd done a lot of serious things. He'd partnered in business with his mother, Cathy, after she'd moved to Fishers' Harbor late in summer to work on real estate developments. He'd partnered with Al Kvalheim, our sewer-and-water guy in the village, to do plumbing jobs. He'd partnered with me to refurbish the Blue Heron Inn. He was taking firefighter and EMT classes with my employee Cody.

But now he said there was an "issue." It had to be about me. He seemed pretty darn perfect. Me? Not so perfect.

This Monday evening he took me a scant five-minute drive straight west of Namur to Chaudoir's Dock and County Park.

After we parked in the blacktopped lot that sat near a trailer park, we raced down to the dock. On the outside pier, a sleek white yacht twice the length of my cabin waited.

The sirens had deadened; I hoped that the sheriff had stopped at the church but hadn't seen us leaving.

I asked, "Is this the issue you want to talk to me about?"

"I suppose you could say that."

Lucky Harbor raced happily down the pier toward the vessel.

The sun had relaxed enough in the sky to paint the water

with a shimmering pink that reminded me of my sparkly fudge.

The sparkles reflected in Dillon's eyes. The way his eyes devoured me shot a hot tingle through my body, awakening the hidden lowlands in my personal geography.

Dillon bowed on the dock, holding one hand out toward the yacht. "Milady, this is practice for when your royal relatives descend upon us."

"Where did you get this boat? How much? I'll pay you back." He started chuckling, and so did I. "Okay. Someday. I'll pay you back someday." I was dirt poor at the moment.

He grabbed my hand to tug me along the narrow pier. "Don't be such a worrywart. My dear mother is renting this for a test run. I'm supposed to take it for a cruise with a lady."

"As soon as I find a lady I'll let you know."

"You're a lady," he reassured me, kissing the top of my hand, which he held.

As we were boarding, I asked, "Is Cathy thinking of getting into the touring business in Door County?"

"Something like that." Dillon smiled into the rose-tinted sunshine, then gave me a sideways glance. "She told me the other day she loved your Fairy Tale Fudge concept. And she's wondering if she could create a fairy-tale fantasy concept for women who wanted to be pampered out on the water for weekends."

"So I'm a guinea pig?"

Dillon laughed. "I told her you'd be the perfect one to test this on because you're practical and know the people here."

"I've been away for eight years."

"If you don't want to try it, we'll turn around. . . ."

That made me growl. "Show me what Cathy has in mind. But let me call my fudge shop to check in."

Cody said a crowd was enjoying the sunset on the Fishers' Harbor docks and he was busy selling fudge. Bethany was helping and Dotty had dropped by. He said he heard on the police scanner that Jordy was heading to pick up somebody at the Namur church.

I told him, "That's not me, because I'm with Dillon on a boat."

But I had to smile. I asked Dillon, "You heard the scanner before, didn't you?"

He nodded. "Wasn't sure I was going to make it in time."

I gave him a kiss. "You're my kind of pirate. But still, what's this about an issue?"

"Go below first. We'll talk after you come back."

To my shock, Cathy had loaded a closet in the stateroom with designer clothing in my size. After a quick and glorious shower, I had my pick of dresses and flowing tops in a rainbow of colors. There were shoes with heels so high Dillon would have to let me lean against him all night long—not a bad thing. There were skinny leggings with Swarovski crystals down the sides of the legs. I was partial to sparkly things because of my Cinderella Pink Fudge. I could almost hear Cody yelling across the fudge shop at me as he was wont to do, "You look all La-La Land, Miss Oosterling!"

I donned an azure blue, flowing silk top that had three-quarter sleeves and a ribbon at the top that held together a boat neckline. I hungered to put on those wickedly tall heels, but I imagined myself accidentally falling overboard. A pair of simple silver sandals looked as sexy as the heels on my basketball-player feet.

A blue ribbon secured my hair into a fresh ponytail. I let a few auburn tendrils frame my face.

Cathy had scads of samples of designer makeup and perfumes on the dresser. This beat Fontana's stuff all to heck. I applied a peachy lipstick that reminded me of the sunset. A spritz of something that smelled like a dewy morning in Grandma's flower garden completed me.

As I headed to the door, a candy dish next to the bed beckoned. It was filled with Cinderella Pink Fairy Tale Fudge. Cathy had thought of everything. Or Dillon had. They cared that much about me. Or was this merely a business deal? What was the "issue" Dillon wanted to talk about?

I was excited about Cathy's business idea. People could stay at the Blue Heron Inn, then board this yacht for a weekend or an afternoon. I'd provide the fudge to complete the fairy tale. But was I prepared for such a partnership?

This sounded more like something I'd do after . . . marrying Dillon.

My stomach did a flip-flop. Was a marriage proposal the so-called issue?

Panic peppered me with heat. But why? Wasn't I ready for something permanent with Dillon and his family? Again? Come to think of it, I hadn't really gotten to know his family or Dillon in that previous marriage. We'd been married only a month.

Maybe I was ahead of myself. I sucked up a deep breath—filling my lungs with the expensive, floral air in the stateroom—and left.

Up on deck, in the covered living quarters with its endless windows, the aroma of something cooking with onions, tomatoes, perhaps some asparagus, made my mouth water, but not nearly as much as the sight of Dillon.

He'd changed into a crisp sky blue shirt with the sleeves rolled up enough to show off his tanned, strong arms. He wore tan pants and canvas deck shoes. The wind off the lake coming through the windows caught his hair, reminding me how rugged he looked these days compared to years ago. His large hands and muscular fingers had nicks and scratches on the knuckles from his carpentry work for me at the Blue Heron Inn.

I suddenly realized that Dillon had grown handsomer with time.

He was different. An edge about him threw my head and heart into a whirl of emotions not felt before.

My heart was pumping so fast and hard and rocking me that I hadn't felt the boat moving. We were easing into the giant bay.

Dillon headed toward the double doors that opened onto the outdoor deck, beckoning me with an outstretched hand and a glint in his eyes.

An exhilarating heat hopscotched up my spine. My legs grew wobbly. I was glad I'd chosen the sandals.

The bay was relatively calm. The breeze buffeted me with the tang of freshwater perfume coming off the gentle froth stirred up by our yacht. With my anxiety fading somewhat, I inhaled the feeling of being Cinderella at her ball.

As we enjoyed the outdoor deck, I ventured, "We *have* changed."

Dillon had a hand at the small of my back. "The chef has wasted his time creating a meal. I have mine right here."

Before I knew it, Dillon let down my hair and had both hands in it as he brought me into a kiss that had me swaying in the rhythm of the boat and breeze. I felt as weightless as the tissue-thin clouds turning tangerine and rosy above us in the sky.

We went inside where an artful dinner awaited us in an elegant dining area decked out with black-and-white linens. The repast came from Door County gardens, orchards, and Lake Michigan. Dillon explained the trout had been caught by my grandfather. Dillon said the chef had preordered it.

"My grandfather knows about this?"

"No. He thinks I ordered it for my mother. I wanted this to be private, only for you and me. Our secret."

Our secret. I smiled. I hoped Dillon had no idea I was thinking about all the many secrets I'd been tussling with lately.

After we'd eaten a couple of bites, the chef appeared. I was shocked.

The chef was Piers Molinsky, one of the guest chefs and bakers who had almost deep-sixed my First Annual Fishers' Harbor Fudge Festival in July. Famous for his muffins in Chicago, he was a portly behemoth with messy brown hair and big fuzzy eyebrows. On one occasion I'd caught him in a fight involving fudge cutters wielded by the other chef, Kelsey King. The two had ended up wrestling in a fight on the floor of my shop, almost knocking over copper kettles full of hot cream and melted Belgian chocolate. As it was, the kettles had boiled over during the fight and Lucky Harbor had lapped up bacon fudge created by Piers.

"Piers? What are you doing back in Door County?"

He laughed heartily as he corralled Lucky Harbor and snapped on a leash. "Don't be afraid of me. I'm not a fighter. I couldn't stand that twit, Kelsey King, who pretended she was a chef. Imagine putting weeds into fudge." He visibly shuddered.

Indeed, the woman guest chef from the West Coast had

almost ruined my festival with her crazy "edible wild-food fudge" ideas.

Dillon said, "Piers is looking around for a location to start a branch of his famous muffin shops."

I told Piers good luck, but I didn't entirely mean it. I sensed trouble brewing again with his return to Fishers' Harbor.

Piers handed me some Goldfish crackers. His thoughtful gesture surprised me. And pleased me a little bit. Good cooks or chefs remember the favorite dishes of their customers. Piers had obviously made a note last July that Lucky Harbor loved cheesy crackers. I tossed a couple of crackers in the air and said to Lucky Harbor, "Want some fudge?"

The happy dog snapped up the crackers. Piers led the dog to the recreation room at the other end of the yacht that had its own private deck.

When we were alone again, Dillon explained, "My mother insisted the chef create a dog-friendly meal just for Lucky. I'm afraid she's to blame for inviting Piers back to Door County. She remembered that he used your Cinderella Pink Fudge in his red velvet muffins and they were all the rage last July."

"Your mother seems quite eager to make this perfect for us. Should we be suspicious?" I was eager to get to the "issue" he'd mentioned.

"It's no secret she wants grandchildren. She figures she had a near miss eight years ago with us, and now she's going to do everything she can to fix that."

"Have you told her we're taking our relationship slow and proper?"

"No way!" he said, guffawing. "I'd get all kinds of lectures on how she's growing old and all her friends have grandchildren. I go with the flow. I told her we'd have at least a dozen children." He winked.

He wasn't serious. However, I was starting to see something new in Dillon that caused me to pause. Did he secretly want children—now? Was that the issue he wanted to talk about?

A wine steward interrupted us. He was nobody I knew. I

was glad, because my face must have gone pale. Somehow leaping ahead to the possibility of having children with Dillon when we were still exploring only being good friends was definitely the "cart before the horse" for me. I decided murder was a safer subject.

Uninterrupted, Dillon and I talked about everything we knew so far over bites of lake trout, cabbage-fried in a red wine sauce, as well as mashed potatoes and a cauliflower jut topped with bubbly yellow cheddar cheese. There was asparagus. Honey-glazed carrots also graced our plates as a waiter in white ferried back and forth to the kitchen. Warm cheese bread from Laura's Luscious Ladle Bakery enticed us bite after bite until we were stuffed. But still we had room for a real Belgian pie—a twelve-inch pan filled with ambrosial chocolate pudding within a brownie crust.

As I finished my large slice, I had to point to the pan with my head shaking. "Plenty for more picnics."

"Or for later? After some exercise?"

Dillon's heated gaze snatched my breath away, giving my mind and heart a quixotic tilting. I loved him—oh boy, did I ever!—but I didn't know if this love could last. It hadn't last time. We'd dived into marriage too fast. Marriage struck me a little like the process of canning vegetables or preserving fruits. If you went about putting up preserves—or a marriage—in haste, the fruit would spoil.

"I probably should get back to my fudge shop." The words sounded inane, but I suddenly wanted to escape Dillon and the boat.

The confidence I'd cultivated over the past few months was slipping away. I started searching for my phone in a pocket, then realized I had no pockets and had left the cell phone in the stateroom.

Dillon reached across our small table to take one of my hands in his. "You don't trust me."

The good feelings imploded inside me, mingling with the doubts. I waved a hand about to indicate the scrumptious, lavish dinner and yacht. "It's not real, Dillon. We promised each other that this time our relationship would be grounded. We'd be more practical."

"And yet you make Cinderella Pink Fairy Tale Fudge.

You like fairy tales, and you want them to happen for you, if you would let yourself admit to that."

He had me. What woman didn't dream of fairy tales now and then? Or pirates stealing her out to sea for a life of coddling and cuddling?

"But my life is more than make-believe. What's happening to my family and friends is real."

I rushed to tell him about finding the "Goldilocks and the Three Bears" scenario at the schoolhouse. "Pauline and I think the killers hid out there that night. They lay low, and when they thought the coast was clear, they got into their car and Cherry's car and drove away."

Dillon withdrew his hand and sat back. "So, who's Goldilocks?"

"Maybe Fontana Dahlgren. And one of the bears is Michael Prevost. He's admitted to wanting Cherry out of the way." I nibbled my lower lip in thought. "And I have doubts about Jonas Coppens, too."

"Another bear. And the Dahlgrens? They're sitting in jail, after all. The sheriff believes they committed the murder."

"On the basis of a shovel? We have to do something to prove they didn't do it."

"Their lawyer is doing that. I saw Parker earlier."

"Where?"

"In Namur going into Chris and Jack's Belgian Bar. Parker said he got inside the church for an inspection. He's representing the Dahlgrens."

"So, what did Parker find?"

Parker Balusek was an expert in historic church renovations and an attorney in Kewaunee County south of Door County. Parker had been the lawyer of Grandpa's murdered friend, Lloyd Mueller. We'd all spent enough time together that Grandpa hinted to me that Parker would be good marriage material.

Dillon said, "Parker didn't get to look as much as he'd have liked. He had to wear the booties and gloves, even a hair net, and Deputy Maria Vasquez escorted him. He said there are often hidden panels in walls in old buildings. Because of the lack of nearby banks back when the buildings were built, secret hiding places abounded. He's sure Saint Mary of the Snows could hold the recipe."

"My grandfather is excited about that, but my grandmother is not so much."

Dillon pushed back his chair, stood, then held out his hand toward me. "I'm working on that secret your grandmother is hiding."

That news got me off my chair. "How so?"

"Thank my mother yet again. She offered to have a talk with your grandmother about our family's secret. She figures if she confesses, maybe your grandmother will confess."

"What secret?"

"It wouldn't be a secret if I told you."

"Stop that." I gave him a playful swat on the chest. "What's your secret?"

He walked away from me a few steps. I watched his shoulders flinch before he turned back to me. "When I was born, my parents gave me away."

I was sure I hadn't heard him correctly.

Dillon nodded. "My mother suffered from postpartum depression and it was bad. Of course I heard about this years later. For much of my first year I was raised mostly by Grandmother Violet and Grandpa Herman Rivers."

"Why didn't you tell me about this before?"

"It was a family secret and I keep secrets. What mother wouldn't be ashamed that she wondered about being a good mother? She said she had horrible doubts and couldn't bond with me at first."

"Oh, Dillon, I'm so sorry." I hugged him tightly. "But she got through it."

Dillon squeezed me back. "Yes. With a good doctor, and much love from my father and her friends, she got well. Now, thirty-eight years later, she feels it's time to help others who are suffering with depression of any kind, particularly women. She mentioned to me the other day that she marveled at the way you're renewing your life. She feels it's time to do that herself."

"Me? I influenced your mother? Wait a minute. She thinks I suffer from depression?"

"No. Remember the word 'renewal.' She sees that you're determined to renew your life here. You're a bundle of energy. She sees herself in you at times. You know she's a whirlwind."

"Indeed."

"And she cares about you and your grandmother."

Breathless with emotions, I went to the windows of the dining room to stare at the lake. My breathing began to match the rhythm of the gentle waves rising and falling. Seagulls swooped by us outside, their wings pumping up and down like a bellows atop the breeze. "I don't think your mother talking to my grandmother will help things."

Dillon took me in his arms again. "Cinderella, I worry about you."

We began to slow-dance to the forward-and-back brush of the boat against the water as we coursed across the bay.

"Why?"

"You can't keep your shop, the inn's remodeling, and the roadside market running while simultaneously trying to save your grandmother, solve a murder, and get ready for the prince and princess. No one person can do all that. You're headed for disaster."

I stopped dancing. Indignation simmered inside me. "You want me to stop doing something? Which thing?"

"I want you to allow me to help with more than what I'm doing now. My mother's interested in helping. Allow me to offer that."

"Allow? Don't I allow you to do things?"

"No, you don't. You watch over me and you keep me locked at the inn pounding nails. Because I'm safe that way."

"Safe from what?"

"Not what. From you. If I'm busy and not hanging around, you don't have to deal with my opinions. There's no opinion involved with pounding nails. It's safe."

"This is silly." My heart said it wasn't, that he'd locked on to some truth I'd missed somehow about myself.

"I sense that you have fear about our relationship. If we did more things together, you might discover I have different opinions. You might be afraid that our relationship will fall apart. Like it did before." The setting sun strafing us through the windows gave Dillon an even more chiseled appearance than normal.

"Exactly what are you asking of me? Is this the 'issue' you wanted to talk about?"

"Yes. I want you to allow me to be a true partner in your life. I want more from this relationship than we ever dared have before. I want to change. Together. Real change. Not pretend change."

"I've been pretending? I haven't changed?" Panic was setting in. My brain searched the universe. Then I recalled Marc's words.

A sudden revelation came to me, as if Dillon had opened a door to a new room of a house, only this house was my brain. "My manager, of all people, told me I'd changed. But he said I was taller than he remembered. He couldn't think of anything else to say. It felt odd at the time, but now I realize I haven't changed enough for him to recognize changes in me. Is that what you're getting at?"

"I'm just worried about you being overextended. That's all I'm getting at."

"So I'm busier than ever, but busy doesn't mean I've changed for the better." This, too, felt like a wondrous truth flowering inside me.

"Sometimes I wonder if you're trying to prove to all those guys on that TV show you used to belong to that you're better than them. Honey, you don't have to prove anything. You're talented in every way. But you tend to become obsessed to prove your points. You're obsessed with this murder. This is Monday night and look where you've been and what you've been doing in just two days' time. You can't keep this up. You have to trust Sheriff Tollefson."

"But the guy often doesn't see motives and clues like I do."

Dillon hiked an eyebrow at me. "Really? Despite his probable six years of school to learn his business and then his decade of on-the-job-experience? You know more?"

Dillon was playing hardball. I sighed. "You're right. We need more time for us, don't we?"

"But do you need me?"

His question slayed me. "Yes." My heart rate was bouncing about like a tadpole struggling to go upstream in a current. "I need you. I need your help, Dillon. I really do. And thank you. I had no idea I was getting so out of hand."

"I bet Pauline was noticing it."

I laughed. "Come to think of it, I think you're right."

Dillon kissed me on the lips. "What can I do?"

"Find Tristan Hardy's missing car. It's a new blue Ford Fusion."

Dillon laughed so hard I thought that he had rocked the yacht. "Is that all?"

"No. Maybe you could hang out at the local bars more to see what the gossip is?"

"Tough job, but I'll do my best. What are you going to be up to?"

"Since I've met Professor Weaver in the past and know him—"

"You're going to wheedle words from Weaver?"

"Pauline would be proud of your alliteration. I have to visit Michael Prevost, too, and ask him the real reason he was so happy Cherry died, and then ask why Michael got my grandmother drunk. I doubt, as Mercy told me, that Grandma was drinking heavily because people asked her about Prince Arnaud and Princess Amandine coming."

"But they could be the simple reason."

"You're right." Working with Dillon was already feeling good. "But my grandma would've merely walked away from that conversation. I suspect my grandmother was asking him too many questions about Cherry and he wanted to shut her up, so he kept asking her to taste-test new bottles and somehow fooled her. Maybe he drugged her—"

"There you go again." Dillon engulfed me in his arms as he planted a more sensual kiss on my lips. "Ava, sweetheart, my Belgian belle, we should try to do something *together*, but not this discussion. Not now. I realize it's not Wednesday. This is only Monday, but . . ."

Some things inside me had not changed and I hoped they wouldn't. Like my yearning for him. I purred, "You're a pirate?"

"If you're a maiden who needs capturing."

We hurried belowdecks to the privacy of our stateroom.

Chapter 17

Refreshed after the best date ever on the yacht, I was at Oosterlings' Live Bait, Bobbers & Belgian Fudge & Beer by five thirty Tuesday morning making fudge.

I vowed to be a new woman. I would simplify my life, relax, and try not to do the sheriff's job plus a half dozen other things.

My grandfather had taken fishermen out and had returned early, fussing about how cold the air-conditioning was on the *Super Catch I*. He also complained that it was too hot and dry outside. He was complaining a lot lately about insignificant things. The opposite of me, he didn't have enough to do anymore. It felt awkward being out of sync with Gilpa.

By ten I'd whipped up two batches of Rose Garden Fudge from petals in the roses behind Lloyd's empty house, plus Cinderella Pink Fudge and Rapunzel Raspberry Rapture Fudge. I tried to think about what my next flavor should be in my signature Fairy Tale line. Goldilocks? Dillon and I had mentioned that tale last night. What flavor would fit Goldilocks and her three bears? I also had many other tales to choose from.

Customers streamed in and out and I enjoyed chatting with them about possible new flavors. Some wanted Snow White. One little girl wanted that to be peppermint.

I couldn't decide. But I knew I had to create divinity fudge for the prince.

Because of the low humidity, at around noon I began whipping egg whites for a divinity fudge recipe I found in a 1930s cookbook put together by a farm family from the Maplewood area of our county and the Ahnapee Trail. The trail was a favorite for those who hiked, biked, or rode horses. The colors in the autumn there made you feel as if you walked inside a rainbow.

My mother called, yelling over my phone, "There's a fire!"

I almost dropped my bowl of egg whites. "Where?"

"Outside Harvest."

She hung up. I called her back, but she didn't answer.

Cody was stocking my shelves with new pink doll clothing the church ladies had made for us when he got the message about the fire on his phone.

"Miss Oosterling, it's a grass fire." He was reading his phone screen. "BUG is arriving already. They'll knock it down."

Cody was referring to the Brussels-Union-Gardner Fire Department—known as BUG. Three townships shared the department that relied on volunteers.

"I should go down there," I said, removing a pink apron with sparkly glass slippers on it.

"It says no buildings were involved, but the fire came up to the back of Ava's Autumn Harvest."

"And if my mother hadn't been there, it might have burned through the wooden doors on either end." My heart was racing.

"Call your mom again," Cody said.

His coolness amazed me. This time when I called her, Mom answered. She said a few cedar trees and wooden field posts had been destroyed. Cinders in the air had landed on the wooden shingles of Ava's Autumn Harvest. Mom had hosed it down before the fire department got there. I was sick thinking about what might have happened if some of the wooden rafters had caught fire and the roof had collapsed. Dillon had spent considerable time repairing that roof and laying a new wooden floor. All of his efforts would have been in cinders, as well as my new business.

My mother was talking in the background to a volunteer

firefighter. She came back on the phone. "Ava, they were asking me if I knew of any reason somebody might want to set a fire here."

"They think arson?" We were close enough to roadsides that I assumed it had been caused by a cigarette tossed from a vehicle into the dry weeds and grasses.

"I don't like this," my mother said, whispering into the phone. I could barely hear her. "This could be somebody warning you to stop asking questions about Cherry's death. What if they ask me about the body?"

"Mom, slow down." Hmm. Dillon's words to me last night were still resonating. Mom was charging mighty fast into the murder case. Just as I'd been doing. "Don't say anything to anybody. Let the firefighters make their conclusions. They're not going to find a clue that scientifically proves a relationship between you, I mean me, finding a body and a grass fire."

When I got off the phone, Cody was staring at me. "Your mother found that body?"

I sank into my steel-toed shoes. "Don't tell anybody."

"You got mad at me once for keeping secrets." He was referring to last May. He'd learned a lot about people who might have been involved with the diamonds in my fudge ingredients, but my lack of trust caused him to run away to Chambers Island out in the bay.

After we sent a few customers on their way with big boxes of fresh fudge, I said to Cody, "You're right. But you know my mother."

"Florine likes to clean a lot. What if she has Asperger's, too?" He was already preparing shiny ribbons for fudge boxes. He enjoyed shiny, sparkly things, which I'd learned could be common with Asperger's. Cody used this to his advantage; he was part artist.

"I doubt she has Asperger's, but I don't think she'd survive a night in a jail cell."

"It'd be a clean jail cell."

His hooting laugh made me smile. I helped fold and ready a few fudge boxes. "Will you keep the secret, Cody? It means a lot to me and my mother."

"Sure, Miss Oosterling. Can I help find the murderer?"

I almost said, "No, thanks, I'll do it myself," but instead said, "If I think of a way, I'll let you know. Thanks for offering."

Within the half hour, as I was getting ready to leave to drive down to Brussels, my grandpa came stomping in through the back hallway. He was covered in black soot.

"Did you hear, A.M.? Somebody tried to torch you."

Although in his seventies, he was still a member of the BUG Volunteer Fire Department. In rural areas, we accepted all the volunteers we could get.

I rushed into the kitchen to get a wet rag and came back. "What're you talking about, Gilpa?"

I handed Gilpa the rag to wipe his hands and face, but he set it aside on his sales counter as he shuffled about in his junk drawer where he kept tools.

"The other volunteers think it was a cigarette, but I saw a spot of scorched earth that looked like somebody tossed a can of gasoline or something. One of those molly drinks." He meant Molotov cocktail. "It was intentional. Lucky your mother was there to put out the damn thing."

Tools—screwdrivers, needle-nose pliers, stubby pencils with erasers long gone—flew out of the drawer and onto his counter while more swearwords flew out of his mouth.

Standing the heck out of the way, I said, "You must have broken all speed records to get back here so fast."

"Yeah, because somebody's trying to scare you and I'm putting a stop to it." He held up a knife in a leather sheath. It was his old Buck knife. "Aha! Found it!"

An edgy feeling tromped through my stomach. "What are you doing with that, Gilpa?"

"That darn Sheriff Tollefson showed up."

"That's good."

"No. He said you'd been in the church and had made a mess."

Before I could explain about Marc tossing the kitchen for some film shoot, Grandpa whipped the knife out, flashing the blade under the overhead light. "I'm going to show this around to people and see who gets scared and who looks guilty. If they look guilty, they usually are."

"Isn't the knife a bit of overkill?"

"Somebody left my son's Buck knife in that church, and then Cherry turns up dead. Now they're messing with you—my granddaughter. I'm gonna solve this murder case just like that." He snapped the fingers of one hand. "Then Jordy Tollefson won't be bothering my family. He's got you and my son—your daddy—under his thumb. I'll cut off his thumb if I have to."

My stomach was doing tricks that would put the Cirque du Soleil trapeze act in Las Vegas to shame. "You can't go around threatening people with a knife, Gilpa. And what's brought this on? You're never like this."

He stood tall and proud—a skinny man with a sooty face and looking like a raccoon, with the knife held out in front of him. His black-streaked white hair stood out every which way like Einstein's. "Ava honey, you've got to understand I'm defending my family. The word is out that a prince and princess are coming. People might be treating us differently now, for good or bad reasons, including offering too many free drinks and getting Sophie drunk."

"So this is about Mike Prevost letting Grandma drink too much. You think he started the fire?" I wasn't tracking on my grandpa's thought process.

He gulped in a big breath while handily sheathing the knife. "Did you find the recipe while you were in the church?"

"No. Maybe we should talk about that—"

"No time for talking. Time for doing. The recipe is there. I feel it in these old bones. You find the recipe and I'll defend us."

With that, he grabbed one of the cardboard beer six-pack carriers we used for the Fisherman's Catch Tall Tale Fudge flavors for men and filled the six-pack with fudge. He then stomped out the front door, pulling it so hard behind him that the cowbell clanked only once before it dropped off the door. I rushed over to pick it up.

Cody said, "I'll fix it."

Grandpa's SUV roared outside. He left the parking lot.

I called Pauline before I realized she was still in school. I felt lost without her. A peek up at our clock told me Laura was probably nursing her babies for their noon feeding. I certainly couldn't call on Grandma to stop Grandpa. Dillon was up the hill hammering away, and he and Grandpa still weren't buddies.

When Moose sauntered down the docks from the *Super Catch I*, I raced outside. "Moose, my grandfather is getting weird. What's going on with him?"

"Beats me. He handles the fishing tours with no problem."

"Never any trouble?"

"No trouble. Nothing goes wrong with my new engines. He doesn't even sweat on hot days, because my boat has air-conditioning."

The sudden weight of the world rested on my shoulders. "Do you think he's bored?"

"Didn't occur to me. Why?"

"He took a knife and some fudge just now and I think he's going to attack Mike Prevost down at his winery."

"Want me to head on down there?"

"No, you've got customers." Fishermen were collecting near the *Super Catch I* at the other end of the dock.

After Moose went into the shop, I called Dillon. "I need your help."

Within two minutes, Lucky Harbor, Dillon, and I converged at my yellow truck parked in front of my cabin on Duck Marsh Street.

The brown water spaniel woofed as I broke speed limits passing cars with tourists gawking at the gorgeous lake scenery and art shops.

My hands crimped around the steering wheel.

Dillon said, "Your grandfather wouldn't use the knife, would he?"

"Grandpa is a tad feisty when it comes to defending Grandma and his family. And he needs something to do."

"Maybe this fire is only some kid thinking he's messing with the family that has royalty in it. Kids do that sort of thing. They get jealous."

"I hadn't thought of that."

"Not everybody appreciates royalty. Some people think they suck from the public trough and sit around eating bonbons."

"Right there's the trouble. They should be eating fudge."

Lucky Harbor pushed his nose in the back of my neck and licked me. I couldn't take my hands off the wheel, so he'd have to wait to get his "fudge."

Dillon reached over to tug at my ponytail in a gesture that never failed to send a tickle down my middle. "Maybe it's not you that somebody wants to scare. It could be the Dahlgrens."

"Because they're murder suspects?"

"Sure. Somebody's upset over Cherry's death."

I thought about Fontana. She had some kind of affection for the man. But would she bother setting a fire? That seemed improbable. A chill did a sidewinder track up the back of my neck, because I wondered if my mother was right. Dillon had said last night I'd been way too active asking questions in the past two days. Could it be true that somebody didn't like me doing that? Had the person started this fire to keep me preoccupied? It was conjecture, but I couldn't help myself.

We sailed over the Sturgeon Bay Canal Bridge, sliding through a red light without anybody stopping me.

In another fifteen minutes we'd turned off Highway 57 and were traveling down the narrow, blacktopped country lane belonging to the Prevost Winery and vineyards. Because it was north of where my market sat, we didn't see the burned area yet.

I didn't see Grandpa's SUV in the parking lot. With relief, I assumed he'd probably gone to Ava's Autumn Harvest after all. But I felt compelled to warn Mike. I got out.

A bright red Mustang convertible with its top down sat near the sidewalk. I groaned. I was sure it was Fontana's car.

Lucky Harbor raced off.

Dillon said, "Don't worry. I'll get him. He always circles buildings looking for animals to flush."

I shivered. The last time Lucky Harbor circled a building lickety-split, it had been the Eagle Bluff Lighthouse outside Fishers' Harbor where he'd discovered my grandpa's friend Lloyd Mueller dead. Lloyd had been pushed off the tower. Later, Lucky Harbor showed up to help save me from the killer.

Shaking off the memory, I focused on finding Michael Prevost. In addition to the attractive, two-story stone building, there was an old farmhouse Mike had fixed up with tan vinyl siding. Behind it was a white barn used for a machine shed. Around us, the rolling hills were striped with rows of grapevines, many with leaves starting to turn autumn colors. On a far slope several workers picked grapes. I also saw Jonas Coppens's sheep grazing in a couple of rows to feast on weeds and old grape leaves.

Inside the winery, to my surprise, Fontana Dahlgren stood behind the cash register ringing up a customer. I sniffed the air; it had the taint from Fontana's distinctive homemade, spicy perfume that reminded me of hot, mulled cider boiled with lilies perhaps, or lavender.

Once the customer had moved on, I said, "Did you close your roadside market?"

"No. I put out a sign for people to come here today. Mike's letting me sell my products here."

"Is Mike around?"

"Not at the moment. He left me in charge."

She fluffed her red hair, which I begrudgingly had to admit was gorgeous. Her face was flawless, too. A dress in autumn gold fit just right.

Fontana looked me up and down. I was wearing a white T-shirt and denim shorts and still had on my heavy work shoes with the steel toes. My ponytail was half undone because of the wild ride in the truck with the wind whipping in the windows.

Fontana reached behind the counter, then handed me a small lavender-colored bag. "Free samples. Nail file. New goat milk soap I made yesterday. It'll help take some of the red out of your complexion."

Ignoring her jab, I accepted the bag and looked inside, then coughed from the pungent aromas of those lilies and maybe pickling spice. "Made from Jonas's goats?"

She nodded.

"My dad caught you trying to break into Jonas's roadside chapel the other day."

Her freckles faded. "I was thinking Adele's fudge recipe was hidden in there."

"Nice comeback, but that chapel isn't that old."

"The recipe can be anywhere. Maybe it was stolen from that church long ago and hidden somewhere else."

"Pardon me while I call Michael." I took out my phone.

"He said he had an errand to do in his back forty somewhere. He went off in his truck."

I put my phone away, but I wondered what else she could tell me. "So, you two are an item?"

She flipped her red hair off her shoulders. "He cares about me."

"No, you care about him helping you escape the blame for Cherry's death. A whole busload of people saw you arguing with Cherry the day he died."

Her gasp told me a lot. "Keep your voice down. I already gave my story to the sheriff."

Leaning over the counter, I asked, "Did you have anything to do with Cherry's death?"

Her gaze flickered about, but I couldn't tell if the action was from guilt or pure embarrassment. "What is wrong with you?" she hissed. "I'm scared to go into any church, and I'm certainly not going to go *down* into a church basement. That direction is Hell." She pointed down to the floor. "There's fire down there."

"It's interesting that you would mention a fire. Did you set the fire next to my market?"

One of her hands covered her gasp this time. "I just gave you a gift and you treat me this way?"

"Did Mike kill Cherry? You were with Cherry. You had to be there." She blinked hard while I continued. "Did you have a tryst at the schoolhouse, then drive off? You drove Mike's car, and he drove off in Cherry's. Right? I suppose Mike is off in the back forty hiding Cherry's car?"

As I said the words, a realization that felt like a bucket of ice being tossed down my back startled me. "Did you kill Cherry in his car? Is that why the car had to disappear? There's blood in it? Who helped you? Who dragged the body into the church and put it in the basement?"

With her hands shaking, Fontana fumbled for her cell phone from a designer purse sitting behind the counter. "I'm calling the sheriff."

"Go ahead. He enjoys talking with me."

I walked out of the winery on rubbery legs, incensed and still carrying the obnoxious lavender bag in one hand. My conscience scolded me to remember Dillon's words about my obsession with the case. But I felt certain Fontana was hiding something. She was neglecting her own roadside market and cozying up to Mike for some reason.

I had little time to think it over, though, because in the parking lot Dillon was smack dab in the middle of an argument between Michael Prevost and my grandfather. My grandpa was pointing dangerously into the air with his Buck knife.

Chapter 18

Grandpa had the knife in one hand while the six-pack loaded with fudge dangled off the other hand. He was railing at Mike about the way he'd treated my grandmother.

Dillon had both arms out, trying to motion them to back off.

Grandpa hollered at Mike, "You bastard. Taking advantage of a good woman like that."

Mike's face wrinkled in red rage. "She willingly took every drink I gave her. Sophie is a lush."

Grandpa lunged around Dillon and almost caught Mike's arm with the dangerous Buck knife.

I filched in the lavender bag and within a blink was spraying Fontana's awful spicy perfume at everybody as if it were pepper spray.

Lucky Harbor started barking at our feet, making us jump.

Grandpa halted to sneeze three times. He lowered the knife, replaced it in its sheath, then handed the knife and the fudge to Mike.

Mike said, "What the hell is this for?"

Grandpa sneezed again. "It's a gift. That's my old knife. I always give my enemies a gift. To butter them up. And to forgive them for being assholes."

Dillon smirked.

I wasn't sure what to say or do. Grandpa was not himself. Amid batting at the perfume in the air, Mike handed the knife back. "Thanks, but you keep the knife. I'll keep the fudge, gladly. You know your granddaughter was always good in my classes. Ava, sorry about everything with your grandmother."

Grandpa waggled a finger at Mike. "You're covering up something, Mike. Why was my wife drinking too much?"

"Sophie asked me for advice about going to Chicago."

I asked, "Why?"

"I mentioned I was going to Chicago soon to visit wine stores. Your grandmother said she wanted to look into some family ghost."

Grandpa harrumphed. "You're making this up. You got her drunk and then she started seeing things."

Mike said, "No. She talked about the ghosts first, then started slamming wine." Grandpa stalked away to his SUV, then drove off.

Lucky Harbor sneezed, then raced around the corner of the stone winery building again. He stopped to peer back at me, then disappeared. I refused to think lightning could strike twice. The dog must have found a cat or woodchuck that interested him.

Mike was about to walk away, and I tried to hold back my questions, I really did, because Dillon was standing there, but I was bursting. "Wait. Mike, did you or Fontana set the fire? Did you have anything to do with Cherry's death?"

Dillon groaned.

Mike took a moment, creating suspicion in my mind. "No. I . . . I just don't want Fontana taking the fall for it. She's . . . fragile."

Dillon said, "Listen, what you do in your spare time isn't my business, but she was with Cherry last Saturday night."

I said to Mike, "And you were out in your car and hit John and my manager from behind. Maybe you hit one of them on the head from behind in the church later."

Mike blinked. "Your manager?"

"The Hollywood kind of manager. They drove on instead of confronting you because my manager is from a place where gang members might be in the car behind you. You don't mess with people."

"Unlike your grandfather." Mike held up the six-pack of fudge.

Dillon asked, "So, Mike, what gives? Did you follow them? Why were you headed in that direction, the opposite way from your property?"

I asked, "Did you go to the church in Namur that night?"

"Stop, both of you." He clutched the fudge to his chest. "I didn't go to Saint Mary of the Snows. I went to see Jonas that night."

"That late?"

"It's not like we're old people. Heck, it wasn't even past midnight at that time. I thought maybe Jonas and I could find a compromise about the chemicals. I should have brought him your fudge."

I ignored his limp smile. "So you talked?"

"We didn't talk. There was somebody else at his house."

"Who?"

Sweat popped onto his forehead again. "A woman. I saw her through the window."

"Jonas didn't see your lights as you came in the driveway?"

"Well, my one headlight was out. I shut off my lights as I coasted closer because I was curious. I could tell there was a woman in the living room with him."

"Who?" I asked.

"I already told the sheriff."

Dillon said, "Tell us."

Mike's face grew redder. "Kjersta Dahlgren was there. Jonas was kissing her."

Dillon whistled for Lucky Harbor. The dog came but kept flicking his head toward the corner of the winery. Mike lingered at his doorway, watching us. I wondered if he was concerned we might go behind the winery for a look at what was attracting the dog.

When I mentioned Lucky Harbor's behavior to Dillon as we drove away from the winery, he lifted up the lavender bag sitting on the console between us. "Probably someone shot down by this perfume. It put a stop to the fight in everybody, including me, in an instant."

"Fontana doesn't know what she's doing. She's like my contest chef Kelsey King this past summer trying to make fudge with fungi. Dangerous."

Dillon said, "What's dangerous is your grandmother drinking so much. Does she believe in ghosts?"

"She believes in guardian angels and the Holy Spirit. She's a staunch Catholic. She believes Sister Adele Brise really did see the Blessed Virgin in the woods near here."

"Where was that exactly?"

"Southwest of here along the bay."

"Has she mentioned going to Chicago before? To find this ghost in your family?"

"Never. This is very strange of her, Dillon."

"I wonder why Chicago. Any connection to Sister Adele?"

"Not that I know of. A good question, though."

"I'm learning from the best. What or who is in Chicago that would tell her about ghosts?"

"I haven't a clue."

On the way to Ava's Autumn Harvest, we stopped alongside Highway 57 as soon as we saw the scorched grass. Grandpa was right. It looked as if a small bomb had been dropped. We got out of the truck for a closer look. Lucky Harbor immediately set to work with his nose, snuffling and sneezing. Fencing wire had been cut in one area to let the fire pumper trucks through to douse the fire before it reached nearby cedars and maples or spread farther into the Dahlgren orchard.

Oddly enough, I smelled Fontana's perfume intermingled with the lingering taint from the grass fire. "I'm going to have to shower. We smell awful."

Dillon said, "Lucky Harbor, too."

The dog was rolling around in a patch of blackened grass. Before I let him in the backseat, I spread an old towel across it.

We drove around the corner onto Highway C. I parked in the grass next to the stone barn. This side had been untouched by the fire.

My mother looked worried as she came out of the stone barn. She had a broom in her hand. As I drew within a couple of yards of her, she puckered up. "What's that smell?"

"Fontana's perfume." I held up the lavender bag. "Want some?"

"Sure. I'll spray it around the porch at home to keep the skunks from nesting under there."

She took the bag from me and I grabbed her broom. "Mom, you go home. I think Grandpa's at the farm showering. He was fighting the fire and got mixed up in that perfume, too."

Florine gave Dillon her evil-eye look. "You'll keep watch over my daughter? And keep your hands in your pockets and not on her?"

I burst out laughing.

She gave in to a smile herself, then headed toward her Holstein-motif minivan.

I said to Dillon, "She's getting used to you."

"Not quite a vote of confidence yet, but that was progress."

There weren't any customers. The scorched ground was probably scaring them off. I locked up.

I wandered over to the Dahlgrens' large garden, a field really, behind the house. Pumpkins needed picking. Some plump, ripe tomatoes were on the verge of rotting on the ground. I was sure several restaurants could use them. The garden shed had yellow tape across its doors, though, indicating I couldn't get access to the tools. Or shouldn't, anyway.

"Why don't we get the word out to friends and neighbors that we're going to pick this garden for Kjersta and Daniel? Let's try for tomorrow night. Wednesdays are always quiet." Thursdays were when the tourists started threading into the county for their long weekends.

"Sounds good."

Dillon turned to go back to the truck, but I headed to the house.

Dillon caught up with me, grabbing an arm. "Oh no you don't. You're addicted to yellow crime scene tape. You have to stop this." But he let go of me.

I hopped up the steps. "I need to get into the house."

"Why?"

"Because Mike must be lying about Kjersta and Jonas. Kjersta loves Daniel. There would not be kissing going on with Jonas. There must be some reason Mike would lie. And

Fontana was definitely covering up for Mike, too. I want to look through Kjersta's papers and notes, to see if there's anything about the feud with the neighbors."

"You're assuming the sheriff left behind something."

"Yes."

"I don't think you need to get into this house. Start with Jonas. Ask him what he knows."

My instincts said something was about to explode with all this subterfuge by my friends here in my old neighborhood. I explained to Dillon that my former teacher hadn't been trustworthy. He'd cooked our math grades a couple of times. "That's why I think he's lying."

"He gave you an A when you didn't deserve it?"

"I deserved the A. But some kids hadn't made the grade, and if they hadn't, they would have lost scholarships to college."

"That sounds half-bad and half-good."

"But he cheated, and that's what bothers me. He could be lying about Kjersta and Jonas for some reason. Maybe to protect Fontana. And why the heck isn't Fontana in jail yet?"

"Obviously, the sheriff hasn't found a solid connection between her and the murder."

"Yet."

Dillon went back down the front steps, his heavy work shoes clomping against the wood. "So you think Mike and Fontana killed Cherry in his car, Mike dragged him to the basement, and then Fontana and Mike drove off with Mike hiding the car somewhere."

"That's about right." But it still bothered me that Fontana could hop in bed with Mike so soon after Cherry's death. At least, I assumed they were sleeping together. I came down the steps, defeated.

Dillon put an arm around me. "What'd you find out from Fontana?"

"Not much. All I can assume is that she's looking for the divinity fudge recipe. She thought it might be hidden in Jonas's roadside chapel."

"That's not a bad idea to inspect all the chapels. How many are there around here?"

"Dozens. And many are part of old garages or in the back rooms of houses built in the 1800s. Every Belgian immigrant back then maintained a private chapel."

"It seems impossible to find a recipe that Adele scribbled on a piece of paper."

"But my grandfather insists it's in the church. Gilpa is always right when it counts." I kissed Dillon on the cheek. "Thanks for helping me. It's fun working together and being together."

He hauled me into his arms and kissed me soundly until my toes itched.

When we got back into my truck, Lucky Harbor's gaze was piercing and steady, as if he were asking me to do something. The eerie feeling that he wanted me to go back to the winery brushed across my brain. I shook it off, giving the Dahlgren house one last look. The yellow tape was calling to me, just as something was calling to Lucky Harbor.

Chapter 19

Dillon and I returned to Fishers' Harbor to get back to work. Several customers in my shop enjoyed watching me stir Belgian chocolate in my copper kettles. When it spun in the air just so, I poured the batch onto the white marble table and gave several customers loafing tools. For a time, I forgot my worries.

But the fudge making got me to thinking about the possible lies and cover-ups going on among Jonas, Mike, Fontana, and perhaps Kjersta.

At five o'clock, I begged Pauline to drive me down to the Dahlgren place in her clunker nondescript gray car so we wouldn't be detected. Laura was along. The plan was that we would pick vegetables for Kjersta and Daniel, but I would find a way to sneak into the house.

Cody's girlfriend, Bethany, was babysitting Clara Ava and Spencer Paul.

During the entire journey, the *clinkety-clunk* rattle in the undercarriage or hubcaps of Pauline's sedan continued.

Pauline said, "Why don't you drive this car from now on since you wrecked it anyway, and I'll take your yellow truck? Fair exchange."

"No, thanks. I like my truck. It has sentimental value."

"You crashed your other truck with me in it. Yeah, that's sentimental, all right."

"Dillon found this truck on the Internet for me. Pauline,

you forget that John is involved in all this. I'm doing this to help prove his innocence."

Pauline growled, "You always know when to pull that card."

"Is he remembering anything more about late Saturday night or early Sunday morning?"

"I haven't seen him much."

I exchanged a look with Laura in the backseat, then said to Pauline, "He's not sleeping at your house?" He hadn't stayed with Dillon last night.

"No."

"Mercy Fogg's?"

Laura burst out laughing in the back. But I saw that I'd gone too far. Tears were shimmering in Pauline's eyes as she drove.

I offered her, "He's going to be fine, Pauline. John wants to prove himself worthy of you. Let him and Marc chase this TV show idea for a while. Everything will turn out okay. You'll see."

"They're lawless, just like you. Nothing's going to be fine. Your manager trashed the church kitchen to create a scene they could film. Nothing's going to be all right when they pull stunts like that."

Laura and I shut up. The car felt mighty chilly the rest of the drive.

We parked the car behind the stone barn so it couldn't be seen from County Trunk C. Trees blocked it mostly from view from Highway 57.

The redbrick Dahlgren house was an old farmhouse, the kind with a storm cellar entrance outside in back and low to the ground. I guessed there'd be no yellow tape across it, and I was right. I used the jack from Pauline's car to bust the lock. We descended the concrete steps, lowering the door above our heads.

The basement was dry and pleasant smelling, a larder filled with canned vegetables, jars, Christmas decorations in plastic boxes, and other things that didn't interest us.

Upstairs on the first floor I went to the desk in the living room alcove. I riffled through the drawers while Pauline and Laura walked through the house looking for notes, file cabinets, and anything having to do with the neighbors or the university's research.

Laura reported back first. "There's not even a laptop or computer tablet left anywhere."

I said, "Jordy's thorough." As I said that, the desk yielded papers from the university extension service in Green Bay from Professor Wesley Weaver. They were under a stack of sales slips for apples and vegetables to local restaurants.

The papers were correspondence revealing that Professor and Dean Wesley Weaver wasn't pleased with Professor Hardy's research, which was having a negative impact on the entire department as well as their two teaching assistants—Nick and Will—who were working on their doctorates. But Weaver informed the Dahlgrens that the research project would end by September 30.

Laura said, "The papers show that Professor Weaver was upset, not that the Dahlgrens were upset with Cherry."

"And it's fairly common that research projects would end by October, because that's the month when federal budgets end or renew. I remember that from college. Professors were always worrying about federal grants running out in the fall."

Pauline sat down in a nearby olive green leather chair. "What irony. The project is about to end, and he gets murdered. The person murdering him maybe didn't know it was over."

With elation, I got up and went over to hug Pauline. "You're right. This proves the Dahlgrens didn't kill him. There's no motive. We can take this evidence to Jordy and they're freed."

Laura sat on the arm of the Dahlgrens' green leather couch. "But that letter is dated a couple of weeks ago." She tucked a wisp of her blond bob behind an ear. "Cherry knew his project was about to end but didn't tell anybody."

"Out of pride," I said, defending him.

Pauline asked, "But why didn't Kjersta and Daniel tell your neighbors? Including your parents? Why did they let Jonas stay mad at them? And Mike?"

Her question made me twist my ponytail around in my

fingers. "Obviously, something else transpired in the past two weeks. And if what Mike said is true, Kjersta was at Jonas's the night of the murder. She saw cars on the road, she says, but she said that sighting was from her house."

Laura let her lithe body slide off the couch arm and down onto a cushion. "So she's wide-awake that night. Where was Daniel during all this?"

Pauline tapped her hands on the leather chair arms. "Sleeping like the rest of us? It certainly was one busy little country road that night."

I walked back to the papers on the desk. "We need to talk with Kjersta and Daniel and that professor. What about tomorrow? We need to pick vegetables anyway."

Pauline said, "That was supposed to be our cover tonight. And you forget I'm teaching thirteen kindergartners. Tomorrow we're painting a mural about Snow White and the Seven Little People. I have to keep track of twenty-six hands filled with finger paints making pictures of Grumpy and Sneezy."

"Now it sounds like we're talking about Fontana's perfume and soaps."

Laura said, "She gave me a bag of that stuff after my twins were born. I had to double-bag it before putting it in the trash can behind the Luscious Ladle. But it kept the raccoons away."

On Wednesday midafternoon, Lucky Harbor showed up at my shop with a note in the orange floatable key holder secured to his collar. *Piers helping me with claw-foot tub. Progress being made for the prince and princess. XOXO.*

The letters meant hugs and kisses. I glowed.

Dillon inspired me. If he'd commandeered Piers to help him refurbish the inn, perhaps there was hope it'd be completed in time for the visit by my royal relatives. When there was a lull in the afternoon, I took the time to do more research online for divinity fudge information. I also remembered I wanted to look up Jane Goodland.

On the Internet, none of the images and references said anything about any Jane Goodland being a lawyer. One photo was a mug shot of a dark-haired woman who'd been arrested for bank robbery a few years ago. Another photo depicted another dark-haired woman in England who wrote children's picture books. She seemed like a possibility for buying our bookstore, yet she was in England. The final image was of a blond exotic dancer. Because there'd been hints around town of the lawyer being a bombshell, I wondered if the dancer was also a lawyer. I refused to believe an exotic dancer was taking over the Wise Owl bookstore.

After school was out for the kindergartners at two thirty, I decided that I could satisfy my curiosities about Kjersta by talking to her directly in jail. I also wanted to talk with Professor Weaver in Green Bay. He could shed light on what was going on among his colleagues and Cherry.

Lois and Dotty had come by with new fairy-tale-fudge-themed aprons they'd made for sale and agreed to work in the store until Cody could drop by later. Dotty said, "We're working on new fudge flavor ideas for you. We think we have a good one. But it's a secret for now."

Everybody had secrets lately.

I hopped into my truck, then picked up Pauline. Laura had driven down from Sister Bay with her twins, whom Bethany was babysitting at Pauline's house.

Pauline said, "The only reason I'm going with you is that you promised this would be the end of you getting into trouble."

"What possibly could happen at the Justice Center?" I said.

Laura laughed in back.

Sheriff Jordy Tollefson arrested me on the spot at the Justice Center.

Jordy didn't see matters the way I did.

He recited my Miranda rights, which I waived. I had to turn my pockets inside out, leave him my wallet, cell phone, and shoelaces, and succumb to fingerprinting. Maria Vasquez was with us the whole time. Jordy was performing my arrest by the book.

After I was stripped of anything that could harm him or me, he took me to his interrogation room, a room I was unfortunately too familiar with. This time we were alone at his six-foot brown table. We sat in the maroon plastic chairs. The only decoration was the clock behind him above his head.

"What did you do with Pauline and Laura?" I asked.

"They're in the dungeon." He kept his face fixed on the papers he was filling out in front of him. He handed me the papers.

My eyes scanned words like "broke in" and "defied police order" and "illegal entry."

"I'm not signing this," I said.

"Why not? You did all those things."

"I need a lawyer. Is Parker Balusek here? I heard he's repping Kjersta and Daniel."

"Why do you keep breaking into property?"

"Because I'm doing your work for you, Jordy."

"Address me, please, as Sheriff, while we're inside the jail."

"Sheriff, did you know that somebody camped out at the schoolhouse? Probably the suspects after they killed Cherry. We've concluded there are two suspects."

"We?"

"Dillon and me. Or me and Pauline and Laura. Or you and me. Take your pick."

Jordy tapped his pen on a pad of paper he'd brought along. "You broke into the schoolhouse as well?" He pulled the arrest record back from me, then added "entered locked schoolhouse." He shoved it back again. "What else have you broken into?"

"That's not important. I need to ask Kjersta if she's having an affair with Jonas Coppens."

"Why?" He eased his lean frame back in his chair, his holster scraping against the plastic seat.

"Because Michael Prevost, the neighbor behind her place with the vineyard, says he saw her with Jonas the night of the murder. She might have been out in her car and may have seen more than she's told you. I still think she's innocent of Cherry's murder, but she may be scared of somebody. That might be why she ran over to Jonas's house the night of the murder."

He sat forward, interested now, a keen look lacing his brown eyes. "Shouldn't she be scared of Jonas?"

"They don't always see eye to eye, but why should she be scared of him?"

"The guy keeps to himself. That's what I've heard, anyway."

"He lives by himself. There's a difference." I clasped my hands together in front of me on the table. "You think he's a killer because he lives by himself?"

"I didn't say he was a killer at all. You said that." He made a note.

"I've known him all my life. Kjersta might be scared of Michael Prevost or Fontana Dahlgren and she was over there talking to Jonas about one of them. Maybe to ask his help in getting Fontana off her back. Everybody in my parents' area knows about Fontana, Daniel's ex. She can't stand the idea of him being married again."

"So you think Fontana's trying to make sure Kjersta is put away so she's out of the way."

Misery trickled through me like a muddy creek. I wasn't liking the feeling of blaming any of my childhood friends and neighbors for Cherry's death. "Why isn't Fontana in jail?"

"That would indicate we don't have enough on her. Yet."

"Nothing like blood on a shovel for her, huh?"

"No."

"But you mentioned the perfume on Cherry's clothes or body."

"Yes. That intrigues an officer of the law."

I leaned forward, my hands still clutched together. "Your idea that the perfume is evidence isn't as flimsy as I first thought. Yesterday I sprayed that stuff around and almost laid my grandfather and others flat. What if Cherry were allergic to some ingredient in that perfume? Maybe Fontana's perfume was intentionally used to subdue him."

Jordy nodded. "An interesting thought. Or maybe somebody besides Fontana was there who wore her perfume. I have all the receipts from her business this summer. We're poring over them."

I had to admire Jordy. He was working hard on this case. "How many receipts? How many possibilities of a murderer with that perfume?"

"About three dozen," Jordy said.

"That's all? Her market is doing miserable business. I had no idea."

"She says you have an idea. You're to blame because you've been successful."

"Jordy, Fontana's been open since the summer. I opened my market at the first of this month for the Labor Day traffic. She's had plenty of time—much more than I have—to test the market."

"None of this proves Fontana Dahlgren could have murdered somebody. In fact, you're proving she couldn't have done it. She's incapable of running a business. How could she be capable of a murder? She contends she really enjoys making soaps and perfumes and makeup for women, so why would she waste it on a dead man she said she loved?"

Hmm. Jordy was good. "But you have Kjersta in jail. Based on perfume and blood on a shovel. But Daniel seemed to be implicated by the shovel. You must have other evidence against Kjersta, enough to hold her."

"Which I'm not telling you."

"I sure am getting tired of secrets. Did you ask her if she and Fontana were working together?" I thought about the papers I'd found and how Kjersta knew two weeks ago that Cherry's research was ending, yet she hadn't told anybody. If I told Jordy about the papers, it would cause big trouble for Kjersta, possibly cement a guilty verdict in a trial. Sooner or later he'd likely learn the truth on his own, so I stayed mum.

Jordy was writing a note. "I'll ask Kjersta about Fontana again. I heard that Cherry was annoying a lot of people. You, too?"

I rubbed my arms. The room was chilly. "The man was an irritation to everybody. Except Fontana, though I saw her arguing with him on Saturday at my market."

"So you're thinking that Kjersta wanted to be free to have Jonas, and Fontana wanted Daniel? They both just needed to get rid of Cherry, who was too nosy for his own good?"

The sheriff made it all sound smooth, easy to believe. "I don't know."

"What about Daniel, the cuckolded husband?"

"You think he whacked Cherry with the shovel. But why? Sheriff, I can't believe Daniel would commit murder. Certainly not out of concern for Fontana."

"He might murder if he thought his property values would plummet. Cherry was, after all, saying he thought their land was tainted with chemicals or bugs."

"And Cherry's talk could just as easily have scared the local workers, who thought they'd be without a job. Any of them could have murdered him."

Jordy said he'd already questioned them. They were seasonal workers who lived in a local motel. The motel manager had verified seeing the workers come home. He hadn't seen them leave later. None of the workers had problems with Cherry or Weaver, or Nick or Will or any other university faculty and students they encountered regularly.

My fingers began involuntarily tapping the table. "Dillon's dog was sniffing around yesterday behind the winery and seemed to want me to follow him."

"Dillon was with you?"

Jordy's brown eyes held a spark. I had to admit he had a certain allure when he was in uniform, but my heart had room enough for only one man.

I ignored his question. "The dog has a good nose. Better than your German shepherd K-9 unit, I bet."

"We don't have a K-9 unit at the moment. Tight budget doesn't cover kibble. I'll leave the sniffing behind the winery to you and your dog."

"Dillon's dog." I hoped that Jordy was forgetting that he was in the process of arresting me. "Do you have any fingerprints from the knife yet?"

"No. Whoever used it likely wore gloves."

"What about the circuit breakers in the basement?"

"We found a couple of prints on them. One print belonged to Kjersta."

My stomach went into turmoil. Kjersta was in deep trouble. "Who does the other print belong to?"

"We don't know. It was a thumbprint, but small, belonging to a woman probably."

My mother's thumb? "What about the fire in the organ

bench? I don't think it's connected to the murder. I don't see how it fits."

I told him about John Schultz winning a spot in the choir over Fontana Dahlgren, and that John had sworn me to secrecy about being able to sing "Ave Maria" during the upcoming kermis for the prince and princess.

Jordy said, "So you think Fontana set that fire?"

"She might have. If she was mad enough about not making the choir."

"Mercy Fogg drove the bus that day. Any thoughts about her?"

"Mercy always seems to be on the periphery of what's going on, as if we're all marionettes on strings and she controls us. She gives me the creeps sometimes." I told him about her finding John on her bus and keeping him overnight in her bed.

"Hmm. She didn't tell me that. I'll have to have another talk with her."

I said, "If she offers you meat loaf, decline."

The page in front of Jordy was filling with leads I'd given him.

I pointed to the pad. "If you let me go, I could find more stuff like that for you. Pauline, Laura, and I were on our way to Green Bay to talk with Professor Wesley Weaver. We think he might have valuable information."

Jordy squinted at me. "How so?"

I relented and told him about the papers Jordy and his deputies had missed at the house.

He said, "Did you break through my crime scene tape?"

"There was no yellow tape over the cellar door. I could mention this to the reporters lurking about, how possible evidence hadn't been properly secured."

Jordy's neck and face blazed red. "Talk to the professor. Then tell me what you find out. Do we have an understanding?"

I nodded.

He ripped up the arrest papers.

Chapter 20

With my friends along, I pointed my yellow Chevy truck toward the city of Green Bay. In my rearview mirror I spied a county squad following us. It turned off when I left Door County and entered Brown County.

At around five, we met Professor Wesley Weaver after a lecture on the university campus that had been open to the public. He'd published a new book about the health benefits of cherries. We grabbed paper cups of free coffee in the back of the room while he signed a few books. When he was done, I introduced him to Laura. Pauline had met him and his PhD students before when I was setting up Ava's Autumn Harvest.

We walked down the hallway of the older brick building that held a rabbit warren of offices and plant pathology labs. The place smelled acidic and musty at the same time, but all in a good way, like dirt and plants and experiments.

Once behind his desk, he said, "What can I do for you all?"

We sat in metal folding chairs. The professor was slightly taller than I, maybe six feet even, so he was looking down at us. He was in his fifties, with neatly kept dark auburn hair graying at the temples. A deep tan reflected his research work outdoors.

The professor said, "I hear your fudge shop is doing well. What about the new market? Your mother said business has been a little up and down."

"Hot lately." I told him about the fire.

"Dry weather is predicted for a while. A lot of people are talking about conditions mirroring that summer of 1871, though we've had more rain than they did back then. Door County went months without a drop that summer."

With the niceties over with, I asked about Tristan Hardy's research. "He even took samples of my fudge. What's become of those samples?"

Professor Weaver's face soured. "We're analyzing them, but only because he was on a federal grant that said he'd do that. He had two assistants and they get paid to finish the work until October 1. Let me take you across the hall to the lab. Laura can meet them."

Nick Stensrud and Will Lucchesi were both in their mid-twenties.

Their lab made me salivate and want to be back in school studying science. The lab had state-of-the art equipment, it appeared to me. My gaze zoomed in on the prettiest sight of all—my sparkly Cinderella Pink Fudge inside a large, clear glass test tube. It looked like precious gems.

Nick got up off his chair to shake our hands. He was a tall beanpole with thick hair the color of rich brown soil, trimmed neatly and with a side part. Nick was finishing his doctorate. Will, another doctoral student, came over to greet us. Will was shorter, with a boyish mop of dark hair with summer highlights. His intense brown eyes darted among us, which made me think he was nervous.

Will said, "I heard you found Cherry's body. Awful."

"It's been awful for everybody who knew him, especially my family. That's why we're here. We wanted to know more about his research near Brussels and Namur."

Will and Nick peered at each other, as if wondering who should talk.

I said, "So you weren't excited about his research in my family's neighborhood?"

Professor Weaver interjected, "Professor Hardy was pushing things too fast. He was making assumptions about what was going on with the chemical feud."

"What did he think was going on?"

Nick said, "He had a new theory, one that was rather preposterous."

"And that was what?" I asked.

When Nick and Will hesitated, the professor glanced about the lab, seemingly to assure himself that nobody was nearby listening. "He felt the Dahlgrens were contaminating their own land as a way to blame their neighbors and drive them into selling."

I shook my head. "I can't imagine Daniel harassing his neighbors that way. Are you sure?"

"Two weeks ago I wrote the letter assuring them he'd be out of their hair by October 1. I had my own firestorm to put out here, too, with him."

"What do you mean?"

"Professor Hardy was sure he was correct about the indiscriminate usage of chemicals in that area."

Nick said, "But he couldn't prove it. I don't know if you're aware of this, but ever since your market opened, he's been bringing fudge back to the lab for testing, and when Will and I are out doing our research, he made us bring back fudge."

No wonder my fudge sales were so good at the market. "My mother clerks at the market a lot, and she didn't mention this."

Professor Weaver said, "When he brought back your fudge for testing as a way to test the cherries for chemical residue, the other professors in our department sent up a howl. Dissecting fudge looked frivolous."

I wanted to take offense at that, but couldn't. Fudge should be eaten, not dissected. "What was your interaction with Cherry, I mean Professor Hardy, concerning my fudge?"

Will said, "He put your fudge in the test tubes, as you see, so we didn't even get to taste it."

Professor Weaver said, "My questioning him at all wasn't welcomed."

"But you and Professor Hardy traveled together now and then throughout the area counties doing your research."

"Because my colleagues wanted nothing to do with him."

Nick said, "The other faculty thought he was a lightweight."

Professor Weaver added, "I have to admit I questioned his approaches to research, too, but that's my job as both a colleague and his dean."

I asked Nick and Will, "So he was being unreasonable somehow?"

Professor Weaver jumped in. "He threatened me with taking this all the way to the chancellor's office." He leaned back against a counter and crossed his arms. "He said I was interfering with his academic freedom."

Nick sat down in his chair again by my fudge. "Professor Hardy threatened to sue the entire department for trying to get him to change what he was doing with his federal grant. He got really mad when I called it the 'federal fudge fiasco.'"

Pauline perked up. "Cherry was causing my friend John a lot of trouble on his tours lately. Cherry would follow the bus. He kept hogging the microphone and presentations. He got worse as the summer went on."

Nick said, "That sounds like Professor Hardy."

Professor Weaver grimaced. "We couldn't reason with him."

Nick said, "From day to day his personality would change. Will and I didn't much like getting stuck with him in a car visiting farmers."

Laura muttered, "Was there anything wrong with him healthwise?" She pulled out a lab chair to sit down.

"What do you mean, Laura?" I asked.

"I had a great-uncle who became erratic in his behavior when he suffered from early onset dementia. He wasn't focusing well, drifted from one project at home to the next without finishing any of them. But once they diagnosed him, medications helped."

Professor Weaver said, "That didn't seem to be Cherry. Sure, he was becoming a nuisance at times, but he was quite focused on helping farmers and others."

I offered, "Maybe it was only a personality clash?"

Nick shrugged. "Well, yeah, for sure. But we're left with this. Oh, sorry."

He'd pointed to the test tube with my fudge in it.

Professor Weaver said, "They're obligated to finish

Cherry's research. It's part of their theses for their doctorates."

I almost said I was sorry, but then I realized I was talking about my own fudge and should be proud it was associated with Will and Nick becoming new faculty members. I thanked them all for their time.

When the three of us walked out of the building and then headed for my truck, Pauline said, "Maybe Cherry following John's tours around had nothing to do with dementia. Maybe Cherry was stressed-out."

We got in my truck, then drove back into the Green Bay streets. I said, "I would be stressed, too. Sounds like his colleagues were pressuring him to quit, and his students didn't seem thrilled with him either. It's hard to get rid of a tenured professor."

"Not if you murdered him and made it look like self-defense," Pauline said.

Laura said, "I've pulled up the department listing." In the rearview mirror I could see her tapping her smartphone. "It has nine faculty members, but only Weaver is doing orchard and grapevine research like Cherry was doing. Nick Stensrud and Will Lucchesi are the only students assigned to Cherry and Weaver."

Pauline said, "Nick and Will seem nice enough. Somebody who says 'federal fudge fiasco' doesn't strike me as a killer. Ava, I think you need to keep those other colleagues of Cherry's as suspects, because bullying is a serious issue."

"The ones we didn't meet yet."

"Yeah, seven other profs. What if one or two of them had agreed to meet Cherry that night in the bar next to the Namur church and got in a fight? What if right there on the road the colleague pushed Cherry and he stumbled backward and hit his head?"

Laura added, "They panicked, stuffed the body in the basement, ran into Marc and John accidentally, and everybody ran."

Their story sounded so plausible that none of us said a word more. Horrible accidents happen in real life. I cringed thinking what could have happened with my grandfather brandishing that knife at Mike. However, moving Cherry's body had been the fatal mistake. It looked like murder.

I pulled into a Walmart parking lot so I could stop the truck and use my phone to call Jordy.

Pauline decided to buy her class some cheap supplies. Laura and I pitched in with cash to help purchase watercolor sets, crayons, whiteboard markers, cleaner for the board, ruled pads, and a full cartload of paper towels. I invited Pauline to bring the class to my fudge shop tomorrow. I'd have the kids build a lighthouse tower mimicking one of Door County's eleven lighthouses and canal lights using squares of fudge. We could put one of the Rapunzel dolls at the top and let her long golden yarn hair flow down. It'd make a perfect weekend window display. I offered to give a portion of the proceeds from the Rapunzel Raspberry Rapture fudge to Pauline's class fund.

Pauline asked, "What's your next fairy-tale flavor?"

"I don't know. But we need to come up with a new one, because Dotty and Lois are dreaming up something."

Laura said, "But aren't you already making divinity fudge?"

Pauline said, "That's in honor of Sister Adele. She needs another fairy-tale flavor, one for every season of her first year in business."

I said, "Dillon and I came up with Goldilocks."

Pauline shrugged. "Golden fudge? Yellow? Pineapple? Not your best yet."

Back in the truck, we returned to the murder case.

Laura said, "They did an autopsy, right? Maybe they already know if Cherry suffered dementia or had any health problems."

"Whatever was wrong with Cherry's behavior, I'm starting to believe he was likely killed in his car, and then his body was put in the basement to hide it." I reminded them about the missing Ford Fusion and the apparently handmade bloody smudge on the basement wall.

Pauline, in the front passenger's seat, said, "If Kjersta was having a fling with Jonas, and if she was complaining to Professor Weaver about Cherry, it does seem to point back to her and Daniel possibly wanting Cherry out of the way. You said Jordy suspects Daniel feared that his place was losing value. So Cherry was ruining them or perhaps threatening to do so. Plus, his weird behavior was weirding them out."

"Sadly, you could be right," I conceded.

It was around six thirty by the time we were driving into Door County. It was dusk, with sunset only an hour away. I was intent on watching the roadsides for animals that could leap out when Laura said from the backseat, "Isn't that smoke over there?"

Black smoke curled above treetops maybe a mile ahead of us.

Ava's Autumn Harvest?

I pressed the gas pedal to the floor.

Chapter 21

A fire had destroyed most of Jonas Coppens's goat barn by the time we arrived. I had pulled into the Dahlgren place and next to my own barn before I realized nothing was on fire. We barreled next door.

The BUG volunteers were on the scene, including my grandfather. He'd stuck around the farm that day and since our farmstead was within view, he'd seen the flames and called it in, then rushed over with my father to help put out the fire using water hoses.

Jonas wasn't home, but somebody said fortunately he'd loaned his goats to Michael Prevost's workers for the day to clean up weeds around the winery building. The sheep were housed in another shed and fenced yard. They were okay.

The fire department was able to locate Jonas by phone. He was on his way.

Pauline, Laura, and I stood out of the way in the stubble of the nearby hayfield. The goat barn was an old machine shed only yards away from the house that Jonas had weatherized years ago.

My friends and I pitched in with my father to take Jonas's twenty goats in a stock truck over to our farm for safekeeping for the night. Dad had built a rather large chicken run with wire over the top to keep hawks out. It was perfect for goats because they loved to climb fences and escape.

It was eight o'clock and dark by the time Jonas arrived.

After helping with the goats, Pauline, Laura, and I had stopped again on our way back to personally offer more help to Jonas.

In the eerie silvery light of the farm's floodlight on a pole in the driveway, Jonas leaped from his truck without even shutting the door. He stood in shock while accepting hugs from us all. I told him we'd moved his goats.

He hugged me tightly, not letting go for a long while. "Thanks, Ooster."

In a daze, he said he'd been in Fishers' Harbor picking up spare parts for a tractor and had even stopped at the fudge shop to say hi. He'd visited with my grandmother.

As he looked about the commotion of firefighters packing up and neighbors coming and going, he said, "Do they know what happened?"

I snagged my grandpa. He was as black as the shadows around us. The whites of his eyes shone like headlights. He smelled of scorched wood and old asphalt shingles. His white hair was mostly black with soot and melded with the night.

"Jonas, sorry. What a shame. It appears to have started in the southeast corner, not too far from the doorway."

"The old outlets?"

"Could be. Did you keep the goats away from them?"

"Of course. Wire cages over anything that way."

"Anything stored there that might have spilled?"

"Spilled? You mean like gasoline? I never keep that in the garage. Hey, you're not saying this looks suspicious, are you?"

Standing beside Jonas, I sensed his body tensing.

My grandpa slapped a hand on one of his shoulders in a friendly man-to-man way. "Jonas, it's just something we have to consider. Especially since there was a fire next door yesterday on your neighbor's property."

Jonas sagged. "This is awful." His voice was a whisper. "Who would do this?" Then he growled. "That bastard."

He probably meant Michael Prevost. His other enemies were in jail or dead.

Grandpa gave Jonas's shoulders a shake. "Don't go there. This is probably only lousy bad luck with an aging electrical receptacle."

Grandpa followed me, Pauline, and Laura to my truck.

Jonas pulled a flashlight from his truck and went off to inspect his shed. The darkness of night was now filled with dots of light roving about the site.

After I slung myself in the truck seat and closed the door, Grandpa poked his head close to mine through the open window. I turned on the overhead light. He said, "I want you girls to be careful. And, Ava, don't be alone anymore over at your market, you hear me?"

A chill pierced me like a sharp icicle.

Grandpa patted my shoulder. "Honey, this is all my fault."

"How can that be?"

"For the want of a nail, a kingdom was lost." He referred to an old poem about a shoe falling off a horse and the horse not being able to run and save somebody. "If I hadn't invited that prince and princess, there wouldn't be all this furor. We wouldn't have people messing with us. Big events like royalty visiting always bring out the weirdos. We have to worry about security and people trying to get attention."

"By setting fires?"

"Yes. Everybody's on edge. Your grandma's right. She knew there'd be trouble. That poor woman."

My heart went out to him. "No, Grandpa, don't talk silliness. You had nothing to do with these fires. We'll fix this."

"This'll take more than you and me fixin' somethin'."

Pauline pulled out the buttons with the picture of the church and fudge on them, explaining how they'd been blessed and were lucky buttons.

Grandpa harrumphed, but added, "Keep rubbing them. Can't hurt."

It was close to eight thirty that night by the time I got Pauline and Laura home in Fishers' Harbor. The warm air had escaped out of the atmosphere, but I eschewed a sweatshirt in my hurry across my back lawn. Grandma was closing up Oosterlings' Live Bait, Bobbers & Belgian Fudge & Beer.

"Grandpa might take a while in getting home, Grandma."

I told her about everything. But my mother had already called her about the fire.

Grandma said, "Jonas bought some of your beer fudge when he was here earlier. Said some of the hired hands love the stuff. He also bought your Worms-in-Dirt flavor for their kids."

Children loved the chewy gummy worms sprouting out of the dark Belgian chocolate fudge.

Grandma was laying clear plastic wrap lightly over the fudge in the window for the night. "The only thing right around here these days is your fudge."

"Thank you, Grandma. You're so sweet."

That gave me an idea. From the shelf under my counter, I dug out a few of the vintage cookbooks. "Would you help me make divinity fudge, Grandma?"

"If you're making it the old-fashioned way, you need egg whites and you're out of them. Want me to run back home for some?"

"That'd be great. Thanks."

I was heartened that Grandma appeared to be in a happier mood. Maybe Dillon's mother wouldn't have to be pressed into service to talk with Grandma. As I paged through another old cookbook put together by a Lutheran church group long ago, I admitted to myself I wasn't sure I wanted a former mother-in-law—who might be a future mother-in-law—helping with my family's affairs. But why did I have that feeling? Weren't Dillon and his mother going to eventually be my family? Was I feeling that things were happening too fast between Dillon and me? Or worse yet, was I not trusting my relationship with Dillon to last?

My silly doubts brought me to thoughts of Fontana. She flitted from man to man with nary a worry. Or did she?

A scratch at the front door told me Lucky Harbor was visiting. After putting the cookbook down on my counter, I checked to make sure I had crackers in the pocket of my denim shorts, then went to the door. He had the floatable key holder on his collar.

Dillon's note said *Wish you were here. Cuddlier than Piers. Finished plumbing the tub. Treating him to sandwich at Troubled Trout. Miss you.*

The note indicated how full our lives were. We had a commitment to help each other thrive within the community of Fishers' Harbor. The commitment felt like pleasant glue holding our relationship together. I suddenly longed to be back on that yacht floating under the moonlight with Dillon.

I put the wishes aside to herd Lucky Harbor out the door. The harbor lights illuminated the area. No boat was docked at our pier and hadn't been since my grandfather sent his fishing trawler, *Sophie's Journey*, to a salvage yard. A twinge of sorrow struck me. I knew that Grandpa was still feeling pangs of loss for his boat.

I tossed the crackers into the air over the water. Lucky Harbor's nails scrabbled against the wooden decking as he loped down the pier. He leaped far into the water, landing with a big splash.

What made him happy was so simple. Maybe Dillon was right. The key to my happiness was simplifying. But how? I liked everything I was doing. Everything I was doing was building my future and laying the groundwork for a day when my grandpa and grandma could retire for real and not worry about me.

Grandma came in through the back door with a carton of eggs. "Your mother delivered these today. Her Brakels sure are prolific. Divinity fudge needs the freshest of eggs."

Brakels are handsome Belgian chickens with golden feathers on their necks and breasts. We'd had chickens all my life. I'd been told long ago the chickens were from a flock that came from Grandma's relatives as a wedding gift. When she and Grandpa moved to Fishers' Harbor, they'd left the chickens on the farm where there was more room for them. The descendants of those chickens were entertaining goats tonight.

My grandmother and I went into the small galley kitchen. I pulled out the sugar tub and measured out a couple of cups while Grandma separated two egg whites from their yolks. Grandma also blanched a half cup of almonds.

The recipe also called for a half cup of water and a half cup of corn syrup.

I said, "Since corn syrup wasn't common here during Sister Adele's time, do you think there's a way to make this fudge without it?"

"We can sure try. But we need a stiff product. We don't want white soup." Grandma knew, as I did, that corn syrup had its own scientific properties and helped create candy. "Let's add more egg whites to the last stage instead of corn syrup and see how that turns out. I've always used corn syrup for divinity at Christmastime, so this is new to me, too."

"I'll go lighter on the sugar so it doesn't weigh down the whites. We can work on beating it enough to work the air amid the sugar crystals."

We let the sugar and water boil longer than called for in the recipe, though I wanted to be careful I didn't turn the sugar brown with caramelizing.

Soon, my thermometer showed we'd reached a light crack stage at two hundred sixty-five degrees Fahrenheit. Grandma used an electric beater to create a fluffy cloud of the egg whites. I drizzled the hot sugar over the whites, with Grandma beating nonstop. Then I added the almonds, along with a touch of lemon extract.

We poured the frothy white mixture into a buttered pan. Then we stared at it.

"It looks a little soupy to me," I said. "I'm not sure this is going to set up. Corn syrup has a different scientific principle in its makeup. We're missing that element."

Grandma was wiping her hands on a towel, mostly to think. "Do you have any marshmallows?"

The word made me think of Mercy Fogg's evil meat loaf that Dillon's dog had scarfed up, to an unpleasant ending.

Grandma said, "Didn't you tell me that marshmallows were invented back in Sister Adele's time?"

"Maybe even in the time of the ancient Egyptians with those marsh plants."

"Well, then, this is authentic with marshmallows. Let's pretend the immigrants from Belgium got them from France and brought some on the boat. Maybe they roasted them over fires on deck."

She was so earnest that I laughed heartily. "I like your style, Grandma."

We melted marshmallows enough to fluff them up and

add them to the mix in a bowl. We poured the mixture again into the pan.

"Looks stiffer," Grandma said. "Give it time."

It looked like a mess to me. "It'll be cool by morning. We can make frosting out of it if it doesn't set up."

"I'll whip up cinnamon rolls in the morning. We'll use it on them. Now let's go home. I need to get to bed early. Got a big to-do tomorrow."

"Oh? What's that, Grandma?"

"For some gol-darn reason your boyfriend's mother wants to treat all the Namur church workers to a breakfast at Al Johnson's."

She was referring to Al Johnson's Swedish Restaurant in Sister Bay. It was near Laura's bakery and cooking school, the Luscious Ladle. The food at the restaurant was divine, including Swedish pancakes topped with Swedish lingonberries, and with butter from my parents' cows, plus Al's homemade syrups. The green grass roof sported a couple of grazing goats, too, always a draw for tourists and their kids.

"That sounds like a wonderful thing, Grandma." I wanted to work up to asking her about going to Chicago and finding ghosts. "You could use a minivacation. You've been working hard lately."

We began cleaning up the kitchen.

"I wouldn't be going, but your mother said she'd be along. I figure she can protect me from Cathy Rivers. She's acting like your mother-in-law already and I feel that's premature. Sam thinks so, too." Grandma slapped a cupboard door extra hard.

She still hadn't forgiven Dillon for his role in my jilting Sam Peterson eight years ago.

I asked, "What does Sam say?"

"He hasn't said anything. I can see the words in his eyes."

"Does he have a PowerPoint presentation about me in his eyes?"

"Bah." She waved me off with a hand as she tidied my kitchen counter.

I was sloshing the beaters in soapy water. "You worked hard on the churchyard. Why not accept this with grace and enjoy the free food?"

"Instead of partying, we should be cleaning the inside of that church. When is that sheriff ever going to take down that tape?"

"That's up to him." I took a deep breath and dove off a cliff. "Grandma, do we have any relatives in Chicago?"

"If we do, I don't know about them."

She slammed another cupboard door. I'd have to take a screwdriver to all my hinges tomorrow.

She gave me one of her long Belgian hugs. "Good night, Ava honey."

She left via the back door. Through the screen, I watched her go. She walked with a slight limp into the dark night. Her image merged into the brackish shadows as she passed under the maple trees by my cabin. Then her silhouette picked up the light coming from outside her house across Duck Marsh Street. Once I could see that she was safely inside her door, I turned back to finish cleaning up.

I hadn't found out anything, but I had high hopes of her eventually confessing this secret about the ghost in her family to me. It might take making several batches of fudge together, but that was something I could easily commit to.

I didn't have high hopes for the divinity fudge. Somehow it looked uncomfortable in its pan. The marshmallows were likely mocking me after I'd dissed them.

After locking up, I walked across my lawn, enjoying the peace of Fishers' Harbor at night. A wet Lucky Harbor caught up to me, poking his nose into my dangling fingers to check for treats.

"Want some fudge?" I asked, already getting the fish-shaped crackers from a pocket. I tossed them ahead of me in the grass.

Crunching sounds followed.

Once inside my cabin, I turned on the light, and within a second Lucky Harbor was chasing Titus, the mouse that had adopted me. "No!" I yelled. "Sit!"

The gray-brown field mouse galloped fast toward the couch. But Lucky Harbor was bigger with longer legs and leaped in front of the mouse. It was a standoff. I knew who would win. One slap by the dog with his big paw and Titus would be in the hereafter.

"Lucky Harbor, sit or you get no fudge."

The curly brown hunting dog plopped his butt down about a yard short of the back of the couch. Titus sat frozen peering up at the spaniel.

Realizing I was forming a barrier for Titus's retreat, I walked around from the back of the mouse to grab the dog. As I did, Titus did an about-face and scurried to the kitchen, disappearing through the wedge in the uneven cupboard door under the sink.

I sighed in relief.

When I called Dillon about his dog, he asked me to keep him for the night, since he and Piers were playing pool and Piers was up five dollars over Dillon.

That unsettled me. Gambling had gotten Dillon into trouble years ago. "Don't both of you have to work tomorrow? At the Blue Heron Inn?"

"Don't worry. Piers said he'd help. And Al Kvalheim is available."

Al had been around forever and was expert at the sewer pipes under our streets but not much else, as far as I knew. I was feeling growly. "I was arrested today."

"That's nice, Ava. Guess where Piers is going to put his muffin shop?"

I stared at my phone. Dillon wasn't listening to me. Noise in the background indicated the guys wanted him back to the pool table. "In the bookstore?"

"Nope. But I heard Jane Goodland is coming again tomorrow."

I heard a bunch of hoots at the mention of the woman's name. Could it be that she was the exotic dancer I'd seen on the Internet? "This doesn't seem right to see our bookstore become . . ." A stripper's place? That'd be one way for an independent bookstore to increase business. "Where's Piers putting down his stakes?"

"In the old mansion my mother's fixing up for the spa."

The faded yellow, rundown mansion was where Grandpa and Cody had almost met their maker last May.

Dillon rattled on. "She plans a nail spa, a massage spa, and a muffin spa on the first floor. I'll be helping Piers with the carpentry for his front counter. We haven't come up with a name yet."

We? Dillon sounded way more excited about this than the Blue Heron Inn. Jealousy acted like a torque wrench twisting me. Was I competing for Dillon's attention now with his mother? And with Piers? With gambling? Having a relationship with Dillon again was taking more emotional strength and work than I had expected.

We said good night as he got pulled back to the pool game.

Within minutes, I climbed into bed, my head spinning about fires, relationships, ghosts, the empty spot at our dock, and Grandpa's warning not to be alone at Ava's Autumn Harvest anymore. I felt saddened by it all, and oh so lonely. I had nobody to talk to about it all.

Lucky Harbor must have sensed the ache in my heart. He hopped onto the bed, then crept gently across the covers to come to me and sniff my face. He slurped my cheek, then went to the end of the bed, twirled in several circles near my feet, finally plunking down with a throaty dog groan.

Chapter 22

A loud rapping at my door woke me at seven on Thursday morning. I'd overslept by two hours. I panicked. I never overslept. The foggy gray autumn morning outside my bedroom window looked as sleepy as I was.

Pulling on a sweatshirt against the chill in the cabin, I headed to the door. Lucky Harbor padded behind me.

Before opening the front door, I peeked out the window next to it. A limousine longer than my cabin was wide was parked between my yellow truck on this side of the street and the other side of Duck Marsh Street in front of my grandparents' cabin. The limo's front end was pointed toward the marsh end of the street.

I opened the door to Mercy Fogg standing there in a sharp black uniform with a white shirt and tie. Her curly blond mop poked out from under a billed black cap.

Mercy said, "You're not dressed yet."

"Was I supposed to be dressed for something?"

With a thumb, she pointed behind her. "Aren't you going to breakfast with your mother and grandmother?"

I'd forgotten about the breakfast. "No, I wasn't invited. I believe it was for the church ladies that regularly take care of the Namur church."

"So you don't go to that church? What church do you go to?"

"Mercy, why do you need to know?"

"So I can avoid it." She laughed.

I was still half-asleep and couldn't throw a punch. She was safe. "Thanks for asking, but I'm not going with. I have to go to the fudge shop."

"No, you're not. I need you to move your truck."

"Why?"

"I can't turn around in this narrow street, and when I started backing up with the ladies, my back bumper scraped a tiny part of your truck. But it's tiny."

I woke up. "You scratched my truck? Are there dents?"

"Not yet, but there will be if you don't move your truck."

After grabbing my keys, I hurried out to pull my truck up onto my lawn. I had no driveway or garage. The limo was filled with chattering ladies. My mother was in back jabbering loudly about the fire at the Coppens place, the goats, and the fire at my roadside market.

Cathy Rivers poked her head out of a back window and winked at me. "We're having so much fun already, dear. Talk with you later."

She waved as Mercy backed up the long black limousine until it edged into the end of Main Street.

The front fender on the driver's side of my yellow truck had a strip of black paint about a foot long above the wheel well. I'd have to take it to the body shop and incur a bill that Mercy wouldn't pay.

Eager to see how the divinity fudge turned out, I changed into a pink, long-sleeved T-shirt, jeans, and heavy work shoes. I tossed on a zippered hoodie sweatshirt and headed to the shop. Lucky Harbor followed me until I told him to go to Dillon and pointed back toward the cliff where the Blue Heron Inn nestled above us. The dog took off in a furry brown streak.

I entered the fudge shop's galley kitchen, shedding my sweatshirt and pushing up my sleeves, ready for cutting fudge. It was gone.

I rushed to the front of the shop. No divinity fudge. But Grandpa was there. Had he sold my fudge?

My grandpa was busy with several fishermen, so to kill time I threw dry ingredients for a new batch of Belgian chocolate fudge into a copper kettle.

After the fishermen left, Grandpa began whistling. This

seemed odd; he usually talked or was swearing and grum-
bling about something.

"Gilpa, I had white fudge in the kitchen. Do you know
what happened to it?"

He came over to me with a piece of paper, flapping it in
front of my face. "See this?"

It was for a new Savage Bros. stove and kettles. "What's
this about, Gilpa?"

"Your equipment arrived for your new kitchen in the
Blue Heron Inn."

"What equipment? I thought I had everything."

"You ordered used equipment. But this is new."

I ripped the paper out of his hands. Indeed, it was a delivery slip for new equipment signed with today's date in
September by my grandfather.

"Gilpa, I thought we agreed to make do with used equipment?"

"I'm the only used equipment you have to deal with."
He was grinning. He liked mischief.

"But we can't afford this."

"I have it figured out."

I couldn't resist the twinkles in his eyes. That's the definition of love. "Just as long as you didn't rob a bank," I said.
I hugged him and gave him a big kiss on both cheeks. He
still smelled vaguely of smoke from last night.

Heading over to feed his minnows, he said, "Why don't
you get on up there and check out that stove? I sent the
fella up there to the inn in his big truck. Can't believe you
didn't hear him hauling ass in first gear up that steep hill."

"I was busy with Mercy. You see her in the limo?"

"Taking your grandmother to that breakfast thing. Exactly what she needs."

He didn't know it was a plot by Cathy Rivers and me to
soften up my grandmother. After tossing a towel over the
top of my copper kettle to protect the sugar and chocolate
pellets, I left.

I ran up the steep hill and was panting by the time I
charged through the grand entrance door of the Blue Heron
Inn.

The foyer and welcome hall sparkled, which shocked me.

There wasn't a speck of sawdust anywhere. The chandelier above me threw rainbow prisms into the air. The stairwell's powder blue carpeting had been vacuumed. The wood floors had been buffed. On a nearby accent table, the cup with AVD on it that had started all our troubles with Grandma but that had given birth to the upcoming visit by the royals sat in an honored spot under a glass dome.

I intended to head straight through the dining room for the kitchen but was stopped by a wondrous sight. On the table—covered with a white Belgian lace tablecloth that belonged to my mother—sat the twelve antique cups and saucers with their pink roses that my mother had been keeping at her house. The precious collection we'd been bequeathed by Grandpa's friend Lloyd Mueller looked as if it'd finally come home.

But what was going on with this overnight transformation of the inn?

My mouth was hanging open when a man I didn't know walked in from the foyer behind me, startling me.

He bowed slightly. *"Bonjour, mademoiselle."*

He was taller than me by a couple of inches, and had the most magnificent, wavy coppery hair perfectly clipped at the sides. His eyes were blue-gray, calm as our morning fog and mesmerizing, though they competed with a dazzling smile. A sky blue cashmere sweater over a blue pin-striped, collared shirt enhanced his perfection. He wore expensive slacks and shoes, the kind of which I'd only seen on Rodeo Drive in Los Angeles. Perhaps he'd stepped from a photograph? An advertisement? A dream? Maybe I was still asleep. I was tempted to slap my face.

Our awkward meeting was interrupted by the clomping feet of Dillon and Piers emerging through the kitchen door at the other end of the dining room.

In contrast to the man standing before me, they were smudged with dust and dirt, maybe a little oil, and wearing T-shirts with sports team logos. They had on holey and frayed work jeans.

Piers grunted, "We got the stove put in already. Savage Brothers is a good name."

Dillon loped over with a big grin as he spread his arms

apart. "How's it looking so far? Piers and I worked until midnight after we played pool. Then we headed to the airport for this guy. I see you've met."

"No," I said, "we hadn't gotten to names yet."

Dillon ran a hand through his shaggy hair. "I guess your grandfather didn't tell you what's going on."

Uh-oh. "He said he had a new stove delivered."

"But your grandpa didn't buy the equipment. This man bought the stove and copper kettle for you. As a gift for the Blue Heron Inn. You don't know who this is?"

"No."

Dillon bowed. "Let me present Prince Arnaud Van Damme."

Chapter 23

The prince was here? My "cousin" in Grandma's lineage? Prince Arnaud took my hand, bowed again, and then kissed the top of my hand. "*Enchanté.* I am pleased to meet you, Ava Oosterling. Your fudge is saintly. I can taste the holiness of Sister Adele Brise. Her fudge—your fudge, *mademoiselle*, is light as the wafer we receive during Communion."

Oh boy. No—*oh crap*. What was I going to do? Evidently, Grandpa had brought that batch of experimental fudge up here to the inn this morning early and told a big fat lie.

After a fevered, panicked glance at Dillon, I smiled for my relative. "I'm charmed to meet you, too." Did I just say "charmed"?

I took a deep breath, then got back to being me. I gave Prince Arnaud a big hug. "When did you get here? Why are you here early? Can I get you something?"

Prince Arnaud laughed again—a rich, melodious song from his throat. His perfection amazed me. He even had the Belgian nose with its slight hump in the middle of the ridge.

Dillon came to my rescue. "Your grandfather brought us the holy fudge this morning before he opened the shop."

Piers said, "We tried the fudge because we couldn't resist, but I set the table with the cups your mother dropped off a few minutes ago. I thought we could offer coffee after breakfast in them, then chocolate. Arnie says he likes some kind of chocolate drink at breakfast."

Arnie?

Prince Arnaud stepped to the head of the table. "It is very pretty. *Merci.*" Then he nodded at me. "I would love to see the recipe for the divinity fudge, the paper that Sister Adele touched. That is where my hunger lies—with knowing the past and connecting the Van Dammes to history, to connecting our two continents and countries, and our families. All accomplished with a confection recipe."

Sweat was trickling down my spine. "The recipe?" I said, stalling to give my brain time to think of some lie.

Dillon grimaced. The man was no help to me at all.

I said, "I, well, you see, to protect the recipe I put it in a bank vault and asked them to seal it until the kermis a week from Saturday."

The prince's face was like the sunrise breaking through clouds over Lake Michigan. "That is smart. You can show me where you found it today. I would enjoy a tour."

Piers stepped up. "Hey, guys, I'm starving. Why don't we head up to Sister Bay to Al Johnson's for pancakes? The prince will get a kick out of those goats."

Panic exploded inside me. "I'll make us breakfast here. We'll christen the new stove. Prince Arnaud, I'm so honored you're here and so thankful for your gift. Would my cooking on the new stove—your gift to me—be acceptable?"

"Of course. May I help?"

"No, thanks. Perhaps you'd like to go outside and look at the gazebo for a few minutes while I get things started. Dillon, can I speak to you in the kitchen about the menu?"

I marched ahead of Dillon into the kitchen.

Once the door was closed, I whispered, "We can't go to Al Johnson's, because Grandma is there with your mother supposedly talking about why she doesn't want the prince here on our soil. I assume Grandpa hasn't told her about Prince Arnaud's arrival. You picked him up this morning?"

Dillon took me in his arms. I wasn't in the mood for lovey-dovey stuff and wriggled, but he wouldn't let me go.

Dillon said, "Your grandfather told me this was the prince's idea. The prince called your grandfather a few days ago about arriving early so that he could experience life here without a mob of people following him and without the obligations of being a good son and escorting his mother and seeing to her comfort."

"A mob is going to follow him with the way he's dressed."

"Piers and I will fix that with a stop at the farm store."

"Where did he stay last night?"

"Here, in the suite. Piers and I settled him in, then cleaned up things until about three or so in the morning, then sacked out at my mother's condo."

"You and Piers are suddenly mighty chummy." I was jealous. I felt ugly even saying that and wanted to take it back.

Dillon kissed me soundly on the lips, with a little tongue action that tasted like marshmallows.

I said, "What am I going to do about the recipe? The prince thinks that fudge concoction Grandpa brought over here is the real deal. And boy, am I going to have to give Gilpa a talking-to!"

Dillon nuzzled my neck. My body was going limp. This was not going how I wanted the discussion to go.

Dillon said, "The only people who know it's not the real thing are you and me, and your grandpa."

"Wrong. My grandma, too. She helped me make it. Dillon, there are ordinary marshmallows in that stuff. Marshmallows," I repeated, trying to extricate myself from Dillon's arms.

He let me go. "We won't tell your grandmother anything. She doesn't have to know he's here."

I found Dillon's coffee beans in the refrigerator and silenced him by grinding for a few seconds. After tossing the coffeepot together and turning it on, I said, "But she's going to see this guy. Isn't he going to be at the shop and meet her sometime soon? This is awful because she was in a really good mood last night. Except when I brought up the ghost thing. Why is Grandpa so happy about this? This could blow up his marriage. He did this last July with his lies about not paying taxes like he should on the bait shop, and now this? Grandma's going to divorce him—"

Dillon kissed me again.

Then he began pulling pans from the hooks in the ceiling over the island he'd created for me. "Prince Arnaud wants to experience life here. Haven't you listened to me? The prince came early so that he could work as a farmhand for a few days on your family farm. He wants to explore life as it was experienced by the Belgian immigrants. Your grandfather plans to take him fishing, and he called Parker Balusek about some lumberjack he knows who can show him how wooden shingles are made by hand, just as your ancestors did after the Great Fire."

"Wait a minute. Do my father and mother know about this?" I reached under a counter cupboard for the flour tub. The menu in my head called for Belgian waffles.

"Your grandpa told me your father knows, but not your mother. Yet. She thinks you merely wanted the cups and saucers because the inn is nearly done. So she brought them with when Mercy picked her up in the limo."

"This isn't going to end well. I can feel it. Grandpa does this all the time. We were swimming along so smoothly, too."

"Very smoothly. Fires, a body you found in a basement, wrecking Pauline's car, Jordy wanting to arrest you—"

"Dillon, this isn't how I want a future husband to help me."

Dillon tugged my ponytail lovingly. "I'll keep doing that until you see the bright side to all this."

"What bright side? The prince thinks a mere marshmallow concoction is something from God, and I've got to figure out what to show him as the place where we found the recipe. And how in the heck am I going to find a divinity fudge recipe written on paper that can be authenticated as coming from the 1850s or 1860s? You know the Vassar College girls didn't even make it popular until the 1880s."

"Maybe check with Milton at the Wise Owl. Maybe he's got collections of old letters from that time. Maybe some of them contain recipes for divinity fudge. We can try to convince Arnie that Adele and her family would have shared in those recipes."

"Brilliant. None of the cookbooks from Lloyd go back to the 1800s. They all start after 1900."

"You called me brilliant." Dillon dipped me into a kiss that held promises for later. His arms were strong and reassuring, holding me snugly against his muscular chest.

After we popped up, I asked, "Is Jane Goodland a stripper?"

"Huh?"

"Don't 'huh' me. I've heard the rumors that she's good-looking. And I looked up the name Jane Goodland online. There's a convict and an exotic dancer. Milton said the lady was a lawyer. Somebody who's been in prison can't be a lawyer, so our new tenant in Milt's building has to be the stripper."

Dillon was quiet for too long, fussing around with pouring cream into a small pitcher.

I said, "So, is Jane Goodland the lawyer also Jane the stripper?"

"That may have been something she did years ago. I saw the pictures, too. All the guys have. Erik helped recruit her." He referred to Erik Gustafson, who bartended at the Troubled Trout bar and was our village president, too. "You should be glad he's making sure the Main Street buildings stay full of tenants. And you shouldn't hold her looks against her. And she has a dog."

"Sheesh. Because she has a dog makes Jane the stripper all right?" I shook my head, trying to clear it. "Too early for this discussion. I'll ask her myself when I meet her." Beating the waffle batter, I said, "What does the prince want for breakfast? Besides hot chocolate? And Belgian waffles?"

"He definitely wants to try American bacon. He said in his castle they don't eat much meat and he'd heard that our bacon was pretty good. And of course he'd like to enjoy more of your fudge."

"Now, there's a breakfast menu. Fudge and bacon. Piers tried to make that bacon fudge last July. I suppose I should ask him to make the bacon."

The kitchen became a communal event with Piers and "Arnie" joining Dillon and me. An odd joy set in, a joy I hadn't ever experienced, not having any siblings or relatives here my own age.

We talked nonstop. Arnie loved his nickname. He lived in a small castle in the countryside of Belgium near a stream where he fly-fished. He told us about riding show horses and owning foxhounds. Arnie was eager to flush birds with Lucky Harbor.

He'd played soccer for a short time on Belgium's national team, which made us all awestruck.

He worked now as a fund-raiser for several charity organizations, including the museum that wanted to bring home Sister Adele's handwritten recipe. The deal was they'd get it for two years, and then it would journey back to us. Prince Arnaud and his mother, Amandine, would leave the precious cup with AVD on it for us to display; plus, they'd contribute other royal items to display at fund-raisers. Arnie said he'd travel back here again next summer for Belgian National Day in July. His good looks and friendly manner would easily get people to pull out their wallets.

I asked, "Do you really think the cup our friend John found is authentic?"

"It appears so, but then I'm just a prince." We laughed. "My mother is an expert on the chinaware handed down in our family."

Seated minutes later in the dining room, we enjoyed eggs sunny-side up per the prince's wishes and waffles with whipped cream and Door County cherries on top, and of course plenty of thick-cut bacon. I made a rich cocoa with Belgian chocolate melted in it, which we enjoyed in the beautiful antique cups at the insistence of the prince. He wanted to experience everything full tilt. I began to feel a kindred spirit with him.

We were finishing up our cocoa at around nine o'clock when John Schultz and Marc Hayward knocked on the door of the inn. They walked in with a camera and lights. My heart fell into my stomach. Had Grandpa told them about our visitor?

But I relaxed soon enough when John made it known they were here to ask permission to film in the shop again today. At first he didn't even notice the prince seated with us.

Marc, a bit bleary-eyed, said, "I'm amazed at how many people are at the harbor already. People around here really do get up early."

"With the birds, Marc," I said.

Los Angeles was a ten o'clock town for the TV series

industry, and sometimes people didn't stir until the afternoon because they worked writing their shows and rehearsing with the actors until midnight.

John, who was standing in the foyer, said, "Hey, that's the cup I brought up from the bottom of the lake, isn't it?"

"Yeah," I said. "And these are the cups from Lloyd's collection."

John took a little video. Then he noticed Prince Arnaud. He reached out a hand as the prince stood up.

I rushed over. "This is, uh, Arnie . . . Malle."

My manager said, "Like Louis Malle? The director? You related?"

Prince Arnaud laughed his beautiful laugh, then said in his slight accent, "I belong to another family."

Dillon said, "He's here on business. Just passing through, getting directions to the Oosterling farm. He'll be there a few days, uh . . ."

I said, "Doing a farm diary for a French magazine. They like butter and cream over there, too."

It all sounded inane at first, but Marc and John bought it when I added, "The French like to follow the comings and goings of royalty. Arnie will be here through the kermis."

John said, "Then we'll cross paths a lot as we both get our stories for the media."

Marc said as he was turning to leave, "Say, why don't we all meet on Saturday at the scene of the crime, since that's so close to the farm?"

Prince Arnaud said, "There's been a crime?"

"You betcha," John said, his voice rising. "A murder. Ava found the body. It was a guy that was studying the cherries and orchards out by her parents' farm. I got myself clocked on the head by somebody in that church, too. You should take some notes for your magazine. This is a big story."

"*Oui*, of course, *merci*," Arnaud said.

My insides were going topsy-turvy. I was embarrassed by the crimes that had occurred recently. Door County never had much crime at all . . . until I returned.

I said to Marc, "Better yet, we've been meaning to help clean up the garden at the Dahlgren place. Let's meet there on Saturday afternoon."

"Deal," Marc said. "You wouldn't mind if I took a few pictures? There's a cinematic quality here that I'd like to show a few people back home."

I groaned inwardly, though a part of me felt proud that he'd noticed how beautiful it was here in this part of the country.

John said, "We'll shoot video earlier at your roadside market, Ava. Saturdays are busy for you, so it'll make great color. You won't mind if I interview a few customers?"

"Sounds peachy," I said, concerned.

The duo left. I breathed in deeply to settle the dread already seeded and sprouting in my head.

While Dillon and "Arnie Malle" went to a farm store for suitable farm duds, Piers hurried to the old mansion for a look and to wait to talk with Dillon's mother, Cathy, about his muffin shop deal.

I went back down the hill to my shop to grill my grandfather.

Chapter 24

Grandpa Gil was in high spirits. He was always that way when he hatched some plan like the one involving Prince Arnaud. I didn't believe for a minute that it was the prince's idea to arrive early in Door County and work on the farm.

Grandpa winked at me. "Did he like the divinity fudge?"

"It's not real divinity, Grandpa." I gave him the gist of how it was made last night. "Why did you tell the prince that was the recipe? You know this lie is going to come back and bite you. Your lies always turn into disasters for us."

He gave me such a hurt look that I wanted to shrivel up and disappear under a copper kettle.

Grandpa said, "This lie is going to solve everything."

"Solve a murder case? A ghost in our family? Mere fudge can't do all that, Gilpa."

"Oh, honey, don't you ever lose faith in what you do or your fudge. I'm proud of you."

While my heart melted like Belgian chocolate in my kettles, I had to do something to help Grandpa. He had too much time on his hands and that was why he hatched crazy ideas. I went over to help him load a shelf with bobbers in DayGlo orange and yellow.

Grandpa said, "The prince will get to like it here, and even if he finds out we snookered him with that recipe, he won't care. He's a pretty darn handsome guy, don't you think?"

"Don't you go matchmaking, too. Grandma still wants me to marry Sam."

"I'm partial to tall Parker Balusek. I'd have basketball players for great-grandkids. But the prince has a castle and fly-fishes. I'd like to go over there and try that a time or two."

"I have Dillon and that's enough for me for now. And besides, Arnie is my relative."

Grandpa chortled. "He's so far back on the family tree he's but a tiny twig. He's fair game. Did he kiss your hand?"

"Yes. How did you know?"

"Because he's a prince and you deserve to be treated like a princess." Grandpa put down the packages of bobbers he was holding to settle his hands on my shoulders. "That's all I want for you in life, Ava Mathilde. I want you to be loved and respected by a man for being you."

"You do that for me, for sure, Gilpa." I put down the box of bobbers I was holding for him and gave him a hug.

"You're a good kid."

"Only the best for you, Gilpa."

He laughed.

The shop soon became crowded as the early weekenders started pouring in for their fishing equipment, fudge, and souvenirs. Cody showed.

"Hey, Miss Oosterling! I learned how to give shots last night. Part of my EMT and firefighter training class. Want to watch me give a piece of your fudge a shot?"

Customers giggled.

"So you think my fudge needs saving?" I was giving out free samples at my glass case area.

"Nope. Could I take a batch to my next meeting?"

"Not if you're going to mutilate it with needles."

Cody guffawed. "Heck no. It's to eat. The guys bring treats. I don't know how to make anything but fudge. Bethany knows how to make lots of stuff, but she's just my girlfriend. Maybe after we're married she'll make stuff for me."

That made me pause. My grandfather peeked over at me with hiked eyebrows from across the shop.

I said to Cody, "Have you proposed to Bethany?"

Customers plastered on sly smiles and went quiet.

"No. I have to take these things slow, Miss Oosterling. Dillon told me that."

"He did?" I almost guffawed at Grandpa's face scrunching up.

"Dillon said special women are worth waiting for."

I was starting to swell with pride at what I was hearing about Dillon.

Then Cody said, "I figure I could save the proposal for the kermis when the prince is here. It'll be like a fairy-tale ball. Bethany looks like Cinderella, don't you think?"

"Yeah, she does." Bethany Bjorklund was a blond former cheerleader. "But maybe you should propose in a more private moment. At least consider it."

Cody was blossoming with Sam's and Dillon's advice, but he also had a mind of his own. Bethany was wise at eighteen, but I was beginning to feel anxious about the prince's visit. I wondered if other men planned to use the Cinderella atmosphere for a proposal.

Several customers remarked they'd be returning to Door County for the festivities a week from this coming Saturday. They bought more items than the usual. The shop became a musical concert with register dings and the cowbell clanking on the door.

Around eleven that Thursday morning, I loaded up fudge, Lucky Harbor, and Prince Arnaud in my truck. He was dressed in blue jeans, work boots, and a gray sweatshirt with a Green Bay Packers logo.

"You're official now," I said to Arnie.

My heartbeat still sputtered in the presence of royalty. It felt unreal to think he lived in a castle. I liked that he had eaten my waffles and drunk authentic Belgian thick cocoa from tiny Limoges cups.

We headed south through the county. Our agenda included stopping by my roadside market, then the farm, and then I'd show him the shrine and resting place of Adele Brise in Champion. For now, I'd do what I could to avoid stopping at the scene of Cherry's final day. We'd drive by, of course, but I wouldn't stop.

A squad car was on my tail the whole way as soon as we passed through Sturgeon Bay.

"Our sheriff doesn't know about you; they're following me. To protect me."

Prince Arnaud said, "Do not worry. I will not tell my mother about the murder or your police needing to follow you. Amandine would cancel her trip. For me, I find this exhilarating. My life is boring compared with yours. I enjoy being called Arnie."

Again I sensed a kindred spirit. I ventured, "What would you think about stopping at a local winery first, Arnie?"

"*S'il vous plait*, show me anything you wish. I'm eager to understand the land where my relatives found their joy in life, *joie de vivre*."

The Prevost parking lot was full, perfect for my plan. At this time of day, near lunchtime, I knew it'd be crowded, a good cover for sneaking around. I let Lucky Harbor out of the truck. He shot to the back of the stone winery.

Arnie went inside like any other customer while I excused myself to allegedly watch the dog.

I hustled to the back of the building. Lucky Harbor was sniffing the ground around a massive old freezer chest, the kind used to store extra bags of ice in summer and fish caught in the lake. It stood about hip high and was about five feet wide and three feet across front to back.

Lucky Harbor kept snapping his head to me and then back to the ground as he circled. He sniffed the freezer chest several times. The way the dog kept appealing to me made goose bumps down my arms ripple in place.

A voice said, "Is there something wrong?"

I jumped. It was Arnaud. "No, Arnie. Just watching the dog."

"He's intrigued by the appliance."

"Yeah. I'd like a look inside. But it's locked. A crowbar would help."

"Perhaps that is not wise."

I chuckled. "You don't know me. This is the kind of thing I do."

"But the car following us has arrived."

He meant the squad car with Maria Vasquez. We walked

up the sidewalk along the building. I implored Arnaud to duck into the shop to buy a bottle of wine.

On the sidewalk, Maria growled out, "What now?"

"Deputy Vasquez, hi. Here to taste a little wine? Aren't you on duty?"

Maria's big brown eyes gave me a weary stare.

I pointed behind me. "The dog knows that there's something in the freezer chest behind the winery."

"Like ice?"

"Maybe. Whatever it is, Lucky Harbor thinks I should open the chest."

Maria walked the few yards back to the corner of the building with me in tow to peek. Lucky Harbor was still snuffling about.

Maria said, "So?"

"So do something. What if there's a body in there?"

I meant it as a joke, but Maria sighed dramatically. "With you, I realize there might really be a body in there, but—"

"Let's open it."

"Please, Ava, I need a warrant for such a thing and you also can't go around thinking the worst about your neighbors. Besides, whose body would it be? There's been nobody reported missing."

"All right, it's not a body. But there's something in there the dog doesn't like."

"Or it's something he does like. Michael Prevost might have steaks stored in there. Now get a move on before Prevost finds you and this dog and complains. Where are you headed next?"

"Ava's Autumn Harvest and then my parents' farm. Why?"

"Do you think you can get there without getting into more trouble? I'd like to head back up to Sturgeon Bay to my office. Alone. Without you in handcuffs."

"I don't look good in cuffs anyway. They don't match my outfit."

She managed a smile as she turned to head back to her squad car.

I gathered the dog and prince and we headed to my market down around the corner of Highway 57 and County Trunk C.

The mystery of the freezer bothered me like something in a tooth you can't get out. A couple of times I flicked a glance in my rearview mirror and Lucky Harbor was giving me a stone-cold stare that said everything.

Ava's Autumn Harvest was packed. A thrill shot through me. I could already hear the pleasant ding of the cash register in my head. I had to park six cars down the road. Lucky Harbor tried to do circles in his excitement in the backseat, but I told him he had to stay in the truck this time.

"Word is out that a prince is coming," I said to Prince Arnaud, nodding to the unusual crowd on the rural road as we got out.

"I am—he is—good for your business. *Beaucoup*."

Very good indeed. But I needed to find a lot more help for me and my poor mother. She looked frazzled. Her lovely dark hair was tied back with a red bandanna that was coming undone from its knot at the nape of her neck.

Prince Arnaud played his role of a visiting journalist. My stomach was churning as I introduced him in front of other people and my mother as Mr. Malle. I couldn't even say "Arnie" for fear my mother would think of "Arnaud" and then screech and spoil his wish to be incognito. He took photos of the flatbed wagons loaded down with bags of cheese curds, apples, pumpkins, and several flavors of my fudge. Nobody took a second look at the tall man in the jeans and Green Bay Packers sweatshirt.

When my mother broke from the crowd at the wagons to head off to the stone barn to cash out a customer, I followed her to ask how she was doing.

She said, "That journalist is handsome, don't you think?"

"Very, but I have Dillon."

She grimaced. "Do I need lipstick? Will I look okay in the pictures?"

"You're beautiful. I need to show him the neighborhood. But I'll be back soon. Should I find more help? Maybe Dotty and Lois could help."

"I'll manage on my own. I've seen what they can do to the fudge shop."

We laughed.

Moments later, Arnaud and I were back in my yellow truck with Lucky Harbor.

I drove past our farm and went on to Namur to drive past Saint Mary of the Snows Church. Several cars were parked at it and on the road. Panic swept through me like a gale-force wind off the Lake Michigan bay. Tourists were wandering around the grounds of the church and school. License plates were from Illinois, Indiana, Iowa, and Wisconsin.

Several people were poking about among the headstones under the tree out front.

The crime scene tape was still over the doors, but one person was trying to boost another so he could see through a window of the church.

Arnaud and I got out of the truck so he could take a few shots of the exterior of the church and grounds. He said in referring to the guy in the window, "He is observing the area of the recipe, *non*?"

My body flushed hot. "May I keep it a surprise until the kermis?"

"*Oui, certainement*. I will enjoy the surprise along with my mother."

His response relieved me. I didn't want to reveal a fake place where I'd allegedly found the still-missing fudge recipe that he thought was now in a bank vault. My hands were sweating because of the compounded lies my grandfather and I were telling. Lucky Harbor woofed, which encouraged me to get us back in the truck. I did a U-turn on the rural road and then sped back eastward to the farm.

Arnaud loved our farmstead the moment his feet touched the gravel turnabout between our house and the barn and creamery. My father, Peter, gave the prince a big Belgian handshake that lasted through all the small talk about how he'd arrived and stayed overnight at the Blue Heron Inn and eaten the divinity fudge recipe. My father's eyebrows shot up, but he didn't pursue the issue. *Thanks, Dad.*

Peter escorted Arnaud through the creamery. Arnaud loved wearing the booties and hair net. My father explained how my mother made cheese, butter, and cream, and how next year my family would have cheese ready for the international competition held in Madison, the state capital. Arnaud kept swooning as Dad fed him a white cheddar cheese curd fresh from the vat.

"It squeaks," Arnaud said with glee.

When they got to the cream separator area, my dad promised to use some of the Holstein gold to make hand-cranked ice cream later that night for dessert.

As we walked from the creamery to the dairy barn and modern milking parlor, I felt proud of my father for all that he'd accomplished. Our farm had grown from a few dozen cows when I was young to two hundred highly prized Holsteins now, plus all the calves and special Belgian chickens who were sharing their pen still with Jonas Coppens's goats.

We also showed the prince Mom's big garden, and our small orchard of fruit trees and the berry patch.

Peter explained how we'd gone from a farm relying too much on chemicals to one that was pure organic. My dad mentioned the feud going on and the tragic murder of Cherry.

Arnaud said, "The kermis and introduction of Sister Adele Brise's fudge will have healing powers. Belgian chocolate brings a smile to people who need a smile. Ava will be at the center of bringing peace to a lovely land."

I blinked. So did my father. We were stunned by his eloquence. At first, his words seemed silly, but then I realized Dillon had told me something similar about how I needed to simplify my life. Making the best fudge in the world was good enough for my life. A pleasant new feeling, like a white dandelion blossom being set free on a breeze, stirred inside me.

My father led the prince to the haymow. The ground rose to provide tractor and wagon access to the haymow that was above the milking parlor. I loved the smell of new-mown and baled hay. It was a clean smell that made me take deep breaths.

My father introduced "Arnie Malle, the journalist" to

our hired hands—two college students from the Czech Republic—who had been helping put up the third and last crop of hay off our large alfalfa fields. To my surprise, Nick was there.

"Hey, Ava. Nice to meet you, Mr. Malle."

Nick explained he was taking hay samples back to his lab.

I asked, "You're not thinking there's something wrong with the third-crop hay?"

Nick shrugged, running a hand through his neatly cropped dark hair. "I doubt it, but this hay does come from the area close to the road and across from the Dahlgren and Coppens places where chemical usage is apparent."

"You can't mean to say that our hay isn't purely organic?" I was in shock.

Fortunately, my father had walked onward with Arnie to show him the baling operation.

Nick said, "Whatever my findings are, I'll let you know the results before I publish them."

"Publish?"

"Well, yeah. That's the whole point of a PhD thesis. We publish from our research."

"Cherry focused on the orchards. I thought that was your focus, too. You were testing my fudge."

"I'm testing the fudge in the lab for Cherry's grant. But my focus is on hay. I'm here today to hurry up on my hay research."

"Why the hurry?"

"Because Professor Weaver wants me to have something more going for me than the fudge research when Cherry's grant closes on October one. If I don't have significant research done on the hay, I might not have a chance at a grant for that."

It was all too much about grants for me to pay attention, but something about it all bothered me because it involved Cherry and my fudge in the test tubes. I hurried off to rejoin my father and Arnaud.

My father took the bales off a wagon that had come in from a field, then placed each bale on a conveyor belt with steel teeth on it. The bales traveled up the belt and into the barn, where they dropped atop an already high stack of bales. Arnie shed his Green Bay Packers sweatshirt to pitch in.

My gaze was riveted on the prince. He wore a black T-shirt underneath that hugged his broad shoulders. Somehow I hadn't expected him to be that buff. Dad found him a pair of leather work gloves, then pointed him up the ladder to help stack the bales into rows. I'd done that chore many times in the past. Though it was hard work, there was something satisfying about watching bales fall into place as neatly as big green dominoes. A farmer with a barn full of hay stored for the winter was considered successful.

I left them to the task, eager to call Pauline. It was her lunch hour at school back in Fishers' Harbor. I stood in the middle of our gravel circle at the farm, soaking up the crisp autumn air. The breeze tugged at my ponytail. Lucky Harbor was nosing around the chicken run watching the goats. My parents' border collie was watching over it all.

After Pauline said hello, I said, "Lucky Harbor and the prince and I found a freezer behind Mike's winery. It's locked and it's suspicious."

"The prince is here?"

"Yes. But he's a journalist now and not a prince. I'll explain later. When are you off school? We have to find out what's in that freezer."

"We're done at the ordinary time. Two thirty for the kindergartners."

"Great. I'm going to help Mom at the roadside market for a while. Meet me there."

"What makes you think I want to go snoop in a freezer?"

"Because Lucky Harbor smells something that isn't right."

"Maybe Fontana stored her perfume in there."

I hadn't thought about that. "I would have smelled that stuff myself. But maybe there are other chemicals in there. Or a body. We need to know."

"No, *you* need to know. I don't need to lose my job breaking into a freezer."

"Pauline, bring Mom's holy fudge buttons along and everything will be all right."

"No, it won't."

"Stop being stubborn, Pauline. You're my best friend."

"Why can't you collect something besides dead bodies and trouble? As hobbies go, this isn't a very good one."

"Do you want to meet the prince or not? And by the way, don't tell anybody he's here. He's incognito."

Pauline blew her disgust into the phone. "I'll see you at three o'clock."

Chapter 25

The prince was enthralled with the farm and wanted to go out on the tractor to watch the baling of the hay, so I left. I mentioned it was lunchtime. Arnie took one look at the Brakels and asked for fried egg sandwiches. My dad was thrilled; those were a favorite sandwich, made with sliced tomatoes and stone-ground mustard lathered on home-made oatmeal bread. I made those within minutes and handed their lunch up to them on the tractor.

Back in my truck with Lucky Harbor and heading toward my market, I was approaching Jonas's property when I noticed the roadside chapel was tilted. I stopped across the road. I snapped a leash on Lucky Harbor to make sure he stayed with me.

We crossed the road. The white wooden siding on the front of the tiny chapel was chipped and marred, as if a car had rammed into it. I spotted tracks in the grass. The ditch was shallow here, so a car or truck could easily have pulled over and nudged the small building. I didn't spot big marks in the grass, though, or rubber on the road to indicate some-body had hit the brakes.

Many yards down the road I could see cars still coming and going at Ava's Autumn Harvest. Perhaps a tourist had tried to do a U-turn in the road here and slipped into the chapel.

Lucky Harbor sniffed throughout the grass, then started scratching at the door of the chapel. The door was still locked, but the doorjamb was askew from the impact of whoever hit the building. With little pressure the jimmied lock popped. As I stepped inside, I dropped my jaw.

The chapel was filled with items from my fudge shop.

Dolls, purses, aprons, and Cinderella Pink soaps sat on the floor, the kneeling rail, and the altar. There were glass jars of the blueberry and raspberry jams that I sold for Dotty Klubertanz's son and daughter-in-law, who ran the mercantile store on Main Street in Fishers' Harbor.

Why was Jonas storing things out here? And why did he buy them? An odd, creepy feeling washed over me. I backed out of the chapel.

I drove up Jonas's driveway.

After I parked, and got out with Lucky Harbor, I found Jonas's place oddly quiet. The goats were still at my parents' farm in the chicken run, so there was no bleating. His small flock of sheep was north of the buildings in a pasture.

The wind rustled through the crimson-tinged leaves on a maple tree nearby. The air still smelled of the burned-down shed, now a pile of blackened rubble several yards from the house to the south.

Beyond the rubble, and beyond cornfield stubble and a hayfield, I recognized a stretch of new fencing. Thinking Jonas was working somewhere along the fence, I hiked down the gentle slope with Lucky Harbor.

Crows cawed off in the tops of trees. Nobody was around. I was sure the area used to have a gate to let Jonas's sheep through to Mike's vineyards that lay beyond the woods on the Prevost side. There were no gates now all up and down the fence line. I wondered which of the two men had done away with the gates. Their war had evidently escalated.

I went to the house intending to knock on the front door, but I paused when I heard women's voices. It was a radio talk show playing loudly. A commercial came on for vitamins. I couldn't help myself—I stepped over to the picture window near the front door to peek in.

Fontana—of all people—was in a pink, long-sleeved leotard and tights rolling around on an exercise ball.

I rapped on the window. Fontana fell off the ball, then popped up wide-eyed at me.

I raced back to the door. She yanked it open as I laid my hand on the knob. I almost fell into her lithe body encased in pink, stretchy fabric. Her red hair was in a knot on top of her head tied with a pink satin ribbon. She looked adorable—and sneaky.

"Jonas isn't home, Ava."

"Never mind him. What are you doing here?"

"Consoling Jonas."

"But you said he's not home." I peered behind her. "Where is he? Doesn't it take two to console?"

She hugged the edge of the door, blocking my entry. "He went to the lumberyard to get an estimate for building a new goat barn."

"That still doesn't answer my question. Why are you here?"

"Jonas Coppens is a friend."

"But how friendly?"

Fontana narrowed her eyes. "Don't be this way, Ava. Those frowny grooves aren't attractive."

"Don't you get it, Fontana, that it's easy to be suspicious of you? Don't you care that by your being here like this, people will think you killed Tristan Hardy so you could get rid of the only thing preventing you from getting what you want?"

She blinked in a way that told me I was onto something. But she straightened her spine and stood taller. "What do I want?"

"You want Daniel back and if you can't have him, you'll take the next best thing. Jonas. Or Michael. Both own a lot of land and have thriving businesses. You'd love to get your hands on that land so you can live next door to Daniel, even if it means killing somebody."

"You still think I killed Cherry?"

"Yes. Because his research was disturbing Daniel. And causing a rift between Jonas and Michael. What you obviously didn't know was that Cherry's research grant was up in a few weeks and I think he was about to be fired or demoted somehow."

Tears glistened in her eyes.

She started to close the door, but I stiff-armed it open

and walked in. She was shorter and skinnier than me. I could take her down if I had to.

The living room was immaculate but had her touches everywhere. There were fragrant soaps and flowers on every other surface in bowls and vases. I walked to the coffee table, picked up the remote, and turned off the radio that was telling me to buy a cream that would save me from going through painful eyelid surgery.

When I turned around, Fontana had flounced onto the sofa, her legs outstretched across the cushions, a pillow over her stomach and chest.

I grabbed a pillow from a nearby chair and threw it at her.

She caught it before it whopped her in the face. "What did you do that for?"

"To wake you up. This is not a game, Fontana. Cherry was murdered. Don't you care? You two were dating. You were with him that night. What the hell happened?"

Darn her, but her eyes puddled up big now.

"Stop that, Fontana. I know you're faking."

"I'm not. I wish I could be as strong as you, but I . . . can't get anything right in my life. I never have been able to get anything right."

I sat down in the chair opposite her. "What're you talking about? You always watched out for me in grade school. You were always perfect. You were the best cheerleader, the one with all the dates. You're artistic with your homegrown makeups and soaps and fragrances. And you're in darn good shape."

After a deep breath, I asked, "What really went on at the church last Saturday night?"

She swiped at her eyes, then hugged the pillow in front of her. "Cherry and I made love. It was the sweetest, most tender—"

"I don't need the details."

"But I thought you wanted to know what went on?"

She had me. I sighed. "Okay. Just go easy on the details."

"We made love in the back of his car."

"The blue Ford Fusion, right?"

"Yes."

"Where is it?"

"I don't know." She sniffled. "It disappeared. We were making love in the schoolhouse and after he left to get something from the car, he never came back." She grabbed for a tissue from a flowered box on the table next to the sofa.

"You made love in the car and at the old schoolhouse?"

"Almost. I know he's older than me, but he still has it. We didn't quite get to do it in the schoolhouse. He disappeared before that."

She talked about him in the present tense, as if he were still alive. As if she cared about him. But this could be an act. The schoolhouse intrigued me. I recalled the bedroom upstairs that had looked used when Pauline and I sneaked in to search the place for clues.

"So you went upstairs in the schoolhouse, but then he left. Then what?"

She covered her face with her hands as she cried.

Her actions didn't look fake. I swallowed my misgivings. Still, my head was warning me that Fontana was smart.

"Fontana, how long did you stay in that room? Did you hear anything?"

Fontana's face popped up from her hands. "A car. I thought he was moving the car closer to the schoolhouse. But then I waited. I heard a car again. Then a car passing by on the road. I think I fell asleep then. I only had one tiny drink, but I couldn't believe how tired I was."

"Maybe Cherry slipped something into your drink. Do you know what time you heard the cars?"

"It had to be around midnight or later."

The timing fit with everything else I knew about the case, but I knew people estimated time and could be off by a lot. "So, after you woke up, then what did you do?"

"I got dressed. I was wearing a really nice black silk sheath dress I'd found in Sister Bay—"

"Fontana, please. You got up, got dressed, went outside, right?"

"Sure. It was beautiful out. All the stars. But deadly quiet." She shuddered. "The moon was shining down on all those gravestones by the church. It spooked me out because Cherry was gone. The car was gone. He'd . . . left me."

She began to cry again, but I couldn't take it. "Enough with the tears. You've been bedding Michael and Jonas within days of your lover being killed. You can't be all that sorry he's gone."

After tossing the pillow aside, she launched off the sofa and headed to the kitchen. I followed. She poured a glass of milk but didn't offer me anything.

"I am sorry he's gone. I thought I might have a future with Cherry." She leaned her backside against the sink.

Sliding into a chair at the kitchen table, I watched her down the entire glass of milk. Her hand shook. Was she covering up for helping to kill a man? Or telling the truth? I didn't know.

I tried a different tack. I reminded Fontana that she had always helped protect me from bullies as a kid. Boys and girls had teased me mercilessly for being tall for my grade. They had called me Bean Pole and Giraffe.

Remembering registered a smile on her face as she put her glass on the counter. "If only we could all go back to a life that wasn't so complicated, right? I'd give anything to only be dealing with bullies right now."

It was about the most profound thing she'd said in a long while, which confounded me. "Did you tell the sheriff the things we've been talking about?"

"Yeah."

"How did you get home that night?"

"I walked."

She lived along Highway 57 not far from her roadside market. Getting there was only about three miles or so south from Namur on County Trunk Roads DK and Y. Still, at night, that would be a long, scary walk.

"Did anybody see you?"

"No cars passed me."

"And you told the sheriff all this?" I had to be sure.

"Yeah."

I suspected the sheriff doubted her story. I had my doubts, too. Everything she'd told me was dramatic and interesting, but it painted her as the poor waif abandoned by her man and knowing nothing about his dead body lying in the basement of Saint Mary of the Snows. She'd said before how much she hated basements. But seeing a dead man in one could spook a person enough to make her run down a country road.

I still had two big questions. "Why is there a bunch of stuff from my fudge shop in the chapel by the road? And who hit the chapel?"

She sprang away from the sink. "There's what in there?"

"Cinderella Pink dolls, purses, soaps. Why?"

"I don't know why. But I know who hit the chapel."

"Who?"

"Mercy Fogg in her limo. That woman was here earlier."

"Dropping off my mother after breakfast."

"No, I mean she stopped here at Jonas's and told him to give himself up. When he told her to leave, she did, but she fishtailed the limo out of his driveway, just missing his mailbox. Then she drove right into the shoulder of the road and pushed at the chapel as if the limo were a bulldozer. That woman is crazy."

After I left Fontana, it felt normal yet disconcerting to do something as simple as help my mother sell fudge to tourists.

I buried myself in the joy of talking about how I made my fudge. I gave away coupons to encourage visits to Fishers' Harbor and Oosterlings' Live Bait, Bobbers & Belgian Fudge & Beer.

A few people asked about the scorched ground nearby, but we shrugged it off to a grass fire caused by a cigarette being tossed out a window.

When Pauline arrived, I told her about the chapel. She had to see everything herself.

At the chapel alongside the road, Pauline peeked in, then said, "You didn't tell me about the voodoo doll."

"Voodoo?"

From the altar she picked up a doll with brown yarn hair and a frilly pink yarn dress made by Dotty Klubertanz. A hat pin was stuck through the doll's head.

I shuddered. "I didn't notice that before."

"How does your head feel?"

"Not like it's got a pin through it."

"Somebody's mad at you."

"At me? Why?"

"Because you've been snooping around your neighbors' places trying to find evidence that one of them is a murderer. If you were doing that to me, I'd probably have a doll I'd be poking pins in."

"Thanks a lot, Pauline."

"Hey, we teachers take psychology in college."

"This has to be Mercy's idea of a joke. She hit the chapel after putting this stuff inside knowing that eventually I'd check it out."

I called Jordy. He said that until Jonas called him about the damage he wouldn't stop by.

"What about the doll with the pin in its head? And the fire? Somebody is threatening me, Jordy."

"That's merely a doll with a pin in its head. Maybe it was wearing a hat and the hat fell off. I don't have time to chase down there to look at a pin in a pink doll."

I mentioned that Cherry and Fontana allegedly had a tryst in the old schoolhouse. Jordy asked if I thought Fontana had made that up. I told him the truth: She might have. She was a totally unreliable witness. But I told him Pauline and I had found the disturbance in the bedroom dust.

Pauline and I then drove in my pickup to the Prevost Winery, with Lucky Harbor in the back. My mother and I had prepared a list of wines we wanted to sell at the market. I'd use that as my cover, in case Mike asked what Pauline and I were doing wandering around his place. Lucky Harbor was in the backseat, panting, eager to be on a mission with his nose. I popped him a few crackers as we drove along the highway.

Pauline said, "Lucky Harbor is like a drug addict and you feed his habit. You're an enabler."

"One of my best qualities."

"There is no way you could be a teacher. You'd be a bad influence on every child. You don't have restraint. You lie, poke your nose in other people's business, and enable lawbreakers. No restraint is your flaw."

"I thought not knowing how to trust myself to be happy was my flaw. That's what you told me months ago."

"The lack of trust has to do with Dillon. You're working

on that, though I don't think you should trust him completely yet."

"Why not?" I thought she could see that Dillon and I were making a go of things.

Pauline said, "You're proving my point. You lack restraint. You broke your Wednesday rule for sex already. You now get sex whenever you want it."

"This sounds like you and John haven't been having sex lately."

She shook her big purse on her lap and growled. "He and Marc have a schedule that certainly doesn't include me. They're crisscrossing Door County like madmen, and John's taking Marc out on a boat to fish today. Then they're going to tape cooking the fish later at some restaurant. I asked John where I was on the schedule and he actually looked at the schedule trying to find a minute for me."

I laughed, then realized my mistake. She was right—I had no restraint. "I'm sorry, P.M. John cares about you. Trust me on that."

I ached to divulge John's planned surprise about singing at the kermis but kept my lips zipped shut. Restraint, restraint.

It was going on four o'clock when we pulled into the winery parking lot, prime time for tourists driving up from Chicago to stop for bottles of wine before they headed north to Fishers' Harbor and Sister Bay.

Assuming Michael was inside, Pauline and I headed for the back of the building and the freezer with Lucky Harbor.

"Help me find something to break the lock."

Pauline asked, "Why didn't you steal the key? You're slipping."

"I can't walk up to Mike and ask him for the key to break into his freezer." I grabbed her purse and then crouched down on the ground with it.

Pauline hissed, "Give that back."

I came up with a screwdriver. "You were holding out on me, P.M. You saved me a trip back to the truck."

The lock was small. I stuffed the screwdriver through the eyehole loop, then shoved it at an angle with all my might. It didn't give.

"Now what?" I asked myself mostly.

"We get out of here. You have no restraint at all. Stop this."

Lucky Harbor was whining as he sniffed about the bottom of the freezer. No way was I leaving now.

"Push with me, Pauline. We played basketball in college. You can't tell me that at thirty-two we've lost all our strength already."

She put her hands over mine on the screwdriver. "Grab, grip, grumble, grunt."

"Today was a G day?"

"Yup. We used the goat cam online to visit the goats on Al's restaurant roof in Sister Bay."

After a gargantuan heave, we popped the lock.

"Make sure nobody heard us," I said to Pauline, pointing toward the corner of the building.

She trotted over, then peeked. "All clear." She stayed put, clinging to her purse.

"Chicken," I said.

"If you're going to reveal a human head or something, I don't want to see it. I'll never get it out of my head."

I lifted the heavy, white-enameled steel lid, pushing it back so it'd stay open.

I blinked several times at what I saw.

Lucky Harbor stood on his hind legs, his front paws on the edge of the opened freezer, eager to get a gander.

I turned to Pauline. "We better get the sheriff."

Chapter 26

I called nine-one-one. Pauline backed right into Deputy Maria Vasquez, who rushed around the corner of the winery. Pauline yelped.

With my phone still in my hand, I asked Maria, "How'd you get here that fast?"

"I've been tailing you in an unmarked car. Sheriff's orders."

"When did he give this order?"

"Saturday. When you called in the body."

Pauline said, "Thank goodness. She has no restraint, you know. She's trying to get herself killed."

Ignoring Pauline, I directed Maria's gaze to the freezer chest. "Getting killed could happen with all this stuff. Or start fires with it."

Maria whistled. "Enough stuff to blow up all of Sturgeon Bay." She called Sheriff Tollefson.

The freezer was filled with chemicals in big bottles and canisters, mostly plastic. If the dog had smelled the chemicals, perhaps there were leaks in the bottom of some of the material. I was surprised fumes hadn't made it all blow up already.

Maria said, "Did you touch any of this stuff?"

"No," Pauline and I said in unison.

Pauline asked, "Are you going to arrest Mike Prevost?"

"Right now we just want to know if he owns the material or not. No law against owning this material."

But it looked mighty suspicious to me, considering how

much fuss Mike had made about not allowing chemicals on his land. Maria made a note of every label. There were pesticides, herbicides, fungicides. Bugs, plants, and molds didn't stand a chance.

Maria made us stay put until Jordy arrived in about twenty minutes.

He stalked right up to me. "Now what have you gotten into? Another doll?"

Lucky Harbor sniffed his shoes and pants. His shoes were covered with mud and what looked like dung of some sort. Jordy grimaced. "I was fishing through a pile of manure behind the Dahlgren garden shed."

That information put me on alert. "What were you doing there?" I tossed crackers off in the nearby grass to distract Lucky Harbor.

"Inspecting it again before they arrive tomorrow or whenever."

"The Dahlgrens are out of jail?"

"Released last night on bail. They put their property up as collateral."

"Why didn't they come home immediately?"

"Their lawyer advised them to lie low. He got them a motel room."

"Where?"

"Telling you where they are would defeat the purpose of them getting a secret motel room."

Maria filled in the sheriff on the chest's contents.

The sheriff asked me, "Did you see somebody put these things in here?"

"No, but Lucky Harbor was sniffing around here on Tuesday afternoon when I was here. Somebody might have spilled some of this."

Jordy let his gaze travel the ground. "The grass would show spots if something spilled, but I don't see anything. Probably a leak in the bottom of this thing. Did you talk with Prevost?"

"No. You told me to stay out of your business. Dillon said the same thing."

Pauline said, "She's working on a new skill—restraint. Could we go?"

The sheriff said, "Not yet. Maria, could you go inside and ask Mr. Prevost to come out here? Thanks."

Pauline's bug-eyed look told me she was trying to signal me about something.

When Mike came around the corner with Maria, his round head flushed at the sight of all of us and the opened freezer chest. I couldn't tell if his reaction was innocent surprise or panic because he was guilty. He said he didn't know anything about the chemicals.

Jordy asked, "When was the last time you opened this chest?"

"Months ago maybe. The freezer unit isn't working right anymore. I haven't had a chance to haul this to the recycle center."

I picked up the broken lock from the ground. "Is this yours?"

"Yeah, but I didn't put it on there. Try Jonas Coppens. The punk is determined to ruin me."

I said, "He'd have no reason to bring his chemicals over here. But I did see that you closed off the gate in the fence between you two. Why?"

"Because of Daniel Dahlgren."

Jordy shifted his stance on that name. "What about Dahlgren?"

Mike seemed to shrink by several inches. "My land abuts the Dahlgren property to the west. We've been friends for a long time." His face wrinkled, as if he were in pain.

Jordy scowled at him. "Well?"

"It's personal."

Maria was taking notes.

Mike was sweating. I felt sorry for my former math teacher.

He said on a rush of expelled breath, "I had an affair with Fontana when she was married to Daniel. I love her."

His bedding Fontana came as a surprise. While she had never dated two men at the same time, she couldn't bear to be alone. She moved from one man to the next as easily and swiftly, in my opinion, as water moves downstream. Fontana having an affair meant she must have been at a very low point in her marriage to Daniel. I felt bad for her because of all her mistakes of the heart.

Jordy asked, "What does this have to do with Jonas allegedly putting these chemicals here?"

"Jonas wants me out of the way . . ."

I said, "So he can have Fontana."

"No," Mike said. "Jonas wants this land back. I bought this land from his parents almost thirty years ago. After they were killed in the car crash, he hasn't been the same. It's like he's trying to go back in time and recreate what his parents started with. It's as if he thinks he can resurrect them if he puts everything back in place the way it was before he was born."

Jordy called the BUG Fire Department and requested the Hazardous Materials Unit to come out. Maria went back to her car to retrieve a fingerprinting kit.

Pauline and I returned to my truck and got in. Lucky Harbor hopped in, too.

I asked Pauline, "What were your faces all about?"

"John was here. They're going to find his fingerprints on that freezer."

"How do you know he was here?"

She pulled a man's watch from her purse. "I found this on the ground under the taller weeds the goats somehow missed near the freezer. It's John's."

I smelled the watch. It possessed the piquantness of pesticides. "You better air out your purse. Get a whiff."

I passed it under her nose. Pauline recoiled as I asked, "How do you know this is John's?"

"The words 'Star Sales Promoter' are on the back." She showed me. "This is a watch he got from his old employer, the riverboat cruise company."

"John will love being questioned about why he was out here. You know he was obviously here filming."

"I keep losing him to these little intrigues. Which seem to be your doings."

"Don't blame me for John's adventurous spirit. Maybe you should speak up more, Pauline. Since you met him you've become a mouse."

"I can't believe you said that. Are we fighting?"

"No. Never. But you need to tell John off. Dillon told me the truth to my face the other night. It didn't feel good at first to learn I was going overboard on everything—"

"So true."

"Just listen. I realized he was right. He cares about me. If you care about John, talk to him about what's bugging you. Use your teacher voice, too. I like your teacher voice." Her teacher voice was operatic and authoritative, designed to stop a kid before he ran into the street in front of a car.

Pauline smiled. "Thank you. My kids mind when I use it. But I wouldn't want to scare John."

"Scare him. He needs the real you."

Before we could leave, a fire engine and a Haz Mat truck cruised past us to the corner of the building. Close behind was Dillon's white construction truck with Cody in the passenger seat and Sam in the backseat.

Lucky Harbor and I raced over. The dog was all over Dillon, happier than heck to see him. I was, too.

I asked, "What're you guys doing down here?"

Cody and Dillon had on firefighter gear. Sam was still dressed in his office duds of a white shirt, tie, and tan pants.

Dillon said, "We don't get real-life Haz Mat training much in Door County, so we all got the call. I picked up Cody and Sam was with him and here we are."

Dillon and Cody rushed to observe and help load chemicals onto the Haz Mat van.

Sam came up to me.

I said, "He's growing up."

Sam said, "Who? Dillon?"

I had to chuckle. Pauline did, too.

Pauline called John as I was driving the two of us without the dog back up the county to Fishers' Harbor at around five thirty. Sam had told me the church ladies were handling the fudge shop. They'd brought new sparkly doodads to sell.

Fearful of what I'd find at the shop, I was speeding up Highway 42.

"Slow down," Pauline said. "This is when the deer like to come out."

It was dusk. The sunset was in my rearview mirror. Buildings ahead of us on the crests of hills were painted gold. Sunsets were why some visited Door County. It'd been a long time since I'd gone to Fred and Fuzzy's Waterfront Bar and Grill near Sister Bay to watch the sun drop on the horizon. I mentioned aloud how that little spot in the woods behind the Bay Ridge Golf Course was romantic, that I wanted to grab Dillon sometime and watch the sun drop.

Pauline said, "You'd be bored and find a body floating in their bay."

Pauline called John again. "John and Marc are still out on the *Super Catch I* with your grandpa. John says they were filming earlier at the winery. He forgot his watch."

"What'd he say about our discovery?"

"They'll make it part of a TV story about how international terrorism was foiled in Door County."

"You're at your best when you're being sarcastic, P.M."

"What John needs are mindfulness exercises I use with my kindergartners to bring him back to reality."

"So you don't think he's going to be successful with his TV show proposal?"

"No."

Her answer was so simple that it made me sad. She didn't believe in John? I had to change the subject. "Tell me about your kindergartner exercises."

Mindfulness had been the rage in Hollywood for years. People took expensive classes to have somebody tell them to focus on their breathing.

"We do belly buddy breathing. Kindergartners love their bellies and belly buttons. We practice putting a hand on our own bellies for three or four breaths. It calms them down."

"The thought of you rubbing John's belly is pretty funny."

"If only we were in such proximity for even a minute, I would love rubbing his belly. Anything at this point."

As Pauline and I headed toward Juddville, almost to Fishers' Harbor, an idea popped into my head. "John and Marc have taken a lot of video and photos. I never thought to ask them what they might have shot that night they went to the church."

"But John said the church was dark and he got hit on the head. They ran for their lives. I doubt they were thinking about filming."

"Maybe they were filming and didn't realize it. You know how it is when you panic. If you're holding something, you grip it tightly. They could have been pressing buttons on their phones or cameras in their hands and took shots they don't even realize they have. Marc is Mr. Automatic with his phone. It's always on."

A moment of stunned silence passed as we rolled along behind a car from Illinois. What if solving this was as simple as searching John's or Marc's cell phone?

Pauline said, "You're good at this sleuthing stuff, Poirot."

"Even if I have no restraint, Hastings?" Arthur Hastings was Hercule Poirot's army captain friend.

"I concede I admire your creativity."

"But we still don't know who put that pin in the doll."

"Probably Jonas. Mike seems to think he's gone off the deep end."

"As soon as we get home, I'm calling Jonas," I said.

"Are you going to tell him that Mike's in love with Fontana?"

"I'm not entirely convinced that's true. Fontana is playing the field. I don't think she'd do that if she felt something was unresolved with Mike."

"Do you think she's telling the truth about what happened at the church and school with Cherry?"

"Not the whole truth. She babbled about that whole making-love thing at the schoolhouse, and I doubt she walked home alone on the country roads. Fontana knows how to take care of herself that way."

"Don't you find it weird that she neglects her own roadside market in order to be around you?"

"What do you mean 'around me'?"

"She thinks you found Cherry's body. You were close to him at the end. I think she's watching you. That's why she's working at the winery and over at Jonas's farm. She wants to keep an eye on Ava's Autumn Harvest. She's probably jealous of your relationship with Dillon. She could have set the fires to make you leave the neighborhood to her. She most definitely could have filled that roadside chapel with items from your fudge shop and stuck that pin in the head of the doll that looks like you."

"But Grandma or Grandpa would have said something if they noticed her at the fudge shop."

"But your grandparents aren't there that often. Neither are you lately. Your fudge shop is operated by Cody, or Bethany, or Lois and Dotty or the other church ladies. And sometimes, frankly, there's nobody behind the counter. Fontana could have stopped by one of those times and hauled out an armful without paying."

Everything about her words disturbed something in my soul, but the soap opera of Fontana was shunted aside when we pulled up in front of my cabin on Duck Marsh Street. Across the way my grandmother was struggling to get two large suitcases in the back hatch area of her SUV.

Pauline and I piled out, then hurried over.

"Grandma, where are you going?"

"Now, Ava, don't get all upset. I'm going to Chicago for a couple of days."

"Does Grandpa know?"

"He's busy. I'll be back before he notices I'm gone."

I pushed down the bag she was attempting to lift to the back of the SUV. "That's not true. Grandma, we're all busy, but if you're mad at him, this isn't the way to handle it. One of us should go with you to Chicago. What is this ghost about?"

Grandma was trying to lift the bag again, but I snatched it and shoved it toward Pauline.

I grabbed the other suitcase from the SUV and shut the back hatch lid.

Grandma pushed both hands through her big white hair in frustration. The wind was catching it in a shape that made her look like a tipsy vanilla ice-cream cone. "I have to go to Chicago. It'll clear everything up."

Her normally creamy complexion was ruddy, as if she'd been crying. I dropped the suitcase in my hands in order to hug her. I melded one of my cheeks to hers in desperation. "Grandma, please tell me what's going on. Please. Pauline and I won't tell a soul. We'll help you. If you want to go to

Chicago, I'll call Dotty and Lois and have them take over the fudge shop for the long weekend."

Her body went limp in the cradle of my arms. "You'd go to Chicago with me?"

"If that's what you want. Let's go inside and talk about it."

Pauline and I escorted her with the bags into my grandparents' cabin. My heart was thumping hard against my breastbone.

Grandma headed straight for the kitchen while Pauline and I dumped the suitcases in the bedroom.

When the two of us returned to the kitchen, Grandma was already pulling out a big Belgian pie tin a foot across in size. Pumpkins sat on a board waiting to be cut and scooped for pie filling. She did her best thinking when she made pies.

But all of us were too agitated to be trusted with big knives to cut up pumpkins. Going to the refrigerator where I thankfully found cream cheese, I waved it around and said, "Let's make truffles instead."

Pauline said, "Perfect. My kindergartners love making those. I'm an expert."

Truffles are an easy Belgian treat. The ingredients are simple: eight ounces of cream cheese, three cups of powdered sugar, twelve ounces of semisweet chocolate, and any flavoring you like.

Grandma beat the cream cheese and sugar together while I melted chocolate.

Pauline heated cups of water in the microwave for tea. The thought of something warm felt good. The kitchen window was open and cool air was crawling in like a stealthy cat from the marshland and harbor, dropping to the floor and weaving around us. I closed the window a smidgen, but the crisp evening air would be needed to cool the chocolate down in order to make the truffles.

At first, we settled for small talk about the flowers going to seed out back and the blackbirds flocking to fly south. We speculated on when a killing frost might come.

But then I got to the subject at hand. "Grandma, why were you heading for Chicago?"

"Family ghosts. My relatives aren't real."

Pauline and I exchanged a look across the table. We were

sitting down now, creating one-inch balls of creamy choco-late. We handed them to Grandma to roll in cocoa before placing them in a pan with wax paper in the bottom.

I said, "Now you're confusing me. The Van Dammes are real. They'd have to be real or you wouldn't have been born."

With cocoa-covered hands, Grandma picked up her cup of tea from the table. "I suppose it's time I told somebody. You have to promise not to tell your parents or your grand-father, though."

"Okay. What is it?"

"I hope it's not too late to tell the prince and princess not to come."

So Grandpa still hadn't told her his secret. Indigestion set in. "Why are you so adamant about them not coming here?"

Grandma put down her teacup a little too hard. Tea spurted up and onto the table, just missing a truffle. "I'm afraid we're not related to royalty."

"How can that be? Grandpa found the link. The royals called back to say it was true."

"I don't even think the prince and princess are true roy-alty. The Van Damme bloodline died a long time ago."

Chapter 27

Grandma's words made me drop my truffle on the floor. Adhering to the three-seconds rule, I grabbed it and took a bite hoping I'd heard wrong. "What do you mean we're not related to the prince and princess? They're not royalty? We're not?"

I stuffed the remainder of the truffle in my mouth. Across from me, Pauline did the same with a truffle, chewing like crazy.

To my left, Grandma punished a truffle by burying it under a pile of cocoa in the pan. "It's true. When I was a little girl, one of my great-aunts told me about how a Van Damme had moved back to Belgium with a secret. My great-aunt had been raised in Belgium herself. She said the family secret was that the royal lineage wasn't royal at all."

"Grandma, I looked them up on the Internet. They wear royal uniforms and crowns at special events. They look royal to me."

"They don't know they're not of royal blood."

"I'm confused." And I was worried. My grandmother was the most commonsense person in our family. She didn't lie like the rest of us.

Grandma explained the family rumor she'd heard when a little girl. One of the Van Damme men of royal lineage and his wife—a distant aunt of my grandmother's—had come to Door County and stayed for weeks, enjoying visiting the Belgians around Brussels and Namur and other locales. They took a trip to Chicago a few weeks before their return to Belgium. This woman had been pregnant, but the tale handed down to my grandmother as a girl said our relative lost her own child in childbirth, but hid the fact. The couple traveled to Chicago so that they could adopt a baby.

The story stunned me. "So you believe that baby had no royal blood? But they passed it off as being of royal lineage when they returned to Belgium."

Grandma nodded.

I exchanged a look with Pauline. We popped another truffle ball into our mouths.

Around her mouthful, Pauline said, "But do you know this for sure? It sounds like gossip. The same sort of gossip surrounding the murder of Tristan Hardy. Of course, there's no baby involved with Tristan Hardy's case, but —"

"Pauline," I said, grimacing at her, "this is serious."

"Sorry, Sophie. I'm just trying to help," Pauline said. "My kindergartners get things twisted all the time. They tell me gossip about their parents and relatives, and maybe one percent of it is true. Maybe this is a one percent thing."

"And adoption still means the baby was within the royal family."

Grandma said, "Blood is thicker than water. Because the baby being adopted was kept a secret, I believe they were afraid others would remove the family's or the boy's royal status. A baby not inheriting the royal genes could have been passed over when it came time to ascending to a throne or taking over a position in a royal court or a castle."

Grandma got up to wash her hands at the sink. "I have to make a pie."

What she meant was "I have to think." She took out a big bowl and, standing at the counter, plopped enough flour in it for at least six pies.

Grandma said, "I've never told anyone because I didn't think I had to worry about this. Now your grandfather has invited the royal Van Damme family for next week, and they may not even have royal blood in them."

"For the sake of argument," I said, picking at the creamy chocolate dough in the bowl in the middle of the table, "let's say they adopted a baby boy and that baby went back to Belgium and was assumed to be their biological baby. When was this exactly?"

"The late 1850s. That baby grew up and went on to marry and have children. And those children had children. Clement Van Damme and his friend Bram Oosterling immigrated here. Clement was my great-uncle."

In the many cookbooks I'd inherited from Lloyd Mueller, I'd found pictures of Clement and Bram as young men. My grandpa had said he thought it possible that it was Clement who was betrothed to somebody with an A name, and thus the chinaware in the bottom of our Lake Michigan bay belonged to him.

Pauline and I rolled more chocolate balls into the cocoa dust. I said to Grandma, "Your grandparents didn't have names that started with A. Do you recall anybody with an A name?"

"No," Grandma said, now cracking eight eggs with loud whacks in quick succession. "This hunt for chinaware is all for naught, too."

Pauline raised her hand across the table from me. "What if the cups were for Adele Brise?"

Grandma slid into her chair to join us. "But she gave her life to God. She didn't marry."

"Yes," Pauline said, rolling a truffle in her hands, "but before she became a nun she was a young woman who'd come over on a ship looking for a better life. Maybe she was going to marry a Van Damme here. And it never came to pass."

I said, "Adele's journey was documented pretty closely. She wasn't betrothed. Maybe the cup isn't for a woman at all. Remember that another Arnaud Van Damme in the family married into a royal family. Grandpa told me that back in July. So there is royalty on the other side somewhere back in time."

My grandma shrugged. "What does it matter? We're not of pure royal lineage. It's all a lie. We're like ghosts. And the prince probably doesn't know he's not of royal blood."

Grandma got up and went straight to beating the eggs into the flour in her pan on the counter. Belgians are practical and move on quickly. "This is a terrible secret, Ava, but I guess I can keep it buried in my heart until I die."

Both Pauline and I got out of our chairs to stand next to my grandmother. The cool air from the kitchen window over the sink feathered across our cheeks.

Grandma said, "I suppose I'm sounding old and senile."

"Grandma, you're a vital, smart woman in her seventies. Were you going to Chicago to see if you could find the adoption records?"

"Yes. I found some agencies online and contacted them. Their people said it might be good to consult church records that aren't yet on the Internet and visit the library collections."

Pauline and I returned to the table. I tossed more truffles in the cocoa. "Grandma, you know it doesn't matter to me if we're not blood relatives of the royal line. We're still Belgian. The lineage married other Belgians, even marrying royalty."

"But the Van Dammes aren't pure royalty. They pulled a fast one. Your grandfather doesn't know any of this. He thinks you could be a princess by bloodline somehow. Now what do I do? It makes me ache to think about telling him."

"Don't tell him."

Pauline gave me a cross-eyed look before stuffing another truffle in her mouth.

I said, "Grandma, Prince Arnaud and Princess Amandine are royal people. They live in a castle in Belgium and have horses and do things for charity and wear crowns. That's real enough for me. And it's really not our place to tell them to get a DNA test because of something that happened over a hundred and sixty years ago."

Grandma was pouring cream into the flour and eggs to make her piecrust dough. She put the jug of cream down on the counter. Then she laughed, turning to us. "You're right. Bah and booyah on me. That's what it boils down to, doesn't it? I'd be asking a prince and princess to get a blood test. I'd be construed as a lunatic."

"Not like you at all, so therefore you must keep this secret." I smiled at her. "You're the most sensible person in this family. What if what you heard your relatives talking about long ago was merely a rumor? Gossip, like Pauline said? What if it's not true? There's a fifty-fifty chance that

Prince Arnaud and Princess Amandine are our blood relatives."

Pauline said, "There's a ninety-nine percent chance that as a little girl you heard things wrong."

Another thought struck me. Grandma's worry about this past rumor wasn't usually her way. This thing about the adopted baby was pretty darn insignificant in our lives. But I wondered if last summer was weighing on her. In July she'd found out Grandpa had kept a big secret from her about not paying the taxes on the bait shop for a few years. He could have lost the shop and maybe their house in order to pay the taxes. Grandma had been madder than an old wet hornet, as we say.

"Are you embarrassed that you haven't confessed this secret to Grandpa? I know how important it is that you both share everything. You love each other so much that the sun and moon smile on you both."

Grandma's mouth and nose twitched. Her gaze cast away, then came back to me again. "It's just that he's so excited about this royal visit and you being related to royalty. I should have told him about this long ago."

Pauline said, "I think it's a one hundred percent thing that even if Gil knew about this rumor he'd laugh and ignore it and still believe Ava was a princess."

Grandma laughed. "Those are good odds."

She came over to tug lovingly on my ponytail. "You're a gift. I love you, you little stinker."

Grandma pulled Pauline's hair, too. "I love both of you. How'd you get so smart? Oh, that's right. I used to feed you my booyah when you were tykes."

I said, "And I hope to eat a ton of it at the kermis next weekend. I'll help stir it."

The voices of Grandpa, John, and Marc came through the kitchen window.

I got up and took Grandma by the shoulders and pointed her out of the kitchen. "Grandma, your suitcases. Hurry and unpack. I'll stall Grandpa. He'll never know a thing about any of this. It's our little secret."

Grandma's hands flew to her cloud of white hair. "Bah on me. You're right."

She raced off while Pauline and I lured the men to the kitchen with the chocolate truffles. It made me think of the Hansel and Gretel fairy tale. But what would Gretel's fudge flavor be?

I was ready to stay and help Grandma finish her pies, but Grandpa told me there was a wild party over on the docks in front of the fudge shop. I headed over straightaway.

Pauline, John, and Marc took off for the Troubled Trout for dinner.

In my fudge shop all my fudge was gone from the glass cases and Dotty Klubertanz and five other women in red hats were stirring batches in all six of my copper kettles. They were talking loudly and laughing. Beers and glasses of wine sat on the floor next to their feet or on nearby shelves.

"What's going on?" I felt as if I'd landed on another planet.

Dotty tossed gold glitter into the air. "It's 'Fudge Fairy Tale and Saints Night.'"

"What's that? I hope that's edible glitter." I tasted some of the gold flecks that had landed on top of my empty glass fudge case. It was edible. "How much have you all had to drink?"

Laughter from outside bubbled up within earshot. I rushed to the big bay window on my side of the shop. Outside on the docks the picnic tables were filled with other women in red hats playing cards. Extra strings of lights hung over their heads. Card tables were also set up along the docks all the way down to the *Super Catch I*. I thought I saw piles of money on a few tables. Panic set in.

I turned back to Dotty and her troupe of red-hatted fudge stirrers. The shop smelled of chocolate, cherries, and red velvet cake. My mouth was watering. "Why are you all making fudge, Dotty?"

"We ate all your fudge, so we're making new fudge. Don't worry. Everybody paid."

"What type of cards are they playing out there?" The hoots and cheers were rattling the windows.

"Go see for yourself."

Outside, the women waved at me. "The new princess

among us." There were a few cheers. The locals were enjoying kidding me. "Come sit by me for good luck. Over here, Cinderella."

There must have been fifty women. I glimpsed a bus in the parking lot. Mercy Fogg sat about five tables away from where I stood. I shimmied among the tables. Feather-festooned finery tickled me on the chin and nose.

Mercy was wearing a bus driver's hat covered in red wrapping paper with a big red bow on top. She held a glittery gold star taped to the end of a foot-long toy fishing rod, obviously purloined from Grandpa's shop. Her other hand showed sparkly cards. Glitter was falling everywhere.

"What're you playing, Mercy?"

She waved her cards. "A new card game Lois and Dotty invented. We're trying it out. If it works, we're rich. You are, too. These are saints, the women tell me." She pointed to her cards. "I'm not Catholic or Lutheran or much of anything but ornery, so I wouldn't know about saints, but they tell me there's a saint for each day of the year. Dotty and Lois created this new card game out of prayer cards. They put glitter on them to fancy them up."

"Why are you here?"

Mercy never liked being around the fudge shop.

"Dotty invited the Red Hats over to try out the game. I bus them around every Thursday night. How do you feel about all this filthy lucre in the middle of the table?"

A mountain of cash sat in the middle of the table. "This is gambling and illegal. Right out in the open. This could close down our shop. Oh, damn you, Mercy, that's what you want!"

The other women at her table raised their beers and wineglasses and with sloppy grins, chorused, "Have Mercy on Mercy!"

They were all beyond reasoning.

Mercy said, "Don't get your undies in a bunch. Nobody's shutting you down. That sheriff of ours is tracking a killer and an arsonist after your *arse*. He's not going to come all the way up here tonight to bust a bunch of ladies. Besides, the fudge shop gets a cut of everything under the table."

"A cut?" I groaned. "That's so illegal."

"That was the law Dotty set down. And I'm a very law-abiding citizen. I used to be village president, you know."

I picked up the beer in front of her. It was empty. "You're cut off."

But women were fetching more drinks from coolers on the dock overflowing with ice. The night was getting chilly, but the women had on light jackets, sweatshirts, or sweaters and didn't seem ready to quit any time soon.

I retreated. I'd lost control of my own fudge shop again.

I suspected Marc and John had shot video of this party. I cringed. This was not how I wanted my shop depicted on TV. Drunken women dealing saints? Eek.

When I stumbled back inside, exhaustion overwhelmed me. I decided to follow Grandpa's lead on this and walk on through and out the back door. "You'll lock up for me, Dotty? You can put the fudge on the marble table by the window to cool and cure."

"Oh, sure. But you better take the money in the till and get that to the night deposit at the bank. I'll go outside right now and collect your cut."

The cash register drawer was hanging open because it was so overstuffed with cash. There were no credit card slips. Nothing to trace back to illegal activity. Dotty knew what she was doing.

Dotty came back in from outside with fists filled with greenbacks. "Here's your take on this round." She helped me stuff the cash in the bank envelope. The zipper barely closed.

I said, "I don't feel right about this. This is a fudge shop, not a gambling hall."

"Honey, I was only trying to help. You weren't here, after all." Dotty pursed her bright pink lips in a hurt expression. "I like working here. I found those old saint prayer cards in an attic we cleaned out a couple of days ago for a family after the woman had passed on, and you know how I am with a glue gun. Pretty soon Lois was helping me and we had them all decorated. We made up rules like Go Fish for the game and here we are."

I felt bad for hurting her feelings, so I asked her, "How does the game work?"

"This game uses the September saints. Each month we meet will have that month's set of saints. You have to get five saints from five days in a row. A Monday saint from September's first week, for example, can't be next to a Tuesday saint from a second week of September, but if you have saints from Monday and Tuesday of the same week, you get bonus points and a free piece of fudge. Losers in the round are called sinners and they have to put more money in the pot in the middle of the table to pay off the saint who wins the next time."

"What about the stars on the toy fishing poles?"

"We call them wands. Those are awarded to the woman at the table who's won the last hand. But the wand has to keep moving around the table. When I whistle at any moment in time, sort of like in musical chairs, whoever has the star gets to take extra cards off the pile."

She was so earnest, and looked so cute in her little red hat, that I relented. "It's wonderful what you did for me tonight. Your heart was in the right place, and you're right—I should've been here. If it weren't for you and your friends making fudge right now, I'd have nothing to sell in my shop in the morning. Thank you, Dotty. Did you pay yourself?"

I handed her a few bills.

She handed them back. "Honey, I've been friends of your family a long time. I enjoy thinking up goofy stuff. Letting me do this once in a while is payment enough. Besides, if this game catches on, it'll change the card nights at St. Ann's in a big way. We can donate a lot more to local causes. Treat this as research. Is that okay?"

I wasn't a fan of research lately, but Dotty was sly as a fox. But what harm could come from a bit of craziness now and then? And for good causes? I nodded. "But I'm the boss of my fudge store, right?"

"Of course you are, dear. Whatever you say." She laughed on her way back to her copper kettle to finish the fudge.

"What're you making?" I wandered after her to peek in the kettle. Her fudge was red.

"Red velvet cake fudge. We thought it would have to be

that because we all wear red hats. And with royalty coming, we were thinking about royal red carpets and capes."

"Does it have a fairy-tale name yet?"

"Why, no. We do want to leave you something to do when we barge in like this and take over your shop." She winked at me.

I laughed. "Capes, hats, and keeping the wolf from my door?"

Dotty said, "Little Red Riding Hood Fairy Tale Fudge."

The ladies at the kettles gave it a thumbs-up. Dotty said, "We can sew red capes for the dolls and red aprons for moms. And of course you'll want mini picnic baskets made from local willow twigs and grapevines."

The grapevines reminded me of today's events. "Do you know Michael Prevost?"

"The girls and I have been to his winery many times for wine-and-cheese pairings."

"Do you think he's capable of murder?"

She left the copper kettle to steer me over behind the minnow tank across the way. "He's a nice enough man, but he doesn't have friends."

"How do you know that?"

"Because one of the gals in the group told me. She stops by Chris and Jack's bar often enough with friends and Michael is there evenings. Alone."

I made a mental note of that. The bar was next to the Namur church. "What's wrong with going alone?"

Dotty nodded. "That's unusual in Door County where everybody's so friendly."

"Maybe he's pining. He told me he loves Fontana Dahlgren."

"Pffft. That trollop? Before you returned to Door County, she was dating one of Cherry Hardy's colleagues."

That surprised me. "Who was that?"

"Wesley Weaver."

My insides clenched in surprise. "I spoke with him yesterday. He didn't say anything about her."

"Why would he? Anything he'd say would implicate him in the murder. Remember when I told you this was about revenge? Cherry may have had something over on Professor Weaver that would destroy him."

After I took the gobs of cash to the bank, I was glad to get home to my quiet cabin. But it was too quiet. As I lay on the couch, I could hear Titus tiptoeing across my kitchen floor.

I thought about the issue of being alone. What if I were alone for life? I thought about Mike, in love with Fontana, but it was evidently unrequited love. He hung out at the local bar for companionship. What would I do? Pauline was lonely, too, wanting more from John. And Grandma was lonely with her secret. My mother had her secret of discovering the body. My grandpa had the secret of the prince being here and he hadn't told Grandma. And what about Cherry Hardy, dead now but a loner in his university department where they didn't much like him evidently because he put my fudge in test tubes? Research has shown we can die of loneliness. Humans need friends; we need to be touched and cared about.

It struck me as odd that the only people not lonely at all were people like Mercy Fogg and Dotty and Lois and women in red feather boas playing a made-up, silly card game and eating all my fudge. They lived for fun.

What if that was all Cherry had been doing? Living for fun? I recalled that his colleagues didn't appreciate him having fun or testing fudge. Would the very serious Professor Weaver kill the silly, fun-loving Cherry? Nothing made sense to me.

I called Kjersta Dahlgren, but the call went to voice mail. I left her a message, telling her about the gang coming to her place on Saturday to clean up the garden for her and Daniel. I also informed her that the sheriff had been looking through everything again, even her compost pile. I didn't know what he was looking for, though. What was left to find? They had the shovel as the possible murder weapon.

The sheriff also had my father's Buck knife, which had ended up in the organ bench, obviously stolen somehow from our farm. The knife wasn't used to commit the murder, though I wondered if it had been used to scare Cherry. Did Cherry know about the knife? Cherry was so not himself during that tour, I wondered now if he'd come on the tour as a means to retrieve the knife.

The crimes were all a muddle in my head, but I felt close to putting the jigsaw puzzle together.

A soft knock came at my door. Regrettably, I had to move off my couch.

I flicked on the outside light. When I opened the door, Lucky Harbor dashed in.

On the porch, Dillon was holding a huge picnic basket and wearing a grin. The basket had the distinct, delicious aroma of the fried cheese curds and cheeseburgers from the Troubled Trout. My mouth watered.

A tickle settled into the empty spot in my stomach. "How did you know I forgot to eat today?"

"Because I love you and you're in my heart all day even if you're not beside me."

I was ravenous. For food. For company. For everything Dillon had to offer.

Chapter 28

On Friday morning the sheriff returned my father's Buck knife. The only blood and fingerprints on it were Cherry's. John's blood was on the music sheets, but not the knife.

I called my father. "Did he borrow your knife? Then forget to leave it when he left the farm?"

"Could be. He could have used it to cut some plants to take in for testing and hadn't taken the time yet to return it. I leave it sitting around in the haymow to cut twine off the bales. He'd split open bales and take samples from the middle of the bale."

"Like Nick yesterday. But that still doesn't explain why it was at the church with Cherry's blood on it the morning before his death."

My father sighed. "Ava, be careful with all this. Stick to your fudge. It's safe."

I recalled the line from "Ave Maria" with the blood smeared beneath it. *Safe may we sleep beneath thy care.* "I'll stay safe, Dad, don't worry." He grunted at me but I went on. "Was Professor Weaver out there recently?"

"Yeah. He was here with a few colleagues maybe a week ago to look at our third-crop hay."

That gave me the chills. "Was your knife missing since that day?"

"I never thought about it because I didn't need it. We only started the baling a few days ago and that's when I missed my knife."

"Who were the colleagues with Professor Weaver?"

"Oh gosh, I don't remember all of them. The usual guys from the lab, like Nick Stensrud and Will Lucchesi. You know the bunch."

"Yeah. Working on their doctorates." By examining my fudge. "Was Mike Prevost at the farm recently?"

"Ava, he comes here all the time to pick up cheese. You know that."

I was only making my father more worried about me, so I said good-bye and hung up.

I needed a normal Friday in order to sort through my twisted thoughts. The weather cooperated with low humidity, so I tested a different divinity fudge recipe, this time with no marshmallows. I let it sit in the kitchen to set up while I came back out to the front to cut up all the fudge Dotty and her five friends had left on the white marble slab at the front window.

Edible gold glitter still festooned spots on counters and floors. I was vacuuming when Grandpa charged in from the front door at around seven o'clock that morning. He went straight for his pot of aromatic chocolate-laced coffee behind his register counter.

"What's up, Gilpa?" I wondered if Grandma had confessed her secret.

He slurped his coffee. "My hands are a problem. I can't take this."

Confused, but patient, I kept cutting the red velvet fudge Dotty had made. Its cakelike, sweet chocolate aroma tickled my nostrils. I carved a slice and walked it over for Grandpa to try.

He said, "You didn't make that fudge."

"How can you tell?"

"Your fudge is always extra creamy."

"Because I stir it fast and long. See my muscles?" I showed off my arms, then went back to cutting fudge. "Don't worry about the fudge. I'm going to reheat this and give it a workout with my arm muscles, and if it doesn't meet my standards, then Laura or Piers can use it to moisten some cupcakes or muffins. So, what's your point about your hands?"

"They're clean."

"Yeah, they are. Do you want to help me cut fudge?"

He kept flipping his hands palm up and down. "These are no good."

"What do you mean?"

"How do you remember my hands from the first day you started calling me Gilpa?"

"Dirty with grease and soil from the farm fields or fixing machinery. You always had black crankcase oil under the fingernails and in the cracks of your knuckles. I remember you called them your knuckle rivers. You would tell me your knuckle creases were named after the rivers of the world. The Nile, the Euphrates, the Danube, the Mississippi."

A smile spread so wide on his face I thought it'd reach his earlobes. "That's my point, Ava Mathilde Oosterling. Ever since I got rid of *Sophie's Journey* and took on piloting Moose's brand-new boat, I have nothing to fix. A man has to have stuff to fix."

"You could fix my truck. Mercy put a big smudge on it with her limo. That needs to be rubbed off."

"I'd be happy to. But I need something more substantial to fix."

"Like what?"

"I don't know."

"Dillon could use help in the Blue Heron Inn."

He growled. Before he disappeared through the back hallway with his coffee cup, I said, "Are you and Grandma okay? About you know who?"

"I didn't tell her about the prince being here. She was in a good mood last night. She liked making those truffles with you girls. You and Pauline should come over more often. Bring that Laura friend, too, and her babies. Your grandma gets lonely. She wouldn't mind if you blessed us with a little one."

"Don't push it, Gilpa. Speaking of blessed, why do you believe there's a divinity fudge recipe in that particular church? After all, Sister Adele could have kept it in her church in Champion."

"No way. That church was rebuilt twice. No hiding places left. Saint Mary of the Snows is special. Have you ever sat in the middle pews of that church and watched how the light from the windows crisscrosses the nave?"

"No. We used to always sit up front when I was little."

"Watch the light in there. It's as if angels fly back and forth before your very eyes, sort of like barn swallows swooping. The sun has to be just right, though. Sister Adele had to have noticed the same phenomenon. She would have hidden things where angels roam."

After he left, I wondered if the church warranted another close inspection.

I finished cutting up the fudge and replenishing my shelves.

A scratch signaled me from the front door. Lucky Harbor wore the floatable key holder on his collar. The note from Dillon read *Arnie stayed at the farm last night. Come up for breakfast. Piers not here.*

I wrote back *Have to stay at shop. Will bring new divinity fudge up later.*

I sent Lucky Harbor back to the Blue Heron Inn.

In his wake, Laura Rousseau came through the door with her twin baby stroller ferrying Clara Ava and Spencer Paul. The babies were sound-asleep cherubs. Laura was almost dancing. Atop the stroller she had a box of cinnamon rolls that I could whiff without even opening the box.

"Hi, Laura. You're out and about early."

"Good news. Brecht will be home for Christmas."

"That's terrific." That was three and a half months from now. "How do you manage being alone without your husband?" I immediately regretted my intrusiveness. "I'm sorry. Skip answering that."

"No, that's okay." She took Clara Ava out of the stroller, cradling her and staring down at her sweet face. "Brecht and I keep journals that we share when we get together. We can relive each other's days, as if we'd been together all along. I hope that doesn't sound too silly."

"Not at all. Dillon and I share two-line messages in key holders that Lucky Harbor trots between us. Now, that's silly. Especially when we could text, e-mail, or even yodel at each other up and down that hill like the Swiss do in the Alps."

She laughed. "Whatever works for you. Nobody else should judge you."

Laura always made me happier than I was the minute before. I set the cinnamon rolls inside the glass case next to my register. "These will go fast with the fishermen."

I'd barely said the words when a couple of fathers and their daughters of about ten years of age came in for minnows. They bought fudge and cinnamon rolls to take out on their boat. The girls made a fuss over the babies; then everybody left.

I couldn't help myself—I took Clara Ava from Laura's arms. "Need my fix for the day."

Laura dug Spencer Paul out of his cocoon in the stroller.

Clara Ava popped her eyes open then. Her tiny lips curled into a cockeyed smile. I cooed to Clara, "Say fudge. Fudge."

Laura laughed again.

I offered her coffee. I didn't want her to go. I also didn't want to give up Clara Ava yet. "You know a lot about antique chinaware and cups, Laura. Could cups be designed with letters for men instead of women?"

"You mean first names? Not usually, though the initial can certainly be for the surname or family crest. You're talking about the cup John found with AVD on it?"

"Yeah. Pauline also mentioned our famous cup could have been designed for Adele Brise, the young nun."

"That's not so unusual. Dinnerware can be commissioned by anybody, including us if we had the dough. I would imagine there's an archbishop or two with plates and cups with his initials on them."

Laura put her twins back in the stroller. My arms and hands felt so bereft I reached for a cinnamon roll, split it in two, and shared it with Laura.

Laura said, "Do you think gossip will die down about the murder and the fires enough so that your family can celebrate about finding the cup?"

I told her about the knife being returned to my father

and Cherry's blood and prints being the only ones on it, and that John's cut hand was a separate incident.

"Cherry had to have run up to the choir loft to hide that knife after the choir tryouts were done, unless somebody wearing gloves did it. Maybe Cherry and this person had an altercation? Maybe Cherry had to dump the knife fast because he had to get back to John's tour? Who was around the church early that morning?"

The obvious answer startled us. I muttered, "Jonas."

"Did you happen to notice if Jonas had any cuts or looked like he'd been in a fight with Cherry?"

"I haven't even thought about such a thing. It's so odd that I overlooked the obvious. Like angels in the church."

"Huh?"

"My grandfather contends we might be able to see angels flying around in Saint Mary of the Snows when the sunlight is lined up right."

"So the angels witnessed everything that morning. If only your grandmother could use her belief in guardian angels to ask them."

"Indeed. Jonas had to have been wearing work gloves to work on the landscaping." My gut was churning. "This is adding up too fast and too easily."

"But it is adding up."

We rocked the babies. "Do you suppose Cherry and Jonas came back later for some reason? Jonas maybe followed the car to the church that night."

The whole scenario was making me feel ill at ease. I mentioned to Laura about several neighbors being invited to the Dahlgrens' tomorrow, but added, "Don't come along. Stay home with Clara and Spencer. I don't trust any of my friends down there anymore."

"You really think one of them killed Cherry?"

"I'm not sure of anything at the moment, except my dad was right. I need to stay safe." Saying that out loud brought a sour taste of fear into my mouth. "Why would Jonas do such a thing, though?"

"Fontana."

"Jealousy over her has entered our minds too often. It strikes me that maybe that's what we're supposed to think."

After holding Clara Ava, I tried to remember her innocent smile and put evil out of my mind that day.

Friday turned out to be magical enough. Grandpa cleaned Mercy's limo smudge off my yellow truck with some special gooey stuff; he got the goo all over his hands and was very happy.

Dillon finished an upstairs bathroom in the Blue Heron Inn.

Piers even helped Dillon create a raised garden bed in the backyard.

But at dinnertime, my mother called. She was screeching.

"You didn't tell me Arnie Malle is the prince! I just learned a prince stayed overnight in my house. Your father knew! You knew! You two are dead meat! This house is filthy! I should have been warned!"

"The house is fine, Mom."

"When I thought he was a journalist I didn't think twice about not having vacuumed that guest bedroom for a couple of weeks. But now, well, I need to vacuum the whole house. Prince Arnaud will talk about me back in Belgium." She issued a sound like a mewling calf.

"Where is he now, Mom?"

"Out on a tractor with your father and Nick Stensrud collecting soil samples."

"See? He's okay with dirt."

"I'm going to be vacuuming all night! It's a good thing I bought a new supply of vacuum bags after last weekend cleaning up that church. And please, do not tell Prince Arnaud I discovered a dead body in that church. I'll die myself."

A realization struck. "Mom, what did you do with the bag of old dirt you took from your vacuum cleaner after cleaning the church?"

"That bag is in the trash bin of course."

My brain jerked alive with electric thoughts. "Go get the bag right now."

"But it's in the trash can, under garbage."

"Mom, go get it. You might have valuable evidence in that bag. We might be able to figure out who killed Cherry."

"You mean there might be somebody's hairs in my bag?"

She'd surprised me with her deduction. "Yes."

"I'll get the bag, but you have to take it to the sheriff."

"Yes, I know, Mom. He thinks I discovered the body. I'll lie for you and say I was doing the vacuuming."

"A mother couldn't ask for a lovelier daughter than one who lies for her."

On Friday evening I drove down to the farm to pick up the vacuum bag. It smelled of the fish Mom had cooked recently. She'd tossed the fish bones into the same trash receptacle as the used vacuum bag. Jordy wasn't happy when I showed up with the stinky thing.

"What the hell? Get that out of my office," he said, not even rising from his desk.

"You're going to find the killer's hairs or clothing threads or dead skin inside this bag. I was vacuuming the church on Sunday."

"You have time to vacuum?" His eyes slid into a suspicious squint. "I've heard your mother is the clean one of the bunch."

"She was at Mass. As for me, cleanliness is next to godliness."

Jordy got up to retrieve an evidence bag from a shelf behind him. He had me drop the droopy, fishy, full vacuum bag into it.

"How long will this take?" I asked.

"Could take a week."

"We don't have a week. We have a kermis in a week."

"We?"

"Yeah, Jordy, you and me. We have to solve this. Trust me."

His laugh echoed behind me as I headed back through the reception area with the portraits of officers.

That evening, Dillon and I attended an old-fashioned fish boil behind the Troubled Trout bar.

On the beach, a wood fire had been built under a steel drum filled with salted water. Big fillets of white fish were dropped into the boiling water. At a certain point, the cook tossed a tiny amount of something akin to fuel oil or gasoline on the fire, making it whoosh up around the steel drum as the boiling water surged and overflowed, causing great clouds of steam to rise in the cool night air. It was great entertainment for tourists and locals alike.

Oddly enough, John showed up with Pauline. He'd somehow disentangled himself from Marc for one evening. The four of us acted like so many average normal couples I'd observed in Door County all my life. The normalcy shifted something in my soul. There was a tranquility I'd forgotten existed here. How had I lost that feeling? How could I keep it?

On Saturday late in the morning, with the fudge shop under control by Cody and Bethany, Pauline and I traveled down to the Dahlgrens' place. We wore heavy work shoes, jeans, and sweatshirts. The day was cool, only in the fifties. A few more leaves on trees looked airbrushed with red and yellow and orange paint. Pauline and I set to work in the garden.

In the early afternoon, right after lunchtime, several tourists showed up. Mom was selling my fudge like crazy, as well as any pumpkins we hauled from the Dahlgren acreage.

John and Marc showed up and began videotaping everything instead of helping.

As I suspected would happen, most of the neighbors stopped by to help, including Fontana Dahlgren, Jonas Coppens, and Michael Prevost. To my surprise, Wesley Weaver showed up with Will and Nick. My mother said she'd called Wes to tell him about everybody helping out the Dahlgrens in the wake of Cherry's murder. She thought Cherry's university department colleagues might be willing to lend a hand in his honor. I hadn't told her about the rocky relationships in the department. I noted who showed up and who didn't—those other seven colleagues. I'd mention this to Jordy.

When Dillon and Piers, with Lucky Harbor, pulled to a stop in the yard in a blue Ford Fusion, everybody ran in shock to the car thinking it was Cherry's. It was not. Dillon explained it was merely Piers's rental. But I could tell by the glint in Dillon's eyes that they'd meant to stir things up with the car.

Mike Prevost told him it was an ugly joke to rent a car identical to the missing car of a dead man.

Jonas Coppens strode to the orchard to pick apples alone.

Wes Weaver didn't immediately believe it wasn't Cherry's car and he stalked around it scrutinizing it with Lucky Harbor sniffing at his heels.

Nick and Will took off in a junker car toward Brussels, saying something about getting a beer.

I was rearranging pumpkins on the flatbed wagon, taking in the hubbub.

Fontana came up to me, gasping for air. "What is wrong with your boyfriend? Doesn't he know that car brings back awful memories?"

"Like what memories?" I hoped she'd let slip some new information.

"Never mind. This stress isn't good for me." Fontana headed to the Dahlgren house, which I had assumed was locked. Fontana went inside without hesitation, oddly enough, as if she'd been in there before and knew it was unlocked.

Out of curiosity, I followed her.

To my surprise, Kjersta was sitting on her couch in her living room. The shades were drawn. Fontana was in their bathroom, coughing. I heard water running.

Edging into the dim room, I said, "Kjersta? I'm sorry. I assumed you were still in a motel. Did you get my message about us cleaning your garden for you?"

"Yes." She was flipping through a magazine in robotic motions.

"Where's Daniel?"

"I don't know." Her long lashes appeared to glisten in the meager light.

I sat down in an olive green chair opposite her. There was an element of déjà vu. The desk wasn't far away from where Pauline, Laura, and I had found the information about Cherry's research contract ending. "What do you mean you don't know? Has Daniel . . . ?"

"Left me? I don't think so. He said he needed to get away for a while. Which isn't good, seeing as how neither of us is supposed to leave the county. I came here hoping he might show up at home."

"I won't say a word."

"Is that true? You're chummy with the sheriff."

Her tone was thick with accusation.

"Not that chummy." I felt bad for letting down my friend, yet I wasn't certain exactly how I'd let her down. "Fontana seemed to know your house would be unlocked. She just barged in. How did she know?"

"I'm sure Daniel called her."

"They're not . . . ?"

"Still in love? No. But Daniel knows something he's not telling me. He definitely didn't want to be here today with everybody coming around."

Her curly brown hair was mashed on one side, as if she'd been sleeping on it. My heart went out to her. "I know you couldn't've killed Cherry."

"Thank you. But it doesn't look good when Daniel runs off like this."

"You said he knows something. Trust him, Kjersta."

I was saying that "trust" word more and more to my friends, but did I believe it? "Did Daniel offer to buy Jonas's land? Or any of Mike's land?"

Kjersta's startled countenance told me everything. "They told you?"

"No. I guessed." I decided not to drag Professor Weaver into this. "Cherry spent a lot of time here with Nick and Will right out in front of your house buying fudge from my stand and testing for chemicals on everybody's property. Land values might be dropping. This would be an opportune time to buy more land." I made a note to check on that with our county's tax assessor.

Kjersta seemed to shrink within herself. "Daniel was interested in expanding. Our organics are beginning to sell well to restaurants all over Door County."

I had to ask her one additional tough question. "Had Professor Hardy accused Daniel of contaminating his own land?"

Kjersta gasped.

Fontana chose that moment to wander from the bathroom. She didn't look upset or angry, oddly enough. She walked right up to us and looked down at Kjersta. "I'm so sorry about this. I don't know who killed Cherry, but I know it wasn't you, Kjersta."

With that, she left, closing the front door quietly behind her. I noted she hadn't said Daniel was free of guilt.

Within a couple of seconds somebody yelled, "Fire!"

I bolted out the door. Everybody was pointing across the road to our farmstead in the distance.

Chapter 29

My mother flashed by me in a blur as she raced to her black-and-white delivery van. "Your father's at the top of that barn and he's not answering his phone."

Meaning he could be trapped in the fire. He always left his phone behind when he was stacking bales because it was too easy for it to drop into the hay and disappear.

Everybody at the Dahlgren place and surrounding Ava's Autumn Harvest scrambled for cars and phones to call nine-one-one.

Pauline and I tumbled into my truck.

Dillon was ahead of me in the rented blue car with Piers.

Within minutes, it seemed like a hundred vehicles and people jammed into our turnabout near the barn.

Tongues of fire were shooting from the roof.

On the ground, dust puffed everywhere. Car doors slammed. Smoke tainted the air. My mouth went dry.

Mom cried out, "Pete! Pete! I love you! We're coming!"

My father was leaning out the window in the peak of the barn—a height of about four stories—with smoke billowing out around him. "Dad! We're coming!"

I ran for nearby hoses and yelled to people to get the ladders in the shed.

Wes Weaver and Jonas and a few others raced to the bottom of the barn to herd cows and calves outside to the barnyard and pasture.

Dillon and Piers hoofed it back with the ladders as a

couple of tourists and I manned ordinary garden hoses. We stretched the hoses as far as we could, but little of the water was reaching into the haymow. A new sprinkler system had been installed, but for some reason it wasn't working.

The fire growled inside the belly of the haymow, a ghastly sound that scraped me hollow inside.

Above us, my father was practically floating in smoke.

A sour smell of hay burning rent the air around us.

Sirens screamed in the distance.

Arnaud came barreling in on a tractor from the fields. He jumped down, and along with several others dove with shovels and forks into the alleyway of the haymow to clear it to prevent the fire from moving to the other half of the barn. But with some roof beams now on fire, I didn't know if that would help. Smoke clouds dipped from above.

Pauline and Kjersta were stomping out cinders that had fallen near us.

Dillon was setting up a ladder against the barn wall. I raced to help steady it with Piers. Piers shoved the extension as far up as it could go. It didn't reach my father, who was yelling, "Hot, too hot! My back!"

The sirens were getting louder. I was muttering prayers.

Dillon yelled my way, "Rope. I need rope."

I raced to the machine shed nearby and brought back a coil of half-inch rope. Dillon snatched it and then climbed the ladder that extended partway up the barn. He attempted to toss the coiled rope up to my father. The coil sailed back to the ground like a flailing snake. I tossed it back up to Dillon while Piers steadied the ladder.

The first fire engine roared into the vicinity. It slowed to find a way around all the vehicles.

My father was bent over the window frame above us yelling, "Help me! Help!"

Dillon yelled, "We're coming, Pete!"

The crowd behind me gasped as my father flipped himself out of the window four stories above us, dangling now by only his hands on the sill. Smoke blew off his jeans. His shirt looked split open in back and charred. Red flames licked out at the top of the window, making it look like a mouth about to devour my father.

"We're coming, Dad!" I yelled. "Hang on!"

My mother was jumping up and down in tears, her hands cupped like a megaphone around her mouth. "Pete, you're gonna make it. Hang on, honey, hang on!"

Another fire engine barreled in, skirting the cars by busting right through our pasture fence.

The first fire engine came around the shed, then shoved some tourist's car out of the way, denting the car all to heck. The engine's ladder was already extending as it pulled into place at the front of the barn.

Dillon, who was atop our ladder, leaped over to the extension ladder off the fire engine and then rode it up as it motored into place, stopping a few feet below my father.

Dillon scrambled to the last rung, with a firefighter coming up the ladder right below him. Dillon stretched up to my father's feet.

In a leap of faith, my father let go of the window ledge and fell into Dillon, who crumpled, making all of us scream on the ground. But they grappled for a hold on the ladder and the firefighter with them held on to Dillon.

My mother collapsed on me, crying. "Thank God, thank God."

I clung to her. "He's okay, he's okay."

He was alive, but as he descended, we saw that the backs of his jeans all the way up his legs, butt, and then the shirt on his back had been scorched, splayed open to show raw red skin. The fire rescue crew whisked my dad away in a cloud of dust as three more engines came screaming and barreling down Highway DK.

Arnaud appeared before me blackened from smoke. Nobody would recognize him as a prince.

He grabbed my arm, rushing me around the vehicles. "*Va!* Go to *ton pere*. Your father."

I realized Mom and I had been frozen in shock, numb at what was happening around us. "Thank you," I mumbled, getting my senses back.

Pauline and I stuffed Mom in my truck in the backseat. Lucky Harbor leaped in with her.

We followed the rescue vehicle to the Sturgeon Bay

Hospital. Pauline dug out Mom's blessed buttons and passed one to the backseat.

Mom said, "Who wants to harm us? It's because I discovered the body, isn't it?"

Lucky Harbor whined. In the rearview mirror I glimpsed him licking Mom's face.

Steamy anger roiled inside me as I hunkered two-fisted on the steering wheel, my foot pressed to the floor to keep up with the fire rescue vehicle transporting my father. Dotty's word came back to me: revenge. Who wanted revenge? And for what?

Pauline said, "Ava, it's . . . about . . . you." Her voice was shaky. "The voodoo doll proved it."

Mom asked, "What voodoo doll?"

"Nothing," I said. "It was just a doll I found in Jonas's chapel." I gave Pauline a hard glance to shut her up.

My mother hiccuped. "I should never have called you about finding that body."

"Mom, you did the right thing."

"Honey, this has to be about the recipe. Somebody knows it's valuable. They're jealous."

"Why would you think this has to do with the recipe?"

"Everything goes back to the church in Namur. The body. The organ bench. The knife. The fires could be meant to distract us from the recipe. Somebody wants time to find it for themselves."

Mom had likely been watching too many crime shows on TV, but what she said resonated with me.

Pauline was nodding, too. "This trouble only started about a week ago when news of the recipe leaked out because of Fontana."

My whole body jerked awake.

Pauline said, "What is it?"

"I'll tell you later." With my mother in the backseat I didn't want to talk too much about my suspicions, but I thought I knew who had murdered Cherry and who was setting the fires. But I needed proof.

My father suffered smoke inhalation and first-degree burns on his back, legs, and some fingers. He'd dislocated a shoulder from his aerial feat out the haymow window, but the doctor said he'd be healed mostly within a couple of weeks.

When I drove Mom and Dad, Pauline, and Lucky Harbor back to the farm, I noticed a nondescript gray sedan was following us from some distance. "Deputy Vasquez is behind us."

"Thank goodness," my mother said. She and my father were in the back with the dog between them. They each had their arms around the curly-haired water spaniel and were petting him. Lucky Harbor was smiling, as if he knew calming my parents was his mindfulness job.

It was five o'clock by the time we pulled into the farmyard. The sun was low. The tourists had gone, but neighbors were still there as well as Dillon and Piers and Arnaud. All were filthy with soot and dust. They'd been working hard with the firefighters to remove smoldering and sodden hay from this half of the haymow.

Half the barn roof had caved in. My dad had a sick look. He and Mom had an arm around each other's waist. I had to hold back tears.

Pauline put an arm around my waist to pull me close. "No lives were lost. Look at all the friends you have."

Just behind us a yellow school bus pulled in. Mercy Fogg was driving, to my shock. Several high school guys I recognized trundled out. They set to work putting hoses and ladders away with Dillon and Piers. Others were pushing charred hay into a pile far away from the barn.

My father, with an arm in a sling to ease his dislocated shoulder, took a couple of the young men to the milking parlor to show them what to do.

John was rounding up cows that had escaped from the fence that had been busted by the fire engine. Marc was recording everything going on with John's video camera. I had started to stalk over to him when Mercy Fogg caught me by an arm.

"Hey, Miss Fudge Lady, cool it. This is the heart of what Door County is about, neighbors helping neighbors. Let him capture it on camera. It's not often we capture a soul on film. Besides, that guy is from the big city. He's about as useful helping on a farm as a fifth teat is on a cow."

Mercy left me in shock as she trundled back to her yellow school bus and took off down our gravel lane.

Pauline muttered, "I don't get her. You're not her favorite person, but then she does something like this."

"Yeah, she's a mystery to me, too. But don't play cards with her."

Jordy and his crew were there, too, finishing up looking around.

I asked, "What'd you find?"

"So far, not much here."

"Somebody set a fire in the barn. It wasn't an accident."

"Could be the hay was too wet when you put it up. We have to check for that."

Jordy had to eliminate natural causes. Alfalfa had to be at the perfect dry stage for baling. If too many juicy stems were baled up into the compacted bales of hay, a chemical reaction created heat and the bales could burst into flames. But my father was an expert on hay.

I said, "Why didn't the water system work? It's practically new."

"The firefighters found a couple of valves had been shut off."

"That's not possible."

"It could be your father was repairing something and didn't turn the valves back on."

But Dad told Jordy everything should have been in working order.

When Jordy headed for his squad car, I followed.

Jordy took off his official hat. His hair was sweated up. He'd been climbing around the hay for a while. "Any thoughts on who did this, Ava?"

"I don't believe it was Daniel Dahlgren. Have you stayed in touch with him?"

"No. Balusek is trying to locate him. If Dahlgren left the county, it won't be good."

"My theory is he's so angry about being blamed for Cherry's murder that he doesn't want to see anybody right now. Daniel has a lot of pride. He also doesn't want anything to do with Fontana."

"What do you mean by that?"

"Did you find any perfume smells around our property just now while looking? I thought I smelled an odd sour smell earlier."

"Could be your imagination. You want to blame Fontana."

"No, I don't. But you smelled her perfume in the church, and the smell lingered near Ava's Autumn Harvest after that fire, and it was certainly in the chapel where I found the doll. And now here."

"So she's to blame. Present at all these events."

"Or maybe you and the firefighters are supposed to blame her. It'd be a good idea to confiscate everything you can at her roadside market down on Highway 57 and at her house. Don't let anybody get their hands on her perfumes and perfumed soaps."

"Is she a friend of yours?"

"We knew each other in school. She's a little older."

"Could she be an accessory to murder and arson?"

I hated saying it, but I had to tell the truth. "Could be. She may not realize she's an accessory, though. I have no proof for any of this, Jordy, but the coincidences seem to add up. Did you find anything in the vacuum cleaner bag yet?"

"Women's hairs. Men's hairs that didn't belong to Tristan Hardy."

I wanted to leap and hug him, but then I realized what he was up against. "I vacuumed a whole lot of that church. Is this a needle in a haystack?"

"It could've been, but you managed to get a few hairs with blood on them. Those I'm interested in."

"A man's hairs?"

Jordy nodded. "Fairly short, an inch or so, dark."

"An inch? Dark? Daniel has blond hair and it's longer than an inch."

"I was thinking about Kjersta Dahlgren and Mike Prevost. Both have short dark hair. He's got maybe an inch-long Mohawk at his widow's peak in front."

"I'm sure he dyes his hair. I call the color 'sienna.' Was it sienna?"

"That I wasn't told. I'll ask."

Jordy was being judicious, meticulous. I had to admire that, while I was too quick to jump to conclusions. "You'll have a DNA match soon?"

"In a week."

"Always a week with you, Jordy. We can't have this murder taint the party for the prince and princess."

Jordy settled his hat back on. "Did you find that holy fudge recipe of the sister's yet?"

"No. Why?"

"A treasure hunt always brings out desperate people."

I was about to tell him who I thought was a prime suspect when Jordy added, "Somebody around here thinks they're going to win the lottery by finding that recipe. They're going to great lengths to make sure you're kept busy doing everything but looking for it. Anybody recently become poor and resent it?"

Jordy's theory shot my theory to heck. I was thinking that maybe Professor Weaver or somebody in his department had committed the murder.

But poor people? That was most of us, even Mike Prevost, Jonas Coppens, and the Dahlgrens. We were all relatively poor in Door County. I asked, "What about rich people who want to stay rich? What about jealousy? What about revenge or glory?" I was quoting Dotty now. "Those are good motives for murder."

Jordy opened his car door and stood with his arms resting over the top of it. "So, who's on your short list?"

"Did you get a chance to talk with the rest of Cherry's colleagues? Professor Weaver said the whole department was in serious conflict with Cherry."

"I've got interviews lined up for next week."

Next week. "You might also talk with Mike Prevost and Jonas Coppens about their theories. I get this feeling they're keeping mum about something significant that could break this wide open."

After he drove away, I went to find Pauline. She was closing the gate in the barnyard after John had shagged in a couple of cows.

"Pauline, we have an important errand to run."

We headed toward my truck, wending our way through

smoldering hay, hoses, and around a couple of deputy cars still sitting near our barn.

Pauline said, "I don't like that look on your face. You're starting to look like Lucky Harbor. Brown hair, nose to the ground always sniffing for clues."

"I'll take that as a compliment, P.M."

"Should I toss you some fudge, A.M.?"

Lucky Harbor woofed at the word "fudge." I dug in my pocket for the crackers, and to please Pauline I tossed one in the air and caught it in my mouth.

Pauline shook her head as we got into my pickup truck.

Chapter 30

The yellow tape was gone at the Namur church. There were no vehicles. It was going on six o'clock, the dinner hour for tourists. I needed to see if I could find more clues.

Maria's car wasn't in sight, but I knew she'd be lurking somewhere watching us.

I walked over to the collection of headstones under the tree where Grandma had been working a week ago. There were three ancient stones with the name Coppens on them. I touched the lettering on one, which had weathered to faint, scratchy ripples. Looking beyond to the actual graveyard behind the church, I began to feel certain I knew what had gone on and how Cherry got himself killed.

Pauline said, "You think Jonas murdered him?"

"No. But his history here gives us clues, Pauline. The Coppens family has been here a long time in Door County and they command respect. This murder is about respect."

I told Pauline my theory of who it might be.

She grabbed a headstone to hang on. "We can't tell anybody that. That's, uh, too preposterous, too big. You'll be in the national news. You better be right."

I called my grandmother. She and my grandfather were driving down from Fishers' Harbor. "Grandma, do you or Grandpa remember a man buying a lot of Cinderella fudge and other items in the past week?"

She didn't, and Grandpa said he'd been in and out of his

shop too much to notice. I called Dotty. She recalled men coming in to buy bait and beer.

Cody, however, gave me a clue when I called him. "I saw a guy standing around who looked fat, but like his arms were holding on to things under his jacket. I'm real sorry. Other customers came in, so I didn't chase him down."

"That's okay, Cody." I asked him about my perfume theory.

He said, "Alcohol burns clear and is the hardest to detect by a fire department's sensors."

"What about alcohol in wine?"

"Nope, Miss Oosterling. If there are by-products of making wine that have concentrated alcohol, then that might work. But wine alone wouldn't start your fires. If so, heartburn would take on a new meaning."

"Cody, what have you learned in your classes about timing devices?"

"Pretty easy to do. Alarm clocks, some string, and a candle will do it."

"But undetected? Wouldn't remnants of the alarm clock be found in Jonas's shed, for example? Jordy never found anything."

"Lots of cheap clocks around, Miss Oosterling. A tiny plastic clock would melt and burn to nothing in a big fire. Cheap clocks are everywhere. Everybody has them. In high school, they bought boxes of them because we kids always broke them throwing things around."

After I got off the phone, I said to Pauline, "Fontana may have unwittingly supplied candles and perfume to the murderer."

With my grandmother's key, I unlocked the church door and we slipped inside.

I went up to the choir loft. I opened the piano bench. It had been cleaned.

We looked about the pews in the loft, and around the old organ. There was no blood. If there ever was a mishap here last Saturday night, either the killer or killers had cleaned it up well or Jordy had. I knew my mother hadn't been back.

Pauline said, "I doubt the investigators cleaned it up, and

the church ladies haven't had time to get here. They may not even know yet the yellow tape is gone."

"Very good. So the killer did the cleanup. Or killers."

"Two people involved?"

"Or several."

I went to the railing overlooking the nave. Last Saturday Pauline and I had peered down on Cherry holding court with a crowd. This time, I scrutinized the open floor below us where a few pews had been removed to allow for programs. Behind a pew, a seam in the flooring appeared darker than the rest.

"Come on, Pauline."

I trundled down the narrow choir loft stairs, hurrying into the nave to look at the seam.

Pauline crouched down with me. "You think it's blood?"

I looked back up to the loft, which was only a few feet from us in the small church. "Cherry's head could have been banged against that choir loft railing, with blood shooting down this way. If John and Marc came in right after that, the killer or one of them might have raced down here from the loft to beat John and Marc over the head with anything, even hymnals. The person may have slipped in Cherry's blood and that's why John and Marc got away."

"Then the blood was cleaned up, or almost. But what about the lights being out?"

"Maybe they'd taken Cherry to the basement to kill him, but he escaped at first. They cut the lights from the circuit breaker box so Cherry couldn't see where he was going. He stumbled to the loft staircase, too late to find his way to the front door. He tried to hide in the loft, and that was his big mistake."

"They? Who helped? Jonas?"

"Somebody who liked being up late at night perhaps. Cruising the bars."

"I'm spooked out. Let's get out of here."

"Yeah." I was getting shivers, too.

I gave a glance to the way the setting sun was coming in the west windows. We had maybe an hour of light left.

We went to the old schoolhouse and climbed in again

behind the loose window screen. It was clear to me that if
Fontana was upstairs in that bedroom on Saturday night or
early Sunday morning, she didn't see anything, just as she
said.

"Go and move my truck for me, P.M."

"Why, A.M.?"

"To see how an engine sounded when it was backing out
versus pulling in. Back out onto the road, then pull into the
parking lot. Then pull over here to the schoolhouse. Drive
right across the lawn."

My pickup made quite a bit of noise. Engines in trucks
tend to be noisier than in most cars.

I got back into my truck with Pauline, with me behind
the driver's seat. I began steering us back onto Highway
DK in front of the church. I turned left, toward Brussels.

Pauline asked, "So, what'd you conclude?"

"If a truck had pulled in, Fontana would have noticed.
She said she heard cars."

"But not all cars sound alike. My car has rocks rattling in it."

"Good point. I suppose we should consider what everybody's driving these days." My head rattled through a list of
SUVs owned by Jonas, the Dahlgrens, my parents. The university sent people out in SUVs as well. Nick and Will
sometimes drove around in an old clunker with a muffler
that rattled, but I made a note to call the university vehicle
department to ask if Nick and Will had taken out a company car to drive later on Saturday. The migrant workers
used a minivan.

Pauline said, "Fontana probably couldn't discern between Cherry's car and the killer's car when she was in that
upstairs back bedroom of the schoolhouse. We've already
thought that Fontana probably had to drive away the killer's car. The killer hid Cherry's car. It's a circular argument,
Poirot."

"Not really, Hastings. Remember when Fontana said she
walked home that night? She might be telling the truth.
What if the killer took Cherry's car and dumped it fairly
quickly nearby, then walked back here to get in his car? Or
rode a bike back?"

"Jonas's bike? He murdered Cherry?"

"Or somebody borrowed his bike for the night. Jonas leaves it out. The person rode the bike back to Namur to get his or her car, a car hidden behind Saint Mary of the Snows. It was after midnight, and a lot of people were asleep. Then the killer returned the bike that night, maybe driving without lights."

"Oh my gosh, you're saying that maybe Fontana's still alive because she left before that guy returned to the church for his own car?"

"I think so. She doesn't realize it."

"Could she be in danger?"

"I think so. It's why she's been sucking up to Jonas and staying where there are a lot of people, like the tours and the winery. She's savvy enough to keep protection around her."

"But Mike has to be involved, if your theory is correct."

"He had the chemicals, though he denies knowing anything. But I don't think he has the energy needed to travel the countryside at night dumping chemicals on land."

"Where are we going now?"

"To see about a broken fence. I think I know where the blue car might be, and if I find that, we'll be able to prove who killed Cherry." I smiled as I looked in my side mirror. "Maria's car caught up with us."

"Thank goodness."

When I pulled into Jonas's farmstead, he was busy out in the pasture to the north herding in his flock. I waved to him; he waved back. I felt uneasy.

Maria's car drove on down the road.

I steered through the sloping field and up to the new fencing.

Beyond the fence, brush and trees obscured a ravine. "I suspect the bears have a nice blue Ford Fusion to hibernate in this winter."

"Certainly the Fusion wouldn't have been driven through here. That ravine is pretty steep."

I got out of the truck for a closer look. Grass and brush had been disturbed, but that was likely Mike on a tractor taking out the gate. Did he know if there was a car down in the ravine behind him in the deep woods? Maybe. If so, his silence gave me a chill.

I said, "The car was probably driven in through the south end, not here. The terrain levels off behind Mike's buildings."

"Where our suspects hid the chemicals in an old chest Mike hadn't looked in for months."

"Yes. Mike's been so busy with his grapes going bust that he probably hasn't noticed a thing about his acres of woodland back here. And thus, Mike played a role in Cherry's murder."

"But is he innocent?"

"I'm not absolutely positive about that."

"Good thing Maria's cruising with us. She's going to make this arrest and solve this murder case handily for Jordy. Big raise for her."

"You got that right. And we'll be free of this mess."

I drove with Pauline back up the slope of Jonas's field, past his house, then down his lane and onto Highway C. When I turned onto Highway 57, Maria showed up in my mirror again, but at a good distance behind us.

At the Prevost Winery, a tasting was going on inside. Mike wouldn't know we were snooping. The setting sun was beginning to turn the sky tangerine to the west. I grabbed my flashlight from the glove box and the mosquito spray.

I said to Pauline, "Put those in your purse."

"Maybe we should let Maria do this part."

"She'll be right behind us. She doesn't know the terrain here like we do. Jonas and I used to walk all the deer paths around here as kids. I'll find the car, and then we'll come back and get Maria."

"What about the bears?"

"Good thinking. If only we had some of Fontana's perfume." I dug out my pepper spray and handed it to her.

"Why do I have to carry everything?"

"So that I don't have to."

She wrinkled up her face. "That's not an answer."

I waved my cell phone in the air. "I need both hands to take pictures of the car when we find it. You fend off any bear that charges us."

"That's not funny, Ava."

Behind the stone winery, Mike had cleared about thirty yards of brush where he kept his equipment and mower. Beyond that lay thick forest of cedars, maples, and an understory filled with wild berry vines and ferns. At first, I wondered if I was wrong about the car driving into the thicket. But after wandering the edge of the forest for a bit, I found bent and mashed berry vines where perhaps a vehicle had pushed its way through. The killer had to know this area well, which only cemented my suspicion as to who murdered Cherry.

Dressed in jeans and sweatshirts, we bullied our way through the briars.

Maybe thirty more yards in, the land began to undulate. The forest opened up into pockets filled with ferns. Sumac leaves had turned red for the season, but in the dimming light had begun to look almost black.

We came over a rise, descended, then trudged along the bottom of the ravine. My heart rate was increasing as we saw more signs of disturbance.

We soon discovered a small cave opening not far ahead of us. I retrieved the flashlight from Pauline's purse, then headed right for the cave, making sure to skirt poison ivy vines lacing the ground.

Pauline stayed back. "There could be a bear in there."

"Too early to start hibernating." I flicked on my flashlight. "Whoa. Pauline, come here. Hold the flashlight."

She sidled up next to me. "Holy cow."

A cache of chemical containers sat in the cave. With Pauline steadying the flashlight, I snapped photos with my phone. "Same stuff we found in Mike's freezer."

Pauline said, "This would contaminate a lot of land and crops."

"And keep Professor Weaver's department in business trying to figure out what was wrong on the local farmland."

"But a bigwig professor at the university in Green Bay? Are you sure? He's been on your farm a lot over the past few years. Why would he be messing around with chemicals? He's Mr. Organic, like Cherry was."

"That's what we have to think about. It's why I think Nick and Will are part of this murder plot."

"There are several people in that department."

"True," I said, putting my phone in my pocket. "But it was Weaver and Nick and Will who were always out in this neighborhood. Kjersta said that Fontana had dated Wes Weaver." I took the flashlight from Pauline. "Cherry knew about the divinity fudge recipe because Fontana blabbed about it."

"But murdering a colleague all because of your fudge in his test tubes feels beneath a professor."

"Pauline, murdering a college professor, period, is beneath anybody."

"Okay. But there's got to be more to his motives. And to involve Nick and Will? They're in their twenties and bright, with no reason to murder Cherry."

My friend was breeding doubts inside me. Professor Weaver wouldn't risk his career to murder for a recipe, or even for a grant. Certainly Nick and Will didn't care about the fudge. But maybe dissing my fudge was reason enough to be suspicious of them?

The bottom of the ravine had a few bare areas where it washed out in storms regularly, but it was dry bare ground now. Vines wrapped everywhere. We were focusing so much on not tripping that we almost walked right into the car.

My flashlight illuminated a taillight, which reflected back at me.

The blue car was hidden well under layers of woody brush. I tugged at some of it. A license plate appeared. I handed off the flashlight to Pauline and then snapped a photo.

A rustling in front of the car startled us.

In the beam of my flashlight, Professor Weaver stood up. He'd been hiding.

My stomach did a jerky dance. "What are you doing here?"

"As in why did I kill Cherry?" He said it in a sarcastic way, a confident, conclusive way that told me he was here for the same reason we were—to collect evidence.

I said, "You didn't do it. I know who did. You do, too. You're protecting the killer. Why?"

"Let me explain." The professor's eyes flashed wider in my beam of light as he came around the car and raised a pistol.

Pauline screamed.

A shot exploded and then Pauline crumpled to the ground.

Chapter 31

When I woke up, it was pitch-black night and my face was mashed against the grass.

My heartbeat pulsated like a bass drum in my ears. Somebody had whacked me on the back of the head.

I shook my head to loosen my fuzziness.

Pauline and I were tied up next to each other with our hands behind us. I couldn't tell if she was bleeding from the gunshot I recalled. Was I bleeding? It didn't feel like it. My ankles were encircled maybe a dozen times with masking tape. We were laid out alongside the car on our stomachs. A limb on the ground was poking into my legs.

A person was moving about in the darkness, piling branches on top of us, essentially burying us. Weaver? I tried to speak, but my tongue met with part of my sweatshirt that had been ripped off my person, stuffed in my mouth, and taped. Tape wound around my head and ponytail. My scalp prickled with each movement as the tape pulled my hair.

I shoved my legs enough to nudge Pauline awake. Her eyelids popped open, then went wide with terror. Part of my sweatshirt was taped into her mouth, too.

When I saw that the person was beginning to pour something around us and on the branches, I wiggled madly. I rolled and bucked.

The person's shoe met my head. I let out a muffled "Ow-mmmph." I wanted to say, "You idiot asshole."

He said, "It'll be over soon."

It was Nick Stensrud.

He ripped the tape off my mouth and said, "Do you have the recipe on you?"

I spat out my ripped sweatshirt sleeve. "There is no recipe," I said, feeling like Judas denying my grandfather's belief in it. "You killed Cherry for no good reason. I thought you didn't like testing fudge in your test tubes."

"Sister Adele's recipe is worth money."

"Money you need to replace the grant Cherry ruined for you."

"He was ruining my department."

"No, he was ruining your thesis and your chances of becoming a newly minted professor. You were afraid pretty Cinderella Pink Fudge in your test tubes would make you a laughingstock by your doctoral committee."

He tore the brush back, then roughly pulled me up and slammed me back against the car tire. He thrust Pauline against the car door next to me.

I said, "You bought all the goods from my store and tossed them in the chapel to spook me. And Fontana knew it was probably you, though she might have feared it was Professor Weaver. My father saw her poking around the chapel. I bet she wanted to return the stolen goods. She came to your offices to talk to Weaver about it and you."

I could barely see him in the dark, but his pause told me I was striking the bull's-eye.

Nick said, "He threatened her, told her to stay out of this. It's her fault."

"For being scared? For wanting what's right? You were hoping you could blame her."

"Where's the recipe?"

I scooted to get my back away from the tire's hubcap. My face was itching horribly from bug bites that I couldn't do a thing about. "I don't have the recipe. I'm sure you've been through all my pockets by now."

"That and your friend's purse."

Pauline kicked and gurgled gagged words that were likely the equivalent of "Give me back my pretty purse, you pyro, pukey pervert!"

I said to Nick, "I don't suppose you left us our phones. I was thinking of calling out for the delivery of marshmallows to roast with our fire."

"The bears will pick up your phones when they come to dine on the human barbecue. Without marshmallows. Now tell me where the recipe is."

"I put it in a bank vault. Only my fingerprint can open the vault lock."

Pauline's wide-eyed gaze questioned my answer.

Nick squatted down from outside the cage built of branches. "Which finger?" He snapped a Buck knife from its sheath.

I realized my mistake. He was going to cut off my fingers or at least the tips to get my fingerprints. "Looks like you bought your own knife. You took my father's Buck knife the last time you were at our farm. Did Cherry find it on you or in your lab? Cherry was onto you. Did he take my father's knife from you so that he could return it? I bet he scolded you. And you hated him for treating you like a dumb kid instead of a nano away from being a faculty member."

"Nobody can make a living on a teaching assistant's salary."

"Salary? You were being paid on the grant, and once it was over, you would lose your job."

His silence told me I was right.

"So, Nick, you met him last Saturday morning at the church. You were out together doing research before the tour maybe? At some point you stopped by the Dahlgrens' and borrowed a shovel for digging. It came in handy later at the church."

"That unused church was a good place to talk. That's all we did."

"I'm not a fool. You meant to kill him in the church, didn't you? You probably heard Jonas come to work on the landscaping and got spooked. But Cherry got cut on the arm with the knife. I bet if we looked at your hands closely or pushed up those long sleeves you're wearing, we'd find a nick or cut."

"Shut up."

"No. You like listening to me because I figured it out.

Maybe I amaze you? Maybe you feel sorry that I got mixed up in this?"

"I like your family. Please ... shut ... up."

"I'll take that as a compliment." My brain was trying to figure out how to get out of this mess. But all I had for a weapon was words. "You like smart people. I'm smart. But Cherry was smart, too. Your career was about to be over because he knew you were spreading chemicals around the countryside and dosing orchards and grapevines so your research could stay on track. You were hoping the feds would renew your grant and your job. Because you're so smart."

He turned his head away and I heard him spit off into the ferns. When he turned his face back toward me, the starlight spying through scudding clouds illuminated his forehead, cheeks, and chin in blue light. He looked crazed.

I continued, still conjuring an escape. "You made up some story to get him to meet you at the church Saturday night. Maybe you thought the knife would still be inside the church? You told him it was still there and you were going to report him? Maybe you reminded him that his blood and fingerprints were all over it?"

"I didn't know he was hopping aboard that tour and would come back or that you'd be there. I drove by a few times while you and your grandma were cleaning the buildings and graveyard."

"Did it make you nervous to think I might have found the knife, considering I've got a reputation for being like a dog on a bone with crimes?"

"I'm sorry, Ava. I have to do this. I don't have a choice."

My throat was too parched to swallow in fear. "You killed Professor Hardy, didn't you, because you knew he was going to report you to the chancellor? Cherry knew that Weaver was scared, maybe scared of you, and didn't have the guts to stand up to you."

The only sound was the whispery rustle of leaves in the trees hugging the ravine's slopes.

"Where is Weaver?" I asked.

"Dead."

Dread seized me. Anger came next—a hot, molten fountain rising inside me like one of my copper kettles overflowing. We were all going to die because of a selfish, pyromaniac punk.

He put the knife away, then brought out a pistol. Nick parted the twigs he'd stacked over me, then shoved me forward to the ground. My face mashed into trampled grass. Nick then placed the pistol in my hands behind me. He pressed my fingers around it.

I asked him, "You really believe the sheriff will think I killed Weaver?"

"Why not? You were driven to do it to protect your friends and family. I'll tell the authorities how Weaver was dosing the land around here, how he set the fires. Heck, he even stole clocks and timing devices from our lab to do it."

After getting my fingerprints on the pistol, he set it aside somewhere on the forest floor. Where Jordy would find it after I'd been toasted to a crisp.

Setting my body up to a sitting position against the car again, Nick said, "Professor Weaver is in the trunk of this car, where you put him."

I could smell the sour fear on Nick's body. I spat at him. And missed.

I said, "Tell Grandpa and Grandma I love them. Mom and Dad, too. And Dillon. And Cody. Sam, too. And Moose and Milt. And Lucky Harbor. And—"

"I bet your grandpa can tell me exactly where to find the recipe. He loves a good story. I listened to my share of them when he was visiting on the farm or when I happened to stop by the shop in Fishers' Harbor. I'll buy him a beer and console him, tell him I was sweet on you."

"You bastard. My grandpa knows nothing." Fear crystallized over every inch of my skin like hoarfrost.

"I'll tell him about how I'm the one testing your fudge in my test tubes. He'll reveal where the recipe is. I'll ask him to donate it to our Belgian collection at the university. The chancellor will reward me handsomely."

I scoffed. "Then you'll have to fight over it with the prince and princess coming from Belgium. That recipe was promised to them."

Nick scowled, clearly confused. If only I could get him to leave for some reason.

I said, "It's true. My grandfather has an agreement with Prince Arnaud and his mother, Princess Amandine Van Damme, to put the recipe in a museum in Belgium for two years after we find it. Go check it out with my grandpa. The recipe will return here to our Door County Belgian Heritage Foundation in Namur after that. It's Grandpa Gil, not you, who will be honored by your chancellor."

He made motions to put the torn fabric back in my mouth, so I grasped at something that had been niggling at me. "Why did Fontana break up with Professor Weaver?"

"He broke up with her. She was going to ruin him. I told him what she was really like. She flirted with everybody, including me."

"You bastard. Are you stupid enough to think you could be good enough for Fontana?"

"That's not it at all. Now you're being stupid. I hate stupid people." He stuffed the ripped sleeve in my mouth, then twisted more masking tape around my head to hold it in place.

Within minutes, the trickle of chemicals and the thud of plastic containers touched my eardrums. I smelled gasoline, too. And spices.

Nick disappeared from my view. From a rustle I heard, it sounded as if he was to my right and in front of the car. Pauline and I were near the back driver's-side tire, with the darkness and something like an eagle's nest worth of sticks between us and Nick. After a sharp slap of his hand on the car hood, I heard feet hitting the ground and branches snapping, receding fast. He had to be running to get away. A chill came over me. He must have struck a match.

The whoosh came. It was at the front of the car. Tongues of fire ignited and skipped along a ring on the ground surrounding Pauline and me.

Within minutes the fire would climb the branches laid over us. Then we'd be smothered in flames when the gas tank exploded.

Chapter 32

The fire fed on the dried branches webbed over us and the car.

I was scared but not a fool. I dumped myself over to lie low below the branches above me that were catching on fire. Pauline went prone, too.

Our only way out was to bust through the branches. But I had to roll right at the fire. I rolled. The branches didn't give. I rolled back, hoping I'd rolled out anything on fire on my person. My taped-down hair seemed to be okay.

I rolled and shoved again, squeezing my eyes closed. Putrid smoke stung in my nose. Smoky branches slapped across my head, hitting the masking tape.

On the third try, Pauline and I synchronized. Our bulk toppled the fiery mass of branches in our wake as we wiggled and rolled across the ground heading down the slight slope behind the car.

I expected gunshots but nothing came. Nick must have taken off or he simply didn't see us behind the car.

We squirmed along the ground like inchworms, doing accordion moves to get away from the car now engulfed with branches on fire. I thought about Wes Weaver in the trunk but couldn't do a thing about him.

The fire's glow was causing eerie shadows to dance on the nearby foliage and up the smooth trunk of a maple tree. The fire was so far down in the ravine that it would be impossible for anybody to spot its glow. Even if anybody in their houses nearby peered out a window into the night, the black smoke wouldn't be seen, either.

Pauline and I lay under ferns catching our breath and listening again. No footsteps. Nobody killing us. Yet.

I scratched my face against a root until the masking tape gave way. I spat out my sweatshirt sleeve.

"Hang in there, Pauline. Let me get at your face."

My hands were still taped behind my back, but I wiggled to her face, then chewed through the masking tape. Once I got it loose, she spat out the fabric and asked, "What do you use for laundry detergent?"

"You want to talk about laundry now?"

"It smells a lot like all the stuff Fontana makes. And did you smell Nick? He smelled like her, too. Like lavender and all kinds of pickling spices."

"My guess is he sprayed a bottle of her stuff all over the trees and bushes around the car, and on us. He wants to blame Fontana for the murder and arsons. He probably sprinkled the stuff over Cherry's dead body to make sure Fontana was a suspect."

We wriggled about and even flipped over so our hands were on the ground and under our backs and butts, but we couldn't find purchase on roots.

I flipped back over onto my stomach. "Who wants to do the chewing first? We have to chew this tape off."

Pauline said, "I just had my teeth whitened."

"Crap, P.M., you always have an excuse."

"A.M., I need excuses for sticking by you. This is not fun."

The fire was worrying me. I couldn't bear the thought of Weaver's body going up in smoke. Maybe he was alive in that trunk. I gnawed on the tape on Pauline's wrists. I felt like little Titus chipping away on acorns, a sound that never failed to wake me up at two in the morning.

In between spitting out tape, a realization banged inside my brain. "Crap, we have to save Fontana from him."

"What're you talking about?"

I spat more tape. "Nick must want her dead or gone, too. He's going after her next."

"Because she knows too much."

"That and because she's pregnant with Tristan Hardy's baby."

"When did you find that out?"

"Just now." I recalled all the signs and enumerated them for Pauline: the drinking of milk; the episode in the house of rushing to the bathroom—not to cough as I thought, but to toss her cookies.

Pauline said, "But is it Cherry's baby? She was playing the field."

I conceded that. And chewed harder.

In minutes, we'd freed ourselves. Panting, we stared at the car engulfed with burning branches. We had no phones.

"We have to get the rest of those branches off that car," I said.

Grappling in the dark, we snapped off a couple of saplings, then used them to shove at the burning branches. They weren't too effective.

I wrapped a bunch of fern fronds around my hands for protection and finally pulled and pushed at the burning branches that were too big and not moving. With Pauline's help, we opened up the space over the driver's door. The windows had been closed, which wasn't the brightest thing on Nick's part because it had saved the interior from catching on fire. I opened the front door and hit the button to pop the trunk.

Pauline and I grabbed Weaver—dead or alive we didn't know—and then dragged him off, stumbling and falling over him twice before we got him far enough away that any explosion wouldn't harm us.

Weaver was still breathing, but the breaths were shallow. In the dark, with only intermittent starlight coming through the cloudy night, I couldn't detect the location of his wound at first. Then my hand found an oozing on his chest. Pauline and I took off his belt and tied it around his chest hoping to stanch the flow of blood.

By then we were drained, almost collapsing. We were scratched and probably bloodied.

We couldn't head back to the winery where we'd parked, because that was where Nick probably left his vehicle.

"Come on," I said, dragging myself up off the ground, "we can't be far from Jonas's place."

"What about that pistol he put in your hands?"

In the dark, I looked about but couldn't see it. I assumed it was under the burning branches.

We pressed into the deep woods.

After we clawed our way up the rim of the ravine and reached the new fencing between Mike's property and Jonas's land, we collapsed for good this time, heaving for air.

Seeing the lights on in Jonas's house revived us. We could call the sheriff from there.

But that thought evaporated when we got close enough to spy through the living room window. Jonas was sitting in a chair while Nick was stalking around him waving a knife in one hand. We crouched down and crawled away from the window's light.

I whispered, "He's going to kill Jonas."

"Because he believes Jonas saw him at the church last Saturday."

"Nick also knows that Jonas must have gotten an earful from Fontana about Weaver and that whole department, including Nick. Nick's afraid she's told Jonas too much."

Pauline said, "We can run to the Dahlgrens' place. Should take us only fifteen minutes to get to a phone."

"That might be too late."

The pile of old wood from Jonas's burned shed was illuminated by the yard light. There were splintered two-by-fours and charred chunks of eight-inch beams.

On my nod Pauline and I ran to the woodpile, then raced back to the house, onto the porch, and then we slung our projectiles through the big front window.

The glass crashed in a deafening explosion.

My wood chunk caught Nick on the back of the head. It was like watching one of my three-point shots from center court swish the basket.

Nick turned as Pauline's big square of wood clocked him straight in the nose.

We ducked and ran.

Jonas tumbled from the house. He hooked up with us

while punching at his cell phone. We ran for our lives into the maw of darkness.

By ten o'clock that night it was all over. Jordy and his backup team had taken Wes Weaver to the hospital. Jordy found Nick in the living room, dazed with a gash across his broken nose and blood streaming down his chin. Evidently, Pauline's blow to his nose had knocked him out. Nick had the appearance of a bloody wraith when he came out of the house in handcuffs and met the glare of the squad car headlights.

After Nick was hauled away, Jordy stood with Pauline and me in Jonas's living room interrogating us. Jonas was sitting in the chair where he'd been minutes ago, while Pauline and I sat opposite him on the couch.

To our surprise, Fontana poked her head into the room from the kitchen. She screamed with relief and ran to hug Jonas.

She was saying over and over, "I'm so sorry. I'm so sorry."

Fontana's red hair looked as if she'd been pulling at it. Grime sullied a pretty yellow top she was wearing and her blue jeans. She explained that as soon as she had heard Nick's voice, she'd hidden in the basement by squeezing behind an unused refrigerator.

I got up to let Fontana sit in my place on the couch. "Fontana, we know what's going on and why you were so scared."

Jordy was watching us, taking notes.

I knelt in front of her and took her hands in mine. "You're pregnant, aren't you?"

Her lower lip trembled.

An awful thought came to me. I made her scooch closer to Pauline, and then I sat beside her. "Is it Nick's baby?"

"Oh no. Thank goodness, no. I never had sex with him or anybody since my divorce, except for Cherry. It's Cherry's." She retrieved a tissue from a pocket. "I made the mistake of telling Nick about the baby a few weeks ago. I thought I could get rid of him that way. Instead he became obsessed. He kept appearing everywhere with Wes, always ending up at my roadside stand, and he was following Cherry, too. He said . . . Oh my gosh, I just remembered what he said to me once. He said that I had a 'fiery' attitude to match my fiery hair."

All of us stared at her red hair.

Jordy stepped closer, towering over us. "Why did he set the fires?"

Fontana choked up. "Nick was mad and scared." She glanced my way. "I overheard your grandpa talk about the recipe with your mother while I was visiting Ava's Autumn Harvest one afternoon. I told Wes about it. I'm sorry. I was mad at Wes for how he was treating Cherry in the university, and I told him off and said Cherry would be rich and famous because he was helping the Oosterlings find the holy recipe. Nick must have overheard me, or Wes told him."

She worried the tissue in her hands. "I tried to make you leave, Ava. I wanted you to shut down your market and get away from here. I didn't want to tell you everything, Ava. I was embarrassed and I wanted to protect you. You're like my kid sister. I knew you'd be ashamed of me if you knew I'd gotten myself pregnant."

I hugged Fontana. "Nonsense."

"But you and your family thought Wes and Nick were wonderful. I'm so sorry."

Shame came to me. How had I misread so many things? Dillon's words came back to me. I was too busy with too many things to listen. I peered down at myself. I was full of grass stains, scratches, black soot, and blood, and one sweatshirt sleeve had been ripped off. There were untold mosquito bites on my face. I touched my hair—it was full of cockleburs.

I asked, because I just had to know, "Fontana, you weren't really dating Jonas or Mike, were you? I mean, well, you kissed them. I jumped to conclusions and thought you were . . ."

"If I kissed a friend, it was a friendly kiss and nothing more. I was scared. Scared for Cherry, and then scared for me and the baby. I wanted to be sure I was never alone." She sucked in a big breath and said to Jonas, "Sorry that I used you. But I needed you. Still friends?"

Jonas nodded. "Friends."

Fontana said to me, "Thanks for saving me."

On the other side of her, Pauline piped up, "Hey, I was the one who hit him square in the nose with a full-court shot."

Jonas said, "You saved my life, Pauline." He came out of his chair to shake her hand.

"What about me?" I said. "Tossing the wood through the window was my idea."

Jordy held up a hand. "Ava, call me first in the future, okay? You almost . . . got yourself killed tonight." He choked on the words, which made us all exchange glances. Then he headed to the door. "Stick to your fudge."

Pauline said, "That'll be the day she does that."

Chapter 33

On Sunday morning I felt as if a tractor had run over me. My skin burned from bug bites and scratches. But I woke to the smell of pancakes, bacon, eggs, and coffee. I had stayed overnight with my parents rather than drive through the wee hours in deathlike shape back to Fishers' Harbor. Pauline had stayed in my grandparents' old room.

After breakfast and a shower, Pauline left for Fishers' Harbor. Maria Vasquez gave her a ride; Maria wanted to get more details about what had happened in the woods.

Despite my scratched face, I went to church in Brussels with Mom and Dad. I hadn't been to church in a long time, but I'd been telling a lot of lies and Dad needed some healing prayers. Mom needed me to fend off people asking questions about the murder. We stuck to our story that I'd found the body, but neighbors knew about Mom's penchant for cleaning, so they knew the vacuum cleaner I'd allegedly used was hers. Mom was a hero by association; I knew she'd really solved the case. Jordy would eventually figure out some of those hairs belonged to Nick Stensrud.

After the service and outside the church, Dillon was waiting for me. I barely recognized him in a blue shirt and dark tie. An involuntary smile pushed creases into my itchy cheeks.

Sun blessed everything and us with a glow. The smell of fresh-mown hayfields for that final crop of hay before winter arrived was one of the best perfumes I'd inhaled in several days.

From the front seat of Dillon's white construction truck, Lucky Harbor woofed at me out the window.

It gave me déjà vu to see Dillon waiting for me outside a church. The last time he'd waited for me like this, we eloped. That hadn't ended well, though.

With most of the congregation talking with Mom and Dad and offering them help rebuilding the barn, I was able to take Dillon aside for a private talk.

His hair had grown over the summer. He had it groomed neatly now into a short ponytail at the nape of his neck. It gave him rakish appeal and injected my libido with a touch of wanton excitement.

Feeling awkward, I touched my hair. It hung loose and felt good after my ordeal. It had taken Pauline and me an hour last night to get the burs out. I was wearing Mom's red jersey knit dress with long sleeves to cover my scratches. Black tights covered my legs. No amount of makeup could cover up the bug bites and scratches on my face, though. I supposed I probably didn't look too kissable, though I would have loved one of Dillon's dip-and-kiss routines right now.

I asked, "Were you sitting in back during Mass? Did I miss seeing you?"

"No. I checked Mass times on the Internet, then calculated when you'd be coming out." He took a deep breath.

"You're dressed up. Is there an occasion?"

"I got to thinking about things."

"This sounds ominous, Dillon."

"I was thinking how I selfishly suggested you slow down and ditch a few things to simplify your life. That wasn't fair of me. In fact, it was pretty darn obnoxious, egotistical, as if I know everything. I don't. If we're going to start over, we need to start at the beginning, at Saint Mary of the Snows. Together. I haven't been inside the Namur church yet."

"I understand. I had trepidations, too. I had to force myself into the church a week ago."

"That's nice to hear, I mean, not nice exactly, but nice that we think alike."

The man was trying hard to please me. "You look nice. I like you in a tie."

"This old thing?" He flipped his tie offhandedly. "I'd like you to come with me to Saint Mary of the Snows, Miss Oosterling."

"Cody is rubbing off on you."

"It's those EMT and firefighter classes we're in together. We're learning procedures for resuscitating hearts."

I felt like a baby bird he was feeding and he was feeding me all the right things that made me want to take flight with him.

I agreed to meet him in Namur after I drove my parents home.

We met outside the church. Lucky Harbor loped about the grounds, tongue lolling out. I unlocked the church. The three of us went inside.

Dillon chose a pew in the middle. It was neutral territory, not too close or too far from the holy business at the front of the room.

For a few moments, we appreciated the beauty and quiet.

There wasn't a sound. Not a horn or a whoosh of tires outside. A crow cawed in the trees outside. Dillon's breathing then feathered to me. I listened to my own breathing. I remembered Pauline talking about mindfulness.

Dillon and I were sharing a certain serenity. A rare thing in our hurly-burly world.

I was amazed in the moment. Dillon had made me stop the world. He'd performed magic.

I gave him a glance. He was looking straight ahead at the altar and angel statues. The side of his face was tanned, freshly shaven. I wanted to touch him but didn't want to interrupt him. I curled my fingers into my palms in my lap.

The church had that churchlike smell of polished wood. A hint of Fontana's awful pickling spice perfume lingered, though, along with the faint tincture of smoke.

The breeze outside was tossing the trees about enough to play with the light inside the church. Fractured colors flitted in flight. *Like angels*. My grandfather's angels.

I took Dillon's hand next to me. His knuckles were roughened and his hand was warm. "We've never sat together in a church."

"Feels strange, and new . . . and nice," he said, his dark eyes searching me in a way I'd never seen or felt before.

"I know."

We chuckled.

Dillon asked, "Do you ever regret not marrying Sam?"

I squeezed his hand. "No, Dillon. Sam needs somebody far more sensible than me."

"You're the most sensible person I know." He lifted my hand, then kissed it. "But sometimes you scare the hell out of me."

"But you've always liked gambling."

His laughter was a raucous reverberation in the cavernous church.

Lucky Harbor chose that moment to leap in the air on the altar's steps, probably to snap at a fly that had come in with us. His body twisted and then hit one of the tall angel statues with the candles on top, knocking it over.

Dillon raced from the pew. "Lucky, shame on you. Sit."

I headed over to pick up the tall angel statue.

Dillon said, "Stop, Ava. Look."

Crouching on the floor, he reached inside the bottom of the statue. He pulled out several yellowed pieces of paper.

At the top of one in cursive script were the words "Divine Confection."

I called Jordy.

He yelled back, "You want me to . . . try to establish the fingerprints today of a revered nun who died in 1896?"

"This recipe is at the center of the murder case, Jordy. You have to help us find out if this recipe is authentic. You'll be famous if you find the fingerprints or DNA belonging to Sister Adele Brise. Think about the Shroud of Turin, Jordy. This will be the Fudge of Namur."

Jordy cursed, then hung up.

Dillon drove the two of us, Lucky Harbor, and the papers to the Justice Center. I was pleased to see Jordy's evidence in the murder case included the test tube with my pink fudge.

When we left Jordy's office, Dillon said, "Your fudge is going to end up on front pages everywhere."

The thought made me buoyant. "We better make sure the Blue Heron Inn is ready for guests. I think we're about to be busy."

During the next few days, fudge flew off my shop shelves and the wagons at Ava's Autumn Harvest.

Door County was abuzz with tourists, press people, history buffs, and church officials.

I'd copied the recipe before we handed it over to Jordy. I was still amazed at the secret ingredient. It was lavender. When I mentioned this to Dotty, she said, "Of course!"

"Why?" I'd asked her.

"Lavender comes from the Latin word *lavare*, which means 'to wash.'"

"Washing a confection?"

Dotty had looked at me as if I were blasphemous. "My dear, the story comes from religious stories, not your fairy tales. The Virgin Mary hung her child's washed clothing on a lavender bush. They dried smelling crisp and clean, pleasing the Christ child. Lavender is a calming scent. Isn't it bountiful in fields in France and Belgium and used in chocolates? Perhaps the sisters were homesick and used it in their cooking, too." Dotty leaned close to me with a big grin on her face. "Maybe the Holy Mother of God traveled all the way to Door County just to deliver lovely sprigs of lavender to Sister Adele. Her life had to have been very hard. She would have deserved a gift of lavender."

True or not, the story enchanted me, and it also planted a wry smile on my face when I considered all the times I'd maligned Fontana's affection for lavender. My childhood mentor deserved more respect from me. I immediately called Laura, who had a little of everything on her shelves because she taught baking classes. She had plenty of lavender to give me for making fudge.

Fog rolled in during the mornings, but dry days were helping me hone my divinity fudge skills. I packaged every last morsel for the kermis fund-raiser.

By Wednesday, Jordy was happily retelling the press about the murder case and "his" call for trying to find fingerprints after all these years as well as analyzing the recipe.

We found out Nick Stensrud had been fudging on his research about my fudge. He'd spread bugs and chemicals everywhere, and even inserted some into the test tubes. Professor Weaver had been lax in overseeing him. Cherry had found out about both of them. Weaver wouldn't be prosecuted for the murder, of course, but he lost his job.

Parker Balusek was representing Nick's buddy Will Lucchesi. Parker told me Will had asked Nick to change his ways. Will had also been convinced by Nick that Michael Prevost and Fontana had murdered Tristan Hardy. Many of us had almost fallen for that theory.

Maria Vasquez got overtime hours. She showed up several times at the harbor parking lot to direct traffic. The entire populace wanted to meet the prince and they'd begun to camp out at the harbor waiting for him.

By Thursday, Prince Arnaud revealed himself as the prince. It was Dillon's idea to have Mercy Fogg drive him from the farm to Fishers' Harbor in her limousine. We pretended he'd arrived at the Green Bay Airport that day. His mother would arrive on Saturday.

At my invitation, Piers took over cooking at the Blue Heron Inn. He became the prince's private chef.

The prince insisted we not reserve the entire inn for only him and his mother. He wanted to experience a real inn, with people who were there to fish and vacation. That Thursday afternoon, after I had inspected the beautiful new rooms upstairs, I raced down the blue-carpeted staircase and ran smack dab into a tall, curvy blond woman. She was out of breath and appeared in distress. She was covered in splotches of apple green paint.

She said, "Have you seen Barkly?"

"There's no guest here by that name."

"He's a Bernese mountain dog. Size of a bear. Hard to miss. About one hundred twenty pounds, black with a white stripe on his face and fawn-colored eyebrows. He was chasing a curly brown dog and they came this way."

"That's my dog, Lucky Harbor."

"I'm sorry about this. Your dog poked his head in my door. I was painting the store. I spilled a can of paint and said, 'Oh, fudge' and your dog took off and my dog tailed after him."

I laughed. "No need to be sorry. They're probably at my fudge shop or swimming in the harbor together by now. I'm Ava Oosterling."

"I'm Jane Goodland."

"The stripper?" It came out before I could stop myself.

She laughed. "Yeah. That's a long story. I'm the new owner of the Wise Owl. Come over soon and I'll show you the new stripper pole in the back of the store. Gotta go find my dog now."

I had no idea whether that stripper pole thing was a joke or not. I put it out of my mind for another time. I had my relatives to worry about.

Grandma Sophie was charmed by the prince, but not so charmed by Grandpa's keeping his presence a secret.

Grandma also confessed to me that it saddened her to think all this could be for naught. She worried that the savvy national reporters in town might look into the past and find out the prince came from a baby adopted in Chicago in the late 1800s.

Pauline, too, was out of sorts. Neither Jordy and his crew nor we had found her purse in the woods. I'd given her a sparkly Cinderella Pink Fairy Tale Fudge cloth bag from my shop that Dotty had made, but still Pauline fussed.

Worse yet, John left town with my manager, Marc Hayward, on that Thursday.

Pauline bolted into the shop late that afternoon. "He's gone, Ava. Gone for good." Tears of fury steeped in her eyes.

My insides twisted. I didn't dare say, "I told you so." I called Marc on the spot but only got his voice mail.

I was loafing a batch of my new Red Riding Hood Fairy Tale Fudge, but abandoned it to take Pauline out back. We stood next to the burning bush that was scarlet with autumn leaves.

"You confirmed he left?"

She nodded. "I called. He's in Los Angeles. Working on his TV deal. He said he didn't know how long it would take."

That disturbed me. He'd been so excited about surprising Pauline by singing "Ave Maria" this coming Sunday. But I blamed my manager for John's taking off.

Pauline sat down on the grass. "I'm so dumb. You were right about him all along."

"You're not dumb." I sat beside her.

"I am dumb. My purse that's lost? It had my diamond ring in it."

I screeched, "John gave you a ring?"

"Shh. No, I bought it myself."

"He asked you to marry him?"

"Not exactly. He said he wanted to get married sometime. He said I deserved a ring the size of a baseball. I thought he meant I should go ahead and shop for one."

I looked at her cross-eyed.

"I was excited, and stupid. Eager. I found a ring I loved at one of the artists' shops here. One of a kind. I was sure John would sell his TV series idea and he'd pay me back."

"Pauline, this isn't how an engagement is supposed to unfold."

"I know, I know." She sniffled. "He's not the type to have time to shop for a ring, which he of course proved by leaving me."

Pauline flipped her long hair off her shoulders. She seemed small now sitting next to me, not the tall friend who always looked down her nose at me.

She said, "Him leaving me is only part of the bad news. I might have to sell my house to pay off the loan for the ring."

"You took out a mortgage on your house?" Her house was a tiny ranch house, but still . . . "That's some ring."

She was trembling. "I love him. Loved. Past tense."

"No insurance?"

"I hadn't added the ring to the policy yet."

I got to my feet, pulling her up. I shook her shoulders. "Don't give up. On the diamond or John."

She sniffled. "Do you think I'm a complete fool?"

"Of course. But who am I to judge? I was once married to a bigamist. And I'm dating him again!"

"You say the sweetest things." She flung her arms around me.

*   *   *

Pauline's diamond debacle wasn't my only problem. Grandpa wasn't himself the rest of that Thursday, Friday, and Saturday.

Sure, he was busy with customers and lines of people asking him to pilot the snazzy *Super Catch I*, but Grandpa seemed to be going through the motions. I remembered his wish to have dirty hands again, but I didn't know how to fix that. About the only way we'd gotten dirty lately was with fires, and I certainly wanted to douse even the thought of another five-alarm fire.

Grandpa wasn't at the center of the murder investigation, either, and I could tell he was out of sorts because of that, too. He and I were used to working together on such adventures. I believed Gilpa was thinking we'd drifted apart. I, too, was missing the closeness we'd had in the summertime.

My only hope was that the recipe in Jordy's hands would turn out to be authentic from Sister Adele Brise. That would please my grandfather.

Chapter 34

On Sunday, the kermis in Namur was an incredible festival with a polka band, a beer tent, and Belgian pies that stretched down picnic tables all the way between the church and the old school. The school and Saint Mary of the Snows had been cleaned to a sheen by my mother and the church ladies, including my grandmother.

Over five thousand people showed up in the tiny burg to tour the church and school. Cars lined the country roads for miles.

My mother had two thousand of the fudge buttons made with the logo "Ava's Fudge—Fit for Royalty." All were sold after she told visitors how rubbing the buttons had helped us solve the murder. She took orders for a couple thousand more at least.

The visitors also went on a tour of the many roadside chapels in our county. Mercy ferried the visitors in the yellow school bus. She wore her snazzy uniform and one of Mom's buttons, which I found a generous gesture by Mercy.

Princess Amandine Van Damme, who had arrived yesterday and stayed at the Blue Heron Inn, was a vivacious, beautiful woman of my mother's generation with white blond hair and exquisite, milky skin. Upon spotting the cup with AVD on it in the foyer of the inn, she said she was certain it belonged to the Van Damme ancestors. She'd brought a similar piece with her for comparison.

I was very excited to tell Pauline and John but realized

John was gone. Despite my concerns about the guy, I was sad.

The princess and Dillon's mother, Cathy, got along famously in an instant, which meant that my mother and Cathy were put into a proximity of each other that they'd never before experienced. The princess had a way of making everybody laugh and enjoy camaraderie, so I thought there might be hope for Dillon's family and mine eventually getting along.

At the farm, the princess toured everything with my grandmother on one arm and my father on the other. She encouraged the press to take pictures of her stirring the cream and tasting fresh cheese curds.

"They squeak," she said, laughing.

At four o'clock at the Namur church grounds during the kermis, Sheriff Tollefson showed up. A murmur reverberated through the throng because word had gotten out during the week that he was examining the divinity fudge recipe.

I rushed through the crowd to get to him. "What did you find out?"

My grandfather leaped to my side. "Jordy, any fingerprints from Adele Brise?"

"In due time," Jordy said.

Jordy pushed through the crowd with my lawyer friend, Parker Balusek. Parker was a Lincolnesque figure dressed in a suit and carrying a briefcase. The two of them proceeded to the dais as our governor stepped up to the microphone.

Rows of folding chairs on the lawn filled instantly. My family and I took honored seats on the dais with the prince and princess. They were dressed in full royal regalia, the prince in a uniform and the princess in a long, ecru-colored gown with a sash.

I felt hot with the thousands of pairs of eyes on us. I'd worn a simple red sheath dress, with a triple strand of pearls borrowed from Grandma. Plenty of makeup helped hide my scratches. My hair was down, fluttering in the breeze.

People were standing out to the road. Little kids were riding their dads' shoulders.

Dillon and Pauline had found seats in the second row below us.

Our governor took the microphone. "Welcome to the Namur kermis, honoring our connection to Belgium with our honored, distinguished guests, Prince Arnaud and Princess Amandine."

The governor blathered on about how Grandma, Dad, and I were related to royalty. I didn't even have to look at Grandma to feel the tension within her heart because of her secret.

Then the governor motioned Jordy to the microphone, amid great applause.

Jordy said, "I asked Attorney Parker Balusek, who specializes in church rehabilitations and church history, to take charge of the authentication of these papers. He and I traveled to the State Historical Society in Madison—"

My grandfather piped up, "Just tell us what you found out, Jordy. I'm collecting cobwebs sitting here."

A chuckle rippled through the crowd. Even the princess seated to Jordy's left on the dais giggled.

Jordy motioned for Parker to come forward. The sheriff removed a shadow box–style frame holding the precious recipe.

A thrill went through me. My hands were shaking.

Parker said, "I'd like the princess and prince and Gil and Sophie Oosterling to read the wording at the bottom of each picture."

The crowd clapped. My grandfather's silver hair stood out against the backdrop of Parker's dark suit. Grandma was on the other side of Parker. The princess stood next to her. Gilpa took up his post next to the prince.

Grandpa read, " 'This authenticated divinity fudge recipe was written during the time when Belgians first arrived in Door County. They were served by Sister Adele Brise, who traveled among settlements during the 1850s and early 1890s. The recipe was discovered inside the angel to the right of the altar in Saint Mary of the Snows Church, in Namur, Wisconsin, by Dillon Rivers, Ava Oosterling, and her grandfather, Gil Oosterling.' "

The plaque's words were so "fudging" that the crowd—

including me—sat there for a moment absorbing what wasn't said.

Parker took over. "'While we cannot say for sure that Sister Adele created this recipe, we do know the paper is from that era. We did not find fingerprints. But we did find our imaginations making connections.'"

Grandpa crowed, "I imagine that Sister Adele liked fudge and that's good enough for me!"

Prince Arnaud accepted the framed recipe from Grandpa. "And it's good enough for me. This unique document represents the beginning of an important partnership between Namur, Belgium, and Namur, Wisconsin. I'm honored to accept this and it will be kept in an honored place in our royal museum in the home country."

His mother walked over to the microphone. "I choose to believe that Adele Brise made fudge. It is that simple. Life is simple." Her voice was silky smooth and cultured. "Adele knew the beauty of Belgian chocolate in the home country. She had to have passed down her love of chocolate here, because after all the best fudge is made in Door County. I've come all the way from Belgium to declare it so!"

The crowd was on its feet, hooting and applauding.

Amandine went on. "Now shouldn't we partake of the recipe? I'm told that Ava Oosterling has made several batches of Adele's divinity fudge recipe that I'm to raffle off as a fund-raiser for a steeple to go atop this lovely church next to us."

Before the crowd could break up to buy raffle tickets, thunderous organ music stopped everyone.

The music swelled from inside the church. It came out the open doors.

Then a deep, rich baritone voice was singing "Ave Maria."

The voice made me think the church was a giant awakened from a deep sleep and glad that he had rediscovered sunshine.

To our surprise, a singing John Schultz strolled from the doorway at the front of the church. He turned east toward the dais on the lawn. As he sang the hymn, the crowd parted to let him amble in song onto the raised platform where he performed like an opera singer. "Ave Maria, Ave Maria . . . Safe may we sleep beneath thy care."

Pauline was a mess of tears. Dillon and I wrapped an arm around her and held her between us as we were transformed by John's beautiful baritone voice.

The choir strolled out of the church two by two, like an ark in reverse. They joined John. They were dressed in red and yellow robes—the colors of the Namur flag. Their voices rose into the air, lifting us all in a tribute to our community. There wasn't a dry eye in the crowd by the end of the hymn.

The Saint Mary of the Snows divinity fudge sold out fast. I'd made it in the shape of bite-sized snowdrifts. People compared the little snowdrifts in their mouths to eating pieces of "clouds" and "Heaven."

Dillon murmured to me, "This little church will have its steeple by the holidays."

Later that Sunday evening, I traveled back to Fishers' Harbor, where the party continued on the docks outside of Oosterlings' Live Bait, Bobbers & Belgian Fudge & Beer.

Cody and Bethany danced longer than anybody. Cody held back from proposing to her, which made Sam Peterson and all of us proud of him. He was only nineteen, after all. Deep in my heart, I wanted Cody and Bethany to have their own private moment someday in the future. Maybe because I wanted such a moment for me, too.

Pauline and John were finally together. Marc called them to say that a decision would be made about John's TV show idea next week. In secret, I promised Pauline we'd search the woods every day until we found her purse with that diamond in it.

Grandma and Grandpa danced cheek to cheek, but I knew the issue of the secret baby in her lineage was not a dead issue with Grandma Sophie.

My mother danced with the prince while the princess kept my dad company.

Dillon surprised me with his skills at polka dancing. He pumped my arms and flew with me around the harbor and then in the new gazebo behind the Blue Heron Inn up on the cliff overlooking the Lake Michigan bay.

Pride crept into me like a sunset, warming me, settling me as if my inner crystals had been stirred properly. I felt rich beyond compare. I was part of a great family that extended beyond Fishers' Harbor and into our peninsular county.

The next morning I welcomed getting up at five because it was peaceful. Not a thing stirred, not even my mouse. I was alone, savoring the afterglow from yesterday.

My grandparents were sleeping in. I'd told Grandpa to stay home with Grandma and I'd take care of the shop. I spent an hour or so restocking shelves.

I was hauling supplies out to the copper kettles when a scratch at the front door made me smile. Lucky Harbor wore the floatable key holder on his collar. When I opened it up, a key fell out. A note read *Come outside.*

I grabbed a sweatshirt to toss on over my pink shirt.

The morning was chilly, a harbinger of things to come. I wondered how I'd fare over the winter after spending so long in a sunny clime. The thick fog reminded me of the many batches of divinity fudge I'd made in the past few days.

"Where are you?" I called. I could only make out sepia shapes in the fog.

"Right here at the end of your pier," Dillon called back.

I tromped through the thick white mist, discovering the ugliest vessel I'd ever seen. "What's this?"

"A boat."

"I know that, but what is it doing here instead of a junkyard?"

Rust was keeping the forty feet or more of the hulk together.

The shop door slammed shut behind me. Grandpa yelled, "What the heck? Who's in my boat slip?"

I held my breath.

Grandpa materialized out of the fog. He hadn't stayed home with Grandma as I hoped he might. But old habits die hard, the saying goes, and as sure and regular as a heart beats he'd always been at the harbor or in his bait shop every morning early. He spotted Dillon and his dog inside the boat, just past the gunwale railing. "What's going on, Rivers?"

Dillon said, "I bought a boat."

"Without eyeglasses on, I see." Grandpa's hands were running along the rusted boat railing as he walked to the stern to peer at the engines. "Are you an idiot?"

"Probably." Dillon grinned at me on the sly so Grandpa didn't notice. "My mother sent me out to buy a boat for her business. I saw this on the Internet. It got towed here overnight."

"A rust bucket," Grandpa said. "Did you try to fire the engines at all?"

"I don't really know that much about engines. Like I said, it got towed here."

Grandpa climbed over the gunwale and into the boat. He was shaking his head as he zeroed in on the important stuff. "Well, these engines are older than the hills, but Wisconsin-made. That's a plus. Probably need to be totally taken apart and put back together again. That'll take ya all winter. We'll need to soak off the rust in cans of oil. You got any oil?"

"Yeah, I can get you oil."

Grandpa hollered to me, "Ava, you got any old coffee cans? We'll need plenty of cans for the oil and parts."

"Yeah, Gilpa, I've got a few old cans you can have."

Grandpa said, "I can see if I can get 'er started today . . ." He was climbing all over the twin engines.

Dillon winked at me, then turned to pay attention to my grandfather.

Grandpa's voice faded as he tutored Dillon on the finer points of the engines on the rust bucket.

Lucky Harbor hopped back onto the pier, wagging his tail. We wore mutual smiles on our faces, and in our hearts, too. We began making our way back up the pier.

I whispered to the curly brown dog with the golden eyes, "They're going to be working on that boat for a long time, all winter and spring, and I hope years. Are you up for this long-term relationship?"

He stared at me expectantly.

I gave in. "Do you want some fudge?"

Lucky Harbor barked. I tossed him fish-shaped crackers, and then he followed me into Oosterlings' Live Bait, Bobbers & Belgian Fudge & Beer to start a new day.

Recipes

Red Riding Hood Fairy Tale Fudge

In the fairy tale, the wolf disguises himself as the grand-mother. This fudge disguises itself as a rich, red velvet brownie when you first make it, but then over the course of a day or two or more it matures and becomes denser in texture, thus revealing itself for what it really is—fudge. It also freezes well; cut into individual pieces before freezing.

PREPARATION: 10 MINUTES
COOKING TIME: 30 MINUTES

Before you cook: Prepare a 9-by-9-inch pan by either greasing it with butter on the bottom and sides, or lining it with wax paper so that the wax paper comes over the edges. Spray the paper lightly with nonstick vegetable cooking spray.

Use a large microwaveable bowl for the mixing and cooking of the ingredients.

Ingredients
   2½ cups red velvet cake mix
   2 cups powdered sugar
   ¼ cup evaporated milk
   1 stick of butter (8 tablespoons), cut into pieces
   ¾ cup semisweet chocolate chips (can use white
      chocolate chips)
   ¾ cup dark chocolate chips

For the frosting:
   ⅔ cup white chocolate chips
   4 ounces cream cheese

Directions
Mix the cake mix and powdered sugar together in the bowl. Add butter and milk. Microwave this for 2 minutes.

Add the chocolate chips, stir until everything is melted and combined. (You may want to soften the chips slightly beforehand before putting them in the bowl, but don't let them dry out.)

Pour the mixture into the pan and flatten with a spatula. It will have the consistency of brownie dough.

In a medium microwaveable bowl, heat the white chocolate chips for 30 seconds, stir, and heat them again if needed to melt them. Add the cream cheese and stir. Pour over the top of the Red Riding Hood fudge. Let it cool before cutting.

Saint Mary of the Snow's Divinity Fudge

This fudge looks like tiny snowdrifts. Divinity fudge is airy and light as snow or clouds, and all about the weather. Don't try to make it on a humid day. On the day I made my latest batch, I checked the local weather statistics. It was a September Saturday in Wisconsin, with the barometer at 30.13 inches; don't try making divinity fudge if the barometric pressure is over 50. The day was sunny, 73 degrees Fahrenheit, and the humidity was at 44 percent.

PREPARATION: 15 MINUTES
COOKING TIME: 45 MINUTES

Before you cook: Prepare a large cookie sheet or the equivalent in pans by placing wax paper on the surface. Spray only lightly with nonstick vegetable cooking spray.

Ingredients
2½ cups white sugar
½ cup light corn syrup
2 egg whites (I used powdered egg whites)
1 teaspoon vanilla*
¼ teaspoon salt
½ cup water

*Flavoring options:

For lavender divinity fudge: Instead of the vanilla flavoring, add 1 tablespoon of ground dried organic lavender flower heads to the white sugar and mix well. If using fresh buds, use about 12 organic lavender blossom heads and chop them well or grind them.

For maple nut divinity fudge: Replace the vanilla flavoring in the recipe with one teaspoon maple flavoring. Add one cup of finely chopped walnuts right after pouring the liquid sugar into the beaten egg whites and fold them in.

Directions

In a 2-quart heavy-bottomed saucepan, combine sugar, corn syrup, salt, and water. Cook to a hard ball stage (260 degrees), stirring only until the sugar dissolves. Set this aside when it reaches 260 degrees.

Using medium speed or a hand mixer, beat the egg whites into stiff peaks. Gradually pour the syrup over the egg whites, beating at high speed. Add the flavoring (and nuts if you're making maple nut divinity fudge), then beat and fold by hand until the candy loses its shine and becomes dull and doughlike; this will take about 10 minutes.

Using a teaspoon, drop the divinity dough quickly onto the prepared cookie sheet. Makes 40–50 pieces.

Ava's Jack-o'-Lantern Pumpkin Fudge

Like the smile on a jack-o'-lantern's face, this fudge puts a smile on two faces: the cook making it, and those eating it. It's easy to make, and the tasters at my office at the university raved about it, noting it had a rich pumpkin flavor.

PREPARATION: 10 MINUTES
COOKING TIME: 45 MINUTES

Before you cook: Prepare a 9-by-9-inch pan by either greasing it with butter on the bottom and sides, or lining it with wax paper so that the wax paper comes over the edges. Spray the paper lightly with nonstick vegetable cooking spray.

Ingredients
    2½ cups white sugar
    ⅔ cup evaporated milk
    ¾ cup canned mashed pumpkin*
    2 tablespoons butter
    7 ounces marshmallow crème
    1½ teaspoons pumpkin pie spice
    1 cup white chocolate chips
    1 teaspoon vanilla extract
    Optional: Edible gold luster dust or candy corn to top
        each piece

*Mashed pumpkin has less sugar than pumpkin pie puree. I did not test this using puree.

Directions
In a 3-quart heavy-bottomed saucepan, heat the evaporated milk and sugar over medium heat. Bring this to a bubbly, rolling boil. Stir with a wooden spoon now and then; there is no need for continuous stirring.

Fold in the mashed pumpkin and pumpkin pie spice and bring it to a boil again. Then stir in the marshmallow crème and butter; bring it again to a rolling boil. Cook for 18 minutes or slightly more, stirring intermittently, until it looks thick and glistening.

Remove it from heat. Add the chocolate chips and vanilla. Stir until the chips are melted. Pour it into the pan. Cool. Dust it with edible gold dust or dress the top with pieces of candy corn.

Dessert serving idea: Chop into chips of fudge and sprinkle the chips onto vanilla ice cream; top it with whipped cream, and enjoy.

Acknowledgments

Many thanks go to these wonderful people:

My readers who have told me they love Ava and Gilpa, and who share recipes with me.

Door County's amazing residents and business operators. Most settings in my books are real. Thank you for creating a paradise that I can write about.

Al and Theresa Alexander, for the tour of the Saint Mary of the Snows Church in Namur; and Bill Chaudoir for his assistance at the Namur kermis; and Christine Chaudoir, who operates Chris and Jack's Belgian Bar next door, for the good information about the cemetery.

Retired Fire Captain Greg Renz and Emergency Response Specialist Thomas Jones answered my questions about fires. Thanks, guys.

My neighbor Jane Adams—a super fan of this series, touting it to friends across the country and to book clubs. Many thanks, Jane, for your tireless support.

Kjersta Holter, of the *Isthmus* newspaper, Madison, Wisconsin, for helping me name a character.

Bookstore owners and managers—you're special. A shout-out to Joanne Berg at Mystery to Me, in Madison, who hosted my launch parties. Thank you!

Danielle Perez, my editor extraordinaire, and Danielle Dill, my hardworking publicist, both at Penguin Random House/New American Library/Obsidian.

Artist Neal Armstrong and designer Katie Anderson, who do my great covers.

Copy editor Dan Larsen, who saves me a lot.

John Talbot, my agent, for keeping me on track.

My colleagues Laura Kahl, for taking photos of fudge that look luscious, and Laurie Scheer, for cheerleading me all the way.

My taste tasters this time: Bob Boetzer, Judy Brickbauer, Laurie Greenberg, Vanika Mock, Kimary Peterson, Sybil Pressprich, Glen Schubert, Robert Toomey.

The writers in my master classes at the University of Wisconsin-Madison — your kind words echo in my ears constantly and spur me onward. Recipe hounds among them included Roi Solberg and Lisa Kusko.

Peggy Williams, author (MJ Williams) and friend, who is always there when needed.

Special, supportive friends Tom and Carol Airis, Anne and Joe Purpura, John and Betty Qualheim. You rock.

My lovely aunts who helped with research on Belgian things: Cheryl DeSmet, Janet DeSmet, Janet Lydon.

My family — your support means everything. Thank you.

And Bob Boetzer — the man who "suffers" through research visits to luscious Door County fudge shops and more. Thank you!

Author's Note

Adele Brise was a real person. According to many historical accounts, in 1859, as a young woman immigrant to Door County, Wisconsin, from Brabant, Belgium, Brise experienced three visions of the Virgin Mary telling her to teach children. She became a nun of the Third Order (secular) Franciscans.

Adele's father built a small ten-by-twelve-foot chapel at the apparition site at Champion, Wisconsin. It was enlarged once, and then a brick chapel was erected in 1880. Saint Mary's Academy for teaching children became part of the site in 1867.

On December 8, 2010, the apparition known as "Our Lady of Good Hope" was declared the first Marian apparition authenticated and recognized by the Roman Catholic Church in the United States. The decree for this is listed at the "Our Lady of Good Hope" Web site.

Today, many make the pilgrimage to see the church and Adele Brise's grave. You'll note on the grave marker "Brice," an American version of her name.

A search online for "Adele Brise" will bring up many details about her life.

The Great Fire of 1871—also known as the Peshtigo Fire—was also real. It happened the same day as the Great Chicago Fire. Many online references, including those of the Wisconsin State Historical Society, give vivid details of the tragedy.

Did Adele have a secret fudge recipe? That part is pure

fictional speculation by the author. Fudge was popularized in the United States in the 1880s—during Sister Adele Brise's lifetime. I like to think the Belgians of Door County who loved their desserts and chocolates were at the fore-front of making that new confection called fudge.

The real Namur, Wisconsin, kermis is held the third Sunday of September. But always check with the Belgians of Door County for the current dates. Many communities hold a kermis in the autumn.

Don't miss the first Fudge Shop Mystery
by Christine DeSmet,

FIRST-DEGREE FUDGE

Available now from Obsidian.

I was cutting a pan of Cinderella Pink Fudge into twenty-four bite-sized squares on the white marble-slab table near the window that fronted the docks when my friend Pauline Mertens burst through the door, rattling the cowbell hooked to the knob. Snow flurries and cold air rushed in to stir the chocolate-scented air.

"Ava, she's here!" Pauline said, not bothering to take off her coat. "Can you believe it? Oh my gosh golly giddy-ups, I saw Hollywood's voluptuous, *von vivant* vixen vamp!" She whipped her long black hair back over her shoulders, acting the part herself.

Pauline is a kindergarten teacher, so over-the-top alliteration and other word games often spilled into our conversations.

But an excited tickle was running through me, too, because this was the day my fudge would debut for a celebrity. "You saw *the* Rainetta Johnson? Where?"

"At the Blue Heron Inn. Isabelle said she stayed overnight. Oh, that looks luscious."

I slapped her hand away before she stole a piece of pale pink cherry-vanilla fudge, which had my own mouth watering. The gustable air in the shop smelled like cotton candy and freshly made vanilla waffle ice-cream cones combined. My little shop had already seen a dozen fishers and early-season tourists duck out of the unusual May cold because of the smell they said hit them yards away along the Lake

Michigan docks of Fishers' Harbor in Door County, Wisconsin.

"This fudge is for the party," I said, "but here, I'll give you a taste from the new batch. Tell me if it's creamy enough."

I moved to the next area of my six-foot marble table, where I'd poured warm but cooling creamy pink fudge straight from the copper kettle nearby. I'd whipped the pink confection fast for the last fifteen minutes with four-foot walnut wood paddles. My shoulders were still aching.

The next step was working the white chocolate with my small wood spatulas until it stiffened enough for my hands to take over in a process called "loafing." I would then knead the pink pile of sugar crystals until they transformed like magic into just the right consistency for slicing. Fudge was all about chemistry—and the aromas emanating from melting sugar, butter, and Belgian chocolate. I found a clean spoon and carved into the pale pink cloud of fudge, handing the treat to Pauline.

Pauline set the smidgen of pink cherry-vanilla fudge on her tongue.

Her eyes melted like dark chocolate as an ambrosial smile curved onto her face.

I hopped on my feet like one of her kindergartners. "Well?"

She blossomed in rapture, looking down on me. She was six feet tall—two inches taller than me, which bugged me when we played hoops over at the school.

"This is yummy, better than cherries jubilee!" She dipped the spoon into the fudge loaf again before I could catch her. "Once they taste this at Isabelle's fund-raiser, they're all going to descend on this place. Did you make enough? What if Rainetta wants to mail some right away to all her Hollywood friends?"

My head spun with sugarplum visions of grandeur and glamour for myself. "Can you stay and help? I've never made this much fudge so fast in my life."

"I'm sorry. I have to get over to the school." It was Sunday, and Pauline frequently prepped her classroom for the week on Sundays. "Isabelle was wondering why you weren't at the inn yet with the fudge."

"I'm waiting for Gilpa to get here. He took some of the inn's guests on the lighthouse tour. And then this storm came up." Gilpa was what I called my grandpa Gil Oosterling. He was the co-owner of my shop.

"He's too crusty to let anything happen."

I hoped Pauline was right. I returned to cutting the hardened Cinderella Pink Fudge into one-inch squares. "What's Rainetta look like?"

"Aging well. Big boobs and bodacious at sixty-five. Rainetta's already holding court like the movie star she is—or was. And after one bite of this, she'll be recommending your pink treat for all the swag bags given away at next year's Oscars."

My hands shook with anticipation, so much that I thought for a second I'd cut off a finger in the pink fudge, but it was only a cherry popping up under the blade.

For Cinderella Pink Fudge, I'd married the best white Belgian chocolate with tart red cherries that grow in the orchards surrounding our little town of two hundred or so permanent residents.

Rainetta Johnson now lived in Chicago, having retired from films years ago, but everybody my parents' age remembered her movies with Elvis and Cary Grant. I'd spent a few years in Los Angeles before moving back to Door County recently, and I knew that Rainetta put money behind plenty of upstart indie filmmakers. So why not my Fairy Tale Fudge line? I'd never met her, but I'd heard she liked vacationing in quaint Door County, called the Cape Cod of the Midwest.

I felt bad about our inhospitable-weather welcome for Rainetta. On this first Sunday in May, the day had started in the fifties. Trust me, it really did. Now, nearly noon, snow spit past my fudge shop windows. Tulips alongside buildings bent under the frozen betrayal. The sudden storm on Lake Michigan was churning our bay with wind gusts up to forty knots, enough to shred the flags outside on their posts. Whitecaps splashed foam and spray over the dock in front of my fudge shop.

My just-opened fudge shop was the last stop on the docks of Fishers' Harbor before you boarded a boat or your first stop after you disembarked following a day spent sight-seeing among the ten lighthouses dotting the shorelines of our peninsula county. Lighthouses attracted people who loved to buy souvenirs, including homemade, handmade fudge. I figured my location would give me a pretty good chance of success.

My place used to be called Oosterling's Live Bait, Bobbers & Beer. In Wisconsin everything ends with "& beer." But when I moved home a couple of weeks back, my grandpa let me tack up a temporary sign and share his space. He moved both his live minnow tank and the apostrophe on "Oosterling's." We're now Oosterlings' Live Bait, Bobbers & Belgian Fudge. There wasn't enough room on the building to keep "& Beer." In these parts, beer is assumed to be on the shelves and in the coolers.

I said good-bye to Pauline, then tried Grandpa Gil's number again. Still no answer. My stomach bottomed out. I took out my worry on the pink fudge cloud, working it with the wood paddles, watching for just the right sheen and mirror-like look before the final loafing.

It was my fault Gilpa had taken the chance to go out today. He wanted to be out of the way so that I could have my fudge debut all on my own. I'm thirty-two, and he feels sorry for me not finding my "thing" in life yet. He was the first to warn me about my ex-husband, too. To say he doesn't have faith in my fudge fantasies and judgment is an understatement.

My assistant, Cody Fjelstad, startled me by calling from across the small room, "Miss Oosterling, hurry up. We got only ten minutes! This isn't La-La Land!"

Cody always called me "Miss," which made me feel old or like my schoolmarm friend, Pauline, who was forced to wear thrift shop dregs that kindergarten kids could throw up on with impunity. I didn't think I looked particularly like an old-maid "Miss." Or did I? My brown ponytail was put up in a twist with a wood chopstick hung half undone over one shoulder of my faded yellow blouse and my long apron. My jeans were ripped from the real wear and tear of fixing up my shop and not the fake tears you buy in the store. I always wore work shoes now—boots, really—with lug soles for safety's sake, in case I needed to step out onto the wet docks or help Gilpa haul equipment onto a boat. And then there were my copper kettles—don't dare drop them on bare feet!

Cody was eighteen and challenged with a mild form of Asperger's and obsessive-compulsive disorder, according to what Pauline knew. He'd worked long and hard on his speech patterns, eye contact, and his sense of humor and sarcasm. Calling me "Miss" made him happy, so though it made me feel old, I also knew it was a sign of him working on his goal to be a happy and well-adjusted adult someday. He was sweet and sincere and ten times as good as any intern I'd had to deal with in Los Angeles, or La-La Land.

Cody had red hair and freckles and liked to be called "Ranger" because he dreamed of being a ranger at a local park, particularly at the Chambers Island Lighthouse, where Gilpa was supposed to have taken those four guests of the Blue Heron Inn. That lighthouse was seven miles into the bay, smack-dab in the middle of the shipping lanes and this upstart storm.

"Sorry, Ranger. My mind is racing today."

"You should race faster or you'll miss your party and we won't be famous after all."

I sped up my fudge-loafing operation. "How's the wrapping going?"

Pink cellophane crinkled and squeaked.

He said, "I'm catchin' up to ya. Hurry up, Miss Oosterling."

He came over to take the pan of fudge I'd cut into pieces and moved it to the register counter, where he was wrapping. "I'm gonna make it beautiful for you. Fairy Tale Fudge is the best!" he crowed. "Divine, delectable, delicious!"

"Pauline would love those D's. Go easy on the fairy dust."

"You got it."

He did a fist pump in the air to make an invisible exclamation point.

Fairy Tale Fudge was my girlie brand of fudge. I was also developing ideas for a Fisherman's Catch Tall Tale Fudge line—male fudge (fudge with nuts!).

For the Cinderella Pink Fudge, I made tiny bite-sized

and edible marzipan fairy wings and glass slippers, which Ranger and I placed atop each piece. Ranger loved sprinkling on the fairy dust—edible pink sugar glitter—before wrapping each piece.

I reached for my lightweight red spring jacket, already feeling chilly. I should've watched the weather earlier that morning and brought my winter coat and gloves, but that's how I was about too many things—spontaneous. It's not good advice for getting married, by the way.

Snow flew thicker now outside the big glass windows, obliterating the docks and bay. I called the Coast Guard; the guys assured me they'd look for Gilpa. The fishing season had officially opened yesterday in Wisconsin. Every year we had people overboard on the first weekend. They didn't always come back alive. At this time of year, hypothermia developed in a person within minutes.

I forced such thoughts away as Ranger flipped the lid shut on the big box that held Cinderella Pink Fudge for fifty. He offered to carry it up the hill to the Blue Heron Inn.

After declining his offer, I said, "When Gilpa comes in, you take the people by the hand to help them off the boat. Wait until each one is steady before assisting the next one."

I had to be exact and literal with Ranger. Sometimes he hurried too much with his tasks; a guest could end up being flung by him from one side of a pier into the water on the other side.

When I burst into the blustery outdoors, the wind nearly whipped the heavy fudge box right out of my hands. The coat I'd put on but failed to button flapped all over the place. Snowflakes stung my cheeks and pecked at my eyes, making me bend my head as I walked blindly up the narrow blacktopped street that threaded up the steep hill. The Blue Heron Inn was only a couple of blocks away, but with it sitting on a small bluff, the street had a pitch that made me step half sideways like a skier travailing up a snowy slope.

As I drew closer, my heart began to pump faster. Besides Pauline and Ranger, no grown-up had yet seen or tasted my Fairy Tale Fudge, each sumptuous, sugary piece dressed with slippers or wings and glitter. Was it too silly? Was it tasty enough? Would it impress Rainetta?

I had hopes after Isabelle Boone—owner of the Blue Heron Inn—had stopped by earlier.

"I can smell the vanilla all the way up the hill to my inn!" she'd declared.

I had shooed Isabelle to the back room, where she'd picked up her usual supplies for the next week of cooking at the inn for her guests. We shared the same delivery service, which brought bulk sugar, flour, and other ingredients to the bars and restaurants in the area. The drivers didn't always like going up the steep, narrow, winding street to the inn when conditions were slippery. Even rain freaked out some drivers.

Ranger's social worker, Sam Peterson, had also come by earlier, offering to help. Sam and I went way back; Ranger didn't understand why we weren't married. Sam had never liked my ex-husband, and I was still embarrassed from the experience even though eight years have passed since the debacle.

I had intended to marry Sam eight years ago, at the end of the summer, but the day before my wedding, I got cold feet and ended up with another guy I'd met in college. He was like a prince whisking me off to a castle. We did the Vegas-wedding thing and settled in Las Vegas, where he pursued his career as a stand-up comic. I worked as a waitress at a casino, then got a job making the desserts for its buffet. It wasn't but a month after our wedding when two women informed me that they believed they were also married to Mr. Dillon Rivers. Bigamy puts a damper on a marriage. I got a divorce and an annulment soon after. I had become enamored enough of the bright lights that I went to Los Angeles, where I worked as a waitress and then a baker in Jerry's Deli while writing my experience with Dillon into scripts. After a year, I submitted a couple of scripts to a new TV series on a little-watched cable channel. I toiled at my writing craft, hoping for fame, but I worked for an anxiety-ridden executive producer. I wasn't his favorite writer on the staff. Mostly he favored the guys and their ideas. I hung on to pay my college debt and to pay back everybody here for the wedding expenses, including Sam for his tuxedo rental.

Sam was going to be at the party. I had to expect people

to talk. In small towns, people tried to pair you off with the same vigor they used for betting on Packers-Bears games.

The Blue Heron Inn's lights were particularly inviting by the time I reached it. My fingers had become frozen wires bent around the edges of the cardboard box.

Isabelle Boone's cream brick and powder blue–trimmed B and B was two and a half stories of history. The original wood boardinghouse had burned in 1871 in a great fire that ravaged the peninsula, killing more than a thousand people. The inn was rebuilt of Cream City brick hauled here by ships from Milwaukee. The brick comes from the clay soils in that area of Wisconsin. The high levels of lime and sulfur in the soil turn creamy colored when fired. The firing of bricks interested me as much as the chemical formula for fudge; I'd taken chemistry classes in college just for the fun of it.

I'd been in the house only once since I'd left town eight years ago in a hurry, but that visit had been a quick nighttime errand in low light. I'd heard customers rave about the collection of Steuben glass Isabelle had assembled. The famous Steuben glass artists out in New York had ceased operations in 2011, so I knew the value for Isabelle's collection must have gone up considerably. I was eager to see it all under bright lights.

As I reached to ring the doorbell, I heard heated debating from within.

When Isabelle opened the door, her normally sophisticated gamine looks were pinched and she was out of breath.

I asked, "What's going on?"

"Rainetta." She took the box. "I leave for a minute to go upstairs to turn down her bed and put chocolates on her pillow and come back down to find Rainetta has everybody arguing over what needs money first in Fishers' Harbor."

I stripped off my jacket and shook off the snowflakes before hanging it on the coat tree. "How about you put my fudge on their pillows from now on? And how about she invest in my fudge?"

"She'll love your idea. Fairy tales and Hollywood? A perfect match. And I'm tired of hearing Al Kvalheim talk about spending Ms. Johnson's money on new storm sewers and grates."

I laughed. I eagerly sent my gaze searching for the famous actress. I didn't see her at first amid the throng of at least a hundred townspeople wearing their Sunday church clothes and enough aftershave and perfume to scare even a skunk. Panic set in. I couldn't breathe.

I whispered, "I didn't bring enough fudge, and the new batch isn't quite done."

Isabelle whispered back, "We'll make sure Rainetta gets the first piece. Others will just have to bid for the rest. I'll tell everybody it's part of the fund-raiser."

"You're a genius, Izzy. Thanks!"

I still couldn't breathe much, but now it had to do with the beauty around me. The two-story-high reception hall was packed with displays of expensive glass. Everybody kept their elbows tucked in and barely moved while talking.

Glass is made of amorphous crystals, which means they're random molecules and light can go through them. Glass sparkled from every surface high and low, with rainbow chips of light in flight under the overhead chandeliers. There were crystal birds and animals—many life-sized, including a seagull. Other items were smaller abstracts or vases, swirls of fire-roasted molecules of sand that bent the light into colorful beams splashing on the cream-and-blue wallpaper. Making glass was probably like making fudge—only a few thousand degrees hotter.

But my appreciation of Isabelle's collection was interrupted by the loud discussion near the magnificent blue-carpeted staircase dead center in the house.

"That's Rainetta Johnson," whispered Isabelle, nodding with raised eyebrows toward an impeccably coiffed blond woman of a regal age wearing an expensive lavender pantsuit.

To my surprise, the object of Ms. Johnson's animated discussion was Sam Peterson.

I asked Isabelle, "What're they arguing about? Seems like Sam's taking the wrong tack to get his donations."

This party wasn't just the opening of the refurbished inn or my fudge debut; it was a fund-raiser to help purchase and redo another historic home in town. It would become a group home for people like Ranger who wanted to live independently. So Sam's being here was logical, seeing as how he was a social worker. I'd never known Sam to raise his voice. I could see that the arguing was mostly one-sided, though. Rainetta was smiling and embracing others with some funny asides even as Sam kept pressing some point with the actress.

"Let's not worry about it," Isabelle said. "Sam's overly eager, perhaps, to sell her on the group home."

"Poor Rainetta. Sam should relax. You told me she loved Door County."

"She does, but she's a shrewd business lady. Come with me and I'll show you."

Isabelle and I skirted the edge of the fray to the round serving table that Isabelle had reserved for the Cinderella Pink Fudge. After she put the box of fudge down gingerly, she lovingly picked up a six-inch glass unicorn from the back of the table.

"My favorite piece," she said with glistening eyes. "I wanted it here on the table with your fudge. Fairies and unicorns go together in tales. I thought maybe it would bring good luck to your Cinderella debut."

"Thank you, Isabelle. That's a lovely thing to say." I gave her a hug, though a careful one so as not to break the unicorn.

"Rainetta loves this piece," Isabelle said.

"She has good taste." The unicorn had the exquisite definition of a horse with a horn. Little girls could easily imagine fairies riding on its back.

"That's the problem. She wants to buy it."

"Then sell it to her," I said, feeling a speck of jealousy as I stood among Isabelle's riches.

"I can't. She wants to buy it for half what it's worth. That lady isn't rich because she gives money away. She drives a hard bargain. And she's making that known to everybody."

"And doing it with a smile. She looks radiant. As if she's truly come home here in Door County and Fishers' Harbor."

"Indeed. But some of the locals don't trust her. They think she's got to have a hidden reason to help us."

The odd thing about it was I'd heard that Rainetta was

always generous. So something wasn't jibing here, particularly with Sam's behavior. If he was getting her upset over a group home investment, it didn't bode well for selling her something as silly as fudge, even though I was determined to elevate it to an art.

Isabelle set the unicorn back down. "And Ms. Johnson was perfectly charming to our new village board president, but I overheard Erik say he thinks she's a stuffy old lady."

Through a slim fissure in the crowd, I caught a glimpse of our new president—Erik Gustafson, a wunderkind of nineteen who'd shocked the town in April by deposing the fifty-something Mercy Fogg. Mercy, who was milling about, voicing her opinion to Erik about our lack of a stoplight, had reigned supreme here for more than twenty years. I groaned, turning back to Isabelle. "Mercy wants the great Rainetta Johnson to buy us a stoplight?"

Isabelle nodded. "Decidedly boring."

"Hmm, but suddenly Sam doesn't look bored," I noted. "If anything, it looks like he's given Rainetta some kind of green light."

Rainetta had a hand cupping his chin. The legendary dame looked like she was about to kiss Sam! I squelched a gasp.

Sam was only a couple of years older than me. Sure, he was good-looking. He was six foot, still had his football player's physique, and had Adonis blond hair in crisp, thick waves. What woman of any age wouldn't want to be on the guy's arm and set her fingers to walking through that hair? But Rainetta? She was more than thirty years older than Sam.

I asked Isabelle in a quiet voice, "Where's the reporter when we need him?"

Isabelle had told me earlier that Jeremy Stone was staying at the inn. I wondered why he was still upstairs when the action was down here. Stone worked for the *Madison Herald*, a daily morning newspaper out of the capital. He roved the state reviewing everything from A to Z: arts to zoos. He loved "quirky." I had high hopes for him finding pink cherry fudge with fairy wings on top "quirky."

Isabelle said, "He's probably sending in a story already

about how hideous my party is. Sam is ruining it by hogging Rainetta's attention."

"I won't let him."

I flipped open my fudge box sitting on the table, grabbed a pink cellophane-wrapped and winged bite-sized morsel of Cinderella Pink Fudge, then wended my way through the throng. I was getting looks, and only then realized I'd forgotten to change clothes. I still wore my messy long baker's apron dotted with pink cherry juice, which looked like bloody finger smudges.

I held out my hand with the fudge in it and delivered my memorized Oscar-winning speech to Rainetta. "Hello, Ms. Johnson. I'm Ava Oosterling, from Oosterlings' Live Bait, Bobbers & Belgian Fudge. I'd love it if the guest of honor would have the first bite of Fairy Tale Fudge. This flavor is the Cinderella Pink Fudge. I hope it lets you feel like you're Cinderella at the ball, Ms. Johnson."

My eyes were sucked out of their sockets by the circle of purple amethysts the size of dollar coins that she wore about her neck. They were inlaid in a museum-quality setting of gold leaves. Certainly she could afford to endorse my fudge fantasies.

"Fudge?" she said, her blue eyes soaking up the purple in the amethysts. "How quaint and perfectly wonderful, but I'm allergic to chocolate."

The blood drained from my head. She hadn't even tasted my fudge.

I prayed like any sane Cinderella would and tried again. "This isn't dark chocolate. This is white, made from sugar and soybean oil. No caffeine, either. The texture is creamy and smooth . . . like your skin."

The woman raised her eyebrows at my inane and all-too-spontaneous words. She stared at the pink confection in crinkly cellophane I was placing in one of her hands.

Sam huffed at me and said, "Excuse me while I find the little boys' room." He marched up the staircase.

Sam obviously was miffed I'd interrupted him and Rainetta. He wasn't normally brusque with me, except about my boyfriend choices in the past.

Isabelle rushed up with a crystal goblet of pink wine

made from Door County cherries, which Rainetta didn't take. Isabelle persevered. "Ms. Johnson, please come with us to the dining room, where we can toast you."

"I recommend the cherry wine," I said, indicating the proffered glass in Isabelle's hands. "My fudge is made from cherries from that same orchard."

Rainetta tossed her head back in a genuine laugh, relaxing me a little. Her helmet of blond waves didn't move a speck. "I'm impressed by your homework. I love the orchards here in spring."

Then she ripped off the pink sparkly string and opened the pink cellophane to reveal the tiny sugared fairy wings. The crowd was so quiet I heard the furnace kick in.

Rainetta nibbled a corner of my pink confection. Then to my horror, she winced. "Perhaps I'll finish this in my room. I'm not feeling well."

She spit the fudge back into the crinkly pink cellophane. Then, with my fudge still in one hand, she hurried up the stairs, disappearing into the upper hallway that ran down the center of the B and B.

My mouth went dry.

People began to murmur. And stare at me. With ugly frowns, the kind we use around here when somebody spills a beer or the Packers miss the Super Bowl.

Isabelle had gone so pale I could see blue veins under the winter white skin of her temples.

The chandelier above us bombarded the Steuben glass figurines and all of us with rainbow darts. Rainetta's lingering perfume billowed into an invisible cloud that was suffocating me. My dream of talking with her about actors' swag bags evaporated.

I muttered to Isabelle, "She hates my fudge."

Isabelle laid a hand on my arm. "Of course not. This is Sam's fault."

"How so?"

"Whatever they were talking about upset her. I better go see to her. But first, egads, we need music, don't we?"

She flipped a switch on the wall beneath the staircase before hurrying up the stairs. Hot jazz jolted us. Even the glass figurines on the shelves and tables vibrated.

The crowd kept staring at me.

Our wunderkind board president, Erik Gustafson, said, "This isn't going the way I expected."

From the outer edges of the crowd, Mercy Fogg croaked, "You can still resign if you like, Erik. It takes a grown-up to handle the likes of Ms. Johnson."

Mercy bullied her way around a couple of men in suits and lumbered up the stairs.

I felt sorry for Erik. A year ago he had been playing football with the high school team, and now he was in the middle of this groveling for money that small towns have to do in order to survive.

I told Erik, "Maybe you could serve wine and stall a little by talking about new things you want to do for the village."

"Like the new playground equipment we need?"

"Perfect idea," I said. I silently prayed Gilpa would be coming soon with the other four guests to resuscitate the party and charm Rainetta Johnson.

Erik called out, "Who wants cherry wine? I'll pour."

"I'll help," I said, wanting to slam back a glass fast.

Erik and I had passed along only a few glasses of wine when Isabelle's scream sliced through the jazzy sax riffs.

I charged up the powder blue carpeted stairs with several people in tow.

In contrast to the glittering brilliance downstairs, the upstairs hallway was dimly lit with only two blue glass globe sconces. But doors popped open from the guest rooms, their lamplights helping to illuminate Isabelle standing in horror at the other end of the hallway.

Rainetta was laid flat on her back on the carpet, half in and half out of her room.

I rushed down the hallway. A woman screamed behind me. A door slammed.

Isabelle trembled. She shook her phone in her hand. "I called nine-one-one."

"What happened?" I asked, going immediately into action to pump at Rainetta's rib cage.

Isabelle said, "I used the bathroom; then I knocked on her door, and she staggered out, choking. On your fudge."

ALSO AVAILABLE
FROM NATIONAL BESTSELLING AUTHOR

Christine DeSmet

First-Degree Fudge
A Fudge Shop Mystery

New candy store owner Ava Oosterling specializes in making heavenly homemade fudge. But she's just found out that her newest flavor is to die for....

Between getting her store up and running and uneasily settling back into her charming Lake Michigan hometown, Ava has her plate full. She hopes she can tempt wealthy ex–film star Rainetta Johnson to try her newest creation called Cinderella Pink, so her road to big-time success will be short and sweet. But when Rainetta chokes to death on a stolen diamond hidden in the fudge's fluffy depths, Ava is pegged as the prime suspect. Now she must figure out who the real culprit is fast, or face a very bitter end....

"An action-filled story with a likeable heroine and a fun setting."
—National bestselling author JoAnna Carl

Available wherever books are sold or at
penguin.com

32953012464089

OM0151